Z9 City

Book 1

Champion of Daoqin

D.C. Hightower

Z9 City
Book 1: Champion of Daoqin

D.C. Hightower

First Edition
December, 2022

Consultant: Linda Marie, MFT

ISBN
978-1-887400-69-5 (paperback)
978-1-887400-70-1 (kindle)

Earthen Vessel Productions
www.earthen.com

Contents

To Jeremiah and Joshua

Chapter 1
Arrival

No one is on the bridge to see the blue luminescent object growing steadily larger in the forward window or hear the woman's voice calling sternly over the radio, "Warning! Unidentified spacecraft, you are entering the restricted space of Z9 City. Identify yourself or you will be fired upon… Warning! Unidentified spacecraft…"

A young man rushes in, snatches the mic from the comms console, and says quickly, "Control, this is Mirage."

"Bobby, is that you?" asks the woman.

"Oh, hi, Sonja. Yeah, it's me."

Sonja sounds relieved but concerned. "Bobby Johnson, you need to be more careful. You're going to get yourself blown out of the stars one of these days."

"Sorry about that," says Bobby. He sits down in the pilot's seat, spins around to the equipment rack behind him, and flips a couple of switches on a device in the rack. "I guess our transponder is acting up again." He taps the device a few times with his fingers. "I'm checking it right now and it looks dead."

"Okay, understood," says Sonja. "You coming in?"

"Yeah, just in time for dinner. Want to join me?"

Sonja gives a quick, playful laugh. "Nice try, handsome. You're cleared for home—Deck 7, Bay 1."

"Roger that, Sonja. Talk to you later."

"Take care, Bobby. And get that transponder fixed."

Bobby is writing in the ship's log about the radio call when Tran Moore walks onto the bridge. "Oh good, we're here," he says, looking out the window.

Bobby asks, "Where were you? You missed all the excitement."

1

"Doing laundry," says Tran. "What happened?"

"Z9 threatened to launch a missile on us."

Tran glances out the window again. "Really? A missile? What for?"

"The transponder's out again, so they couldn't identify us," says Bobby.

Tran frowns. "They would have sent ships out to identify us first, don't you think?"

Bobby shrugs. "Who knows? They're getting kind of paranoid around here these days. Anyway, I took care of it." Bobby gets up and stretches. "Go ahead and take us in, will you? I'm going to go get ready."

"Ready for what?" asks Tran, taking the pilot's seat.

"Well, I don't know," says Bobby, "I just might meet the girl of my dreams, so I want to look my best."

Tran rolls his eyes.

With the flight controls in hand, Tran takes the ship out of autopilot. He's relaxed in the pilot's seat. To him, Mirage is a familiar friend. When he was ten, his grandfather insisted he start learning to fly her. Now, six years later, piloting the ship is second nature to him.

Even though Mirage is classified as a luxury cruiser, her top speed is up there with some of the fastest ships ever built, and her maneuverability rivals that of smaller more nimble vessels. The inspiration for her design came to Tran's grandfather in a vision more than seventy years ago when he was hunting meteorites on Earth in the Mohave Desert. He came around an outcropping, and there she was, right in front of him—long, sleek, dark blue like deep water. He thought she was real. Every detail of the ship was instantly in his mind, or at least the idea for them. Many of the technologies didn't exist until he finished developing them some twelve years later, finally enabling him to fulfill his vision.

Tran has heard his grandfather tell the story many times. Is it true? He doesn't know. It's hard for him to imagine, but hearing it and the passion with which the old gentleman tells it always gives him goosebumps. Mirage is unquestionably an extraordinary ship, unlike any other, and well before her time, so he chooses to believe in her story and the man telling it.

Z9 City now fills the forward window, its luminous cobalt blue color shifting in random patterns of light and dark like ripples on a wind-swept ocean. Twice as wide as it is tall, Z9 was affectionately dubbed "the tuna can" when the original settlers first saw it, though that name was soon forgotten.

Tran throttles back and switches on the landing lights. Slowly he maneuvers Mirage counterclockwise around the nine-mile perimeter of the station until he reaches Deck 7, its lowest level. He lines the ship up parallel to her Home bay. The space door for Bay 1 slides open, and Tran gently manipulates the thrusters, guiding the ship sideways into the docking bay. Hovering Mirage steady off the deck, he makes final adjustments and, with the lightest touch, smoothly sets the ship down and mag-locks her to the deck. An alarm sounds and red lights flash inside and out until the space door seals and the bay is pressurized. Over the intercom, he tells Bobby, "We're in."

"I'll be awhile yet," answers Bobby.

"I'm not surprised," says Tran. "I have stuff to do anyway. Where do you want to eat?"

"Rodgers," says Bobby. "But we have to stop by the Service Center first to schedule the repair for the transponder."

The buzzer for the dryer goes off just as Tran arrives at the laundry room. Clutching the warm clothes to his chest, he pushes his cabin door open and dumps the laundry on his bed. Expertly he shakes out each piece, methodically folding it the way his mother taught him. As his hands do the work, his mind drifts to her in their old flat on Z9. She'd be sitting on his bed, her hands folding his clothes, her attention on her young son. "Spell cytoskeleton," she'd say. Tran would repeat the word, then speak each letter quickly and distinctly, then say the word again. "Very good, Tran," his mother would say with obvious pleasure. "You're so smart!"

Sometimes she'd pull a shirt out of the laundry that Tran had never seen before. "What's this?" she'd say, acting surprised. "Oh, Tran! This might look really nice on you. Come over here and let me see." Holding the shirt up to his chest, she'd tilt her head from side to side evaluating the size and color. "It's perfect!" She'd smile, giving him a hug and a quick kiss on his cheek. Then it was back to spelling and laundry. "Spell peptidoglycan," she'd challenge. And he would, without missing a letter or tripping over the pronunciation.

But even at seven years old, Tran knew he wasn't going to be a biochemist like his parents. He didn't exactly know what a biochemist did, except that they liked using long, confusing words, but he was sure he didn't want to be one. His mother knew it too. She recognized his craving for adventure. He longed to be like the explorers and pioneers he had read about in his history adventure books—Marco Polo, Ferdinand Magellan, John Cabot, Lewis and Clark. He yearned to explore Earth's wildernesses and sail its oceans. His shelves were full of books about wildlife and wild places. The walls of his room were covered with giant posters that his father had brought back for him from his trips to Earth. Tran would lie on his bed and stare at them, imagining himself there, maybe happening upon the fierce-eyed eagle perched in its high place, or watching a waterfall thundering over a sheer granite rock face 2,000 feet high.

Tran sighs as he puts his clothes neatly away. Their fresh smell and the movement of folding them brings back a time of security and love, but only briefly, and it leaves him sad. The posters are rolled up and packed away with the books in storage now. He hoped he might visit those places someday, a dream that may never come true, but kept safely tucked away nonetheless.

Born and raised in the Zenith Colony, Tran has never been to Earth. He has never smelled the ocean, walked in the woods, breathed fresh uncycled air, or felt real gravity. The Zenith Colony has incorporated as many of Earth's natural systems as possible in each of the colony's fifty-one space stations, especially in its capitol, Z9. But Tran has never felt the mist from a waterfall or the heat of summer sand on his feet, nor the sun as the blazing source of that heat. He's only known it as a bright, distant star.

He puts the last shirt in his dresser and glances at his watch. It's time to go.

Chapter 2
What's on Deck 6?

"Friday's the soonest we can get to it," says the short, bald fellow standing behind the worn service counter. Bobby studies the paper calendar the man reluctantly lets him see.

"Look, Dave," Bobby says, tapping on the date with his finger, "just move the hull repair on the Scraper to Friday and give us Wednesday for the transponder."

"Business repairs before personal," Dave says firmly. "You know that, Bobby."

"The Scraper's just body work, Dave. What's the big deal?" Bobby taps the calendar and says more emphatically, "I need a functioning transponder. The repairs you guys did last time didn't hold up, so it should be scheduled first anyway."

Moving the calendar out of Bobby's reach, Dave locks eyes with him and attempts to make his round, friendly face look menacing. "You know what I think, Bobby? I think you're trying to get me fired."

"That would be doing everyone a favor, you old ship monkey," says Bobby. After years of dealings with Dave, Bobby is well-aware that the man knows where everything is, but he gestures around the cluttered office with its stacks of papers and overflowing file cabinets, and says in mock dismay, "I mean, look at this place! You should have retired ten years ago."

"The wife didn't want me home," Dave says sadly.

"Well, who could blame her?" Bobby says, heading for the door. "See you later."

Dave mumbles, "Unfortunately."

Grinning, Bobby adds, "Oh, and say 'hi' to your daughter for me."

"Not a chance in the heavenly stars!" mutters Dave, somewhat loudly. Bobby laughs. The door closes behind him with a click.

Tran is talking with three shop technicians out on the mezzanine. Sounds of tools and smells of maintenance fluids rise from the large service center below. When Bobby walks up, the oldest tech gives him a big smile. "Hi, Bobby," he says, "what's going on?"

"Hi, Ron," says Bobby. "Just trying to get our transponder fixed but your boss is playing hard to get."

"I'll do it off hours for you if you want," says another tech.

Bobby looks at the thin, sandy-haired boy with the shy voice. He's the youngest tech Bobby's ever seen. "You think you can handle something like that away from the shop?" he asks.

"I'm pretty sure I can," says the boy. "Honestly, I'd work on the sewage system for a chance to get onboard Mirage."

Bobby chuckles, "Well, thank goodness that's working." He holds out his hand, "And your name is?"

"Oh, I'm Dengie," says the boy, shaking Bobby's hand.

"Dengie will do a good job for you," Ron assures him. "The kid knows his stuff. He's our new communications expert."

"Really?" Bobby gives the boy a closer look. "When do you think you can come check it out? We're kind of in a hurry."

"I can come by tonight at 2200, if that's okay."

"Sounds good to me," Bobby says, motioning to a small lounge area. "Let's go work out the details."

Tran and the other techs wander over to the mezzanine wall and look down into the shop area. A massive Class-A Transport is docked there, its huge bulk dwarfing everything around it. A service cart packed with techs and equipment is driving up the loading ramp leading into the open nose of the ship. It makes Tran think of a shrimp swimming into the gaping mouth of a gigantic whale. "I'd love to fly that monster," he says, leaning a little farther over the wall.

"That thing's like a garbage scow compared to Mirage," Ron says.

"I hear they're quite a challenge, though," says Tran.

"Yeah," quips the other tech. "You have to turn a parsec before you need to." The techs share a knowing chuckle.

But Tran's eyes stay fixed on the behemoth in the shop below. "Still..." he murmurs wistfully.

In the lounge, Bobby and Dengie quickly settle on a price for the transponder repair—300 tags. "Then I'll see you at 2200?" asks Bobby.

"Yep. I'll be there," says Dengie. "Thanks for the work."

"Well, that's settled," Bobby says as he and Tran pass through the bright blue double doors that lead out onto Mechanics Row, the busy thoroughfare of the service district. On each side of the Row are factories and shops for manufacturing, maintaining, and repairing the ships and equipment needed to support the Zenith Colony's magtronium mining operations. Many are open-bay shops with large roll-up doors, the sound of power tools and the faint tang of solvents coming from the work going on inside. Staying out of the main traffic, Bobby and Tran skirt tables and chairs outside the shops where workers gather to take their breaks and eat.

"I want to show you a new way," says Tran, turning down a side street on their left, then into a corridor with an inconspicuous access door in its wall. Deftly opening the hidden latch, Tran climbs inside. "This way's faster," he says. Bobby follows without protest. Even considering the labyrinth of hidden tunnels and corridors within Z9's walls, he's not worried about getting lost. He's convinced no one knows the intricacies of the city's layout better than his brother. The dimly-lit passageway smells musty from what Bobby recognizes as old, overheated lubricant, most likely used for the machinery he hears clattering in the dark. He follows Tran through the maze of tunnels, careful not to let his clothes touch the grimy walls. Tran has no such concerns. He presses on, ten paces ahead.

After a while, Bobby yells, "How much more of this, Tran?"

"Almost there," Tran shouts back. "This is at least ten minutes faster."

"Who cares?" Bobby mumbles, but suddenly there is a flood of light and the two boys step through an access door which opens to a spectacular view of the station's Hub. They're only thirty feet from a Smartcart queue.

"See?" Tran says triumphantly.

"Uh-huh," Bobby murmurs with not much enthusiasm. "Now, let's go eat!"

Bobby enters the destination code for the West Gate into the Smartcart control panel and sits back. The cart lifts and hovers slightly off the deck, accelerates with the faintest whisper, and smoothly maneuvers across an overpass, then merges onto Ring 6, the avenue which encircles the two-mile wide Hub. Tran stares up at the massive cream-colored structure towering more than a thousand feet before reaching the top of the deck. After sixteen years, he never tires of these soaring heights that are characteristic of every deck of Z9.

Bobby turns to Tran in the back seat and asks, "Do you know that Dengie kid?"

Tran looks at him blankly. "I'm sorry. What?"

"That Dengie kid. Do you know him?"

"No, not really," Tran says, searching his memory. "He was two years ahead of me in school. Some of the guys used to pick on him because of his small size, but it never seemed to bother him and the teachers put an end to it pretty fast. That's all I know."

"He's even younger than I thought," muses Bobby, now feeling unsure about hiring such a young kid for such an important job. But his attention quickly shifts to his stomach. "Man, I'm starving! I can taste that Triple right now."

Tran's not listening. His eyes are on a familiar stand of trees and a walking path off in the distance to their left, one of his favorite places on Z9. Because Deck 6 is mostly business and the people who work here live on other decks, the only time Ring 6 is even remotely busy is during the three shift changes. The rest of the day there's hardly anyone around. Tran comes here often to walk and think—and not think.

There are birds here—starlings. The only birds on Z9, and one of the only live animals Tran has ever seen. The birds' ancestors, smuggled onboard a transport long ago, were released here in the hopes they would survive and multiply. They did, thanks to the volunteers and maintenance crews who make sure they have food. When he can, Tran enjoys sitting under the trees, listening to the starlings' varying calls and the soft rustling of leaves when the vents come on to circulate the air.

At the West Gate, the Smartcart slows and pulls off to the right. Even before it stops, Bobby and Tran jump off and run toward the bank of lift doors along the wall of the Hub, but suddenly Tran veers to the left. "I'm going to take the Freetube," he says.

"Aw, come on, Tran," Bobby protests, "I need to eat!"

But Tran shouts over his shoulder as he sprints away, "I'll catch up with you!"

Bobby kicks softly at the wall and tries to guess which of the four lift doors will open first. Just as he picks the one on the left, the one on the right opens. Shaking his head, he steps into the circular shaped car. Since there are no other riders, he ambles the twenty feet across to the open door on the opposite side where he can see into the infamous, deserted Dome 6. Just as the lift doors slide shut, his eyes catch something. *Was that someone running? A woman? A woman carrying something and running toward the lift?* Convinced it was, Bobby punches the "Door Open" button several times, but it's too late. He feels the lift rise, his balance adjusting instinctively as the car shakes and shudders from gravitational irregularities. There are comfortable seats along with stability poles and hand straps for passengers to hold onto, but no young, self-respecting Z9er would ever use them, choosing to ride freehanded instead.

The thirty seconds it takes to get to the next deck seems like forever. When the doors finally open, Bobby dashes into the noise and foot traffic of Dome 5, dodging pedestrians in his hurry to find a lift going down. He sees one, rushes in and punches the button for Deck 6.

Noticing Bobby's haste, a man asks with concern, "Are you okay?"

"Uh, yes, sir," Bobby says, giving him a quick, reassuring smile. "Just in a hurry."

"Not enough hours in the day, eh?" says the man kindly.

"That's for sure," Bobby laughs.

Delicious aromas waft torturously in from nearby restaurants as Bobby waits impatiently for the lift doors to close. His stomach is growling so loudly he's sure the other passengers can hear it. Rodgers is close by. He could take a step forward, turn to the right, and be there in a couple of minutes. He considers not going back down. Maybe he didn't really see what he thought he saw. The doors close, deciding for him, and after another thirty seconds of what seems like forever, he hurries out into Dome 6, leaving the other riders to wonder why anyone is actually going there.

Stepping into the interior, Bobby is immediately reminded just how creepy it is within this silent, lifeless dome. In such a thriving, pleasing city as Z9, Dome 6 is an astonishing horror. A tangle of deformity where PiMar technology had gone very wrong. A mutation in the resin's build code resulted in miles of buildings folding in on themselves like melted plastic, or bolting high like twisted grotesque arms reaching for the top of the dome, and a labyrinth of chaotic chambers and passageways, many leading nowhere. The development of Z9 was almost completely abandoned due to these architectural nightmares, but repair codes were injected into the resin and the PiMar adjusted itself. Arching over the pale, misshapen structures, the dome shell took shape perfectly, and the rest of Deck 6 grew outward without any major flaws. In the end, only the interior of Dome 6 was affected.

Quickly scanning the scene, Bobby sees a flash of movement beyond a shallow jog in the wall. Cautiously he maneuvers to get a better angle. It's a man—a tall, thin man forcing a young woman up against the wall, his left forearm pressing just below her throat. The woman's hands are shielding her face—palms out, fingers spread in the gesture for stop. The man screams, "What have you done with her?"

Without thinking, Bobby shouts, "Hey!" and sprints toward them. Alarmed, the man takes off running.

"Walter! Wait!" the woman cries, running after him, but he dashes away in long, lanky strides and disappears around the corner of a deformed building. Breathless, the woman calls, "Walter! Please! Come back!"

Bobby runs up to her. "Are you okay?" he asks. The woman takes no notice of him, keeping her eyes focused on where the man went out of sight. Finally, she lets out a long, defeated sigh.

"I'm fine," she says dully. And with that, she walks back and starts picking up groceries. Bobby retrieves a few scattered items and offers them to her. She slams them into a bag. A strand of her long auburn hair falls over her eyes. Impatiently she pushes it back.

"You sure you're okay?" Bobby asks.

Without looking up she says cooly, "Listen, I appreciate your concern, but I really don't need your help."

Bobby takes a step back. "Hey, I'm sorry. It looked like that guy was hurting you." When she says nothing, he ventures, "Is he your husband or boyfriend or something?"

The woman slumps, her voice exasperated and sad. "He's my brother. He has… problems. But he wouldn't have really hurt me. Now please, just leave me alone."

"I'm sorry," says Bobby, "but brother or no brother, I don't feel right leaving you here. It isn't safe. Dome 6 isn't known for its hospitality."

The woman doesn't answer. She shoves a few last items into the bags, stands and shouts toward the building, "Walter! I'm leaving these things here for you. You can come get them after we leave. This man won't hurt you. He was only worried about me. I told him you wouldn't hurt me. I will be back to see you in a few

Chapter 2: What's on Deck 6?

days. Please eat. Please stay safe. I love you!" She scans the distance hoping to catch a glimpse of her brother, but sees and hears nothing. For a brief moment, she seems to fold in on herself like the PiMar structures before her, then she straightens, smooths her clothes, and says with tired resignation, "Okay. I'm ready to go."

"Which deck?" Bobby asks, his finger hovering over the buttons.

"Two," she says. The lift shudders as it ascends. The young woman grabs a stability pole.

"You're from Earth," Bobby observes

"Aren't we all?" she retorts with a slight scowl.

"You know what I mean," says Bobby. "When did you arrive?" He sounds friendly and genuinely interested, but she keeps looking straight ahead. Her words are a wall.

"Why? Why would you want to know that?"

"Just curious. We don't get many newcomers from Earth these days. How did you even get clearance?"

"My gosh!" she scowls. "Are you an Enforcer or something?"

Bobby chuckles. "Far from it. It's just nice to meet someone new from Earth, that's all."

The woman pauses, considering his words. "I arrived two days ago, if two days ago was Thursday. I don't even know anymore."

"Space lag?" Bobby suggests.

"The worst! And the extra gravity! My legs are lead. I could fall on my face any moment."

"Don't worry," Bobby says. "it will get better soon."

They travel the rest of the way in silence. When the lift doors open, they step out only moments before twilight on Dome 2. The projected sun sits low on the horizon. Streaks of wispy, pinkish clouds spread across the darkening blue of the gracefully domed sky. Stretching out beyond and below are wide, well-lit streets with Smartcarts silently floating past blocks of buildings—most in the style and colors of the Old Southwest. Earth-toned buildings with turquoise accents terrace the bowl-shaped incline up to the wall of the dome. Even in her exhaustion, the young woman can't help but gasp at the beauty. She glances back to say something to Bobby, but a girl has stopped him and he seems involved in conversation. The woman walks farther into the dome, letting its quiet peace surround her.

"Sorry," Bobby says, catching up with her. "Listen, I have to go, but can I see you home first?"

"That's not at all necessary," she says.

"Well, I'll see you later then. Take care." There's reluctance in his voice.

"You, too," she says, turning to go.

Impulsively he says, "Hey! Just in case we see each other again, my name's Bobby."

The woman takes a few steps back to him. "Eliesia," she says, meeting his eyes for the first time. Gently touching his forearm, she adds softly, "Thanks for your help, Bobby." Her eyes are deep tiranium green.

He tries to say, "Anytime," but his tongue gets twisted and it comes out something like, "Utt-a-tie." It doesn't matter. She's gone.

Punching in an eight-digit code, Tran unlocks an access door to the freight tunnel in the outer wall of the Hub. He steps inside and waits for his eyes to adjust before starting down the cavernous, dimly-lit passageway. After thirty yards, it ends at a wide opening, the side entrance to the Freetube. Used for moving freight and other large, heavy objects weightlessly between decks. The Tube is forty feet in diameter, a cylinder that extends vertically a mile-and-a-half to all seven decks of Z9. Small lights illuminate its off-white interior, revealing the checkerboard pattern of dark gray antigravity plates inset into its wall. A bright red fluorescent safety buoy tethered to the wall floats inside the Tube.

Years ago, a maintenance worker, not knowing that his co-worker had shut off the power to the antigravity plates, jumped into the Tube to his death. Safety buoys were added at each deck level opening after that—reminders of the tragic accident and the need to look before you leap.

Chapter 2: What's on Deck 6?

From a beat-up, old locker nearby, Tran pulls out orange coveralls and a helmet and puts them on. He smacks the top and sides of the helmet hard with his palms to make sure it's secure—a ritual he does to get himself ready to take on the Freetube. It's him against time, against chance, against his best. Tran gives the helmet one final smack and goes to the edge. Making sure the safety buoy is still in place, and satisfied that it's safe to go, Tran takes a few steps back, then sprints forward launching himself into the Tube with arms and legs outstretched like Superman. He drops at first, but only a little. Momentum takes him forty feet to the other side where he grabs a handrail marked by a splotch of bright green paint. Floating weightless, he gets into a squat position, switches his watch to stopwatch mode, and pushes off the wall hard for the other side.

Body position and flight angles are the keys to reaching the deck 1,100 feet above in record time—body straight and streamlined when gliding between walls, thrusting his feet forward and curling into a full squat just before reaching the wall, then pushing off again with all his strength. Too shallow an angle and there isn't enough upward momentum. Too steep, and too much speed is lost before reaching the other side.

Finding his rhythm, Tran zigzags swiftly up towards Deck 5. He's halfway there when gravitational turbulence causes him to lose weightlessness for fractions of a second. He fights to regain his rhythm and make up for lost time. Push-off, glide, squat, push-off, glide, squat—like Spiderman jumping from building to building.

Now with just a few hundred feet to go, major turbulence hits, tossing him like a butterfly in a windstorm, dropping him at least 75 feet. Using everything he's learned in his years of Freetubing, Tran stabilizes himself as best he can during the sporadic freefalls, careful to avoid being bashed into the wall. Finally back in rhythm, he pushes off again and again, making his way to Deck 5 more tired than usual for a single-deck run.

Being so light, it's difficult for Tran to get out of the Tube. The antigravity acts like suction not wanting to let him go. He feels like a sock being sucked into a vacuum cleaner hose and strains to pull himself free. Pressing his palms firmly down on the freight tunnel's floor, he takes a deep breath, and, having years ago figured out the movements necessary to escape, methodically extricates himself, then lies winded on his back and checks his watch. It's a full minute and a half over his best time. *Can't be helped,* he thinks. *Turbulence happens.* So does hunger, and he realizes it's been too long since his last meal. He hangs the coveralls and helmet on a rack, and heads off for Rodgers.

When Tran arrives, the restaurant is already half-filled with Saturday-evening diners. "Hi, Tracy," he says, "Have you seen Bobby?"

"Not today," says the waitress, setting some dirty dishes into a tub.

Tran glances across the patrons looking for Bobby's light brown hair. *Nope. Not here yet.* But he's happy to see that the booth in the back corner is available. He slides across the burgundy-colored bench seat, careful not to catch his pants on the strip of duct tape covering a tear. Tracy hands him a menu and places a glass of water and basket of fresh breadsticks in front of him. "Bobby's supposed to be here," says Tran.

Tracy says, "He'll probably have a Triple."

"I think that's what I'm going to have too," he says, handing her the menu.

"You want fries with that?" Tran gives her a look. "Right," she says, "Silly question. I'll make sure you get your salad right away."

In a few gulps Tran downs his water, then pulls a soft, warm breadstick from the cloth-covered basket. Rodgers is famous for its breadsticks, their taste matching their heavenly aroma. Tran wonders what the secret is in making them taste so wonderful. Every bite has layers of flavor. Revived and refreshed, he looks towards the door, hoping to see Bobby's friendly face. He's surprised that he's beaten him here. Then, with a start, he sees a neatly dressed middle-aged man enter the restaurant. The man surveys the surroundings, then approaches Tran's booth, seemingly nonchalant,

Chapter 2: What's on Deck 6?

but not quite. He moves with latent power, like a man who keeps himself fit just in case he needs to be. Tran sits forward with alarm.

"Good evening, Mr. Moore," says the man. His voice is cordial, but formal.

Anxiously Tran asks, "Is everything okay?"

"Yes, sir. Everything is fine. Your grandfather would like a meeting with you and Mr. Johnson on Wednesday afternoon, if that's possible."

Tran sits back and lets out the breath he didn't know he was holding. "I'm glad to know he's returned," he says, "Wednesday is fine for me and I'm pretty sure that's okay for Bobby too. What time?"

"Sixteen hundred hours. The location is Vidmar Delta."

"We'll be there," says Tran.

"Very good," says the man, "I'll let him know to expect you. Good-bye."

Tracy refills Tran's water and sets his salad in front of him. He chews the buttery lettuce without noticing its delicate flavor, his mind pondering the meeting with his grandfather, wondering what it might be about. Half his salad is gone when Bobby collapses into the seat opposite him and says, "I'll give you 20 tags for that if you let me have it right now."

Tran laughs. "Where have you been?"

"Believe it or not, Dome 6."

"Really?"

"I know. I'll tell you about it later. Right now I just want to order and eat." Bobby cranes his neck looking for the waitress.

"You can have my Triple when it comes," Tran offers. "I'll order another one."

Bobby's voice drips with exaggerated gratitude. "Have I ever told you what a wonderful person you are?"

Tran threatens, "Hey, if you don't want it…"

"No, really, thank you. You're a good person. Too good. Your girlfriend was crazy to leave you."

Tran retorts with irritation, "She didn't leave me. She moved to Earth with her parents. But thanks for bringing it up."

"Oops! Sore spot. Sorry…" says Bobby.

"Here's some news," says Tran, "Mr. Shapiro was just here. Grandfather is back at Vidmar and wants us to meet him there on Wednesday. Do you know what that's about?"

Bobby shakes his head and reaches for a breadstick. "Haven't a clue. Did he say how Grandfather is doing?"

"He said everything is fine. I was really worried when I saw him, though. I was afraid he was going to say Grandfather was dead."

"I would have thought the same," says Bobby.

Tracy arrives with the Triple. Bobby pronounces her an angel of mercy and dubs her with a breadstick, then devours the Triple like a Labrador pup gulping a pound of ground round. Sighing, he sits back and looks at his watch, "Oh, I've got to get going. I have shopping to do, and I have to meet that Dengie kid at 2200. Are you staying on Mirage tonight?"

"No," says Tran. "I'll be at the compound for a few days. We have church tomorrow and Monday I coach the kids."

Bobby slides out of the booth. "Okay. I'll see you tomorrow then. Thanks for the Triple."

"Hey, wait!" says Tran, "You were going to tell me about Dome 6."

"I'll tell you later," says Bobby. He takes one last gulp of water, waves good-bye to Tracy, and hurries out the door.

Chapter 2: What's on Deck 6?

Chapter 3
Dengie and the Master

Pressing the call button on the boarding platform's intercom, the young tech calls, "Dengie here. Permission to come aboard."

Not long after, Bobby leans out from the open boarding hatch on the port side of Mirage. "Permission granted," he says.

As the platform rises, so does Dengie's anticipation. He has admired the beauty and exterior design of Mirage since he first saw her during a class field trip to the docks in the 2nd grade. The experience sparked a desire in him to work on the ships of Zenith Colony, and now, ten years later, he's about to step inside this famous ship.

Bobby welcomes Dengie aboard and offers to carry his toolbox, but Dengie declines. "I'm used to it," he says.

Bobby wastes no time with small talk. Hurrying Dengie towards the bridge, he tells the young tech, "The transponder was acting up for about three months. After two failed repairs, I had it replaced. The new one worked fine for a few weeks and now it won't transmit at all." Dengie shifts his backpack and struggles to keep up. "Sorry," Bobby says, slowing down, "I'm just so ready for this to be over. It's mystifying. No one's been able to track it down and it's way beyond what I can do."

When they reach the bridge, Dengie glances around and lets out a low whistle. Setting down his toolbox he exclaims softly, "Perfection! She's even more amazing than I imagined." He's been in many ships, from streamlined Screamers to bulky Transports, but this isn't just a ship; Mirage is a work of art. Every inch, from the gracefully curving passageways to the layout of the bridge, is designed to please the eye as well as meet the needs of the crew as efficiently as possible.

Dengie swings his backpack to the floor and rolls up his sleeves. "I'll figure it out," he says with confidence.

"I hope so," says Bobby. Pointing to a small alcove somewhat hidden in the rear of the bridge, he says, "I'll be right over there if you need me." The young technician seems trustworthy enough, but Bobby's not about to leave someone he's barely met alone on the bridge.

Dengie has already removed the access panel under the console. Bobby watches him slide inside, pulling his backpack and toolbox in after him.

Lost in his book, a fictional piece that famously predicted the War Of The States, Bobby begins to hear Dengie's voice, somewhat muffled, coming from under the console. He's saying things such as, "Oh, no you don't. Not on my watch!"

Bobby calls, "Excuse me?"

Dengie calls back, "Uh, nothing. Just talking to myself. Sorry."

Bobby glances at his watch. It's 0030 hours. He ignores further comments from the bridge, knowing they're not meant for him.

Just past 0200 hours, Dengie emerges from under the console, wipes his face with his handkerchief, and announces, "Okay, I think we got it."

Bobby jerks awake. "Yeah. Yeah, I'm here. What did you say?"

Dengie calls, "I think I got it figured out."

"Oh, okay. Good!" says Bobby.

"Uh, well, unfortunately, it's not so good. I found a major problem."

"What's that?" Bobby asks, rubbing his eyes as he walks back to the bridge.

"Your transponder has been hacked," Dengie says.

"Hacked?" Bobby is suddenly wide awake. "What do you mean 'hacked'? How do you hack a transponder?"

"They gained access through its carrier wave. It looks like they were trying to get into the nav system."

Chapter 3: Dengie and the Master

"For what purpose?"

"I really don't know," Dengie says, "but if I were to take a guess, I'd say to gain access to the ship's navigational history."

Alarmed, Bobby asks, "Did they get it?"

"We won't know until we can tap fully into the system," says the tech. "I'm just seeing the surface. I can't go any farther without an Overseer."

Bobby's mind is quickly processing this disturbing information. The ramifications of someone knowing everywhere Mirage has been are staggering. Grimly he grabs the mic. "Z9 Control, this is Mirage, Deck 7, Bay 1."

Immediately a voice comes back, "Mirage, go ahead."

"Control, this is Bobby Johnson. I am requesting an Overseer. Priority 1."

"Affirmative, Mirage. Will contact you shortly with ETA."

"Roger that." Bobby looks back at Dengie. "Are you absolutely sure about this? Could it possibly be a bug or some other anomaly that's causing whatever you're seeing?"

Dengie shakes his head. "I double and triple checked it, Bobby. It's clear to me that someone cracked the transponder. I just don't know how far they got before security measures shut it down. At least that part worked." Sliding a tool into its slot in his toolbox, he adds, "Whoever it was, they're highly skilled and they have the right type of equipment—expensive equipment. It took a lot of power to overtake the carrier wave. I don't know anyone with equipment like that."

"I don't either," says Bobby, "But I aim to find out. Can you come with me to a meeting on Wednesday afternoon to explain what you've found?"

"I work on Wednesdays," says Dengie.

"Don't worry about that. I'll clear it with Dave."

"I can't afford to lose pay, Bobby," Dengie says.

"I'll pay you triple what you make on your shift," Bobby says, "and I'm doubling your pay for this job. We're into way more than what I hired you for."

"I appreciate that," Dengie says, snapping the latches of his toolbox closed. "As long as you clear it with Dave, it's okay with me."

"Great!" says Bobby. Then he adds quickly, "But you can't mention this to anyone. Not your parents, your friends, not your girlfriend or coworkers, not your grandmother, or…"

Dengie laughs and holds up his hands. "Don't worry, Bobby. I won't say a word."

The voice comes back on the radio. "Mirage, this is Z9 Control."

"Go ahead, Control."

"ETA 0330 hours. Name: Goldwyn Turry."

"Affirmative. Thank you." Turning to Dengie, Bobby says, "Well, we've got a little time to kill. Let's get some tea."

Dengie sits at the table drinking his second cup of tea, admiring the design and artistic attention to detail that is evident even in such a utilitarian area as this ship's galley. Bobby moves around the orderly space, opening cabinets that reveal innovative compartments with easy access to everything. Normally, he would be engaging Dengie in conversation, but his mind is on other things. He doesn't tell Dengie he's met this Overseer before, a hard-nosed, no-nonsense, by-the-book type, and he's feeling intimidated about having to deal with him. As he sits down, Bobby absentmindedly fills Dengie's cup again and asks, "How long do you think it will take before we know how far the hack went?"

"I'm not really sure," says the tech. "It's not like I have a lot of experience with hacks. I've studied books about stuff like this happening on Earth, but that's all I know. My guess is it probably won't take long once we plug into the system. Maybe an hour or two. It all depends on the queries we send."

Bobby is surprised when the call bell rings. "He's early," he says, glancing at his watch. He heads for the boarding hatch, mentally preparing for whatever comes.

Chapter 3: Dengie and the Master

Goldwyn Turry enters Mirage with the easy authority of a man who has long known his worth. "Hello, gentlemen," he says, removing his hat, overcoat, and scarf. Even at 0315 hours Turry is dressed meticulously in a dark blue suit. He hands the outerwear to Dengie, who holds it awkwardly, wondering what to do with it. "Is your grandfather onboard, Mr. Johnson?"

"No, sir. He's been on an extended trip."

"Without Mirage?" Turry's tone holds a hint of challenge. "That's quite unusual isn't it?"

Evenly Bobby replies, "As you know, he has many ships.

Turry fixes his eyes on Bobby. With a slight frown, he says, "I have to say I'm extremely uncomfortable with your grandfather being absent. It's quite unorthodox."

"I assure you I have full autonomy and authority on this ship," says Bobby firmly. "I have the commission papers to back that up, if you would care to see them."

Turry studies the young man standing unflinching before him. "That won't be necessary. I have seen you with your grandfather and have on occasion heard him speak very highly of you. We can proceed."

Bobby steps into the passageway, saying, "Please come this way."

Dengie starts to follow, his arms still full of the heavy clothing, but Turry notices, gives him a kindly look, and says, "Young man, there is a coat closet right behind you."

"Oh, yes, I see," says Dengie, quickly hanging everything up. "Sorry, sir."

The walk to the bridge is brisk, Turry keeping pace effortlessly with Bobby though he's more than three times his age and is carrying a large, official-looking black case.

"Please sit down," says Bobby, directing Turry and Dengie to seats across the aisle from the control console, then taking a seat behind them.

Turry pulls a clipboard from his bag and, in an official tone fluid from decades of repetition, opens the session. "Before we begin, gentlemen, you must be aware and agree to the following conditions: I, the Overseer, will monitor all your coded queries and will pass them on to the system only if they meet my approval. In no case are you allowed to modify any of the existing programs of the system, the only exception being if malicious code is found and verified. That code may then be eradicated, if possible. If I suspect any of your queries contain hidden or covert command codes, and believe me, I will know if they do, I will immediately terminate this session and alert the Enforcers.

"This session is private and my report is confidential, unless needed for legal reasons in the courts. I am not to divulge any information to any other agent or agency. However, I do inform you that Enforcers are aware of my whereabouts and will act swiftly if I do not report back in a timely manner. I must also inform you that while I am onboard, the space door will remain locked by Flight Control and this ship will not be allowed to leave the dock." Holding out the clipboard, Turry asks, "Do you understand and agree to these conditions?" Bobby and Dengie sign the form and Turry slips it back into his case. "Very well," he says, "to which systems would you like me to connect?"

"The comms and nav please," says Dengie.

From his case Turry removes two hand-held coding terminals and a metallic keycard with a black interface formed as a grip on one end. With long, thin cables he connects both terminals to the keycard's interface and inserts the keycard into a slot in the console. Offering one of the hand terminals to Dengie, he says, "I'm assuming you're the coder here."

"Yes, sir," Dengie says, taking the device. "Thank you, sir."

With the other terminal in hand, the Overseer says, "You may begin."

Dengie quickly enters his first query into the hand terminal and sends it. Turry reviews it on his terminal, approves it, and passes it on to the system. The system replies back. Dengie sends query after query. In some cases Turry suggests a different or better syntax, reminding him that he's dealing with an older system.

Dengie is extremely impressed with the man's mastery of code and how unbelievably fast he can read, interpret, and improve it. He starts calling him Master Turry, which the Overseer neither acknowledges nor deflects.

The procedure continues at a furious pace. From where he sits, Bobby can't see the expressions on the young tech's face to ascertain how things are going, but he knows better than to ask questions or disrupt their concentration. Finally, Dengie pauses and asks, "Master Turry, can you verify that the transponder has been hacked?"

There's passion in the elderly gentleman's reply, "Oh, yes! Quite certainly! Without question. Would you like me to eradicate it?"

"That's okay," says Dengie, "I'll do it." Then he quickly adds, "That is, if you don't mind."

"Please," Turry says magnanimously, "go right ahead."

Dengie enters the code he's been compiling in his head and sends it. Turry carefully examines what the young coder has written, approves it, and passes it on. "Your code is sublime," he says. "Many of our Junior Overseers cannot write code this well or this fast. You truly have a gift, young man. You may want to consider Overseeing as a career." Dengie blushes and stammers, trying to brush it off. Turry bristles. "Listen here, young man, you must learn how to take a compliment without showing false modesty or self-deprecation. I know what I'm talking about when it comes to code. You cannot discount it. Accept it with dignity from now on."

Humbly Dengie replies, "Yes, sir. I will try, sir."

For just a moment, some of the hardness leaves the Overseer's eyes. Then, confirming that the hack has been removed and the transponder is functioning properly, Turry ends the session and packs up his devices. Bobby is anxious to know how far the hack went, but Dengie is feverishly asking the Overseer questions and Turry is answering with obvious pleasure. Abruptly Bobby interrupts. "Thank you so much, Overseer Turry. I appreciate you coming here at such an hour. It is very important to me and my grandfather that you did so. We are in your debt."

"Nonsense!" Turry retorts brusquely. "I'm doing my official duty. Twenty-seven years ago I came to the colony, and thanks to what your grandfather has built, I've been employed here ever since. I can't do enough to repay him for what he's done."

Dengie brings the Overseer's hat, coat, and scarf, handing them back in the reverse order that they had been removed. This attention to detail is not lost on the man. Settling his hat on his gray head, he says, "I wish you a good morning, Mr. Johnson." Then, with a slight nod, he adds, "and to you, Mr. Dengie." For a brief moment he looks like a master craftsman who has just encountered a gifted young apprentice worthy to be his heir.

Bobby presses the button, the hatch slides open, and chill air rushes in. Turry tightens his scarf. "It's cold down here in the docking bays," he says. Then, case in hand, he steps onto the boarding platform and turns to face the boys. Fixing his eyes on Bobby he says, "Oh, by the way, I recognize that hack. It's based on an old hack from Earth. Best be careful." He tips his hat as the platform lowers to the deck.

Bobby latches the door and gives Dengie a searching look. Blankly, Dengie stares back, then says, "Oh, right! Sorry. Everything is okay. No harm. They didn't get into the nav history. It remained secure."

"You're sure?" asks Bobby.

"Positive. No doubt about it." Dengie gives him a reassuring grin. "Hey, the Master says I'm gifted. Relax!"

Bobby laughs and pats Dengie on the shoulder. "Good work, my friend. You really came through for us." Then a new worry passes over his face. "So… what do you think about that last thing—you know, about the old hack from Earth?"

Dengie shrugs, "I don't know. I'll take a look in the library and see if I can find anything."

Chapter 3: Dengie and the Master

"I'd appreciate that," Bobby says. "But for now, thanks to you, we're good to go." Bobby smiles gratefully. "Hey, you want to see the rest of the ship?"

"I would love it!" Dengie says, his eyes suddenly bright even at the hour.

"Great! What do you want to see first?"

"Well," Dengie says with a wry smile, "considering all that tea, how about a bathroom?"

Chapter 4
Baseball to Nothingness

Shouting, "Bring it home, Jeremiah!" Tran hits a lazy fly ball to shallow right field. Jeremiah goes back on his heels, catching the ball and throwing it weakly towards home plate. Tran calls out to him, pantomiming his instructions, "Get yourself back and come in on the ball as you catch it. That gives you momentum to get off a good throw. Try it again. Bring it home!" Tran tosses the ball up and swings. The ball cracks off the wooden bat. Jeremiah drifts back, then moves forward to make the catch and fires a throw on two hops right to the catcher's mitt. Tran shouts, "There you go! Nice! Now you've got it!" Jeremiah grins, pleased at the words and the nod of approval from his coach.

Tran yells, "Okay, everyone, bring it home and come on in." With precision, he hits the ball to each fielder in turn. One after another, they throw it home, then run in and line up in front of the third-base dugout. They're feeling their successes and jostle each other, silly and a little rowdy, but as soon as their coach walks up they give him their full attention.

"Good work today," Tran says. "I'm proud of you. You're getting the movements down, learning how to play the ball and throwing it where it needs to be. All of that is important. But there's something just as important, and I saw you doing it today. You stayed focused and made very few mental mistakes. That's important if you want the team to do well. We practice and do drills over and over again to cut down on physical errors, but they're still going to happen from time to time. We're not perfect. But mental mistakes don't have to happen. Out on the field, you need to be prepared before each pitch—thinking ahead and figuring out what you'll do if the ball's hit to you hard or soft or in-between, on the ground or in the air, or where you're going to cover if it's hit to someone else. And what's the first thing you need to know before each pitch?"

They shout in unison, "How many outs and who's on base!"

"Right! You don't want to get caught daydreaming. You want to be prepared before every pitch. And when you are, it frees your mind up for that play so you no longer have to think about it. All you have to do is see the ball and play the ball.

"I had a difficult time with that when I was first learning. I didn't want to have to concentrate that hard. It was a challenge I didn't think I could overcome. But the more I did it, the easier it got until it was perfectly natural to me and not hard at all. It actually makes the game more fun. Do you guys understand all that?"

"Yes, Coach!" they shout with one voice.

It makes Tran chuckle. They're earnest and enthusiastic, but also so happy and free—*The way kids ought to be,* he thinks, remembering when he was like that—when his biggest challenge was learning to keep his mind on where he was and what he was doing right that minute. He didn't realize how special those times were, days when baseball and other things he loved were giving him skills for life he didn't even know he was learning.

"A short announcement," Tran says. "Mr. Moreno is going to run Wednesday evening's practice so I'll see all of you back here next Monday. Now let's get the gear picked up."

Baseball has a long history in the Zenith Colony. One of the main challenges with artificial gravity is how to make objects in the air react as they would on Earth without increasing the gravitational effects on objects near or on the surface. The early settlers adjusted the gravitational systems according to how a baseball reacted and how natural it felt when they played the game. Among those first inhabitants of Z9 City were astrophysicists, engineers, chemists, artisans and artists. Because they loved the game, they wanted their baseball fields to feel as genuinely authentic as possible. They knew there were limitations to what they'd be able to imitate of the natural material world, but they refused to settle for what was quick, cheap, convenient, and artificial. Combining their efforts and aesthetics, they created both a convincingly supple green grass and a good, red dirt that felt satisfyingly real. Teams and ball parks started appearing on most of the stations, and baseball became the colony's favorite pastime.

Leaving the ballfield, Tran settles into an easy running pace toward home. It's a quiet Monday evening in Dome 2. The lights of the ballfield are still on. Tran glances at them shining in the dark. It looks friendly to him. Lots of good memories come from baseball at night.

Some of the players call out and wave wildly as they glide past in Smartcarts. Tran smiles and waves back. It's his second year coaching a junior team and he's surprised to find it as enjoyable as playing the game himself.

Tran's love of baseball came early. His father started it, tossing a soft white ball to his four-year-old son for an easy catch. Before baseball, if his father wasn't at work in the lab, he was locked away in his study at home, wrapped up in his research where Tran couldn't get to him. But Tran's mother insisted that her husband find a way to spend extended, meaningful time with their son, not just a moment here and there.

Tran's father was bewildered. He didn't know how to relate to the boy. But the science of baseball intrigued the man and he found it worthy of his examination. When Tran showed aptitude and enthusiasm for the game, his father designed a full training program for him and took joy in instructing him in all aspects, but especially in the precision of physical movement, and the strategies and psychologies that give baseball its finesse.

Drill after drill, hours and hours of practice—first with only his father coaching him, then on his own or with friends or in the school league so he could show his father how much he had improved. Many young children might have complained, gotten bored or discouraged, or quit. But Tran had good reasons for investing so much of his time and heart in baseball—he had de-

Chapter 4: Baseball to Nothingness

veloped a deep love and appreciation for the game, but most of all, he treasured the connection it made between him and his father, the only significant involvement they had in each other's lives.

In the distance, the ballfield lights go off. It's darker now. No projected moon crossing the dome, only stars. Tran angles across the avenue and turns left onto a wide walkway, its edges illuminated with soft white lines of light. His footfalls make rhythmic, muffled thuds in the quiet of evening. After a few blocks, he passes some flats on his left, his eyes swiftly moving to the fourth floor where he can see light through the blinds of the place where he once lived with his parents. It seems strange and unnatural to him that others live there now and call it home.

Eight years ago, Tran said good-bye to his parents, grabbed his book bag and scampered downstairs, banged out the front door of the complex, and ran the three blocks to school. That afternoon, the Principle came to his class and escorted him to her office. Tran was mystified. He was an exemplary student. His parents expected that of him, and he would never do anything to jeopardize their approval. Still, he worried that he had done something wrong and was in some kind of trouble. When the Principle opened the door to her office, Tran was surprised to see the Monsignor of his parish there. "Hello, Tran," he said. "Please sit down. I have something to tell you…" The Monsignor hesitated. There was grief on the man's face. Dread began to crawl over Tran's skin. Haltingly, the man continued, "Son… there's been a terrible accident. An explosion…"

Tran's mind went numb. Words hit him like heavy objects. Then he was falling, falling through the darkness, falling like the worker who jumped into the Freetube expecting to find the antigravity working as usual, expecting to do his job as usual, expecting his life to go on…as usual…

"So sorry… your parents… so sorry…"

Everything was a blur after that. Arrangements were made for him to stay with foster parents. He went from one foster home to another. They all wanted to help, but he had problems they weren't prepared to handle and it didn't go well. He had horrible dreams of explosions that made him afraid to go to sleep, and when he was awake, grief shot through him, wracking his heart until he wanted to scream and tear himself to bits. He fell under the delirium of a spiking fever that left him unresponsive to the outside world. He heard voices near and far. He saw light and shapes and shadows, but his brain could not translate any of it. At one point, he sensed he was traveling on a very powerful, fast-moving ship. *Where am I?* he wondered. It was his last coherent thought before slipping into nothingness.

Chapter 5
New Life

Tran was sinking, darkness surrounding him, blocking out all else. Was he dreaming? He tried to move, but his arms and legs would not respond and he couldn't make a sound. His heart beat wildly. *This has to be a dream,* he thought. *If I can just open my eyes...* He willed his eyes to open, fighting with all his might, and finally there was light and the dark weight slowly lifted.

Where am I? he wondered. He saw faint blue—the pale first light of morning. Maybe he was in his room, but the light panel was on the wrong side and the bed was wrong. It smelled clean, but different, and everything was white. Then he noticed breathing—quiet and even, and close. Cautiously he turned his head and looked. Asleep in a bed a few feet away was a woman, her long hair like black brush strokes on the white pillow. *Who is that?* he thought in alarm.

The woman seemed to sense him and was instantly awake. She looked at him with kind brown eyes. "You are thirsty," she said. And he realized he was, terribly. She rolled off her bed and tied back her hair with a couple of swift twists of a red band she took off her wrist. Tran stared at her. She was wearing something that looked like pajamas. They were white and seemed to float about her as she moved. Then a thought hit him. Maybe he was dead. But his throat was so sore he figured he probably wasn't. Still, who knows what you feel after you're dead?

"Are you an angel?" he croaked.

The woman laughed lightly. "No angel. I am Mei," she said, touching over her heart, "here to see you well."

She still looked like an angel to him. He wondered, *Do angels wear pajamas?* He didn't know. Besides, why would an angel lie? Tran decided she was telling him the truth.

Mei moved effortlessly—graceful, yet strong. He thought she would make a great shortstop. She returned with a glass of water. Carefully she slipped a supporting arm under his shoulders and held the glass to his lips. "Drink slow," she said. It hurt him to swallow, but after a few sips his throat began to feel better. With a gentle hand, she felt his forehead. "Fever is gone," she said. "You will be better now."

"Is this a Health Station?" he asked.

"This is home," she said, settling him back on his pillow. "We will not talk now."

Home. The very sound of the word and the way she said it made Tran remember. He'd been in so many places, one after another. The people seemed to belong there, and though they welcomed him and were nice enough, he didn't feel he ever fit in. Now, in Mei's home, he suddenly remembered the dark, endless falling and knew he would not be going home again. There was no way to get there, and even if he could, no one would be there. He knew that now. Tears filled his eyes. It hurt too much to be alive. He turned his face away, his tears soaking into the pillow. Darkness returned—heavy, relentless, irresistible. But before it could engulf him completely, Mei dispelled it as swiftly as a light in the night.

"You will eat now," she said, propping him up with pillows. Mei held a small white bowl up for him to see. "Gold broth," she said. "You try it?" She encouraged him with her eyes. It was a pale golden color, clear and smelling of herbs he didn't know. He sniffed it tentatively, not convinced he could get it down, but when he tasted the first spoonful, his body welcomed it as something it needed and was hungry to have. However, after a few more spoonfuls, there was a problem. Terribly embarrassed, he confessed, "Mei, I have to go to the bathroom."

She was overjoyed. "Good!" she said. "I will carry you. Call me when you are done." And that's how it worked.

Chapter 5: New Life

Days passed. Tran mostly slept, drank water, clear soups and teas, and slept some more. Mei was always nearby. Sometimes he heard soft singing, though he couldn't understand the words. He would lie quietly, letting the sounds bring pictures into his mind, and though sometimes the songs seemed sad, they were beautiful, and it always made him feel better.

When the partition between the bedroom and kitchen was folded back, the two rooms became essentially one, and Tran, propped on pillows, took comfort in watching Mei cutting things to put in the various pots on the stove. He liked her precise movements. She did a lot of cooking, and everything she did was always followed by thorough rinsing, wiping, and drying. *A Clean Bean,* Tran thought. That's what his mother would have called her. He wondered how old she was, but he had been taught it was impolite to ask, so he didn't. He especially liked her skin—dark, smooth, clear, like it was brand new. He decided she must be a little younger than his mother.

It was frustrating for Tran to stay in bed, but he was no longer the healthy eight year old he had been. The high fevers had left him prone to crippling headaches so intense he could barely open his eyes. His legs that had easily run countless baseball drills were now practically useless.

Lovingly, Mei continued her vigilant care. The broth began to come with little pieces of tender vegetables. Teas were steeped with healing herbs. She wrapped Tran's limbs in soft cloths that had been soaked in strong-smelling liquid and massaged his hands and feet, gently but firmly squeezing where the energy lines ran. "Energy is like water," she said, explaining in her way how his body was brilliantly designed with circuits of nerves, networks of blood vessels, and energy moving in meridians like rivers up and down the body. "When rivers stop, troubles come," she said, pressing her thumbs along Tran's calf. He winced under her strong fingers. She paused, pressing down on the sore spot, then releasing the pressure suddenly. He felt energy rush into his feet. "River is free now," she said, "Body can heal."

One day while Mei was busy In the laundry room, Tran found himself eyeing the bathroom door. It was only a few steps from the side of his bed. He assessed the distance and his present condition. He was definitely feeling stronger, even somewhat coordinated. *Hmmm,* he thought. *Maybe I can make it...* Carefully he eased out of bed and stood braced against the mattress, steadying himself with palms flat on the covers. He ventured a small step, then another. By the time Mei had returned and noticed he was up, Tran had made it to the bathroom door. Flashing her a huge, triumphant smile, he stepped inside and shut the door. He did not see her astonishment melt into relief and profound fondness. He never knew how very worried she had been.

As the weeks went by, Tran's health continued to improve. One morning as Mei was bringing fresh towels to the kitchen, she found him pretending to field ground balls in the living room, then scrambling up the four steps to the dining area to catch an imaginary fly ball, all the while giving a play-by-play description of his efforts. He was a little slow and unsteady on his feet, and out of breath from the effort, but his blue eyes were bright with happiness. By that night, the two of them had converted the living room into a workout area.

Mei was a methodical teacher. Her instructions were as deft and precise as her cooking skills. For Tran's exercises, she alternated slow movement which maximized the strength of muscle fibers and balance with fast, sharp movements for agility and carefully directed power. Tran liked repetition. He enjoyed the feeling of muscles that remembered how to move together in a fluid motion, and breath that came from the bottoms of his lungs, exhaling all deep wastes, then inhaling fresh, good air. He happily stretched, lunged, and jumped, translating each movement she taught him into something useful for baseball.

After breakfast one morning, Mei led Tran to a room just down the short hall from the living room. "This is your room," she said. "You are well now. Time to have your own quiet place. Things are here from your old house. Do you want to see?"

Tran was startled. "From my house?"

"Yes," she said. "You want to see?"

Together they began to open boxes and put things in place. They hung his posters on the walls and organized books on the shelves. His baseball stuff was put in one corner, and they made up his bed with blue baseball-theme sheets, covers, and bedspread. His collection of figurines of Earth animals was arranged on top of a blue bureau with its shiny round brass drawer pulls, and the matching oval throw rug was on the floor. It looked a lot like his old room. Even the light panel was in the right place. It gave him a strange sense of security and peace.

It was evening by the time they finished. They ate dinner and completed the cleanup Mei always insisted upon, even if they were tired. Tran yawned. Fondly Mei touched his cheek. "You get ready now," she said. "Tomorrow is big day." Tran wondered what that meant, but he also knew better than to ask. He figured she'd tell him when she told him.

Soon he was back, smiling in his old baseball pajamas, face washed, teeth brushed.

"First night in your new room," Mei said, escorting him down the hall. "I am happy for you." She tucked him in under his blue bed covers. They smelled like home. "Sleep now," she said. "Tomorrow you will meet friend who brought you to me."

"Who's that?" he asked, stifling a yawn.

"Dr. Gransom," she said.

Tran snapped suddenly awake. "Dr. Gransom brought me to you?" Mei nodded. His voice rose an octave. "The Chief Director Dr. Gransom? Why?"

"We will not talk now," said Mei. She kissed him lightly on the forehead, turned off the light and left the room.

It was difficult for Tran to sleep that night, not only because he was in an unfamiliar room without the soothing rhythms of Mei's gentle breathing nearby, he was nervous about meeting the founder and Chief Director of the Zenith Colony. Doctor Gransom was enormously famous, someone Tran had learned about in school. Someone bigger than life. Someone so important that everyone in the galaxy knew of him. He wondered, *How does he know me and why did he bring me to Mei?* There were no answers, and at last he drifted into sleep.

At midday Tran and Mei left the flat, walking down a long, well-lit corridor with doors to flats on either side. He was excited to be out for the first time since he came to stay with her. Two men walked well ahead of them and two walked well behind. Mei had already told him they would be there. When he asked why, she said, "You stay young boy now. Not worry like old man."

Tran frowned. He liked answers, not postponements. *Maybe they're guides like Lewis and Clark,* he reasoned. He began to imagine Mei and him trekking through unknown realms. In a way, it was true. For him, everything was new. He had no idea where he was or where they were going. Maybe Mei didn't either. Maybe that's why they needed guides—two ahead to lead them, two behind in case they got separated and wandered off.

Their soft shoes made hardly any noise as they followed the men down a long ramp that spiraled into a courtyard dotted with a number of conveniently-placed tables situated amongst numerous potted trees, flowers, and shrubs. Nearby was a large pond about twenty feet long and almost as wide. It was shaped in the graceful curves of a natural pool, the glossy dark water edged all around with white undressed stones. In the center of the pond, a silver stream cascaded down the rugged face of a black space rock. Tran yelled, "Mei! Look! Fish!" He pulled her over to the water's edge and stared down at the huge multi-colored koi, excited to see living fish for the first time. "Why are they all over here looking at us?" he asked.

"They want food," she said.

Tran begged, "Please, can I feed them?"

"We will come back," she said, taking his hand. "We must see Dr. Gransom now." Reluctantly, Tran trotted beside her, though he looked back over his shoulder as long as he could.

They walked quickly past many doors with signs that he didn't have time to read. Then they turned down a hallway and went up a short flight of stairs to a pair of thick white doors. The men unlocked and held them open while Mei and Tran stepped into a wide, quiet room carpeted in rich burgundy with flowers and vines woven throughout in intricate designs. The walls were filled with paintings and there were intriguing sculptures of animals set in small, rounded alcoves. The room was softly lit and empty except for a few padded chairs and a shiny black grand piano with its lid down.

Tran would have liked to linger and look at all the animals, but the men were moving on. They passed through another corridor and unlocked a door that opened into a large room crowded with so many free-standing shelves of books that Tran thought they must be in the stacks of a public library. The shelves filled most of the room, but there was a pleasant area with cushioned chairs that invited a person to read and rest. It reminded him of his father's study, homey with comfortable old furniture from Earth, and it triggered a pang of grief that made him feel small and insecure. Just then a deep voice boomed from behind one of the shelves. "Come in, you two. I'll be right with you."

Quietly the men closed the doors leaving Tran and Mei alone with the voice. Tran tried hard to keep the butterflies in his stomach under control. Sensing his nervousness, Mei whispered, "He is just a man." Tran took a deep breath, squared his shoulders, and hoped he looked braver than he felt. He wanted to be strong for Mei.

From behind the stacks of books, an elderly man strode towards them. Tran recognized him from pictures in his textbooks, but Dr. Gransom was much taller than he expected, and more energetic too. His strong movements were evidence of decades of exploring in mountains and deserts in hostile conditions.

"Hello, Mei," Dr. Gransom said with a welcoming smile. "Good to see you again." Then, holding out his big hand, he said to Tran,"And hello, young man. I'm so pleased to finally meet you." Shyly Tran offered his own small hand, which the doctor shook gently, bending his frame considerably to do so. "Mei has kept me informed of your progress. I'm amazed at your determination to recover. We were all so worried about you. Has Mei taken good care of you?"

Tran glanced at Mei and then looked up at Gransom. "She saved me," he said quietly.

Gransom studied Tran's face, then straightened up and said simply, "Yes, I believe she did." In the doctor's light gray eyes, Tran saw concern and kindness, but they were sharp too, like the eagle in his poster. With his bright white hair and brown sweater, Dr. Gransom reminded him of one of those mighty birds, but mostly it was his bearing and the keen, penetrating gaze that could discern the truth of what he was seeing even from a long way off.

"Come let's sit down and talk," Gransom said, taking his seat on a high-backed chair. "We have a lot to discuss." Mei and Tran sat on a couch facing him across a low table strewn with books, papers, and miscellaneous space rocks. Tran stared at the rocks and worried about what he might hear. When grown-ups said, "Sit down, we need to talk," it usually meant something bad was coming.

Gransom settled himself in his chair. "Let's see. Where to begin?" He paused, considering his words. "Did you know your parents worked for me?"

Surprised, Tran answered, "I thought everyone worked for you."

Gransom chuckled, "I mean did you know they worked directly with me? They were two of the most brilliant scientists I've ever known. We spent a great deal of time together on many important projects. I take it you didn't know that."

"No, sir. They didn't talk about their work."

Chapter 5: New Life

"Well, there were good reasons for that. Good for them for keeping things secret. Not many do." Gransom leaned forward and lifted a large book from the table, running his hand over its old, brown cover. "This book is very special to me," he said. "I wrote it over fifty years ago on my voyage here to start the colony. It took eight months to get here in those days. Can you imagine that? I find the majority of space travel extremely boring, so I like to fill my time writing. This particular volume is the first copy of the first printing of this book. I want you to have it because of what your parents meant to me. I respected them and miss them a great deal. Their passing is a substantial loss to me and the entire Zenith Colony, but our loss is nothing compared to yours." Dr. Gransom held the book out to Tran. "Please accept this as a token of my honor to them."

Carefully Tran took the book in both hands. In embossed letters it read, "The Future of Magtronic Space Travel by Dr. Joseph Gransom." He felt its weight and smelled the aged paper. It seemed as if Lewis and Clark had just handed him one of their original journals.

Gransom continued, "The technologies and concepts in that book helped open the doors to deep-space travel. I'm very proud of it. I hope you'll read it someday."

"I will, sir," Tran said. "I promise. Thank you."

Gransom nodded approvingly, then cleared his throat and straightened himself in his chair. "Now then, there's something of great importance that we need to discuss." Tran stiffened at the new tone in the doctor's voice. "Ever since your parents' accident, the question has been what will be best for you. You don't have any next of kin, and your parents did not leave a Will or Trust of any kind. Mei asked me to bring you here so she could care for you, the doctors all being at a loss of what to do for you. But what happens now that you're well?"

Tran's mind began to race. Where would he go? Was he leaving today? Would he ever see Mei again? Tears started to roll down his cheeks. He hung his head and would have hidden his face In his hands except he didn't want to embarrass Mei. She moved closer to him and put her arm around him. Softly she said, "Joseph, you frighten the boy."

Chagrined, Gransom said, "I'm sorry. I'm just an old scientist who doesn't know how to be subtle or talk to youngsters. Please forgive me." He came around the table, sat down on the couch next to Tran, and put a reassuring, though somewhat awkward, hand on his shoulder. "What I'm trying to tell you is that, upon your approval, I will become your legal guardian. You are to stay here with Mei who will watch after you. No one is going to force you to live anywhere else. You belong here now. Will that be all right with you?"

Tran wiped his eyes and found himself breathing again. Without looking up, he whispered, "Yes, sir. I want to stay with Mei forever."

"Good!" Gransom replied, patting Tran's shoulder. "Then it's settled. Problem solved." He let out a sigh, as if he, too, had been holding his breath. Then, in a lighter tone, he said, "Now, why don't you and Mei go explore your new home? For the time being, I'll take that book off your hands so you don't have to lug it around with you. I'll make sure it gets to you safely when you're done. In the meantime, I'm sure you'll find Vidmar Delta to your liking, and with some pleasant surprises I hope. I'd go with you myself but I have work to do." With that, the doctor straightened himself to his full height, smiled at Tran and Mei, and disappeared back into the stacks.

It looked the same as when they were led there—the long corridors, two flights of steps, two sets of doors, the soft burgundy carpet in the room of art and music, but the trip to Gransom's study had taken forever, and it seemed to Tran the trip back to the courtyard took no time at all.

When they reached the courtyard, the men who guided them slipped into their surroundings like watchful silent shadows, but Tran never noticed. He knew exactly where he wanted to go. He

42

Chapter 5: New Life

ran straight to the koi pond and bent over the water, his eyes fixed on the fish. "Would you like to give them some food?" A maintenance worker asked, holding out a cup of little green pellets. She watched with pleasure as Tran carefully sprinkled the pieces so everyone would get some. With their big round mouths, the fish greedily scooped up the pellets, splashing Tran's face as they jostled each other, churning the water with their powerful tails. He squealed with delight. It was rare to see a child on Vidmar Delta, and the maintenance worker allowed herself a moment to enjoy Tran's happiness before taking the empty cup and bidding Mei and him good-bye.

The fish did not know the food was gone. They continued to crowd together in front of Tran, looking at him hopefully. He put his fingers into the water to see what they would do. When they mouthed his fingers, he giggled. "It tickles!" he chuckled. He was so happy he couldn't stop smiling.

There were many fish, but a few in particular caught his attention. "Look at that one," he said, pointing at the koi whose smooth, sleek body was splotched with black, white, and rust. "I'm calling him Calie because he's calico colors like the cat in my book." The white one with a bright red patch on its head he called Spot, and the golden one with big metallic scales became Dragon. His favorite was the blue one that flashed a startling orange belly when it darted away. "I'm going to give it a name," he murmured, "but not yet. I have to think about it first."

Tran stood up and looked around, absently wiping his wet fingers on his pants. People were sitting at the round white tables eating their lunches. Beyond them, at the far side of the courtyard, he saw an opening to a wide passageway. He pointed to it and asked, "Can we go through there, Mei?"

"Yes," she said, "That goes to front of station."

Excitedly he ran straight to the entrance and skipped around as he waited for her. They were about to enter a new unknown. What would he see on the other side? He could hardly wait to find out.

Chapter 5: New Life 43

The passageway was only about fifty feet long, but all he could see through the opening on the other side was black. The closer they got to the end, the more curious he became. At last they stepped out of the passageway into Vidmar's main concourse, and what he saw stopped him in astonishment. Before him rose an enormous window three stories high. On his left the window ran all the way to the east wing docking bays. To his right it ran beyond where the concourse curved left into the west wing, disappearing out of his sight.

"Wow!" Tran shouted, "Is that PiMar glass?" He hurried to the window and looked up its smooth face. There was not a seam or a pane or any kind of bracing or support to reinforce the transparent expanse. Z9 had windows too but they were nothing like this. He stared out at the stars. They seemed closer and brighter than ever. But when he looked to his right, what he saw made him gasp. The shape of the station curved like a boomerang around a cluster of huge reddish-gray asteroids strategically lit to reveal their eerie otherworldly beauty. Tran ran west towards the middle of the concourse to get a better look. The asteroids were breathtakingly close. When Mei caught up with him, he exclaimed, "Look how big they are! Do these have magtronium in them?"

"You ask doctor," she said. "He knows."

On the other side of the concourse, the wall also rose up three stories. On the main level were shops, offices, and passageways, ramps, corridors, and doors leading to parts unknown. Tran could hardly wait to go exploring. He'd mapped as much of Z9 as his mother had allowed, but Vidmar Delta was a whole unexplored territory, a truly new frontier.

Looking up, he saw people leaning over the second level mezzanine wall watching the activities on the concourse below and enjoying the window wall. The top level didn't have a mezzanine, but the face of the wall was designed with many windows that took advantage of the spectacular view. Above was the slightly domed ceiling with a projected sky like Z9. He knew it would be synchronized with the Capitol, as were all the other stations in the colony, and when evening came, the pleasant sunlight would warm into sunset colors before darkening into night. Then the lights in the lamp posts would come on as they did in some areas on Z9, a comforting look he knew would feel like home.

Tran and Mei walked around the curve at the center of the concourse where the east and west wings met. Tran tried to look out the window from the west side to see through the window on the east side, but it was one-way glass. All anyone would see from the outside was black. In fact, he noticed that the whole station was practically invisible. It gave him a delicious shiver of secrecy and mystery.

Because Vidmar was a place of research, invention, and engineering, it could have been utilitarian and intimidating, but it was the opposite. And it was uncommonly beautiful. Tran was as thrilled as if he'd happened upon the Grand Canyon, stunned by its vibrant colors and sculpted stone. His future now looked vast and wonderful where before he had seen only foggy unknowns. Since those horrible days of staying in unfamiliar houses with unfamiliar people, he had wondered if there would ever again be a place where he belonged. Now there was no more terrible uncertainty. Vidmar Delta was his home, Dr. Gransom's private station. But very best of all, he would be with Mei. Not that she replaced his mother; there was room in his heart for both, and he knew his mother would want it that way. He felt as if nothing else would ever trouble him again.

When they neared the docking bay at the west end of the window wall, Mei stopped. "Look," she said, pointing at something beyond the glass. "Your Z9 City." Tran squinted his eyes.

"I don't see it," he said.

Mei knelt behind him, her eyes at his eye level, and put her fingertip against the smooth surface. "Look here," she said, slowly pulling her finger away. Looking past where her finger had been, he saw it then, so tiny, just a pinpoint of faint blue. How strange to see so small and far away the only world he had ever known. For a long time he stared at the tiny bit of blue. It made him sad. That was his past. It would never be again.

Mei watched him silently. She understood that longing for home you could never have again. Finally she touched his shoulder, saying, "We go now, Tran." She led him down several corridors and up a ramp, turning deep into the interior towards the back of the station. Finally she stopped in front of a large, dark green door. "You close your eyes," she said. "Do not open till I say open." Tran heard the door slide back, felt a rush of air on his face, then Mei's hands guiding him slowly forward, up a fairly steep ramp onto a flat landing. There she stopped and stood behind him, her hands on his shoulders, adjusting his position. "Open eyes now," she said.

They were up behind home plate looking down on a new pristine ballfield. The ceiling was so high it looked like a sky. In fact, the interior was finished to look like one of the Z9 stadiums, instead of the big empty warehouse it used to be.

"Wow!" Tran exclaimed.

"Doctor had it built for you," Mei said.

Tran gasped, "For me?"

"Yes. He said it will be good for you."

"It's beautiful!" Tran said, barely able to contain himself. "Can I go down?"

"Go! Go!" Mei laughed.

Tran ran down onto the diamond. It was set up for Junior League play with shorter base paths and a closer pitching mound, but it could easily be converted to Senior League specifications. There was a pitching machine on the mound and a net to catch the balls behind home plate. Tran drew his hand over the Zenith grass, then grabbed a handful of red dirt, letting a little spill through his fingers, then rubbing some between his hands. Surrounding the field were foot-wide walls, six feet high, along with bleachers and dugouts all in standard, true baseball green. "It's perfect!" he declared.

Mei came out of the third-base dugout carrying a glove, ball and bat. "You hit ball for me?" she shouted.

Tran ran over and took the ball and bat from her. "You go to left field over there and I'll hit you some fly balls. Do you know how to catch?"

"I will try," Mei said, tying back her hair. "But you not make fun."

Tran stood on the grass in front of home plate, stretched his arms and back and swung the bat a few times to get loosened up, then called, "Okay, here comes!" He hit a fly ball. Mei put the glove up, but as the ball was going over her head, she jumped up and snatched it out of the air with her bare hand.

"Wow!" Tran yelled, almost in shock. "How'd you do that?"

Mei shrugged. "You said catch ball."

"You're supposed to use the glove," he laughed.

"You come show me how," she said.

Tran ran out and stood beside her, demonstrating each move as he explained it. "Put the glove a little out in front of you and off to the side by your cheek." Mei listened intently, her eyes studying his every move.

They played the rest of the afternoon. Mei was a willing and gifted student. Tran was surprised at how fast she learned and how athletic she was. Finally, sweaty and happy, they put everything away and headed home.

A package addressed to Tran was there in the mail drop. When he unwrapped it, he found a beautiful box of smooth, dark wood with a single clasp of antique brass. Inside, wrapped in Mirage-blue linen, lay Dr. Gransom's book. Carefully, Tran unwrapped it and opened its cover. In simple, bold handwriting, the doctor had written, *To Tran, son of two very gifted scientists who were also my friends. Welcome home. —Dr. Gransom.*

After dinner Tran and Mei were too tired to enjoy their usual reading time. "I'm pooped," Tran said with a yawn.

"You are a good teacher," Mei said. "I like baseball." She gave him a hug and kissed him good night.

That night Tran dreamed he was running onto the field to play in the Zenith Colony Championships, his parents, Mei, and Dr. Gransom cheering him on from the stands.

Chapter 6
The Trap

Tran's strides are rhythmic, strong, and long as he continues his run home from the ballfield on Deck 2. His eyes linger on the lighted window four stories up. Has it really been eight years since he called it home? A lot can happen in eight years—half a lifetime of changes. Some have been quite good, and some… well… not… He forces his eyes from his old flat and his thoughts to other matters. He has things to do. There's that meeting with Gransom coming up. It's been awhile since he's seen the old gentleman, and he wonders what it could be about. But then, knowing his busy creative mind, it could be anything. *Anyway, that's not till Wednesday. This is only Monday. Stay present,* he reminds himself, recalling his words to his young team. As he starts the incline heading up to the house, Tran increases his pace. *Half a mile to go,* he thinks.

Suddenly two dark figures charge from behind a garden wall. A large, stocky man slams into him from the side and tackles him to the ground, muscling him hard onto his back. Tran's head hits with a thud and for a moment the world spins and he can't focus his eyes. The big attacker is quick as a cat. He's on Tran in a moment, digging his heavy knee into Tran's chest bone. As Tran tries to twist away, the attacker pushes down harder. Tran gasps for breath. Strong thick thumbs dig deep into the tendons just below his shoulders, sending lightning bolts of pain to his brain. The masked face comes menacingly close, and for a brief moment Tran can see the malice in the attacker's eyes. Just then the second attacker digs some kind of hard object into Tran's shins. Tran lifts his head to see what the object is, but the first attacker head-butts him hard. Warm blood flows from Tran's nose. A low voice growls in his ear. "Listen to me, Tranny boy. You hearing me?" The masked face presses hard against Tran's cheek. "Tell Gransom we're coming for him. Tell him his days of calling all the shots are over." The object digs deep into the most sensitive points of Tran's legs. He tries to relax into the pain, refusing even to groan. One last excruciating dig and the men are gone.

Slowly, painfully, Tran rolls onto his side and tries to catch his breath. He wants to get up but his arms and legs refuse to cooperate. A thought comes to him through the pain. *Tranny! That guy called me Tranny!*

The walkway is cool under his cheek. He lies dazed waiting for his strength to return, remembering former, harder hurts, feeling the dark, thinking of Mei.

Chapter 7
Emergency Response

A blaring alarm blasts into Bobby's sleep, incorporated for a few disturbing moments into his dream before jarring him awake. Groaning, he rolls out of bed and stumbles to the wall, feeling for the button that shuts it off. Still groggy, he quickly pulls on his flight suit, secures Mirage, sprints to a Smartcart outside Bay 1, and punches in the code for Bay 23. As the cart glides towards the emergency staging bay, he yawns and rubs his eyes, wondering what type of emergency it could be, thinking it's probably just a drill. He looks at his watch. It's 0312 hours, much too early on Monday morning. *Ugh!*

As soon as he arrives at Bay 23, Bobby rushes inside with others who have responded to the call. On the launch pad are two ships, each with two large engines in front and two in back—no-frills vessels specifically designed for speed and fast deceleration. Their purpose? Get there fast, assess the problem, report findings immediately. Speed is their specialty. They're not called Screamers for nothing. Even as they sit motionless on the pad, these ships look fast.

"Listen up, people!" a woman shouts. There is authority in her voice and more emblems and patches on her flight suit than on anyone else's. "This is not a drill. This is the real deal. Z17 has radioed in with reports of a collision, an explosion, and a possible fire inside the station. Information is sketchy right now. Screamers need to get there fast to evaluate. Growlers will follow for containment, and a Transport for evac, if necessary. We know what to do. Now let's go do it. Load up!" The Flight Leader is already striding to Screamer 1, her crew not far behind.

50

Bobby and his crew hurry to their ship and make their way down its narrow center aisle to their individual flight pods. Bobby climbs into the pilot's pod, seals it closed, and pressurizes it. He activates the heads-up display on the wraparound window, adjusts its brightness and contrast, and switches on the comms, quickly running through the pre-flight checklist with his copilot Beth and instruments technician Jason. As soon as they give the "All go," Bobby fires up the rear engines. They hum, rumble, rise to a threatening growl, then settle into a throaty purr. Bobby reports over the radio, "Flight, Screamer 2 ready for launch."

"Roger that, 2," replies the Flight Leader, "Follow me out."

As the bay door opens, both Screamers lift off the pad, hover in place, then move forward out the door one after the other.

"Thirty-second spacing," says Flight. "Screamer 1 leaving in 3, 2, 1." Bobby watches as Screamer 1's exhaust glows blue, then turns purple just before the ship streaks off and disappears into the black. He makes a final check of his instruments and calls to his crew on radio, "Here we go, folks. Launching in 3, 2, 1." The rear engines scream as the craft shoots forward, the g-forces pressing them back in their seats. The air pressure and anti-g forces in their pods automatically adjust to help counteract the effect. "How's it look, Jason?"

"All clear, Cap," reports the v-tech.

"Okay, Seven minutes to deceleration," says Bobby. "I'll count it down when it's time. Until then, enjoy the ride."

Bobby's eyes dart over the heads-up display. All readings are normal, right down the middle. "Three minutes to deceleration," he reports. Suddenly the ship banks hard to port. The g-forces are so intense he nearly blacks out. Then the ship self-stabilizes and banks back slowly on course. He shakes himself alert. "Everyone okay?" Beth and Jason respond with well-trained affirmatives.

"Small rock, Cap," says Jason. ODS didn't pick it up until we were nearly on top of it."

"Roger that," replies Bobby. "Let's hope that's the only one." He checks his readouts once again. "Deceleration in 10, 9, 8…"

The pods in the Screamer rotate 180 degrees. "…3, 2, 1." The rear engines shut off. There is a brief period of complete silence. Bobby calls, "Reverse thrust in 3, 2, 1." The front engines wind up and fire, slamming the crew hard against their seats. The engines spin up to a loud scream. Even with their pods' anti-g and air pressure adjustments the crew members groan from the pressure on their internal organs. Bobby's readouts are a blur to him now. He senses the ship is close to maximum deceleration and manages a strained, "Hang in there" over the comms. His crew is impressed he can talk at all. Their lungs feel pressed flat against their bones. The ship shakes violently as the engines roar even louder, then gradually begin to spin down. "All right," Bobby reassures them, "five minutes more of decel and we're there. Make sure your instruments are ready." The crew says nothing. They have five minutes to breathe and recover before they do their jobs.

In what seems like mere moments, they hear Bobby saying, "Coming out of decel in 3, 2, 1." The front engines wind down to a beautiful silence. The pods rotate 180 degrees, facing forward again.

In his display, Bobby can see the lights of Z17 in the distance. He switches the ship to manual control. "Here comes separation," he calls to his crew. They hear loud clunks and hissing as the middle section of the ship detaches from the main frame and lifts away from the large engines, leaving a much smaller, more maneuverable vessel with a large window in front and one on each side.

As they approach the station, Flight comes on the radio. "Screamer 2."

"Go ahead Flight," replies Bobby.

"You check the bottom two decks. I'll take the top two."

"Roger that." Bobby adjusts his course and lines his ship up with the station's vertical positioning. He tells his crew, "Okay, let's see what we've got." Expertly he guides his ship close to the station and circles it counterclockwise, tapping the thrusters to point the ship's front window straight at the station's side.

Chapter 7: Emergency Response

"Cap, instruments are picking up excessive heat centered around Bay 3 on Deck 4," reports Jason.

"Roger that."

It doesn't take Bobby long to fly the Screamer around the station. "I'm not seeing any collision marks," he says, "Anyone else picking up anything?"

"Just that heat, Cap," replies Jason.

"Affirm," says Bobby. "Flight, this is 2."

"Go ahead," says Flight.

"We're picking up heat near Bay 3, Deck 4, but we're not seeing any collision marks."

"Roger that. Seems to be an internal fire," says Flight. "But take another look."

"Copy that." Another pass around the station reveals no external damage to the bottom two decks.

"Screamer 2, this is Flight."

"Go ahead, Flight."

"Z17's Disaster Team have evacuated and sealed off all of Deck 4. They have no idea what happened in there or how bad it is. You're going to have to take a look inside."

"Roger that," says Bobby, excited that the Flight Leader has put her trust in him and his crew instead of going in with her own ship.

"Try Bay 2 first," orders Flight. "Let's get a sense of how hot the pot is before you jump in."

"Copy that. Going to Bay 2, Deck 4." Bobby maneuvers his ship to Bay 2. His copilot Beth transmits a code to open its space door. Bobby guides the ship slowly into the station, the Screamer's external searchlights illuminating the deck's dark interior. "Flight, there's a mining Hauler on the pad, but the ship and the bay seem secure and intact. Nothing looks out of the ordinary."

"Roger that, Bobby. Go ahead and take a look into Bay 3. There's definitely heat registering in there, so proceed with caution."

Smoothly Bobby backs his ship out of Bay 2 and maneuvers it to Bay 3. "Go ahead and open her up, Beth," says Bobby.

"You got it, Cap. Opening now."

For a moment, Bobby sees flames but they quickly dissipate. He reports, "Flight, we just starved a fire in Bay 3. Going to have a look." He slides the Screamer into the bay, pivoting his ship around to get a better look. "What in the stars do we have here?" he says to himself as much as to his crew.

There's a scorched Scout with its hatch open. He circles around it to search for signs of casualties. No one sees any. He reports to Flight what they've found.

Flight comes back, "We're going to open the airlock door, Bobby. Get yourself in position."

Bobby backs the Screamer halfway out the bay door. Usually only one of the three doors can be open at a time in order to prevent accidental decompression and venting, but there are override codes that are used during maintenance or emergencies.

Bobby positions the Screamer and reports that they're in position.

"Roger," replies the Flight Leader. "Opening airlock door in 3, 2, 1..."

Suddenly a huge roiling fireball rushes towards Bobby's ship, blasting it backwards, hurling it out and away from the station. The Screamer flips violently end over end, straining, splitting, twisting, cracking. All three crew pods rip from their mountings, their bucking ship flinging them wildly into space, its last wrenching contortions spinning their pods like fastballs as it breaks apart.

Barely conscious, Bobby hears air thrusters firing like a machine gun as they struggle to self-stabilize his pod. A cacophony of radio sounds and static crackles in his ear. His heart beats furiously, pounding in his head. His pod flips end over end, unable to stabilize. Bobby feels sick, but worry presses through the nausea... *My crew...*

Over the radio, people are yelling. Some of their words start to register in his swollen brain—"Explosion..." "Bay 3..." He hears his name. He tries to answer, but no words come out.

The Flight Leader is shouting over the radio, "Everybody, shut up!" Then, in a firm, steady voice, she says, "Any crew member of Screamer 2, please come in." She repeats it several times, a somber silence between. In each pause, ears strain for some response. Again she makes the call.

A small, weak, shaken voice comes over the radio, "Flight... This is Beth. Do you read me?"

Bobby blinks, trying to focus his eyes. *Beth!*

"We read you, Beth." says Flight. "We have you on STS. Growlers will be there soon. Hang on!"

Flight calls again, "Any crew member of Screamer 2, please come in." Bobby hears staticky jumbled mumbling he can't understand, then Flight's voice, "Good! Good! You're going to be okay. We're coming for you, Jason. We're coming for all of you!"

Bobby doesn't try to talk. He knows he can't. It's difficult for him to even breathe. Tumbling wildly in space, he's pleading, *Please, let them be okay. Let them both be okay...*

Chapter 8
Heavy Space

"You're going to stay with Dr. Gransom while I'm gone, sweetie. It's only eight months. I'll be back before you know it." Bobby looked earnestly into his mother's face and tried to make sense out of her cheerful, lilting voice. He had only been back with her on Z9 for three weeks. Why was she so happy to be leaving him again?

Four years earlier, Bobby's mother had led a daring thirty-month flight which succeeded in becoming the farthest manned mission into deep space and broke all the speed records along the way. It made her a household name in the colony. Everyone knew of Cynda Johnson. But while she was off making history, her husband took Bobby from Z9 and moved back to Earth. When Cynda returned, she tried living with them on Earth, but it didn't satisfy her, and she quickly went back to the Zenith Colony to plan and fly more missions.

While his illustrious wife was out chasing her dreams, Bobby's father moved on, leaving his eleven-year-old son to fend for himself in their small apartment. When Cynda found out, she immediately arranged for Bobby's passage back to Z9. After five boring months on a comfortless long-haul freighter, Bobby arrived withdrawn and sullen. Nevertheless, Cynda's vivacious personality soon won him over, convincing him things would be different—and better. But here she was, telling him she was leaving again. He begged her not to go. His mother listened, but not really. She was the mission Commander, the head pilot, the catalyst behind the entire mission. "I have to go, Bobby," she said in a voice that left no room for discussion. "It's my job. My profession. I need you to understand that. Can you do that for me?" Miserably, Bobby nodded his head, but his heart did not agree. All he heard was how important she was, and now he was going to be dumped off with another very important person who also wouldn't have time for him.

It was common for people working on projects to live on Vidmar, but never children. The station had a population of approximately 1200 residents, and another 400 commuted there from Z9 and other nearby stations for work every day, but there was little on vidmar Delta that would interest, amuse, or enrich a child. Though Cynda knew it was not the best place to park her son for eight months, she couldn't think of anything else, so, unbeknownst to Bobby, she threatened Dr. Gransom, saying she would drop out of the mission unless he allowed Bobby to stay on Vidmar under his care. To Cynda's relief, the doctor readily agreed, and they signed legal documents giving him guardianship while she was gone.

Just before boarding her ship, Cynda took her son aside. "I'll think of you every day," she promised, her hands on his shoulders, her face close to his. "You be good for the doctor while I'm gone, and make sure you do your schoolwork. She smiled, looking deeply into her son's sad hazel eyes. "Remember, I always love you." She kissed him gently on his cheek and gave him a hug. He hugged her back, then let her go.

Bobby's whole life had been countless repetitions of one parent or the other leaving for this reason or that. He was used to long periods alone. When he thought of life on Vidmar, he resigned himself to more of the same. But Gransom took to the boy right away, welcoming him and involving him whole-heartedly into his busy life. Surprised, Bobby thrived on the attention and flourished like a wilted seedling getting much-needed sunlight and water.

For school, Bobby needed to go to Z9. Most of the time he was flown there in quick little shuttles called Zippers that were ubiquitous throughout the colony. Sometimes, depending on flight schedules, he caught rides on other, more interesting ships—mining Haulers, Scrapers, Breakers, Growlers, Cruisers, and Scouts. Every type was different, and even ships of the same type had their quirks. Bobby enjoyed that. *Like dogs*, he thought. *They all have their own personality.*

Bobby was good-natured, outgoing, and easy to be around, so he was welcomed as an enjoyable companion rather than an unpleasant chore. On those twenty-minute flights, he came to know the pilots and crews quite well. They let him sit in the cockpit or allowed him on the bridge. He listened and watched intently to everything they said and did, and it wasn't long before he was interested in becoming a pilot himself, and he started hitching rides on longer flights whenever he could.

Most of the pilots and crew members were more than willing to share their knowledge with him. Not only did they teach him how to setup and use the Ship Tracking and Object Detection Systems, STS and ODS, they showed him how to plot and log flight plans, and how to properly call in approaches and departures on the radio. Once he learned those things, they started teaching him the flight controls. They stressed the need to follow the speed limits going in and out of the stations, and emphasized that deceleration was just as important as acceleration.

Once a pilot let him take the controls of one of the faster ships. Speed was in Bobby's blood. He pushed the vessel hard, shooting past Z9 by over thirty minutes before he could decelerate the ship enough to turn it around. The pilot got a huge laugh at Bobby's expense. It was a lesson Bobby would never forget.

When Cynda returned from her mission, Gransom was getting ready to leave on a trip to Earth. Concerned for Bobby's well-being, the doctor asked Cynda if she would be willing to live on Vidmar so her son wouldn't be uprooted again. She agreed. After Gransom returned, he continued to include Bobby in his activities, and the boy settled into a life that was intellectually stimulating as well as secure and comfortable. It was the most stable time of his young life and he couldn't have been happier.

When he was only thirteen, Bobby earned his official certificate of Pilot in Training. He could now pilot ships anywhere in the colony as long as a fully licensed pilot was present onboard when flying in open space, or in the cockpit with him during docking and departure. Noticing Bobby's interest and gift for flying, Gransom had his crew train him to fly Mirage. Bobby had already flown quite a few ships, but Mirage was something completely different. Her reputation was enough to intimidate even experienced pilots. His hands were shaking when he took the controls for the first time, but to his astonishment, Mirage felt more natural to him than any ship he had flown before. After that, he piloted her every chance he could get.

One morning while Bobby was getting ready for school, his mother came to his room. "Guess what, sweetie?" she said cheerfully. "I have to go to Z9 this morning to pick up some scientists, so guess who gets to fly you to school?" Her green eyes sparkled. "We'll have a little more time to catch up!" A few days before, Cynda had returned home from a two-month mission. Now she was back on light duty.

As their Zipper sped toward Z9, Bobby talked happily about the science project he was doing in school. He and his team were trying to develop gravity adjustment collars so dogs could come live on Z9.

"What a great idea!" Cynda said with genuine enthusiasm. "I've always wondered why most animals can't tolerate the gravity here. After I've been on the station a few days, it doesn't feel any different to me than it does on Earth, but I guess they're just much more sensitive. Of course, some people have serious trouble with gravity sickness. I've known a few who had to go back to Earth because they couldn't stand it here. So maybe your collars would be good for them too. Ever think of that? And think of all those who love dogs! I hear people live longer when they have a pet. You're onto something very special." She glanced over at him with pride in her eyes.

"Of course, we don't have any dogs to try it on so it's all just theory and numbers," Bobby said, then added with a laugh, "Good thing my team partners are a lot smarter than me! That's why I picked them."

"Don't you sell yourself short, young man," Cynda chided, "You're plenty smart. Dr. Gransom says you may run this colony someday, and he's one of the smartest men ever."

"He's just being nice and trying to build me up. You know how he is, Mom. He's always encouraging everybody. That's why so many people came out here."

Cynda gave her son a stern look. "Bobby Randall Johnson, Dr. Gransom does not say things he doesn't mean. He said that because he sees something in you and believes in your potential. You would be wise to listen to him. You know, that man loves you. I feel so blessed that you have the guidance of such a good man. And as far as people coming to live out here, they came because they wanted a better life. They came because they wanted a say-so in their destiny. Dr. Gransom didn't talk them into it." She paused, then added with a fierceness in her voice. "It's why I came. Earth no longer offered opportunities in space exploration. Too many regulations. Too many restrictions. Too much red tape. Too much control. Out here we can get things done."

Cynda sighed and fell silent. Bobby sat wordless. He didn't know this side of his mom and he had no idea what to say. After a moment, she cleared her throat and looked at her son. Though they were alone in the Zipper, she lowered her voice and leaned towards him, enfolding him in a privileged private secrecy. "You know what?" she said, "I'm going to tell you what we did on my last mission. It's been top secret. The report is going to be released in a few weeks but I know you can keep a confidence, so I'm going to tell you now. Okay?" Bobby nodded. His mother smiled at him. Then she sat up and, with a ring of triumph in her voice, declared, "We tested the new magtronic pulse engines. They're incredible! Speed like you could never imagine."

"How fast, Mom?" he asked.

Chapter 8: Heavy Space

"Five hundred and thirteen miles per second." Cynda paused briefly to let it sink in. "Okay, I admit, that doesn't sound too impressive, so let me break it down for you. That's 1,846,800 miles per hour. It shatters my old record almost threefold. Think of it this way—four times from Earth to the moon and back in one hour. Or how about this? Earth to Z9 in eleven days at full speed. So about twenty-four days with spool-up and deceleration. It opens up so many possibilities. What do you think of your old mom now?"

Bobby gave a long, low whistle. "You've gone faster and farther than anyone, Mom. You're a hero."

Cynda looked pleased. "Oh, it's not just me. It's the whole team." Then a shadow passed over her face, a conflict of realities and regrets that Bobby was too young to understand. She looked steadily out the cockpit window. "It's so... special... or something. I don't know how to say it... But it has taken something out of me, too." She continued looking straight ahead, and her voice went even softer. "And I don't want you to think it's not hard work, or that I don't know the sacrifices you've made." Bobby glanced at her. She had never said anything like this to him before. In the fourteen months he had been with her on Vidmar, she was forever off doing something. She didn't seem to notice his sacrifices or struggles. All he knew was he had wanted his mom to be home. Why this beautiful, vivacious woman wanted to spend her time traveling in deep space, he didn't know. He wanted to ask her, but couldn't find the words or the courage—afraid also of what the answer might be. All he knew was he loved her, even after everything she'd put him through. They rode awhile in silence. When they talked again, it was only about little things.

As they approached Z9, Bobby asked if he could dock the ship. With a big smile, Cynda surrendered the controls and watched with a practiced eye as her son skillfully maneuvered the ship into the bay. She gave him an approving nod. "Like mother, like son," she said.

Chapter 8: Heavy Space   61

Pleased, Bobby gathered his things and was about to sprint away when his mother called him back. "Bobby, I love you," she said. "Remember that I always love you, no matter what." Then she kissed him on each cheek and on the forehead, gave him a huge hug, and let him go. He never saw her again. Later that morning, on a research station where she had taken two scientists, there was an explosion. No one survived.

Dr. Gransom acted quickly after Cynda Johnson's death. He had his attorneys track down her husband who, for an undisclosed sum of money, happily gave up his parental rights so Gransom could adopt the boy. Gransom and Bobby flew to Midway Station where political, business, and legal proceedings between Zenith Colony and Earth were conducted. There the adoption was finalized.

Neither Gransom nor Bobby said much during the six-week round trip, each dealing with grief his own way. Gransom kept an eye on the boy, but Bobby, trying to shield his mind from his loss, busied himself with various duties and projects on the ship. It worked pretty well. But once he was back to the familiarity of Vidmar, reality began to haunt him. Nothing big—her empty chair, the smell of her shampoo, the dishcloth she'd left irritatingly wadded up in the kitchen sink.

Sleepless in his bed one night, Bobby found himself staring at the doorway of his room, remembering the nights he had wanted to see her there. It felt almost normal, this waiting for her in the dark. He could see her silhouette, backlit by the warm light in the hall. Fresh pain stabbed his heart. "Stop thinking about it," he growled angrily, lying in a flood of conflicting emotions, too overwhelmed to sort it all out. So much of his life had been spent waiting for his mother to come home. And now in the stark reality that she was never coming back, he was painfully aware of the size and burden of it.

Spurred by a mixture of confusion, anger, and pain, Bobby took off in one of the mining ships without permission or clearance, causing quite a panic in Vidmar's Flight Control Center.

Chapter 8: Heavy Space

He turned off the Scout's radio and transponder, pointed it to nowhere in particular, and flew it as far and fast as he could until it shuddered and shook so violently he thought it might break apart. He slammed the ship into full reverse-thrust deceleration, the engine screaming in protest. *Go ahead and blow up,* he thought as the engine struggled to stay intact. *Why should I care?* He sat staring bitterly out the window, ignoring the spasms and tremors as if he wanted the Scout to be in as much agony as he was. Finally he shut the engines down. The Scout creaked and moaned and then was dead quiet.

At Cynda's memorial service, one of her crew members said, "Captain Johnson could handle 'Heavy Space' better than anyone—Heavy Space—when you're millions of miles from home with the blackness of nothingness squeezing the very breath out of you. It's pure terror. You feel so alone and small, like there's no hope and you think you might as well give up right now and get it over with…" He stopped and wiped his eyes. "Not so for Captain Johnson. That's when she was at her very best. That's when she encouraged everyone to keep going, convincing us that everything was going to work out, that we could overcome any obstacle… that we were going to make it home… And because of her, we did."

In the silent Scout, Bobby could hear his heart pulsing in his ears as it adjusted to the physical extremes of space travel—something he knew his mother would never feel again. He listened for a moment, then everything inside him exploded. He screamed, "This is what you did best? Why did you need this? Why did you love this so much? Why did you leave me for this… this nothing? Why couldn't you just be a mom?" He punched at the air and screamed at the void, his rage blasting into the blackness. There was no reply. Bobby's hands opened helplessly and covered his face. He fell to the floor and sobbed a long time, shaking and shuddering as if he would break apart—a thirteen-year-old boy alone in space crying over his dead mother. Desperately he croaked through his tears, "God, please! Help me!" Then he whispered, "Please, take this pain away."

He wept until his mouth was dry and no more tears were possible. Quietly he got up and took a few sips of water and breathed deeply. He was drained, but calm. It was time to go home. Sighing, he climbed back into the pilot's seat and fired up the engine. There was a terrible grinding noise. Horrified, he let go of the ignition switch as if it were white hot. *What was that?* He waited a moment, then carefully tried the engine again. It whirred slowly for a few seconds then locked up, sending a sickening shudder throughout the ship. Moments later, the electrical system failed, leaving him in complete darkness, but before he had time to panic, the emergency backup system kicked in and the lights came back on at a low level. Quickly Bobby got on the radio. He called into Vidmar Delta. There was no reply. He called Z9. No reply. He tried an all-channels Mayday to any ship or station. Nothing. *How is this possible?* he thought. Fear crept into his chest. He willed it away.

He tried the engine again. That drained the backup system substantially and the lights went even dimmer. *Come on! Use your head!* he thought fiercely. *Don't make things worse by doing stupid stuff.* Quickly he turned off everything but the radio and the little light atop the flight console and sat trying to think of what to do. His brain wouldn't cooperate. It only wanted to panic. He wondered how long the air would last.

With every passing second the Scout was moving farther away from Vidmar Delta. The drastic, dangerous, foolish deceleration had slowed the ship down considerably but it still had forward momentum, and he had no way now of slowing it down or steering it. He tried the radio a few more times, getting nothing but dead air and draining the backup system further. Not knowing what else to do, he grabbed a flashlight out of the emergency kit and began rummaging through the ship hoping to find anything that would trigger an idea. He searched the equipment lockers and every compartment. When he found a space suit in the airlock, he knew he had bought himself more time. He checked the air gauges, relieved to see they were full. He didn't really know how long that would last, though he seemed to remember it was something like two hours.

He rubbed his arms through his thin shirt. He had been in such a state when he left the flat that he hadn't thought to bring a jacket. Now, without power, the coldness of space was starting to creep into everything. Awkwardly he wrestled himself into the large space suit. He was glad for the warmth. Despite the chill in the diminishing air, he chose not to put the helmet on. He would wait until the ship's oxygen dropped down to a dangerous level.

Unable to start the ship, he settled into the pilot's seat, his eyes drawn to the one feeble light still on. It felt like a dream, or more like a trance from shock and fear. Time passed without reference. Maybe he slept. How long? When he opened his eyes, the little light was barely on. As he watched, it dimmed, flickered, and went out. He was completely enveloped in blackness.

Mind scrambling, thoughts dwindling like the last breathable air, Bobby turned on the helmet light, put the helmet on, and turned on the oxygen to the suit. "Two hours," he murmured. *Then what?*

He could feel the enormous weight of space pressing in on him. He wanted to scream. He wanted to lose consciousness so the terror would be over. *I'll just take off the helmet,* he thought, his mind sinking into an odd, crazy calm. *I'll just go to sleep.* He pondered this idea seriously for a time. He could see himself suffocating in the ridiculous, oversized suit—some crew finding him months later—if they ever found him at all. He and the ship could slide through space until the end of time.

Against these frightful imaginations, something quiet began to insist, like a faint knocking at the back door of his heart. Something was saying, "No." That's all, just, "no."

No? No to what? he wondered. The answer came, *No to helplessly waiting for death to arrive. No to waiting for life to begin. No. No. No!*

His mind cleared. He knew he wasn't going to give up or give in. Earnestly he whispered, "Thank You, God!" The heaviness lifted. He even felt warmer. He forced himself to think. There had to be an answer. Flashlight in hand, he explored the ship again, quickly studying the contents of every compartment. One of the lockers was full of markers. When activated, these markers sent out a special radio signal that could be picked up by other mining ships. They were used to tag asteroids that had the right type of ore, so the pilots of Breakers, Scrapers, Sweepers, and Cutters could track and collect the rocks. Magtronium ore is rare, only one out of hundreds of asteroids contain it, so not many markers are set out by one Scout during a shift, and they're usually spread out through a wide area. Bobby thought if he activated a lot of markers in the same area all at once, maybe a pilot or two would fly out right away to investigate such an anomaly. But he soon realized a flaw in his plan. Markers were shot from a powerful air cannon which embedded them into the asteroids. There was no power to run the air cannon's compressor, and even if there were, there was no asteroid to shoot them at. Shooting markers into space wouldn't do him any good. He needed another way. Activating markers inside the ship wouldn't work because its hull would block their signal. He had to get them outside and keep them attached to the ship.

Rifling through other lockers, Bobby found a coil of wire, a short length of rope, and about a dozen tie-down straps. There was a total of twenty-five markers, each about a foot and a half long, shiny bright red, missile shaped, but fat. Branching out another six inches from their nose were four shafts with extremely sharp points and small barbs. Bobby set the flashlight on a shelf in the locker, combining its beam with the helmet light so he could see what he was doing. He tried tying the markers together, but the space gloves were not designed for such precise movement. He realized he had to take them off, but then the oxygen would escape through the open sleeves. *Tourniquet,* he thought. He looped a strap just above the wrist of the left sleeve of the space suit and buckled it down as tight as he could. He did the same for the right

Chapter 8: Heavy Space

sleeve. Then, reluctantly, he shut off the air to the suit, unsealed the sleeves' collars, and pulled off the gloves. Precious oxygen vented through the open sleeves. *At least it's slower,* he thought.

With frigid, fumbling fingers, he worked as fast as he could tying markers into a tangled chain. He focused his eyes on the intersection between the two beams of light, a small bright circle in the icy, dense darkness.

Bobby's vision began to blur. His lungs hurt. *Have to get the air back on!* But where were his gloves? In the blackness, with his mind a muddle, he couldn't find them. Desperately he turned the air on. It was enough to get some clarity back, but he could feel the oxygen escaping. Alarmed, he began to hyperventilate. His heart quickened. "Panic can kill faster than circumstance," a pilot had once told him. He forced himself to slow his breathing. His heart slowed in response. Feeling more in control, he reached for the flashlight and right there were his gloves. Hastily, he put them back on and sealed the sleeve collars.

The markers were heavy and slick, and some of them slipped out of their makeshift harness as he dragged them to the airlock, but he couldn't stop. He was running out of air and time. Sealing the airlock, he manually worked the valve to depressurize the chamber and opened the space door. He slipped one of his legs through a safety loop on the wall, leaned out and tied the end of the rope around a grab handle just outside the door, and fed the chain of markers into space. They drifted slowly away, but as the last marker left his hands, he felt something was wrong. Then it hit him—he hadn't activated them. Fighting cramping, reluctant muscles, he pulled them back inside. Even with bulky gloved fingers, he managed to activate each small switch. Then he fed them back into space and closed the hatch. There was no need to pressurize the chamber and he didn't want to waste the energy. He lay flat on his back and concentrated on slowing his breathing, fighting to stay awake, but exhaustion and the cold overtook him. It was a relief to give in.

Out of the deep silence, something jerked Bobby awake. *How long was I asleep?* he wondered. *Was that sound an engine?* He listened hopefully, but there was nothing to hear. He lay in a daze assuring himself, *It's okay. I'm okay. No matter what, I'm okay.* His body did not agree. His lungs tightened with every shallow breath. He felt dizzy and strange. He imagined he could float back home, amazed at how simple it would be. He started to laugh, but instead his back arched violently in a desperate gasp for air.

Sharp needles burned through Bobby's extremities. He stifled a scream.

"Try to stay calm," came a woman's voice. "It won't last much longer. You're doing good."

What is this torture? Bobby wondered.

As if reading his mind, the woman said, "You're in a warming suit. You're thawing out. It's going to hurt for a while but you're alive. What were you doing way out there, young man?"

"Saying good-bye to someone," he murmured, slipping back into a deep, dark sleep.

Chapter 8: Heavy Space

Chapter 9
Brothers

Bobby stood outside the door of Dr. Gransom's study, his stomach in knots, his heart a turmoil, but grateful still to be alive. His plan had worked. Mining pilots had come out to investigate the markers and found him inside the Scout, unresponsive and in grave condition. They transferred him to one of their ships and raced for the nearest Health Station. There he was treated and released. Gransom had mobilized search parties to look for his missing adopted son, and a large number of his ships had fanned out in all directions, but they did not find him, though they searched all night. Then came the call from the mining ship. As soon as Gransom was informed of Bobby's rescue, he arranged for a ship to bring him home.

On the flight back to Vidmar, Bobby had ample time to worry about how the Chief Director was going to react. *Grounded for a year? Never allowed to fly the rest of my life? Sorry he ever adopted me?* No matter what he imagined, nothing played out well in his mind. And now, here he was.

He steadied himself and went inside. He could see right away that the doctor had been badly worried. His face looked tired and strained. Whatever Bobby had planned to say immediately left his mind. "I'm sorry," he blurted, not waiting for rebuke. "I'm sorry for taking the ship. I'm sorry I worried you. I'm sorry for the trouble I caused everybody. I'm sorry for everything."

"It must never happen again," Gransom said in a voice without anger or reproach.

"No, sir," Bobby replied, studying the floor.

"Good. Good. Well, you're all right then?"

"Yes, sir."

"I was told you were completely out of oxygen when they found you."

"I guess I was. I don't remember much."

"Not a bad way to go, I suppose," Gransom said, "Still, I'm relieved you didn't..." Bobby felt the doctor's big hand on his shoulder. When he looked up, he saw gentle affection in the man's tired gray eyes. "Go now and get as much rest as you need. We have important things to do in the coming weeks."

"Yes, sir. Good night."

No more waiting for life to begin—that's what Bobby had decided in the stranded Scout. He realized he could choose how he lived, and it changed him. He found he enjoyed the various facets and interactions of the colony and became more involved in its day-to-day operations. He went with Gransom on as many trips to other stations as he could. Although he didn't have a scientific mind like the doctor, he discovered he had a knack for seeing solutions to problems that others would often miss. He began to use that gift to help improve the colony.

Whenever they were on other stations and Gransom had to attend closed meetings, Bobby visited with the workers, learning about their specific responsibilities, the equipment they used, and how they utilized the different ships. They were eager to share their ideas on better, more efficient, safer ways of getting the work done. Bobby listened intently, later conveying their ideas to Gransom who often implemented them and rewarded the workers with acknowledgements and bonuses.

Bobby decided to leave his mother's flat and move into a single-story suite on Vidmar's top level, only a short passageway from the back entrance of Gransom's flat. Though there were two fine cafeterias on the station, he most often ate dinner with Gransom so the doctor could fill him on anything important that happened during the day. That way he was always up to date on all matters of colony business though he had to keep up with his schoolwork at the same time. He didn't mind. He enjoyed problem solving and could keep complexities in his spacious brain without feeling overloaded, so he relished those evening updates with Gransom. He also loved to eat, and Gransom had an exceptional chef—a thin, elderly woman who never spoke. Her name was Gracie.

One evening after dinner as they were enjoying their favorite spiced tea, Gransom said, "Oh, I've been meaning to tell you, the young boy whose parents were killed along with your mother is now living on Vidmar. I have taken custody of him."

"Oh! I was wondering about him," said Bobby. "I heard he was very ill, but I didn't know he ended up here. How is he now?"

"He's doing well. Almost fully recovered. He's being cared for by a friend of mine who also came to the station recently. She was able to nurture him back to health. I met him only a few days ago. Nice young man. Very polite. I think things will work out well for him. He's going to stay with my friend. They have developed a special bond. The boy needs a mother."

"How old is he?" Bobby asked.

"Let's see," said Gransom. "I believe he's five years younger than you, so if I can do that kind of math, I would say he is eight."

Bobby laughed, "What's his name?"

"Tran," Gransom said. "Tran Moore."

"Well, I look forward to meeting him. It will be nice to see a young person on Vidmar."

Gransom agreed heartily. "Yes! You know, I've always wanted to keep it a serious working atmosphere here, but your mother and you changed that for me. It's nice having young folks around. It makes things…Oh, how would I say it?…Lighter. It makes things lighter. I like it, and maybe we will have more of it."

The very next afternoon as Bobby was walking to the gym, he saw a young boy running down the spiral ramp. He ran after him, catching up with him near the koi pond. "Hi, is your name Tran?" he asked.

The boy looked surprised, "Yes. Who are you?"

"I'm Bobby."

Oh, Tran thought. *The boy Mei told me about.* He walked right up close to Bobby and stared into his eyes. "Are you nice?"

I - I'd like to think I am," Bobby said haltingly, "

"I'm asking because I had a friend who had a really mean older brother. I don't want one of those," said the boy.

"Well," Bobby countered, "I have a friend who has a horrible pesky little brother, and I don't want one of those. Are you pesky?"

"You mean, obnoxious?"

"Yes. Obnoxious and rude."

"I don't think so," said Tran, "but I've never had a brother before to find out."

"Me neither," said Bobby, "I'll tell you what. I'll be nice, and you don't be obnoxious. Is it a deal?"

"Yeah, deal," said Tran. And they shook on it.

Softly Bobby said, "I'm sorry about your parents."

"Me too," said Tran. "Sorry about your mom." They were silent a moment, and afterwards never again spoke a word about it to one another.

"How did you know about me?" Tran asked.

Bobby said, "Grandfather told me."

Tran asked, "Who's your Grandfather?"

"That's what I call Dr. Gransom," Bobby said. "He seems to like it. You should call him that too." Then he grinned. "Hey, little brother, I heard Grandfather built you a ballfield. Can I see it?"

"Sure," said Tran. "It'll be more fun with you there."

The boys ran off together, each feeling lighter and more like children again.

Chapter 10
The Mysteries of Mei

"We celebrate!" Mei said joyfully as she and the boys neared a group of restaurants on Deck 5.

"Yep. Mister Sixteen and official pilot gets to choose," Tran said, thumping Bobby on the back.

Bobby looked pleased. "It's funny," he said. "I didn't think it would be a big deal since I've flown so much, but it feels different now. I wish Grandfather were here. I couldn't have done this without him."

"He will celebrate with you when he returns," Mei assured him.

Bobby grinned, walking tall beside her with light, long strides. After three years of doing exercises with Mei and Tran, countless hours on the baseball field, and running for fun here and there on Vidmar and Z9, he had developed a remarkable ease of movement and the grace of an athlete, and an appetite to match. He led them to the restaurant just ahead on their right. "Rodgers!" he exclaimed. "I'm having a Triple with sweet potato fries."

"What a shock!" Tran said, feigning astonishment.

It was a tradition with them—whoever had a birthday got to pick all the activities for that day. This was the third year of birthdays since both boys had come to live on Vidmar, and this particular day was especially happy because of what Bobby had achieved at such a young age.

For the afternoon's outing, they could have attended the new musical that had just opened at the Main Stage Theater downtown on Deck 4. Each season, a new troupe of actors from Earth was invited to the colony to live and work for one year. They would be augmented by veteran performers and crew from the colony's resident population. The Main Stage Theater was known for having the best of the best, and it was always a big deal when a new show opened. Gransom had a private box at the theater and Mei and the boys often went more than once if they really liked the show. But this day Bobby had chosen a quiet stroll where they frequently went on Sunday afternoons.

After lunch, they made the flight to Z11—a large, 5-deck horticulture station thirty minutes from Z9. Acutely aware that there wasn't another licensed pilot onboard, Bobby was particularly diligent with all his maneuvers. When he set the Zipper down carefully in the bay on Deck 5, Tran declared, "Perfect flight."

"Yes," Mei agreed, "very nice."

Bobby gave the ship a pat on the nose as they headed out of the docking bay on their way to the lifts.

It was hot on Deck 2 when they passed through the heavy green door into the orchard area. Temperatures on most of the Zenith stations were set for mild seasonal changes, but on horticulture stations, both the colors of the light panels covering the 40-foot high ceilings and the air that circulated through the large spaces were coordinated with the seasons and conditions that the plants liked best. At this time, the peaches were maturing and heat was intensifying their natural sugars. The ripening fruit was releasing a heavy fragrance that made the boys long for pyramids of peaches in Mei's kitchen, available to devour fresh and raw, or transformed by Mei into something delectable.

Bobby was happy to see there were no other visitors or workers there, making it wonderfully restful and quiet. All they could hear was the pleasant trickle of rich brown water flowing slowly around the roots of the suspended trees as they absorbed nutrient-dense aquaponic solution from the 20-foot wide channels.

Deck 2 could have been designed for no-frills industrial efficiency, but the planners had incorporated some features that made it more enjoyable for the visiting public. Between the outer channels, a footpath curved up and down over gentle mounds and slopes, bordered by beds of flowers in hot summer colors.

Sometimes the boys would have Mei time them as they raced the 100 yards from the green door to their favorite bench half way down the path. But it was too hot for racing on this day, so they sauntered along the path, Mei singing softly as they savored the sensory overload. Multitudes of peaches hung huge and heavy on the trees. They walked through the orchard, breathing deeply and feeling utterly content.

After two trips around the path, Mei told Bobby, "I have surprise for you at home. Peach cobbler."

"With whipped coconut cream?" he asked hopefully.

"Yes. Special treat for your birthday."

Bobby started for the door. "No time to waste," he said. "Let's get moving! I hope I don't get a speeding violation on the way back."

As they rode the lift down to Deck 5, both boys had cobbler on their minds, intensified by the fragrance of peaches still filling their senses. Bobby was surprised at how happy he felt. He was sixteen years old and a pilot—a licensed, certified, *bona fide* Class-C pilot. He knew his mother would be proud.

It took about a minute for the descent to Deck 5 and only one more to traverse the main corridor to the bay where their ship was docked. Bobby pressed the control to release the airlock door. As he pulled the door open, a blur of figures shoved past him and grabbed at Mei. In a flash, she ducked under their hands, striking one in the groin with a hard, fast fist, then thrusting a side kick upwards to the same strategic spot on another. They dropped to the floor moaning. In one fluid motion, Mei sprang up and released a wheelhouse kick to the throat of the third attacker, sending him reeling backwards against the wall.

Everything happened so fast the boys didn't have time to do anything. They stood open-mouthed, paralyzed with shock. Mei grabbed their hands, rushed them to the lift, and pushed them inside. Quickly tying back her hair, she said, "You go back. Hide by bench." Her voice was strangely calm and fierce. "Do not move from there until I come for you." The boys started to protest but she shushed them, pressed the button for Deck 2, and slipped swiftly out of the lift.

In terrified silence, Bobby and Tran rode the lift to Deck 2, ran to the white bench and crouched behind it. Tran whispered anxiously, "Who are those men? What do they want?"

"I don't know," said Bobby.

"Let's go back," Tran urged.

"Mei said to wait here," Bobby said.

"What if they hurt her?" Tran was in tears.

Bobby put his arm around his little brother. "Did you see Mei? I didn't know she could fight like that!"

"I didn't know anyone could fight like that," said Tran. "Let's go back!"

"No! We're going to wait here like she told us to." But inside Bobby was struggling, torn between Mei's emphatic instructions and his growing anxiety for her safety. He felt totally helpless. More to himself than to Tran, he said, "Anyway, what could *we* do?"

"I don't know…" Tran's voice trailed off. The boys hid in silence for a time, their minds racing.

Bobby's face grew resolute. In a different tone, he said, "I'm going to go look for her."

"I'm going with you," Tran insisted.

"No! You're only ten. I know she wouldn't want me to bring you back down there."

"I'll be eleven next month!" Tran argued.

"I don't care!" Bobby said firmly. "You have to stay here in case she shows up. If one of us isn't here, she's not going to know what happened. I'll be back as soon as I can." He patted Tran on the shoulder, then ran down the path to the lift.

Tran sat on the ground hugging his knees. He could smell the peaches that only a few minutes before had been such a delight to them all. Now everything was awful. He bit his lip and tried to force himself not to let fear overwhelm him, but he couldn't stand the thought of anything happening to Mei.

Chapter 10: The Mysteries of Mei

When Bobby reached the lift, he was surprised to find it had already been called back down. He hid and waited to see if it would come back up with Mei. It didn't. The idea of going down in the lift and having its doors open to the unknown gave him the creeps. He also didn't want to call it up in case Mei needed it. As quickly as he could, he ran to the switchback ramps on the far side of the station and followed them down to Level 5. Slipping stealthily into the main corridor through a gap in a partially open freight door, he quietly made his way back to where the attack had occurred. No one was there and the airlock door was closed. He ran to the lift. Its door was open but the car was empty. His entire body was shaking. He wanted to shout Mei's name. *Where is she? I don't know what to do!* Icy, clutching fear started to crawl over him the way it did when he was stranded in the mining Scout. Fervently he whispered, "Please, God, give me the courage and strength to do this." He breathed deep and exhaled long, then ran back to the bay.

With a pounding heart, he opened the door. The airlock was empty. He stepped inside and carefully closed the door behind him. Taking another deep, calming breath, he flattened himself against the side wall, and pressed the control to the bay door. It opened with a whoosh and a slight clatter that to his mind sounded like bombs going off. He cringed, scarcely breathing, listening for footsteps or shouts of alarm. Hearing nothing, he peeked into the bay. Two unfamiliar spacecraft were docked behind the Zipper. They were a dull gray, with bulky bodies. Voices were coming from somewhere beyond the ships. Disasters flashed in Bobby's mind. He shut them off. Fear was not going to hold him back. Silently he ran to the farthest ship and, keeping low, peered around the back of it.

What he saw shocked him with horror. Near the side wall, a large man was gripping Mei's wrists, forcing her arms straight back behind her. It must have cruelly hurt her shoulders, but Bobby could clearly see her face. She gave no indication that she felt anything—not fear, not pain. A few steps to her left, a tall man pointed a blaster at her heart. In front of Mei stood a short, stocky man. He yelled something at her and struck her with the back of his hand hard in the face.

"No!" Bobby screamed, charging furiously at the man. "Leave her alone!" The striker spun around and strode grimly toward Bobby. Just as Bobby rushed up, the stocky man stepped quickly to the side and clotheslined him with a thick arm, knocking the boy flat on his back.

The man with the blaster was distracted only a moment, but it was enough. In that split second, Mei jerked fiercely forward, yanking the man behind her off balance. Jumping up, she scissor kicked the barrel of the blaster. It hit the tall man squarely in the face. The weapon fired, sending a blue sphere of energy ricocheting off the ceiling before hitting the rear corner of the bay and dissipating. Mei landed on her left foot, immediately jackknifing her body, her head almost reaching the deck, and shot her right leg straight up behind her, kicking the man gripping her wrists directly under his chin, snapping his head back violently. He fell to the floor in a heap. Now free, Mei twirled towards the tall man, who was dazed but still holding the weapon. She landed a spin kick to the side of his head. He crumpled to the floor.

The stocky man was just getting ready to kick Bobby in the head when the blaster went off. He turned and saw Mei make quick work of the other attackers. With a roar he barreled towards her like a bull. When he was almost on her, she dropped to a crouch and knocked his legs out from under him with a swift and powerful sweep kick. As he fell forward, she rolled out of his way. Then, leaping upon him, she power slammed her elbow down into his left temple.

Mei paused briefly, eyeing him, then rushed to Bobby. "Are you hurt?" He shook his head. She helped him to his feet. "Where is Tran?"

With difficulty, he gasped, "At the bench."

"Come," she urged, "There are more men."

Hastily they left the bay and ran up the switchback ramps as fast as Bobby could manage, winded as he was. But he was young and fit and soon was able to run full out, keeping up with Mei. Worried, he asked, "What if those men wake up?"

"They cannot wake up," she said.

In the distance, Tran caught a glimpse of movement. Someone was coming. Through the slats of the bench, he saw two figures approaching over one of the mounds. *They're back!* he thought with relief, but as they neared the crest of the mound, his fear spiked and his heart sank. It was two men. He could see them clearly now. With a shock, he realized, *They're going to see me. I need a better place to hide.* He glanced around. Wherever it was, it would have to be close and he'd have to get there fast.

The path curved and dipped down out of Tran's line of sight. *If I can't see them, they can't see me*, he thought. He waited, watching carefully. When the men reached that dip in the path and he could no longer see them, he crawled quickly to the nearest aquaponic channel and slid silently into the chilled opaque liquid, the cold shocking his little body. Gripping the roots of one of the suspended trees, he hid behind its trunk, submerged in the thick water up to his chin. He couldn't see the men but soon he heard their footsteps coming closer. Convinced they would look down and see him, he held his breath, closed his eyes, and, holding onto the roots, lowered himself under the surface, staying as still as possible. It was so cold. Water filled his ears, keeping him from hearing footsteps or voices. It was hard to judge time. *Has it been long enough?* he wondered. His lungs were already protesting. Soon they would be screaming. Maybe they had already passed by. With numb fingers gripping the roots, Tran was about to pull himself up when suddenly something hit the water just in front of him with a loud splash. His mind screamed, *Someone jumped in after me!* He swam blindly under the dark water as hard as he could away from the sound. Seconds later there was a horrible heavy splash right over him. He wanted desperately to stay under, but he had to have air. A frantic kick propelled him upwards. As his head broke the surface he bumped something. *A body?* Adrenalin pumping, Tran grabbed a gulp of air and plunged back into the darkness, swimming furiously away, sure that someone was going to grab his ankle and hold him under. Panic propelled him, but the cold was draining his strength and his muscles began to cramp. No matter how much he willed himself to continue, his body rebelled. He surfaced, gasping. Bitter, thick liquid rushed into his throat. He choked and coughed. He tried to hold his face above the water to keep from swallowing more, but with no strength left, he began to sink. He managed to catch a quick breath just before he went under. *Where's the bottom?* he thought. *I can push off the bottom.* But he couldn't find it. Then, horribly, hands were grabbing at him. A strong arm wrapped around his chest and dragged him upward. Powerful hands pulled him out of the channel. He lay on his belly on the walkway, too weak to flee, shivering and violently coughing up bitter liquid, his eyes stinging and blurry. Someone was there, but he couldn't see, and he knew he was too weak to get away. He lay helpless, expecting a kick or a blow. A hand touched his back.

Soaking wet, Mei knelt beside him. "You will be all right," she said. "Mei!" Tran croaked. He struggled to his knees and flung his arms around her. "You're here! You're here! I thought I was going to lose you!"

For a few moments Mei held him tight, then helped him to his feet. "We need to go now," she said. "I will carry you."

Tran said hoarsely, "No. I can walk." Bobby looked at him with concern. "You sure, little brother?" Tran nodded, then froze, catching sight of two bodies floating face down in the channel. "Are they…"

"We go now," said Mei.

They hurried to the lift and down the main corridor to the docking bay, but when they arrived at the airlock door, Mei held up a restraining hand. "Wait here. I will come back soon." She went in alone. Tran and Bobby stood near the airlock door wondering if she was going to be safe. They couldn't hear anything, but

Chapter 10: The Mysteries of Mei

they kept listening, just in case. After a few minutes she returned. "Okay now," she said, and they followed her inside.

The gray ships were mag-locked behind the Zipper. Tran stared hard at them. "What kind of ships are those?" he asked. "They look like rhinoceros."

"I don't know," Bobby said as they boarded the Zipper, "I've never seen ships like them before, but Rhino is the perfect name for them."

Mei and Tran were shivering violently from being in the cold aquaponic solution. Bobby gave them blankets from the storage compartment, powered up the ship and turned the heater on high. "Let me know if it gets too hot," he said lightly as he maneuvered the Zipper over the Rhinos and out the space door. He was relieved when they were safely on their way home. He wasn't really as cheerful as he sounded, but he didn't want to let either of them know how scared he had been, and how shaken he still was.

In the back seat, Tran was chilled by more than the cold. He stared at Mei, seated ahead of him in the copilot's seat. He was feeling a growing uneasiness. *How could she do that?* he wondered. He felt he no longer knew her, and he didn't like himself much for feeling that way.

Tran was an inquisitive child. When he came to live with Mei, he asked her many times about her life—where she grew up, where she went to school, what her parents were like, if she had any brothers or sisters, how she came to be in the Zenith Colony, how she met Dr. Gransom. But instead of answering, Mei would either change the subject, give him a chore to do, or tell him "stay young boy." After a while he gave up asking, and, as with most young people, life became all about him, and that was the way Mei wanted it. She devoted most of her time to Tran and Bobby. But there were times Tran could see shades of sorrow pass over her face, and he wondered what pain she had endured and what her life was like before he met her. There was a deep silence about her, just as there was now in the ship as they sped home.

They were halfway to Vidmar when Mei broke the silence, "You did not do what I told you, Bobby."

Quickly he replied, "I couldn't. We were so scared you would get hurt. Tran was begging to go back for you, but I made him stay there like you said. So I did half right."

"You were brave to come back, but..."

"Who were those guys?" Bobby interrupted. "What did they want with you?"

"That is not for you to know now,' Mei said softly. "What you need to know is you must do what I say, no matter what."

Bobby had never argued with Mei before, and there was a tone in her voice that made it clear he shouldn't argue with her now. "Okay, Mei," he said.

"Good. Now, please, radio Vidmar and have Protectors meet us when we land."

When they docked at Vidmar, Mei sent the boys on ahead so she could talk to the two Protectors who were there waiting.

The boys walked to the flat in silence, clouded with their own thoughts and fears, but when they opened the door, they were met with comforting smells that soothed them with a sense of safety and relief. In that privacy, Tran finally felt the freedom to talk.

"So what happened after you left me?" he asked. "Where did you find Mei?"

Bobby recounted what he could remember from the docking bay, and how Mei overtook the attackers by the aquaponic channels. "It's impossible how fast she can move," he said with admiration. "It's like she knows what people are going to do before they do it."

Tran didn't know what to think. He knew nothing of violence, except that it terrified him. But he had seen the swelling on Mei's face and outrage and anger flared up inside his peace-loving heart. He looked at his brother and said solemnly, "Thank you for going back for her. Who knows what would have happened if you didn't?"

"She wasn't happy about it," said Bobby wryly.

Chapter 10: The Mysteries of Mei

"No, but I am," said Tran.

"Yeah, me too. But I'll tell you, little brother, I was scared out of my mind."

"But you did it anyway," Tran said. "That's what makes you brave. And you got clobbered for it. How are you feeling now?"

"I'm all right. It just rang my bell for a while. It knocked the wind out of me more than anything else, landing on my back like that."

After hot showers, a quiet dinner, and the special peach cobbler with fluffy white coconut cream, Mei went to the sink to wash the dishes. The boys got up to help but she said she wanted to do them herself. Tran and Bobby sat quietly at the table. It was hard to talk. Silence seemed the only fitting thing.

After she finished the dishes, Mei brought mugs of Bobby's favorite spiced tea and sat down. She lifted a mug and let the sweet steam warm her face.

Suddenly Tran blurted, "How do you know how to fight like that, Mei?" There was an edge in his voice.

Mei didn't say anything. She stared down at her tea. The boys thought she wasn't going to answer at all, but they sat, waiting. Finally she put down her mug, raised her head, and looked at them. "This I will tell you, if you are ready to hear," she said. The boys nodded, their eyes intent on her face. "I was young girl, three years old, when I started. It is ancient fighting of my people, passed down many, many years. The true name I cannot tell you, it is forbidden. Even I have only heard it spoken twice. But we gave it name that means fastfighting.

"How long did you study it?" Bobby asked.

"All my life," said Mei. "I still study. So much to learn and practice. It cannot be mastered. I tell you this now because I think it would be the right thing, the good thing, for me to teach both of you. Exercises we do made your bodies ready for it. Would you like to learn?"

Bobby said an enthusiastic, immediate, "Yes!"

But Tran burst out in a voice stricken with horror and grief, "Did you have to kill those men, Mei? Couldn't you have just knocked them out or hurt them so they couldn't fight anymore?"

Mei looked directly in his eyes, proud of the boy he was turning out to be. In a steady voice, clear and quiet, she said, "I do not answer to you, Tran. I answer to God only. I have reasons for doing what I do. I know things you do not. When you are older, you will have your own reasons and will decide who you answer to. But now, you are young boy, you answer to me and your grandfather until you learn. Do you understand this?"

"I think so," he said. It had shaken the ground under his feet when he heard the thuds and groans from the blows Mei delivered to the attackers outside the docking bay, and then seeing the bodies floating in the aquaponic channel. *Who was this who was capable of such things?* But now he looked at her and saw the kind brown eyes of the early days, and the same light that shined in them whenever she talked to him about God, honor, right, and good. It *was* Mei. The ground under his feet was solid again—rock solid. She was not one person here and another one there, depending on circumstances. She was the same, though the expressions of that person were different according to the needs. Tran wanted order, consistency, integrity, someone he could trust. Before him sat his beloved Mei. She was herself and only herself. "Is fastfighting hard?" he asked.

"Yes, very difficult," said Mei. "Harder than you can know."

"Then I would like to do it," said Tran. "I like learning hard things."

Chapter 10: The Mysteries of Mei

Chapter 11
Fastfighting

Having completed their stretches, their bodies now warmed up, Tran and Bobby stood on the grass in front of home plate facing centerfield in the ballfield on Vidmar Delta. Mei stood barefoot in front of them in loose-fitting white pants and top. The boys were dressed the same. It was 0530 hours on Tuesday, two days after the attack on Z11, and though they were sleepy from being up so early, both boys were excited to be getting their first lesson in fastfighting.

"Put your feet like this," said Mei, positioning her feet a little past shoulder width apart. "Arms at sides relaxed. Bend your knees a little. Find good balance." Lightly she pushed Bobby's left shoulder directly to the right, checking his side-to-side balance. He was rock solid. Tran was too. "This is neutral stance," she said. Very important for balance and learning. "Now look here." She pointed to the center of her chest near the heart. "Look here and you will see all parts of a fighter's body, parts they can use to strike you—head, shoulders, elbows, hands, hips, knees, shins, feet. Even close, three feet away, you can see them all. This spot we call the key. When you focus on the key of a fighter, we say you are locked. When you hear me say 'lock,' I am telling you to keep your eyes on this spot. Do you understand this?"

"Yes," they said.

"Good," said Mei. "Lock!" She stood a moment checking to make sure the boys were focused on the key. Then suddenly she jumped up and spun twice around so fast that both boys flinched and stumbled slightly backwards. She landed directly in front of them, touching each lightly on the forehead at the same time before they could process what was happening.

"Whoa!" shouted Tran. "I didn't even see you coming!"

"Me neither," said Bobby, shaking his head in disbelief.

"Yes, but now I will teach you how to see," said Mei. "Listen and remember this: Look at nothing to see everything." She paused, reading their blank looks. "Here is what this means: You do not look at eyes, you see eyes. You do not look at hands, you see hands. You do not look at feet, you see feet. Do not look at one thing with busy mind. Stay locked on key, let mind relax and see all things at once. We will try again. You will see much more." She took her stance. "Lock!" she commanded, then she jumped straight up and spun twice around just as fast and high as before.

"Wow! It works!" Bobby cried. "The first time I couldn't make anything out. You were just a blur. This time I was able to see your feet, knees, shoulders, and head. You were still spinning fast but I was relaxed and I could make out much more. Of course, I knew you were going to do it, so that helped."

"Yes," Mei replied, "but you are learning."

"I didn't see a lot," said Tran. "You still looked like a blur to me, but I was wondering if you were going to touch us on our foreheads again and I was going to try to stop you." He laughed at his admission.

Mei quickly touched him again on the forehead. "When you guess, you cannot lock. When you think, you cannot lock. When you cannot lock you cannot see. We will try again. I will throw a hand strike at you, Tran. Are you locked?" Balanced in his neutral stance with his eyes on the key, Tran said he was. Cat-quick, Mei threw a hand strike from her neutral stance. She asked, "What did you see?"

"I saw your hips and knees turn to the right first, then your left arm go out a little bit from your side, and then your left fist came towards my right eye."

Mei nodded approvingly. "What else did you see?"

"Uh, nothing."

"Did you see my right foot almost kick your left knee?"

Tran was horrified. "No. Did it?"

Chapter 11: Fastfighting

"Sure did," said Bobby.

Tran moaned, "How did I miss that?"

"You locked on hands only," said Mei. "To truly see, you think of nothing. You lock on key and let all come to your eyes."

Mystified, Tran said, "So I'm just supposed to stand there and let you throw hand strikes and kicks at me and not do or think anything but lock on the key and somehow I will learn from that?"

"Yes," said Mei. "You learn the truth of movement. You learn what is real to your eyes, not what is in your busy brain. You cannot learn how to block or move away from hand strikes or kicks if you do not know what they look like. You must learn to see and move without thinking. Then you can use it for good fastfighting."

"Oh, I think I get it," said Tran. "If you react, you can't learn to see what you're reacting to. Reaction is distraction."

"Yes, you say it right!" said Mei.

"Reaction is distraction," repeated Bobby. "I like that."

Next Mei sent the boys to opposite sides of the outfield. There they stood, weight balanced in a neutral stance, their eyes on the blank green fence, until she felt they had brought their thoughts under control. Then, one at a time, she had them turn and lock on her as she flipped and spun and kicked bright flashes of white across their line of sight. It was hard for the boys to ignore her exquisite movements, or to not think about how they hoped they could do what she could do some day. But Mei could always tell if their eyes shifted or their attention wavered. Whenever she caught a flicker of distraction, she would remind them to lock.

Tran was dubious, but determined, and as time went on, he found he was able to stay focused better, and then he noticed a strange peace in his heart. He felt more alert and calm than he had ever been. He began to like it.

Mei explained, "When you truly see, you learn to see the early motion of strikes before they are thrown. In fight, your body answers in best way."

When they were done with their lesson, Mei told the boys to run four laps around the field. "Running helps get what you learn inside you," she said. "Concentrate on your breathing. Fall into a pace that is not hard or easy. Think of what you learned and test its truth in your heart and mind. This way, it will be yours."

After two hours of locking and learning, struggling with completely unfamiliar ways of perceiving, the boys were glad to run. Their bodies settled into smooth, comfortable rhythms that drew the new ways from their heads down throughout their entire beings. By the time they had finished their laps, these truths of fastfighting were integrated into the way they processed what they saw. As Mei had said, it had become their own.

Chapter 12
Daoqin

Dr. Gransom was on his way to an important summit on Midway when he received the radio call from the Vidmar Protectors' office informing him that Mei and the boys had been attacked. Immediately he gave orders for Mirage and the two accompanying Protector ships to speed for home. It took three days. Early Wednesday afternoon, he arrived, went straight to his study and met privately with Mei. After she left, he sent for Bobby.

Bobby had been waiting impatiently in his flat, hoping to get answers to the questions that were troubling his young heart. As soon as word came over the intercom that Gransom was ready for him, he hurried to the back entrance to Gransom's study. As soon as he stepped into that familiar place, he instantly felt better. He gave Gransom a quick, relieved hug and welcomed him back, then sat down on the couch facing him as the doctor took his customary seat in his comfortable high-back chair. A teapot and two mugs of tea were steaming on the table. Bobby picked up a mug and took a sip.

At first, Gransom didn't say anything. He seemed to be checking Bobby over, looking searchingly into his hazel eyes. Bobby gazed back, open and trusting. Gransom smiled. "First things first," he said, picking up the remaining mug and settling back in his chair. "You're sixteen now. Congratulations and happy birthday." Bobby smiled back, surprised Gransom remembered, especially considering everything that was going on. The doctor continued, "And I was informed that you passed your pilot's test with flying colors, if you'll pardon the pun. I'm very proud of you, my boy."

Bobby felt a rush of gratitude and love for the man. "Thank you, Grandfather. You're the one who made it possible."

Gransom shrugged, "I gave you the opportunity, but you're the one who put in the hard work. Very few people give any thought to the training and commitment that goes into being a pilot. I find it extraordinary that you were able to accomplish this at such a young age. Well done. We will celebrate this Friday evening with a special dinner. After that, we will go to the theater and enjoy the new musical. I hear it's quite good."

"I would like that," said Bobby, waiting quietly, his eyes on Gransom's face. He knew he was not there just to discuss plans for his birthday. The Chief Director was not one for small talk.

"Mei filled me in on what happened," Gransom said. "She told me you were very brave to stand up to those men."

"It was more anger than bravery," said Bobby.

"I understand. How could anyone strike our beloved Mei?"

"Exactly, but I was kind of useless in there," Bobby said ruefully.

"You distracted the men enough that Mei could get free. I wouldn't call that useless."

Suddenly Bobby's worries came pouring out in a rush of questions. "Who were those men, Grandfather? Why did they go after Mei and want to hurt her? Why did they come looking for Tran and me? I need to know these things, and Tran needs you to assure him things are okay. He thought he was going to lose her. Can you imagine what that would do to him? And Mei won't tell us anything. She just says we don't need to know. But *I* want to know!"

Bobby wasn't afraid to talk to Gransom this way, though it wasn't natural to him. When he was a little boy, he had learned the hard way that he must be very careful what he said to his parents. There was this invisible line…he never knew where it was until he crossed it. Then the offended parent would react—with rebuff, dismissal, blame, rejection, fury, or withdrawal. It was too risky to reveal what was on his heart, so he simply didn't. He might have continued in this way except for his angry flight in the Scout when all his resentments exploded in total foolishness that nearly ended his young life. When he thought about it afterwards, he could clearly see how destructive it had been to hide his feelings

Chapter 12: Daoqin

from his parents, whether they wanted to hear about them or not. After his rescue, Bobby resolved to be as open and honest with Gransom as he could, no matter how uncomfortable it was for the man to hear or for Bobby to say. He didn't want another distant parent figure who was always busy with more important things. He wanted someone to be involved in his life. Someone he could talk to about real things, some of which terrified him.

Gransom was an inspirational leader, but Bobby discovered the man did not share himself easily. He shared his knowledge and vision for the colony freely and enthusiastically, but not himself. Nevertheless, over the years, Bobby had found ways to be heard through Gransom's preoccupation with projects and the distractions of multitudes of competing voices. Bobby was never rude about it. He was polite and respectful, but also insistent. He was determined not to be lost again in the background noise. His commitment to having genuine connection kept the Chief Director grounded in humanity and the things that matter most. Bobby was like a young sapling growing tall and straight that the doctor could see as a kind of hope for the future. The Chief Director never shared his personal fears or the heaviest and most dreadful things he knew were going on, things affecting the colony and Earth, but he was impressed with the young man's character and believed he could handle knowing certain things, especially since he'd recently been thrust directly into the middle of them.

"I will answer some of your questions," said Gransom gravely, "and I'll talk to Tran later to reassure him and settle him down. I know this has been shocking and upsetting for all of you. It's shocking to me as well, but in a different way. As far as Mei goes, I have no control over what she does or does not share with you boys. That is her choice. I can tell you some of what I know, but not everything. And I don't know everything anyway. Mei has told me much of her story, but is extremely private about certain parts of her life, I think the more painful ones. However, now that you're sixteen and such an integral part of my life and my work within the colony, it's important that you see things in a larger context. Mei trusts you implicitly, and she has given me permission to share things I know about her. But I caution you, what I'm about to tell you is extremely sensitive and must not be repeated. I trust you to honor what is spoken to you in confidence. This is for your ears alone. It is not even for Tran's. Mei has decided that she will tell him whatever he needs to know when the time seems best to her. I will be telling him only what she and I deem necessary, so you must promise not to discuss with him any of what I'm about to tell you. Do you understand?"

"Yes, sir." said Bobby. "I give my word."

"Good," said Gransom. "Then I will tell you this long and twisted tale." He sighed, then began…

"We traced the origin of the two ships and the men who attacked you back to a powerful business coalition within the East Coast Legion of States. That coalition is called MedTrust. It's controlled by some of the top bureaucrats in the Eclos government. I have been up against MedTrust for decades because of their nefarious business practices and industrial spying. Like so many others on Earth, they would like nothing more than to crack the secrets of processing magtronium. You already know many of the precautions we take to guard against that from happening."

In his travels with Gransom, Bobby had been introduced to some of what was required in the complicated processes of converting magtronium into its three useable forms—a substance used for gravitational manipulation devices, fusional power cores for spacecraft engines, and slow-depleting low energy cells. The processes for each of these forms were broken down into numerous steps carried out by different processing stations throughout the colony, all of which had strict security protocols. He also knew that primer solutions formulated by Gransom were key elements in creating the final compounds. Only one person knew how all of this was done, and that was Gransom. It was vital to the colony that the information stay protected and preserved so it could be transferred to Gransom's replacement as Chief Director in case of his death, and there were safeguards in place to guarantee that would be accomplished without the risk of outsiders obtaining it.

Gransom leaned forward in his chair and looked at Bobby intently. "An even more concerning issue with Eclos and MedTrust is their totalitarian control over a small undeveloped island halfway around the world from their border. Eclos gained control over the island when one of their first orbital cities was destroyed due to an accidental missile launch by the East Nation. To stop an all-out war from breaking out, the East Nation immediately offered reparations. Eclos demanded that the island be added to the sweeping reparations package. When I heard this, I wondered why Eclos was that adamant about obtaining it. The island was so small it could be crossed by foot in three days. It had no substantial mineral or rare-earth deposits, or any other valuable resources, and since it was only 800 miles off of the East Nation's southeast coast, part of the reparations agreement was it could not be used as a military base or for harboring any type of military vessel, for air or sea, or the East Nation would destroy the entire island. The name of that island is Daoqin—the island of deep caves."

"DAY-o-chin," repeated Bobby slowly. "Like violin. DAY-o-chin. I've never heard of it."

"Most people haven't," said Gransom. "For the most part, their culture had remained virtually unchanged by the modern world. The East Nation had no interest in developing the island. All they had there was a series of docks, a small medical clinic, and a couple of buildings that housed the workers who cycled through every three months to act as conservators. That was about the extent of it. Daoqin was so isolated that even the Black Hack and the second War of the States didn't have an effect on the islanders' lives.

"When I became aware of Daoqin, I was fascinated with it. I started studying its history and culture, though very little could be found in the archives. But what kept me going was one haunting question: Why was MedTrust so interested in this tiny island? That led to years of methodical investigations, some of which I will share with you now."

Gransom took a sip of tea, sat back in his chair, and continued. "Twenty years before the destruction of their orbital city, an Eclos cargo ship crash-landed a few miles off the Daoqin shore. Fishermen from the island were able to rescue some of the crew, taking the injured to the East Nation's medical clinic. There the men were treated, some receiving transfusions with blood donated by the Daoqins. As it turned out, two of those injured crew members had pre-existing and well-documented illnesses. One had stage 2 pancreatic cancer, and the other had mid-level emphysema. The prognosis in both cases was grim—death within three years.

"Astonishingly, a few weeks after returning home from the island, both crew members showed no signs of their diseases. Extensive test results confirmed that no trace of their conditions remained, and their overall health had improved dramatically. That got the attention of MedTrust, and since Eclos still had permission by the East Nation to use Daoqin as the crash recovery site, they imbedded a team of doctors and scientists into the recovery crew in order to secretly study the island and its people, especially those from whom the transfusions came.

"What that team found was extraordinary. The vast majority of islanders native to Daoqin were purebloods. The only pureblooded people left on Earth. Their blood was universal to all types, and its healing properties were nothing short of miraculous. This information was restricted to only top members of MedTrust, who then negotiated a secret agreement with the village elders. For twenty years blood from villagers was smuggled off the island, turned into a serum, and made available to an elite and wealthy few. When the missile attack on the orbital city occurred, MedTrust saw the chance for something big, and they got what they wanted. The East Nation ultimately turned ownership of Daoqin over to Eclos.

"Now in control, MedTrust immediately went to work performing extensive tests on the islanders. It didn't take long before they discovered that the younger the blood, the more powerful its benefits. Then they found that serums made from the bone marrow of children was like the fountain of youth. They studied further and found that the bone marrow of newborn babies produced the quintessential longevity drug. They estimated, and it's been proven since, that the serums could add thirty to forty years to natural life. Not only that, they could cure diseases, providing vibrant health for whomever obtained the drug. This was too much for MedTrust to pass up, and medical science driven by greed ran amuck. Young children were rounded up and harvested. The islanders were forced to have more and more babies who were confiscated and processed. If the parents refused, they would be starved, or any older children who had not been harvested would be taken from them and processed."

Bobby sat back in horror. Gransom looked at him with compassion. "I know. It's hard to comprehend. Do you want me to continue?" Bobby nodded, though his face was pale. Gransom went on, his deep voice steady but sad. "The effect this had on the Daoqins was profound. They loved their children dearly. Indeed, their culture was based on family. After MedTrust began taking their children, many of the parents committed suicide. Those who remained took off their bright island clothes and dressed in the colors of mourning—the shades of shadow, dusk, and dust.

"Meanwhile, MedTrust continued their work. At first it was a small but extremely lucrative enterprise, if one could call it that, but in a couple of years it became big business. Once it leaked out into the public that there was this incredible longevity drug available, people clamored for it. Business boomed. MedTrust could not keep up with the demand. Even when a former MedTrust worker revealed the gristly source of the longevity serum, the pushback MedTrust expected never came. People on Earth accepted it with not much trouble. The argument was, 'Well, the baby already died giving its marrow, that's not our fault, so we can use it without any guilt or responsibility.' After that, the island became nothing more than a baby mill.

"I tell you this, Bobby, and never forget it. Greed has many companions, the most prominent of which is stupidity. MedTrust had a problem. They were killing off future baby makers. They were on their way to making their own business commodity obsolete. Realizing their folly, they started allowing islanders to have more surviving children, the horrible catch being parents never knew which babies would be taken from them. But once the villages were populated with children again, it became possible for them to have unregistered children, 'Secret' children. It was an act of defiance that sprang up from an overwhelming desire to have families again.

"It wasn't long before MedTrust figured out this was going on, but allowing it helped keep the islanders in order, so they ignored it. The two sides entered into what I call a mutual-trust lie. Mei was born into this lie. When her mother was pregnant with her, she drank some herbs which induced labor two months early. She told the MedTrust techs that the baby had been stillborn in the night, and as their custom on the island, was given to the sea. The lie was accepted. Mei was now a Secret Child.

"But mutual trust lies have a way of breaking down, and when Mei was a little over two years old, there was a world-wide viral scare which prompted a higher demand for all levels of the blood serums. In their haste to meet the demand, MedTrust decided that all unregistered Secret Children were to be rounded up and processed. This was beyond the peaceful Daoqins' tolerance and a deadly riot broke out, during which, some courageous teenagers smuggled over forty Secret Children to the mountain in the center of the island and hid them there. One of those refugees was Mei.

"During the riot, many villagers were killed, including Mei's parents, and her eight-year-old brother was taken and processed. When the riot was finally quelled, the punishment by MedTrust was swift and severe—a number of executions, and strict lockdowns and food rationing for the rest. Boats were locked up and islanders were forbidden to fish, and guards patrolled the forest to prevent them from gathering food from the trees. It became impossible for the parents who survived to reunite with their Secret Children on the mountain, so the children had to remain there.

"Now here is something quite interesting, Bobby. Living within the labyrinth of caves, tunnels, chambers, and caverns of the island's long-dormant volcanic mountain was an order of monks—followers of a Daoqin creed from long ago and its sacred form of fighting. This was a strange group of men. They had very little interaction with other islanders, and yet, young men, following some internal call, would leave their families and villages, wander up the mountain and join this order, swearing off all other connections and allegiance. Islanders whose sons chose this rigorous lifestyle were proud of them and received honor from the other villagers. They detached emotionally from their sons, considering them a sacrificial gift to the island.

"The entire society and hierarchy of this order of monks was based on and controlled by fighting competitions. It's how they settled all disputes, made all decisions, and determined who their leaders would be. Confronted with the refugee children, they held a three-day tournament to determine their future. The winner of that tournament was Supreme Master Paag, who had already been serving as their current leader for a number of years. He had been concerned because young men had not been coming to join their order, the harvesting raids having left very few children alive. When Supreme Master Paag won the tournament, he declared that the refugees would be allowed to stay as servants. In return, the monks would become their masters and trainers. This was now the life in which Mei would be raised.

"The monks were hardened, disciplined men who knew nothing about raising or caring for children, especially girls. They looked with distain upon the rag-tag refugees which they referred to as grubs—nothing but worthless eaters. The grubs were no better than slaves, even the very youngest, forced to do the most menial and exhausting tasks, and physical punishments for stepping out of line or not doing their work were swift and severe. Concerned for the well-being of these little ones, the teenagers who had brought them there took it upon themselves to care for the younger ones, and that became their main responsibility. If it hadn't been for them, many of the little ones wouldn't have survived. When I think times are difficult, I often think of those older children and how hard their lives must have been. Much harder than when they lived in the villages and that was already extremely difficult. Of course, the children were not forced to stay in the caves. The monks could have cared less. But the grubs had no other alternative. If they went back to the villages, they would be rounded up and processed. In the caves they had food and a safe place to live. Sadly, it was better than going home.

"Mei's fight training and chores began when she was three years old. She assisted the cooks—grinding herbs, chopping vegetables, stirring pots, stoking the cooking fires—whatever they needed done. The kitchen monks, observing Mei's precise cutting and slicing, reported her remarkable dexterity to their superiors who, when she was only five, sent her to the healer monks who gave her the added responsibilities of making medicinal liniments and salves, and binding the limbs and dressing the wounds of the monks and grubs who were injured during fighting and training.

"You have to understand, Bobby, the monks had no training regimes that accommodated age. They demanded the same discipline from three-year-old Mei as from the young men who wandered into the mountain. That meant she trained 14 hours a day, 6 days a week, and she was still expected to get her work done between those rigorous training sessions.

"One good thing was the monks believed one's body needed time to rest and recuperate, so even the grubs had a free day to do what they wished. The children called these 'Healing Days.' Mei's designated healing day was Sunday.

"Meanwhile, back in the villages, the restrictions imposed on the islanders were becoming more relaxed, and after about four years things were pretty much back to the way they had been before—the islanders even having Secret Children again. Though the grubs could not stay in the villages for fear of being captured, they were able to sneak back in on their healing days to visit family and friends.

Chapter 12: Daoqin

"One Sunday when she was seven, Mei made her way through the rainforest down to where the villages stood. She had no idea where her family lived, but she knew she was from the middle village, the one called Gonqin. Excited, but fearful too, she found a woman with a kind face and asked if she knew her family and could show her where they lived. Sadly the woman said they were no more. Mei told me she had only faint memories of her parents and brother, but her heart was shattered nonetheless. It hit her hard—she was now an orphan with no family to remember her.

"As she left the village, it began to rain, beating against her face, mixing with her bitter tears. She was too devastated to care. Weeping, she stumbled along a narrow trail leading up the mountain, feeling small and alone. Somehow through the downpour of battering rain she heard a sound like singing. Astonished, she followed the sound to a clearing where she saw a makeshift building made out of mud bricks. She stood under the thatch eves and listened. People were singing about a love beyond all loves sent from God and His Son—beautiful melodies carrying words in her language, the meaning of which she did not understand. She said the songs flowed like a clear, rippling river over her anguished heart.

"A woman came out and invited her inside. Warily Mei stood in the back of the small room. After a few more songs, the people sat on the floor. There weren't many, maybe fifteen. A young man went to the front and started to talk. Even though it was many years ago, Mei told me she will never forget what he said—how God will heal the brokenhearted. How no suffering is unseen or unknown to Him. How He has counted and collected every tear and will turn them all to joy. Mei said it felt as if the man was talking directly to her, as if somehow he could read her thoughts. It terrified her. Alarmed, she fled back to the caves. In her confusion, she tried to forget, but she couldn't. The young man's words matched something she had been feeling in the secrets of her heart.

"On her next Healing Day, she worked up the courage to go back, but was thinking maybe it had been a dream and the building wouldn't be there, but it was, and this time even more people were there. She went back every week. She learned the hymns and listened to the young man talk. His name was Taal—a strange name to Mei and the others because all it meant in their language was 'word.'

"I was curious about that young man, so I did some investigation. Taal's story was so remarkable it astounds me. He and his parents were not only brave, they were daring, but I'm getting ahead of myself. Though he had been conceived on the island, Taal was not born there. When his mother became pregnant with him, his parents wanted to escape the island and save their child from MedTrust's horrific roundups. At that time, both of them worked on the docks and had learned a bit of English from the ships' crews and dock masters. One night, they stowed away in a MedTrust cargo ship departing for the Great Continent. It was on that continent that Taal was born. His parents named him Taal because it sounded like some of the English names they had heard. Over time he taught his parents to speak Universal English and they started listening to the radio to immerse themselves in the language. One evening they heard a preacher on the radio reciting words they knew in English. This is what he said: 'In the beginning was the Word, and the Word was with God, and the Word was God.' They took that as a sign, and it changed their lives. They became outspoken, zealous people of faith, and preached in public without fear. Not surprisingly, they were soon in trouble with the authorities and jailed numerous times before being sent to prison for life for repeat offenses of spreading lies and propaganda.

"Devastated and angry, Taal fell into a fury of confusion and despair. Then he received a letter from his father asking him to live up to his name and to go speak the love and forgiveness of God to the people of Daoqin. His mother sent him a letter that said only that he needed to do what God put in his heart. Two months later, Taal returned to the island the same way his parents left it when he was still in the womb. He stowed away on a MedTrust cargo ship, and on the night it docked, he found his way into his parents' village.

"Since he was Daoqin (except for his clothes, which he quickly remedied), and spoke the language perfectly, he didn't have any trouble blending in. Taal was a gentle young man who quietly went about inviting people to his meetings. They found him intriguing because, though his looks and words were thoroughly Daoqin, he wasn't exactly like them, and they were interested to hear what he could tell them about what existed beyond the island and the sea.

"One day Mei was peacefully grinding up herbs in the cooking chamber. Suddenly she found herself on the ground, her cheek stinging painfully from the violent slap that had knocked her off her feet. A tall, angry monk stood glowering down at her. He demanded to know what she was singing. Not knowing better, she said it was a song about God. She saw his face twist. She said it looked like he was being tortured, and when he demanded to know where she had learned the song, she lied and said her mother had taught it to her. He shouted that there was no god but the island and the sea and forbade her to speak or sing that name ever again. If she did, she would be severely punished. After that, whenever she was in the caves, Mei sang silently inside herself. The songs gave her hope, and she knew she needed them.

"Another of the grubs was a little girl around Mei's age. Her name was Fe Lin. She was a happy child, always goofing around imitating the monks, or telling stories and acting them out with dolls she made from the big leaves she folded into little green figures. She and Mei became very close friends. Because both girls were gifted in treating the injured, they eventually earned gratitude and respect, even from the monks. A number of monks were coming to see the advantage of having servants to do the boring, repetitive chores, and warmed to the idea that it was beneficial to have them around.

"Mei and Fe Lin enjoyed each other's company so much that they began to do their training together, often continuing long into the night. When the girls were twelve, Great Master Yaang took notice of their fighting skills and saw that they took it upon themselves to train extra hours. He was so deeply respected that no one objected when he claimed them as his students. It was an unprecedented honor, especially for girls, who were at the bottom of the social and fighting hierarchy. Mei said she thought Great Master Yaang had a sly, secret sense of humor and found it amusing to address them as if they were one person, calling them either Fe Mei or Mei Lin, even when one of them wasn't there. She thought she caught an occasional twinkle in his eye, though she could never find a trace of it on his stern, serious face. Both girls grew to love and respect the man. He was a strict, demanding, but gifted teacher, and though he was quite elderly, he was still a formidable and fierce fighter. But outside the training circle, they found him to be a gentle, kind, caring, and rather grandfatherly man.

"Great Master Yaang was different from most of the other monks who were adamant about adherence to the original forms. He respected the discipline of the ancient ways, but he wasn't a slave to them. Once he was satisfied that his students had a solid foundation, He allowed them to experiment and try new things. Mei and Fe Lin flourished under his guidance, and wanted nothing more than to please him and make him proud, so they trained harder and longer than anyone.

"When Mei was fourteen, an older boy, thinking he could take advantage of a weak girl, picked a fight with Mei and challenged her for her spot in Master Yaang's class. Because he was three years older and much larger than Mei, no one thought Master Yaang would approve such an uneven match, but he did, and the match was scheduled for three days later. Mei was intimidated, but when she went to the master to plead her case, he told her if she didn't think she could win, she should not show up for the match and she no longer belonged in his class.

"When the time for the match arrived, Mei was there. The fight lasted twelve seconds before the boy submitted his surrender. Those who watched the match were astonished. One of the High Masters declared that if anyone said they saw what happened they were lying because Mei moved so quickly there was nothing to see. Ever since then, the moves Mei made in that fight have been studied over and over by students, monks, and masters, the way chess aficionados examine the moves of a great chess match. Word spread quickly about the young girl with so much power and speed and her unusual combinations of moves. Even in the villages her name and skills became known.

"The boy (his name was Park) was shamed by his defeat, not a good thing in their culture, but much worse in a society which determines merit and worth by one's fighting skills. After his bravado and subsequent defeat, his future was dim, but Mei asked Master Yaang if he would take Park as his student. She understood the boy's desperation for wanting the best training, and when she explained it that way to her master, he accepted him into his class. Mei, Park, and Fe Lin became training partners and loyal friends from that day forward.

"When Mei was nineteen, Great Master Yaang died. Though it was the custom for neophytes to submit themselves to another master, Mei, Fe Lin, and Park trained together instead. There were grumblings about this by some of the monks and masters, but no one officially challenged them, so they were allowed to continue. Over the next seven years, the three of them sparred hundreds of the monks and other students. However, some monks refused to engage with them, and some masters forbade their students to spar with them. They considered them insignificant, arrogant upstarts trying to make a name for themselves and unworthy of their time.

"Mei believed it was important to experience all the different styles and movements of all the different fighters. She spent hours upon hours watching and studying them and encouraged Fe Lin and Park to do the same. She became their master teacher, and she methodically developed her own style built on the foundation put in place for seven years by her beloved Master Yaang.

"When Mei was twenty-six, a regime change occurred within Eclos. Those who came into power were dissatisfied with the soft approach MedTrust was taking with the Daoqins and implemented much stronger measures. A number of ugly gray buildings were erected on the outskirts of Gonqin—a prison and some smaller buildings with a compound of barracks for personnel. They stood as formidable, forbidding barricades between the village and the slopes of the mountain, imposing their grim institutional domination on the lush green land. Guards actively patrolled the villages and performed surprise raids. They hauled men, women, and children off to these bleak structures, some never to be seen again. The smaller buildings turned out to be some sort of medical labs. The atrocities that were told by those who returned from those buildings, I will not tell you now. Even at sixteen, you should not hear them, and I do not want to speak the words.

"MedTrust didn't want any more children escaping to the caves, so checkpoints and border patrols were set up around the base of the mountain, and only a few villagers doing trade with the monks were allowed to pass. Violators could be thrown in prison without recourse. Afraid of putting their loved ones in danger, the grubs could no longer risk sneaking into the villages to visit their families.

"Taal moved his meeting place higher up the mountain where the guards dared not go for fear of angering the monks, but the villagers could no longer get to him because of the risk of getting caught by the guards. Attendance at the meetings dwindled to Mei, Fe Lin, and Park on Sundays, and a handful of other grubs during the week. But Taal was determined to stay and support his people, no matter how few. For many years he had taught them, counseled and comforted them, especially Mei, who had absorbed the words of truth like a tree with its roots thrust deeply into rich soil.

"Astonishingly, that year a new group of Secret Children were smuggled past the guards and up to the caves. The adult grubs were well prepared and equipped to take them in, making things much easier for the new little ones than when they went through it themselves. Mei loved caring for the young children and being in their company. She even took time away from her training in order to spend more time with them.

"The new influx of children created a heated rift at the top of the monks' order. Some of the monks wanted to break connections with all of the grubs and have them moved to the windward side of the island. They complained the grubs were no longer servants. They said they had infiltrated the Order's culture and made them soft. Some wanted only the new children to be moved, with a few of the adult grubs appointed to act as caretakers for them. Others wanted them all to stay. Spontaneous fights broke out. Serious injuries occurred. A number of monks and grubs, and even two masters, went missing, no one having a clue what happened to them. Things had gotten out of hand.

"Finally a tournament was scheduled. The monks announced it was to be the largest tournament in over 150 years. Twenty-four masters pairing off in five days of fights. The current Supreme Master chose not to take part, so the winner would be the new Supreme Master, the one who would decide the future for all the rest.

"Two days before the tournament, one of the grubs told Mei that Taal had to move once again because the guards had been patrolling higher up the mountain, but he said he wasn't sure exactly where he was going to make camp. Concerned for Taal's safety, Mei finished her duties and went looking for him. She hiked partway down one of the less traveled trails and back up another, but she saw no signs of him or his camp. Though the sun would be setting soon, she knew all the trails well, so she decided to go down one of the steeper paths. Twisting and turning down an exposed rock cropping, the trail curved to the left and plunged into the rainforest. It was darker under the canopy, but Mei had grown up on that mountain. She knew she could find her way home even on a moonless night so she went on.

"Parrots squawked and complained about being disturbed, their powerful wings whooshing overhead as Mei passed through their territory. Smaller birds twittered and she could hear animals hurrying out of her way, warning and scolding as they fled. When she had gone deeply into the forest, she became aware that the creature calls, and even insect noises were strangely still. She stopped and listened. There was nothing but an eerie quiet. Perplexed, she stood wondering what it meant. That's when she heard faint voices coming from somewhere off the trail. Quietly she followed the sound, slipping through the foliage till her way was blocked by a fallen tree.

"The voices were closer now. She crouched behind the log and carefully peered over it. She was looking down over another trail that ran along the top of a steep green gorge. Four guards were standing relaxed, casually drinking from their canteens, swatting at flies, and complaining about the heat. Something lay on the ground near their feet. In the dimming light Mei could barely make out a pale shape. It was Taal's lifeless body. Stunned, she couldn't think or weep. Then she heard a voice, a voice she recognized—cold, proud, hard as stone. 'Throw him over the cliff and let the vermin have him,' the voice said. 'At least he will have made a small contribution to the island.' Out from the narrow trail, a monk came striding into view, the same monk who had slapped her to the ground for singing to God when she was a child. He was a High Master now, and a powerful one.

"The guards did as he commanded, but grumbled. 'What are you doing, Suun? We get two thousand a head dead, and four thousand alive, Why have us kill this one and then throw away good money?'

"Coldly Master Suun replied, 'I've brought you enough grubs and traitors already, and I will bring you many more once the tournament is over. This one I wanted lost. Never mind why.' One of the guards mumbled something Mei didn't hear and then they hurried off down the trail. Master Suun stood with clenched fists, watching them for a time, then turned and walked swiftly back up the trail.

"Tears started to course down Mei's face. Taal, the dear, sweet, gentle man of God she had known for almost twenty years, murdered, for what? The gorge was deep and covered with dense foliage. The last light was fading. It would be impossible for her to

Chapter 12: Daoqin

find and bury his body. There was nothing she could do for him. She knelt behind the log, her tears falling on the old dead tree. She whispered a long prayer for Taal and his parents. As she tasted her tears, she thought of the first time she had seen Taal and heard God speak to her heart through him. Weeping, Mei walked slowly up the trail, her thoughts a cloud of confusion, her heart crying to her God, the One Taal had faithfully loved to the end. It was completely dark now, but the light of an idea started to grow in her mind."

Seeing the anguish on Bobby's face, Gransom stopped and asked, "Are you okay?"

Bobby shook his head. "No, but I need to know what happened. Please give me a moment." He got up, walked back and forth swinging his arms, then took a neutral stance and a few deep breaths, as if trying to ground himself in familiar reality. Then he sat back down and looked earnestly at Gransom. "I have to ask you, Grandfather. How do you know all these things. How did you find all this out?"

"Good questions," Gransom replied. "Things I've related are so strange one could be inclined to believe it's a fiction made up from rumors and speculation, but I assure you, I have meticulously checked everything I've told you multiple times, cross referencing multiple sources, when possible. I'm telling you this as a researcher, historian, head scientist, businessman, and Chief Director of the colony. As I mentioned, I've been dealing with MedTrust for decades, and Eclos for even longer than that, and when they made a play for Daoqin, I poured a lot of resources and money into finding out why. It just didn't make any sense to me. And then, after I did find out why, I couldn't stop there. I had to investigate further. I myself have interviewed dozens of people from the island—Daoqins and members of MedTrust. I've talked to the foremen and workers who built the prison and medical labs there. I've interviewed villagers who survived being in those facilities. I found and interviewed neighbors of Mei's parents who knew them well. They told me things Mei could not know. I've talked to guards, lab workers, supervisors, techs, doctors. The list is too long for me to remember. There is a massive amount of material in my files. Money buys a lot of access and favor. I've interviewed a number of whistleblowers fairly high up in MedTrust. I've talked to a number of monks and grubs. I've been to the island three times myself, secretly of course, and have even been a guest in the caves. I've had people on the island who have reported to me for almost thirty years. And, most importantly, I've talked to Mei at length.

"Also, these days it's easier to get a spectrum of data. I'm no longer one of the few people interested in gathering information about Daoqin. Once it was unknown, but now there are quite a few scholars, anthropologists, sociologists, and others who are, I would say, obsessed with the island—what has happened there, and why. It's a tragic but intriguing part of history and current events. It holds a great significance to the political and moral structure of our two worlds—Zenith Colony and Earth, and it could very well destroy them both. That's what we are working against." Gransom stopped and looked at Bobby. "Would you like me to continue?"

"Yes," said Bobby, "if you have the energy, please do. I need to know what happened."

Gransom nodded. "Let's see. Where was I? Oh yes... After Mei returned from her search for Taal, she resumed her normal routine until the day of the tournament. She hadn't had the heart or energy to tell Fe Lin and Park what had happened, and she wasn't exactly sure what she was going to do, so she kept it all to herself and tried to act normal.

"On the island is an area where the mountain has a natural formation suitable for a fighting ring. It has a flat dirt area about thirty-feet square with sloping rock walls on three sides where spectators can sit. Since the ancient days, it has been the place where combat had decided the future of the monks' community. That, of course, was the site of the tournament.

Chapter 12: Daoqin

"The only thing Mei told me she knew for sure was that she didn't want to miss one second of even one match. She went to the ring early and climbed high up one of the walls where she knew no one could block her view.

"There was no fanfare or ceremony before the beginning of the tournament. Two masters entered the ring, hung two flags on a pole in their corner, went to the center of the ring, bowed to all four directions and to each other, and started fighting. When a match was over, the loser surrendered one of his flags to the winner. Once both flags of a master were surrendered, he was eliminated from the tournament.

"The last match on the first day was between Master Kie and Master Suun, the monk who had Taal killed. When the match started, Mei could tell right away something wasn't right. Master Kie was holding back. At first she thought he was injured or luring Suun into a trap, but as the fight went on she realized he was throwing the match. It wasn't long before he submitted to a hold. The next two days the same thing happened. Master Suun's opponents did not put out a complete effort. No one watching complained or seemed to notice.

"On the fourth day, Suun's opponent was Master Yu. He had not lost a match and he did not hold back in this one. Mei said his high-low attacks were masterful and greatly disrupted Suun's timing. But later in the match he suffered a powerful side kick to his left hip and came up lame. He tried to go on but was beaten down and knocked out. Shortly after the match ended, it was determined that Master Yu's injuries were serious enough that he would not be able to continue in the tournament. He surrendered his remaining flag. Suun had only one more match to win before being named Supreme Master, and it was against Master Kie, the monk who had thrown him the match on the first day and then had worked his way back up through the ranks.

"Mei said Master Suun was a few inches taller than all the other monks, with a perfectly formed lean and muscular body. He looked and carried himself as if he were created specifically for fighting, and he trained that way. She had studied him over the years when she could, and thought he was the best fighter in the order. When the other Masters threw their fights, she was surprised and dismayed. Why did he stoop to securing his supremacy that way when he could have won legitimately? She carefully observed all these things, pondering them in her heart. It wasn't until late that night that she finally decided what she had to do. Once she did, she was able to sleep soundly.

"The next morning, Mei rose before dawn, dressed and went to the kitchen as usual. After a light breakfast, she began her work. She had to get things ready before the monks started coming in to get their food. She stood at the table facing the back wall, slicing fruit for their breakfast. She filled the big trays and placed them on the long serving table that was a few feet behind her. Since the monks took as much as they wished, She was kept busy slicing and replenishing, careful to make sure there was plenty for them to take. After the monks were satisfied, the grubs would be permitted to eat.

"Mei was slicing up yet more fruit when Master Suun came striding in. The sound of her soft singing stopped him cold. It was the same song she had been singing all those years before. In three strides, he was there grabbing her shoulder, viciously spinning her around, his hand raised to slap her. But Mei was no longer a seven-year-old girl less than half his height. She was a full-grown woman who had trained for twenty-three years, and she was ready for him. Faster than thought, she slapped him hard across his startled face. Then she did it again. No grub had ever challenged him, and for a moment, he froze in shock. Mei threw him to the floor, grabbing the knife on her way down, pressing the blade against his throat. She bent over him and said in a low voice, 'I know what you did. I know everything. When you are victorious today, I will challenge you to a death match. If you do not accept, I will tell everyone what you have done in violation of the honor of your Order. It is treason. They will execute you.'

Chapter 12: Daoqin

"Suun said cooly, 'You are not of the Order. You cannot challenge me. It is not allowed.'

"'But it is,' said Mei, her eyes glittering with purpose. 'If I defeat three of your best masters, I earn the right to challenge. It is in your laws. Great Master Yaang taught me this. You select who they will be. If I lose to any of them, do what you want with me. If I defeat them and lose to you, I cannot speak from the grave. Do you accept or are you the coward I believe you to be?'

"'I accept,' growled Suun. But Mei saw a flash of deceit cross his face.

"Monks and grubs were crowding into the kitchen trying to see what was going on. Keeping the blade to Suun's throat, Mei spoke loudly so everyone could hear. 'I have challenged Master Suun to a death match. He has accepted. If I am murdered before the match, know that he is a coward and should not be followed.' Without another word, she rose quickly and left the kitchen. A monk who was there told me that Suun had calmly gotten up and eaten his breakfast as if nothing had happened.

"After leaving the kitchen, Mei went straight to the training chamber where Fe Lin and Park awaited her. As soon as she arrived, she told them what had happened to Taal and that she had challenged Master Suun. There in that private place, they embraced each other and wept. Then wiping away their tears, the three of them did their training as usual because that's what Mei wanted to do. Neither Fe Lin nor Park asked Mei if she wanted help getting ready for her matches, they knew she was ready.

"By late that morning, word had spread through the caves and down into the villages that there was going to be a death match between a High Master and a lowly grub. No one had ever heard of such a thing. It caused great commotion. When the villagers found out it was the same girl they had heard about twelve years earlier, and that she had to defeat three other masters before the death match, it caused even more excitement. They wondered aloud, 'If she was so good then, how good is she now?' It was all anyone could talk about.

Chapter 12: Daoqin   111

"The rock walls around the fighting area filled up early with spectators from the caves. The overflow sat on the ground on the open side, leaving only a thin path up to the ring. Villagers crowded the boundaries nearest to the caves so they could receive the earliest news about the matches from the young runners who were allowed to go up and down the mountain. But seeing that the MedTrust guards were overwhelmed and distracted, many of the villagers took advantage of the confusion, crossed the border, and hurried up the mountainside.

"After their training, the three friends ate a light lunch Fe Lin had prepared for them, prayed, and made their way through the crowd to the ring. Right before the final match was to begin, Master Kie forfeited and swore his allegiance to Master Suun. The Council overseeing the tournament proclaimed Suun the Supreme Master of the Daoqin order. Suun immediately announced that all grubs would be banished from the caves and young grubs would be relocated to the harsh and desolate windward side of the island. The announcement was met with a mixture of cheers and shouts of dismay.

"Immediately Mei stood up and, in a clear, ringing voice, officially challenged Suun to a death match. The Council denied her request stating that she was not of the order. Mei said she would defeat three masters to claim her right of challenge. The Council had no choice but to accept. Suun named the three masters she would be fighting. Then the Council announced a rule that Mei was not aware of, and that has since been proven not to exist. She had to win each of the three matches within the length of a shadow, which is roughly ten minutes. 'So be it,' said Mei, then walked to her corner and waited for the first opponent. Fe Lin and Park sat on the ground beside her.

"Her first match was against Master Kao, one of the monks who had not objected to letting his students spar with her. She found his students to be well-trained both mentally and physically, solidly strong in the fundamentals. She admired Master Kao's excellent teaching, and now she would meet him in combat. The two of them walked to the center of the ring, bowed as prescribed, and the match began.

"Master Kao wanted to end the match quickly. For the first two minutes he released flurry after flurry of combinations. Mei blocked or avoided most of them, but never countered with much of an attack herself. Some watching thought she was outmatched and the fight would end soon.

"Around four minutes into the match, Kao decided to launch another flurry of unrelenting combinations. In the middle of one of these, Mei ducked under a flying spin kick then sprang up and threw a counter spin kick of her own that arced over Kao's block and struck him on the side of the head while he was still in the air. He fell like a stone, out cold. Monks and grubs alike were stunned. Mei had hardly thrown any strikes and now the match was over. Calmly Mei walked back to her corner and sat on the ground. It took a good five minutes for the Healers to take care of Master Kao, finally assisting him out of the ring.

"Mei now faced Master Tabor. She had watched him teach and spar many times over the years, but he had consistently refused to let his students spar with her, Fe Lin, or Park. Tabor was a large, broad chested man, and deceptively fast for his size. Even the thickness of his muscular arms and legs was intimidating. One did not want to get into a ground war with this man for fear of being crushed.

"When the match started, Mei walked smoothly around the edges of the ring while Tabor tried to cut her off, but she swiftly changed direction and the cat and mouse game would begin all over again. This went on for three minutes. Very few strikes were thrown. Tabor became frustrated and rushed at Mei a few times, but she was always able to avoid him. Then, light and swift as a mongoose, she went to the center of the ring. Tabor now seemed hesitant and didn't try to overtake her. Instead he threw a few hand strikes and kicks to get a feel for how she would respond. Mei slipped most of them but one combination caught her hard in the throat and she reeled backwards. Sensing that she was hurt, he rushed her and tried to sweep her legs out from under her. She jumped over the sweep and sideslipped to the left, landing a hand strike to his right temple, then side-kicking his right knee. When Tabor attacked again, she responded in much the same way—side-slip, strike to temple, side-kick to knee. But when he anticipated that strategy against his next attack, she did not sideslip. Instead she charged him, throwing with precision and dizzying speed a combination of hand strikes to his head and knee strikes to his thighs. He retreated, sideslipped to his left and threw a right cross. Mei's right roundhouse kick came up under it and smashed into his jaw, followed by a left roundhouse kick to the back of his head, followed by a right roundhouse kick to his left temple. Tabor crumpled to his knees. His hands dropped. Groaning, he submitted. It had taken seven minutes.

"Mei would now have to fight Master Kie, Suun's treacherous henchman who was fresh and rested and completely sold out to Suun, a full participant in his sculduggery for power.

"Master Kie was a couple of inches taller than Mei and lean of build. He too was blindingly fast and a powerful striker, but was mostly admired for his defensive mastery and wrestling skills.

"When the match started, he quickly entangled her legs and the fight went to the ground, Mei on her back, Kie hitting her with short, sharp strikes to the face. She worked her legs free and landed multiple skull-jarring knee strikes to the back of his head until he was forced to release her. As Mei rolled over to her hands and knees to get up, Kie dove onto her back, knocking the breath out of her, flattening her face-first to the ground. Even knowing the rule of silence during a match, a gasp of horror escaped from the grubs as Tabor wrapped Mei's throat in a neck hold that everyone knew would end the match. With a mean smile, he tightened his vice around her throat. Everyone knew there was no way out. Mei would have to submit or she would pass out or die. But then, working her legs and hips free, she bent backwards, as if she had no spine, locked her ankles around his throat, and pulled him powerfully back. Both fighters were bent backwards almost double like scorpions locked together stinging one another. Neither one could breathe. Thirty seconds. One minute. Two minutes, and then remarkably, Mei applied even more pressure. Kie slumped unconscious. Mei rolled him off of her, stood up, and went to her corner a little shaky on her feet and still struggling to breathe. It had taken eight minutes.

"The crowd was speechless. They were experienced fighters—monks and grubs who had spent years training. They understood the moves, what was effective, and what guaranteed success, but this was different. Mei had broken a neck hold that had always been unbreakable. Before their eyes, she had done the impossible.

"Furious, Master Suun immediately ordered other monks to drag Kie's limp body away, but he didn't wait for them to finish before he strode to the center of the ring, bowed towards the Council and charged towards Mei while she was still trying to catch her breath. He went straight at her throwing a barrage of swift and powerful kick combinations. Mei tried to get away, but Suun was a predator, treacherous as a jackal, ready to capitalize on her weakness. With a look of pleasure, he rocked her with a couple of kicks to her head. She saw black and red and knew she was in deep trouble, but she lured Suun in close and wrapped up his legs to bring the fight to the ground where she hoped she could catch her breath and regain her senses. She had a hold on Suun, but he worked his way out of it and was able to stand over her and stomp on the back of her head. If there had been a referee, the fight would have been stopped, but this was a death match. With grim determination, Suun drove his foot down for another powerful blow, but Mei managed to move just far enough that his foot hit the ground hard an inch from her head. Swiftly she curled her body up and hooked her legs around Suun's left leg, rolling him to the ground with all the force she could muster. He yelled in searing pain, both of his legs now trapped under Mei. If he tried to shift his position or pull his right leg out from under her, she would roll towards him even more, fiercely applying intense pressure to the nerves of his left leg and he would have to relent. Mei held him there as long as she could, long enough to restore her breath, but the position could not be maintained, so she sprang to her feet. Suun jumped up, his eyes black with hatred.

"They moved forward and back, side to side, coming together in a flurry of strikes, blocks, ducks, spins, jumps and side-steps before breaking away again. Over and over they did this, like master sword fighters looking for an opening. Sometimes Suun was the aggressor, sometimes Mei. Suun was bouncing and bob-bing, agitated as turbulent white water rapids. Mei was smooth as a pool, still, calm, and deep. Her hands began to move in slow rhythmic rotations, her fingers spreading in ever-changing pat-terns, a fascinating dance in the air. Suun slapped at her hands as if to say, 'Quit playing! This is a fight to the death,' but Mei continued. The patterns came faster and faster in front of his eyes. Frowning, Suun threw a combination but his timing was off and Mei countered with hand strikes to his gut, throat, and nose. He threw another combination and was met with a heel kick to the front of his thigh that wobbled him, followed by a swift, precise uppercut to his jaw. Mei's hands continued—flashing, blurring, increasing in speed.

"Grimacing with frustration, Suun leaped towards Mei, his powerful hand strikes aimed at her head, but he missed. She side-stepped and threw a cross-kick to the bridge of his nose, then whipped a side-kick to his left temple. Suun stumbled back. Smoothly she swept his legs out from under him. He hit the ground, rolled backwards and sprang up swinging furiously, but Mei wasn't there. She had slipped to the side, releasing a blur of hand strikes and kicks to the right side of his head and neck. Suun spun towards Mei and was smashed with a roundhouse kick under the jaw. His head snapped sharply back and he wheeled backwards, his arms swinging wildly as he fell. He landed hard flat on his back with a thud that could be felt through the crowd. Mei rushed towards him, but it was done. Suun never moved again.

"Nobody made a sound. A high master, the newly pronounced Supreme Master, was dead. A Secret Child, a grub, had beaten him and the best masters in the Daoqin Order. In the quiet, Mei walked back to her corner. Fe Lin and Park embraced her and helped her sit down.

"When the Council declared Mei the Supreme Master, there was silence. People were waiting to see if anyone would challenge her. When no one did, Mei walked back to the center of the ring and stood motionless while the monks who had conspired with Suun lifted his body onto a stretcher. As they carried him past her, Mei bowed, giving him the respect he had not given to her. All the monks were astonished, and their esteem for her rose greatly, but Mei told me she didn't do it for that. She told me she knew she had to keep her heart clean. Otherwise bitterness at Suun would have defeated her even though she had won the match.

"Mei waited till Suun was carried out of sight. Then she made her pronouncement. Secret Children would continue living at the caves, but no longer as servants. They were to be equal to the monks, but were to continue doing their work with good hearts, allowing things to adjust slowly.

"Villagers told me when news of Mei's victory reached them, a spontaneous celebration broke out. Neighbors pushed their tables together outside to share food as they had in the old days when they were free. Fishermen joyfully hurried into the blue sea and hauled in nets full of thrashing fat fish. Soon a huge bonfire was blazing on the beach while big fish wrapped in thick green leaves were lowered into glowing fire pits. Sizzling plantains released their heavy, sweet smell into the high, wide sky. Children sparred on the wet sand, pretending to be great fighters. Elderly islanders brought out musical instruments and found their old fingers still remembered how to play. At the first sound of those ancient melodies, songs and stories stirred in hearts that had almost forgotten. Joyfully they put on their island clothes, bright in oranges and reds of sunsets and deep and brilliant ocean blues, singing and dancing and feasting far into the night. Those who had dared to cross the borders returned with stories. Some had watched the fights from a ridge above the ring. They described in detail what they had seen.

Their audiences listened, mesmerized, passing what they heard onto others who listened eagerly. Mei's legend began to grow, as did hope. And MedTrust saw it all.

"Now hold on, Bobby, because things are about to get fast and complicated with a lot of moving parts.

"Two years went by, and as the months ticked away, the villagers became more bold and defiant against their captors. Scuffles broke out between them and the guards. Borders were violated daily. MedTrust labs were broken into and equipment was destroyed. Women refused to go to their physical exams and stopped taking pregnancy tests. Couples refused to get pregnant, even though it meant they would be cut off from food rations or thrown into prison. Villagers pulled together and started helping one another by sharing food and shelter and hiding those in trouble. A large number of villagers escaped deep into the rain forest to start over, certain they would be able to make it on their own.

"Significantly, at just about the start of those two years, a humanitarian organization approached MedTrust and offered to build, at their own expense, a hospital on the island and staff it with expertly trained health professionals in order to treat the islanders' ever increasing health problems. As strange as it seems, Daoqins themselves do not have long life spans. At that time, their average natural life expectancy was seventy-two years, and that was quickly going down. MedTrust had no reason to care about the islanders who were past childbearing age, but pregnancy rates were also going down, and more young Daoqins were dying due to health complications than ever before, so they accepted the offer almost without hesitation. Of course, they didn't know I funded the organization and had a number of spies within it.

"The hospital was built just behind and little north of the Gonqin village huts, a few hundred yards in front of the MedTrust labs. Using PiMar technology, the hospital was soon in operation and became something of a sanctuary for the villagers. The staff treated everyone with dignity and respect which earned them the trust of their Daoqin patients. Many of the villagers told the doctors and nurses stories about Mei. I was on Earth at that time and was able to receive immediate reports, so they passed those stories onto me. At first I thought it was legend, but my sources assured me the stories were true.

"Right after that, one of the villagers was able to smuggle his very pregnant wife up to the caves a few days before she delivered their baby. After their little daughter was born the father asked if they would be able to remain at the caves for protection. Mei granted the request. Two masters stood against Mei's decision and challenged her, but she won those matches and her decision held. More pregnant women escaped to the caves after that, and Mei welcomed them all. This was too much for many of the monks. They complained it was unsafe and would put the order in jeopardy. Mei agreed it was risky but said it was the right thing to do and that they were all Daoqin and should stand together. 'The creed you have sworn to is that of a warrior,' she countered, 'not of a coward.' Soon after, a quarter of the order split off and moved to a group of caves farther down the mountain.

"It didn't take long for MedTrust to find out their commodities were escaping to the caves and sent a patrol of twenty armed guards to capture Mei, but before they reached the caves, monks and grubs ambushed them and sent them back beaten and bloodied without their weapons. The next night, MedTrust initiated a raid on one of the smaller villages, but monks appeared out of the darkness, disarmed the guards and forced them back to their compound. The following night, one of the main weapon sheds of the guards' was broken into and emptied.

"It seemed the Daoqins were finally going to take back their island, but they were up against foes with power, weapons, and the means to protect their empires ruthlessly. I didn't know this at the time, but to crush the insurrection, MedTrust requested that Eclos launch an air attack on the monks' caves. A Speedbomber was dispatched from orbit to do the job, but when it came up on the East Nation's threat board, it was tracked by anti-aircraft missiles and turned back by aggressive threats. Eclos apologized to the

East Nation and requested special clearance for the Speedbomber. That was rejected out of hand. Any military presence or vessel on the island would be considered a breech of the Daoqin Agreement and met with harsh and deadly action.

"MedTrust had to figure out another solution, and they did. In a dastardly move, they negotiated a contract with a mercenary group sanctioned by the East Nation to take back control of the island. I've never been able to find out the exact terms of that deal, or how much serum and money was involved, but the mercenary soldiers were soon on their way. The East Nation allowed air transport of the soldiers, but still would not allow any armed vessels near the island, either in the air or on water. I know they had always felt shamed about handing the island over to Eclos, and I think this was a way of retrieving some of their dignity.

"From what I could piece together from reports and radio chatter at the time, I felt things would come to a head fairly quickly, so I sent a number of vessels to the area—some the size of commercial fishing boats and some smaller—all of them looking sufficiently innocuous to avoid attracting any attention. Soon these boats were anchored forty miles east of the island. We wanted to be ready for any rescues or humanitarian action that might be needed. If things went bad, we would try to come in and get as many people off the island as we could. When we were in position, I sent an encoded message to one of my operatives at the hospital, and he passed the word onto others.

"Not long after the soldiers arrived on the island, two hundred strong went up the mountain and set up around the caves. Heavily armed, they fired their weapons and launched explosives into the caves for hours, jeering and challenging the monks to come out. Finally, believing there was no one left alive, the soldiers settled in for the night. When morning came, they were shocked to find twelve soldiers dead. Somehow monks had slipped into their camp and killed them without a sound. Unnerved, the soldiers withdrew and set up camp further down the mountain. That night seven more soldiers came to their end, even though the watch had

Chapter 12: Daoqin

been tripled and everyone was on high alert. Incensed and intimidated, the soldiers reported this sabotage to their commander, Colonel Markson. He was an older man, a career mercenary from the Wars Of The States and other hellish battles. Markson ordered his soldiers down the mountain to help round up all the villagers in Gonqin. He sent a message by the mouth of one of the village men who did trade with the monks. It was clear and unequivocal: 'Surrender within 24 hours or all villagers in Gonqin will die.'

"The next evening, Markson had a huge bonfire lit near the beach in Gonqin's village where their celebrations were usually held. The islanders were forced to wait there crowded together surrounded by soldiers armed with blasters and other weapons. At seven o'clock, thirty minutes before the deadline, Mei slipped past the soldiers and stood with the villagers in the flickering orange light before anyone noticed she was there. Soon some villagers spotted her and started whispering her name. Hope rushed through the crowd and they began chanting and cheering, 'Champion of Daoqin! Champion of Daoqin!' They encircled her but did not crowd her, marveling that she was standing in their midst.

"The soldiers fired shots over the crowd to quiet them down. Then, with his accompanying special troops shoving villagers out of his way, Markson strode towards Mei. The villagers closed quietly in behind them.

"Through a translator, Mei offered her surrender and assured Markson there would be no more trouble. He laughed and said he wanted all the monks to surrender. She told him that would not be possible. She said since she was the Order's Supreme Master, she was taking full responsibility for what had happened and said she alone should suffer the consequences. Markson scoffed at the title 'Supreme Master' and called Mei a little girl. His men laughed. He said he wanted at least nineteen monks to be executed for the men he had lost, and if they were too cowardly to come down, he would kill nineteen villagers each day until they did. Mei said, 'If I am a little girl, have your big men fight me. For each one I defeat, I save five lives until the debt is paid.' Having heard stories about Mei's skills, Markson was amused by the idea. He said if she could beat four of his best men, he would accept the terms of her surrender and she would be the only one executed.

"Four of the biggest, toughest soldiers came forward. To those hardened mercenaries, Mei must indeed have looked like a child. The villagers and the soldiers who surrounded them moved back to make more room for the combat.

"Mei told me she had some difficulty in the first fight because she had never fought a foreigner before, and it was a different style from anything she had previously experienced. She said the soldier would yell before he attacked and she couldn't understand why he was giving himself away.

"Villagers who were there told me not one soldier landed a blow. Mei defeated them all with ease, her opponents overwhelmed and dumbfounded by her speed and power. When the last soldier dropped, the villagers let out a huge roar, then started chanting once again, 'Champion of Daoqin! Champion of Daoqin!' Two soldiers immediately flanked Mei, pointing their blasters at her. Without fear, she stood unflinching before Markson who eyed her cooly. 'Your monks may live,' he said. 'You will be taken to the prison and hanged.' The translator repeated his words.

"Suddenly there was a great cry of Island voices, and the crowd of captured Gonqin villagers began to roil like boiling water. Immediately, all the monks and grubs from the caves and all the villagers who had left for the rainforest and all the monks who had split from the order and hundreds of Daoqins from the other two villages, many armed with weapons that had been taken from the guards, rushed in from all directions and attacked the soldiers. In the mayhem of clashes, screams and weapons fire, Mei dispatched the two soldiers with the blasters and pursued the group surrounding Markson, who were retreating towards the beach and shooting into the crowd. She took out two of them quickly. The rest were overcome by villagers. Markson put up his hands and surrendered to Mei. She assigned villagers with weapons to hold him on the beach while she went back into the main fight.

"The soldiers who had been positioned inside the crowd had been swiftly overrun. Weapons' fire was mostly on the peripheral now, but Mei saw two soldiers with knives cutting their way through the crowd and took them on, incapacitating them both. Soldiers and guards retreated towards the compound but were cut off by a group of villagers with weapons, so they fled to the lab buildings and prison, taking cover there.

"When the bonfire was lit in Gonqin, I received a communication from my source at the hospital that it was time to get underway. All boats rushed towards the island. It was an extremely calm, hot night. The sea was like glass so we made good time. We came around from the backside of the island close to shore, hidden by the forest that came down to the water just before the wide shallow notch of cove and beaches. In the blackness of that moonless night, we could see the bolts of weapons' fire from Gonqin, but we had to stay put until we knew how and when we were needed.

"After some time passed, guards and soldiers from other areas took cover with their comrades at the prison complex. The monks and grubs and islanders held Gonqin, and some still blocked the compound further up the hill. It seemed a standoff for the moment but the aftermath was heart-rending. The village center and the beach had become a battleground. More than sixty lay dead—Daoqins and soldiers alike in nearly equal numbers. Many more were grievously wounded. The staff from the hospital came out to help anyone who was hurt, and villagers carried both their own people and the wounded soldiers into the hospital.

"When Mei returned to the beach to talk with Markson, he said he was a soldier, not a diplomat, but he would get someone to talk to her. Mei said she would be waiting the next morning at the hospital which would be neutral ground. Markson agreed. She and some monks escorted him to the north border of the village near the prison and let him go. Then she headed towards the village center to see if she could help the wounded. On her way, in the light of the bonfire, she saw Fe Lin kneeling on the ground.

Lying beside her was Park, their dear, trusted friend, a black blaster scorch mark on his chest. Fe Lin looked up, her eyes spilling tears and whispered bravely, 'Our brother died a warrior defending his people.' Their cries of sorrow mixed with the anguished voices of others who had found their loved ones dead. Gently the waters of the sea came higher and higher onto the beach, washing from the sand the marks of turmoil and death.

"At daybreak Mei and Fe Lin sat on the ground outside the hospital, waiting. Completely spent, Mei stared blankly at the ground. She had just buried her friend. Villagers, monks, and grubs were dead and wounded. And it was her fault. She had forced everything to happen. She had felt it was the right thing to do—to finally fight to take back the island. To stop the torture and killing of innocent children. To stop the mistreatment and unspeakable cruelty towards her people. To help them take back their lives, their dignity, their freedom, their children. To stop living in fear or hiding in caves. But now, with so many dead and nothing settled, she knew it wasn't worth it.

"A man in a light blue suit with two men on each side of him came down the path to the hospital. Mei and Fe Lin, along with the village translator, went to meet them. His name was Porter. Grant Porter. He told them he was Special Council to the Director of Eclos and had just flown to the island on Eclos 1. None of that meant anything to Mei or Fe Lin. Porter was in his mid thirties, pale with black hair and a wide, flat face. He walked slowly, his enormous soft belly sagging over his belt. The hospital was a frenzy of activity so he suggested they go someplace quiet. They walked to an area near the beach and sat at a table in the shade of a thatched shelter.

"Porter wasn't there to negotiate. He was there to intimidate and he didn't waste any time. Through the translator, he told Mei his people wanted her off the island. They didn't care where she went, they just wanted her gone. He warned her if she didn't leave, more soldiers would come. In fact, they were already on their way and only he could stop them. More villagers would die and that would continue over and over and over again. She must leave the island so it could go back to how it was before she interfered with its operations.

"Mei thought for a time, then she and Fe Lin stood up and started to leave. Porter stopped them and asked Mei what she wanted. 'Stop killing,' she said. 'Use only blood. Don't kill.' Porter asked what would happen if he couldn't promise that. 'We all go into the mountain, into the caves,' said Mei. 'All villagers. Everyone. We stay there and fight until the end and you will have nothing.'

"'Let me show you something,' said Porter. He nodded to one of his men who spoke into a hand-held radio. 'Watch out there,' he told the women, pointing to the sea. Seconds later, a huge explosion shot millions of gallons of water into the air. The shockwave from the blast ripped through the village knocking some people off their feet. The earth shook and shuddered. Mei and Fe Lin stared wide-eyed at one another, frightened and confused. *Who could possess such power?* Porter's men raised their weapons and pointed them at the two women. He declared, 'I can kill you both right now.'

"Fe Lin shouted at the translator, 'Tell him this is neutral ground.'

"Porter smirked when he heard this. 'You are mistaken,' he said smugly. 'The hospital is neutral ground. This is not.'

"But what Porter hadn't counted on were the villagers and their reverence for Mei. There were many hiding in the trees watching her, and once they shook off the shock of the explosion and saw Porter's men draw their weapons, they started calling in a peculiar cry that was both primal and piercing, like parrot shrieks that can be heard for miles. Other villagers heard and, taking up the cry, rushed shrieking towards where Mei was. Soon Porter and his men were surrounded by hundreds of angry Daoqins, many of them armed.

"'If we die, you die,' said Mei. 'Put down your weapons and be honorable men.'

"Porter signaled and his men lowered their weapons. 'You can't win no matter what you do,' he said grimly, 'I will detonate a bomb like that in each village and in the caves if you don't leave the island. All you have to do to stop it is leave.'

"The translator didn't know what a bomb was, so she asked Porter to explain. He pointed out to the sea and made the motion and sound of the explosion. 'And if I die, you all die,' said Porter. 'The bombs will still go off. I alone can stop them.'

"Mei told me it was at this moment she realized she was defeated and would have to leave the island.

"The explosion was so powerful that many of us in the boats were knocked off our feet. We didn't know what was happening, but I felt strongly we needed to make our presence known, so we headed for the middle beach.

"As we approached the beach, we could see many villagers running and gathering near where we intended to land. They were shouting angrily and brandishing weapons. Turns out they thought we were more soldiers and, as we got closer, they became even more hostile and threatening. I waived both arms and shouted, 'Dachee! Dachee!' — 'Fish! Fish!' — the only Daoqin word I could remember. Fortunately, a few of the villagers remembered me from my previous visits and spoke up for me, and then one of the nurses from the hospital told them we were not soldiers but workers like she was. I tell you, Bobby, those peace-loving Daoqins can be formidable! I was a bit worried there for a time. But as soon as they were convinced we were friends there to help, they smiled and quickly escorted us to where Porter stood threatening Mei.

"When Porter saw me he snorted, 'I always had a feeling you were involved in this, Gransom. What do you think you can do here?'

"'Hopefully, save lives,' I said.

"'That's easy,' he said, pointing at Mei. 'Get this woman off this island and I won't blow it up. I have bombs ready to drop on the villages and the mountain, mark my word.'

"'What if they just kill you now right where you stand?' I asked.

Chapter 12: Daoqin

"'The bombs drop as soon as my people know I'm dead. They will carry out my orders. The Director sent me here to win at all cost, and that's what I will do. The East Nation approved my mission. They're growing tired of this whole thing.'

"I knew then that Porter wasn't bluffing. This was the East Nation's backyard. Nothing like this would go on without them knowing about it or reacting to it. I was surprised we had even gotten our boats there without a fly-over or two.

"Porter continued, 'There's a lifestyle I'm accustomed to. A lifestyle I will lose if I go back with the wrong answers.' He mopped his flushed face with his monogramed handkerchief. 'I'm not here to lose.'

"Then, for the first time, I looked at Mei. There was the Champion of Daoqin, straight as young bamboo, standing in the center of the turmoil with grief in her eyes. Through the translator I told her I was a friend who cared about her people. I said I had visited the island before and had been inside the caves as a guest. 'There are many levels of caves, caverns and tunnels that go on for miles,' I said. 'There are no signs telling you where you are. If the rock formations on the walls aren't familiar to you, you could be lost for hours or never find your way out.' I described them to her so she would know I was telling the truth. I told her she must leave the island or Porter would destroy the villages and all the people in them, and I fully believed he would do it.

"'My worry is for my people,' she said. 'All of us will die here if the soldiers do not leave the island first. We will wait.'

"Porter barked out his orders, and the soldiers collected their wounded and dead and left the island. When the villagers saw the transport ships ascend over the trees and fly out of sight they cheered.

"Mei asked Porter, 'Do you know of Secret Children?'

"'Yes, yes. I know all about them, he said. 'They're not really all that secret.'

"'This is what we want,' said Mei. 'They go back to parents or visit villages without fear of being taken or killed, or they can leave with me. You promise this.' The crowd stirred and Porter heard it.

"'No. No. I don't have the power to do that!' he declared.

"Sternly Mei countered, 'You say you will kill us all, but now you say you have no power?'

"Porter scowled, 'Listen, I'm not here to give things away. I'm here to get things back! I won't do it!"

"'Then we all die now,' said Mei. She raised her arm, and the villagers prepared to attack.

"'All right! All right! I give my word,' said Porter. 'The Secret Children or the grubs or whatever you call them have amnesty. But let me be clear, their children do not.' He had to explain what he meant by amnesty because the Daoqins don't have a word for it.

"By this time we had been there for many hours. Porter was tired and hungry, his face was flushed scarlet and his light blue suit had turned dark blue from sweating profusely in the afternoon heat. Mei used his discomfort to her advantage and kept demanding more things. She asked the village elders to make suggestions for improvements to their living conditions. They knew immediately what to ask for—things such as no more unannounced raids at night but orderly inspections instead. No more locking up the fishing vessels. Stop food rationing as a punishment. Empty the prison. Many different things that I won't go into now. Porter didn't agree to all of them, but he acquiesced more than I thought he would. Everything was written down and signed. I could tell Mei knew Porter could go back on his word as soon as she left the island, but there was nothing she could do about that. She had done her best. She had done all she could. Finally the negotiations were over.

"Porter left the island immediately, but he wasn't taking any chances. Once he boarded his ship, Eclos 1 took off and hovered silently a few hundred yards offshore waiting for Mei to leave.

"During the time it took for Porter and his men to walk to their ship, we made hasty inquiries to ascertain if any grubs would like to leave with us. Mei, Fe Lin and two dozen grubs, all of them orphans with no family left, chose to leave the island in our boats. I asked them if there was anything at the caves they needed to get. Mei said she had some clothes there but no other possessions. I told her I would supply them all with clothes. Hearing that, none of them said they needed or wanted to go back to the caves, though I saw them pause, wistfully looking back to the mountain.

"When the orange sun touched the sea, villagers, monks, and grubs began to emerge from every direction. Silently they came, lining the way to the boats. One by one, Fe Lin and the grubs walked solemnly past the islanders, some with tears running down their faces. Mei was the last to leave. I watched her closely. She walked past her people with downcast eyes. When she reached the boat, she turned and bowed to them all, then knelt and kissed the sand. Rising, she brushed the sand lightly from her lips and rubbed it over her heart. Then, turning away from everything she loved, she boarded the boat with the strength and grace of the woman warrior she was. It was one of the saddest and most beautiful things I have ever seen."

Chapter 13
Mei's New Life

The light panel in Gransom's study was showing sunset colors when the Chief Director stopped talking. Bobby's mind struggled to absorb what he'd been hearing—of beauty and valor and unfathomable pain. In the hours since Gransom began, he had heard a lifetime of conflict and suffering on an extraordinary scale, and the center of it all was their Mei. "Did you come straight to the colony after you left the island?" he asked.

"Just me," said Gransom. "I had responsibilities here, so I had to leave right away in order to not miss the orbit window. Mei and the rest stayed on Earth. Taking them off the island and going straight into deep space would have been too much of a shock, both physically and mentally. It was hard enough on them to be transported to the Central States. None of them had ever traveled by air before, or even in a powered boat.

"I put them up in a complex of flats I have there with a special team in place to care for them, teach them English and the social skills they would need to navigate the modern world. From what I was told, Fe Lin was the star student. Mei, however, kept mostly to herself and didn't want to participate, though she did attend the English classes.

"The first obstacle we faced was meeting their dietary needs. Because they were from the caves and not subject to the food rations of MedTrust, they had eaten mostly clean and natural foods all their lives. Their digestive systems were conditioned to receive a certain type of input, so we couldn't just give them whatever. The food we supplied for them had to be clean. I had people traveling all over the Eastern Sea to get what we needed for them. It was very costly. There was no way to maintain that extravagance if they were going to live on their own, so they were slowly introduced to other healthy foods, like the ones we have here.

"There was also a concern about exposing them to bacteria and viruses their immune systems might not be able to fight off, but they never showed any signs of getting sick, which makes sense when you think about the serums made from their blood and marrow.

"To get them comfortable with space travel, the team took them into orbit a few times, and they even went more than once around the moon. Mei and Fe Lin enjoyed it immensely. As for the rest, they really didn't like it. They found it too overwhelming. They said they liked looking at the moon and the stars where they were used to seeing them.

"Eleven months later, I returned to Earth, very eager to see them again in person. They seemed healthy and happy and communicated quite well, all except Mei. She was withdrawn, quiet, and hard to reach.

"I arrived in time to sit in on my team's interviews with them about their futures. While I was gone, all of them had been taught about the Zenith Colony, but none of them wanted to come here to live. It wasn't beyond their comprehension; it was just beyond their comfort level. They liked where they were and wanted to stay there. The exceptions again were Mei and Fe Lin. Mei wanted to come out here. Fe Lin was open to it because of Mei. But Fe Lin had already made some friends, had a social life, and had found an interest she wanted to pursue, and ultimately she decided to stay on Earth. I know that was a great sorrow for Mei, and Fe Lin didn't make the decision lightly, but she also understood her own need to follow the path that was calling to her so clearly.

"A big concern for me was for the safety of them all. I was worried that people would find out who they were and where they were from, and abduct them to use for blood transfusions, putting them right back to where all this inhumanity began. We gave each of them a new identity, and they learned how to answer if they were questioned about their past. They were grateful and relieved to be getting this kind of protection, but Mei refused to change her identity. She was not willing to give up anything more. Since she was coming straight here to Vidmar, I didn't push the issue—not that it would have done me any good.

"Two weeks later, Mei and I left Earth. There were many tears when she said her good-byes, especially with Fe Lin. Now she was truly leaving her people behind. There would be no other Daoqins where she was going, not even her beloved friend. The only thing she had from the island was the red band she wears on her wrist to tie back her hair.

"Once we were underway, Mei told me she enjoyed space travel—that it reminded her of the solitude and quiet of going deep into the caves on the mountain. As Earth became smaller in the windows, she seemed less burdened. We had some good talks on our three-month trip here, and many more once we arrived. That's why I know her story so well. She is the sister I never had, and she treats me like a brother. You may have noticed that she can be rather bossy with me at times. But I kind of like that. It keeps me in my place.

"After we arrived here, Mei mostly stayed in her flat, which, for security reasons, I thought was good. I wanted more time to pass before she started going out. I offered her a larger flat but she liked the one she has now. I really don't know what she did all day because she kept to herself and I was out taking care of the colony.

"Mei had been here nine months when your mom's accident occurred. When I told her about the orphaned eight-year-old boy that the doctors couldn't help, she said she wanted very much to take care of him. I thought about all the people she had treated on the island with medicinal herbs and healing foods, so I readily agreed. It was a good decision, as you know."

"Yes. She has helped him immeasurably," said Bobby. "And me too! I couldn't imagine our lives without her. But, Grandfather, you still haven't answered all my questions. Who were those men who attacked Mei? How did they know where to find her? If Eclos and MedTrust wanted her off the island, why did they come after her?"

Gransom held up his hands. Not unkindly he said, "One thing at a time! I had to give you the full picture so you could understand what I'm going to tell you now.

"As far as I can figure, here's what I think happened: After Mei left, conditions were better on the island for a time, but as she feared, Porter eventually went back on his word, or was forced to by his higher-ups. The mercenary soldiers came back and are a permanent presence on the island now, mistreating the villagers by doing all sorts of despicable things. Villagers are still fighting back, and when they do, they chant 'Champion of Daoqin,' and remind the soldiers how Mei easily defeated their best fighters. The monks stay to themselves and hardly leave the caves. Amnesty for grubs was soon rescinded leaving them open targets once again. In order to avoid capture, all of them had to retreat to the caves. But as distressing as all that is, I don't get the sense from the reports I've received, or from going over the attackers' ships and belongings, that any orders were given to capture Mei, or that Eclos or MedTrust even know she's here, or that they would care if they did know. Instead, I think the men who attacked you were a rogue group of mercenary soldiers trying to make a name for themselves. I've seen it before. It's a very power-driven, competitive fraternity. One of them must have gotten information from who-knows-who that Mei was here and told his comrades, and they thought they'd cash in on that. If they could bring her back, especially alive, they would be top of the heap for conquering the Champion of Daoqin."

"That makes sense," Bobby mused. "But why did they come looking for Tran and me after they had Mei cornered in the docking bay?"

"For money," Gransom said, looking both disgusted and sad. "People know you are my family. That makes you a target for kidnapping for ransom. We have to be aware of that without being paranoid about it. I don't believe anyone in the colony would kidnap you boys. It would be extremely difficult for them to get away with it. But outside forces certainly would try, and we can't stop them all from getting in. Space is a hard place to defend. That's why I'm putting a team of Protectors back on you three. You all complained about them before and I gave in, thinking everything was secure. That was my folly. But now you're getting them whether you like it or not."

"Oh, I don't mind them," said Bobby "It's a small thing compared to what others go through. It makes me sick to think about what's happening to the people on that little island, especially the children. I'm proud of you and what you've done. You've spent decades and extensive efforts exerting yourself so much to help those people and make things better for them."

"Thank you, my boy. I hope and pray someday they will be free."

Bobby stood up. "Well, thank you for telling me everything in such detail, Grandfather. It's pretty overwhelming, and parts of it are hard to wrap by mind around, but I'm glad I know it. I certainly won't ever see Mei the same way again."

"Oh," Gransom said with a small smile, "What I love about Mei is she's always Mei. Nothing will be different between the two of you. You will see."

When Bobby walked into Mei's flat that evening, he was met with the fragrance of one of his favorite meals. Mei smiled at him and asked him to set the table. Then she went back to stirring something on the stove. And she was softly singing.

Chapter 13: Mei's New Life

Ch 14
Shaytown Station

"Batter up!" hollered the umpire. Tran grabbed a bat and waited on the steps of the dugout. He was batting third. It was the bottom of the 9th inning and his team was down by two runs. "Come on, Joshua! Pick one you can hit!" he cheered.

Baseball season in the colonial school league had gone into the playoffs, and Tran's team The Niners were up by one game in a best-of-three series. If they lost the game, they would play this team again. If they won, they would advance to the Championship.

Tran was having a record breaking year. Two years of fastfight training had improved his hitting and fielding skills to such a high degree that coaches from around the colony would come to his games to watch him play.

For most of his young life, Tran had been obsessed with baseball. Now he was thoroughly captivated by fastfighting as well. In fact, he couldn't get enough of it. He committed himself as intensely to fastfighting as he did to baseball, training almost constantly. Mei and Bobby couldn't find enough time to satisfy his desire to work with a training partner, so he did much of it on his own. To help him in this matter, Mei taught him how to envision different opponents in his mind, sparring with them in real time. He didn't know she had taught herself that tactic in the darkness of the deep Daoqin caves. Alone in the ballfield on Vidmar, Tran moved around the outfield with his eyes closed, fighting imaginary opponents. Over time, he learned to keep track of where he was, though he had a few hard run-ins with the wall until he improved that skill.

Two years of training had honed Tran's body, but he still had problems controlling his mind. It was extremely difficult for him

135

to see the first signs of an opponent's upcoming strike, and it was immensely frustrating for a boy who constantly challenged himself to perform with optimum efficiency always aiming at perfection. He had no problem staying locked on the key, but keeping his mind still and not trying to figure out what the next strike would be was almost impossible for him. *Reaction is distraction*, he reminded himself, but it was easier to say than to apply. Mei told him it would come with time.

The stands at the ballfield in Dome 2 were packed with fans from both teams. "Strike," called the ump as the first pitch snapped into the catcher's glove. Tran watched the opposing pitcher intently. There were certain unconscious things a pitcher might do that would give away what type of pitch he was going to throw next. It could be something as subtle as the way he straightened up after getting the sign from the catcher, or even just the tilt of his head.

The next pitch sounded like a gunshot when it hit the glove. "Strike two," bellowed the ump. Tran had studied the scouting report on this closing pitcher, and had faced him a few times before. He was a big fourteen-year-old, a flamethrower. Tran was fairly convinced the kid wasn't going to throw anything but fastballs, though he did have a change-up. Crack! The fans cheered as the ball landed in right field for a base hit.

"Way to go, Joshua!" Tran shouted as he moved up to the on-deck circle. Thomas, the next batter, stepped to the plate. But just as the pitcher was getting set, the ump called time and waved his arms for play to stop. Tran heard the crowd stirring and noticed everyone was looking up. He looked up too, and saw a bright flashing white light coming from a small opening near the center of the dome's roof. Anxiously he looked at Mei in the stands. She was sitting calmly, but the three Protectors positioned nearby were all standing at the ready. When Tran looked back to the roof, he saw something drop from the opening with a stream of red smoke behind it. People gasped when they realized it was a person falling ever faster towards the ground. Some turned away and covered their ears not wanting to see or hear the inevitable impact. But only fifty feet before hitting the ground, the plummet abruptly slowed and the person smoothly lowered out of sight a few hundred feet beyond the center field fence. A mixture of relief, excitement, and disgust spread through the stadium. Some people applauded. Others booed. It had been very disruptive and things didn't settle down for quite awhile.

Though illegal within the colony, jumping with an anti-g vest jury-rigged from scrap pieces of anti-gravity plates had become popular with thrill seekers, and this jump was the most spectacular Tran had seen or even heard about. He wondered how the jumper knew when to activate the vest so he wouldn't slam into the ground. It took a lot of nerve to wait that long.

Due to the disturbing interruption, the umpire let the pitcher take a few warm-up pitches, and then called, "Play ball!" Tran's mind immediately snapped back to the game. Thomas got jammed with the first pitch, hitting the ball weakly just out of the reach of the pitcher towards the hole at second. There was nothing the second baseman could do once he got to the ball but hold onto it. It was an infield hit. Runners at first and second with no outs, with Tran coming to the plate.

In the stadium, there was an expectant murmur and rustling. The manager of the other team asked for time and went to the mound to talk to his pitcher and infielders. Tran stood near home plate taking lazy practice swings to stay loose. *Don't guess,* he told himself. *Just see it and hit it. He has good control, so he may waste a pitch or two to get me to chase. But don't guess. He wants a grounder for a double play, so he needs to keep the ball down and out of my power. But don't guess. Just see it and hit it.*

With the conference on the mound ended, and the players back in their positions, Tran stepped to the plate and dug in. The first pitch was low and outside. An easy take for Tran. He wasn't tempted to swing at all. The next pitch was on the inside corner for a called strike, and the next pitch he fouled off down the right field line, well out of play. *Come on! Get with it!* he chided himself. *You're way late! One and two. You've got to protect the plate.*

Don't leave the bat on your shoulder. The pitcher looked in for the sign and got set. Immediately Tran asked for time and got it. Stepping out of the batter's box, he swung his arms and stretched as he tried to figure out what he had just seen. The pitcher had looked down before getting set. *Why did he look down? He always stares straight into the catcher's glove after getting a sign. His eyes stay on the glove until he checks the lead runner. Why did he look down this time? If he does it again, I have to be ready for a change-up.* Tran stepped back to the plate. The pitcher stared in for the sign, and then glanced down at the ground in front of him before going into his set position. Tran made his final decision—*Change-up is coming. If I'm wrong, he's going to throw a fastball right by me, but we have two more outs to work with.* The pitcher checked the runner at second then delivered his pitch, his body and arm looking exactly like the motion for a fast ball, but the ball came out of his hand much slower and had a lazy spin to it. Tran held back, waiting, staying well balanced, then unleashed his swing, hitting a blistering line drive over the third baseman's head that curved towards the left field line, landed fair, then shot into the left field corner and ricocheted hard off the side and back walls, whistling fast just beyond the left fielder's outstretched glove. The baserunners were on the move. Tran sprinted down the first base line. Running full out, he hit second and was partway to third when the left fielder finally got to the ball and was throwing it to the cutoff man. Tran looked for his third-base coach, shocked to see him down the third-base line waving madly for him to go for home. Tearing around third-base he saw Joshua and Thomas signaling wildly for him to slide to the outside of the plate. He could tell by their actions it was going to be close. Launching himself with all his might, he dove head first, left hand straining for the edge of the plate, fingertips touching just as the catcher's glove tagged his wrist. "Safe! Safe! Safe!" shouted the umpire making the sign three times and then pointing to the plate. It was an inside-the-park home run, giving The Niners a 5 to 4 win. The fans roared and his teammates rushed onto the field with cheers, shouts, back-slaps, and a lot of jumping up and down. They were going to the Championship.

Lining up and shaking hands with the other team, Tran recognized their disappointment. It was something he knew well. He remembered the last two years of being knocked out of the play-offs, and the game they lost in the first year was due to an error he made in the last inning, throwing the ball over the first baseman's head. So when the other team's left fielder, looking crestfallen, shook his hand and mumbled nice game, Tran said, "Hey, there was nothing you could do with that weird bounce off the wall. It's just one of those things in baseball. Head up. Good game!"

Surprised, the kid looked at Tran with a relieved smile, and said, "Thanks. You really smoked that ball. I've never seen one come off the wall that hard. See you next year."

After celebrating with his team, Tran boarded a Smartcart with Mei to take the short ride to Gransom's compound so he could get cleaned up and changed before meeting Gransom and Bobby for dinner on Deck 3.

As they glided along, Tran asked with awe in his voice, "Could you believe that jumper? That guy had guts!"

"He would lose all guts if he hit the ground," said Mei with a frown. "Why risk life like that?"

Tran thought a moment, then said, "I guess because it's daring and you can prove to yourself you have the courage to do it. I'm not sure I'd have enough nerve."

"Don't you do that, Tranny," Mei said with a warning look. "No need to risk life for worthless things. You be smarter than that."

Gransom's compound covered an entire block on the highest tier of the southeast incline of Dome 2, which gave it a spectacular view of the residential area where the houses and buildings were designed in the colors and style of the American Southwest as it had looked before the second War of the States. Because of his love for the old Southwest, Gransom had worked with the designers of Z9 to recreate that harmonious, earthy feeling in the community, and wanted his own dwelling to be part of that style.

All of the buildings in his compound, as well as the 8-foot tall wall that surrounded it, were in reddish-brown terra cotta. The top of the wall was not sharp but rounded, which gave it a friendly rather than imposing presence, and its wide double gates were a deep turquoise blue. An invisible Thumper Shield rose an additional twelve feet from the top of the wall, an effective deterrent to trespassers who might try to climb or vault over it. Inside, smooth walkways bordered with succulents and desert plants curved to the main house and the spacious bungalows where Protectors, staff, and guests were housed. The two-storied main house had a wealth of large windows to provide a generous view of the neighborhood. The compound was only a few blocks from where Tran had lived with his parents and it always felt like home to him. He and Mei stayed in the west wing and Gransom took up the east wing. Bobby preferred one of the bungalows. The grounds of the compound were designed to be restful and refreshing. There were several gardens of various sorts, with flowers, shrubs and trees flourishing in rich Zenith soil. A meandering path led to a small courtyard with a waterfall and koi pond full of friendly fish. In the evenings, Tran liked going there to feed them before doing his fastfight training. As the light darkened, the night-blooming jasmine would open, releasing their rich sweet fragrance as Tran moved silently under the smooth black dome arrayed with changing moon and small white stars.

Now that he was thirteen, Tran was allowed to stay at the house without Mei or Gransom. There were always staff members and Protectors there, but they left him alone unless he needed them for something. Most of the time Mei preferred her flat on Vidmar, and Bobby and Gransom were often away on business or tending to matters on Vidmar, so some weeks Tran would stay on Z9 by himself to attend school and baseball practices without having to commute back and forth. He liked the solitude of the compound while still being in the active city of Z9, and staying there gave him the opportunity to do more exploring. There were areas on each Deck that were still wholly unfamiliar to him and he wished to remedy that. The only problem was the Protectors. Tran disliked being followed when he went on his expeditions, even though he knew the Protectors were there to keep him safe. It still felt to him like a crimp in his style and he sensed the Protectors weren't all that thrilled about it either. In fact, he believed they considered it a loathsome and odious chore. A couple of times he ditched them and went off on his own, which didn't go over well with the Protectors. When Gransom found out, he told Tran if he continued with that kind of sneaky behavior he would no longer be allowed to stay at the compound unsupervised. "Remember what I told you after the attack on the horticulture station?" Gransom said. "People know you're part of my family. That makes you a target. I don't want anything to happen to you."

Of course Tran knew the risk, but argued that since he was able to lose the Protectors, no one else would know where he was either. But Gransom would not budge on the issue. Neither would Tran. He complained that Bobby didn't have to have Protectors so why should he be stuck with them? Gransom reminded him that when Bobby turned eighteen, he had made the decision to no longer have Protectors. "He did that against my objections," said Gransom. "But Bobby is his own man now. You will be your own man in five years, Tran, not before. Try not to rush it."

When Bobby heard of this rift between Gransom and Tran, he proposed a compromise: Only one Protector would go with Tran when he went exploring, and the trips would have to be scheduled instead of happening whenever Tran felt like it. Gransom decided the compromise was satisfactory. Tran wasn't completely happy with the idea, but he figured it was the best deal he was going to get so he went along with it.

Within the Protectors, Tran was known as the difficult assignment. Agents disliked crawling through shafts and old dirty passageways, but a young agent named Phillip said he was willing to take on the responsibility, so he was assigned to go with Tran on these treks. At twenty-three years old, Phillip was the youngest Protector in the elite corps of guards who were trusted with the safety of the Chief Director and other key people Gransom would need them to watch over. Weapons were illegal in the Zenith Colony, but Protectors were licensed to carry small concealed Thumpers, which could incapacitate and immobilize a person without being lethal. Being selected to be a Protector was an honor, and it required extensive clearance before an applicant would even be considered. Because of the weight of their responsibility, Protectors could be grimly serious, so Tran wasn't happy about having even one around. But he and Phillip hit it off right away, and instead of being hindered by an irritating shadow, Tran now was pleased to have an active and interested co-explorer.

Whenever Tran didn't have something going on after school, he would hurry home to change and eat, then he and Phillip would head out to find something new. Except for Dome 6, which Tran wasn't interested in and Gransom had forbidden him to explore, they diligently mapped out as many of the nooks and crannies on each Deck as they could, often continuing into the late evening, discovering all types of passageways, shafts, rooms, chambers, tunnels, crawl spaces, tubes, and vents. But Tran wasn't only keen on exploring the hidden places, he was also interested in the big picture—the neighborhoods, the buildings, the businesses, the layout of each part of the city, what it was for, how it was supported or ignored, and how it all worked together.

Another focus of Tran's curiosity was the mystery of what lay between the top of one dome and the bottom of another. All his life he had seen ships come into the domes through an opening called the Skydoor, but what was on the other side he didn't know, and it bugged him. One day Phillip surprised him by arranging for him to take a ride in a Blocker, a special type of delivery ship that used the Skydoor. When Phillip told him, Tran couldn't get to the docking bay fast enough. Blockers were specifically designed for delivering goods to warehouses inside the domes of Z9. They could travel outside the station from deck to deck, but they had no long distance capabilities. Tran thought they were funny looking—a large box with a small cockpit sticking out the front near the bottom.

Hal was a knowledgeable veteran Blocker pilot who was able to explain every step and procedure of the flight. After the ship was loaded with freight at the distribution warehouse on Deck 1, they left the warehouse docking bay and flew the short distance outside the station to Deck 4. Hal told Tran they were going to enter the station through what was called the Spacegate. "It's a horizontal shaft that goes from one side of the station to the other," he said. "There's one between each pair of decks and there's also one at the top of Deck 1." Hovering just outside Z9's luminous blue exterior, Hal transmitted a special code that opened the Spacegate door and then moved the ship slowly inside.

"What's outside the shaft?" Tran asked.

"Nothing at all, really," said Hal. "It's an unpressurized area. I was told it allows the station to expand and contract as needed, but I'm no structural engineer."

The ship passed through a series of three airlocks, each one taking a minute or so to complete and a different code to operate. Tran recognized the chambers as redundant safeguards so the dome could not be accidentally depressurized. Hal explained there was also a series of airlocks on the other end of the shaft so ships could enter and leave from either side.

Tran noticed a dark window in the wall of each airlock chamber and asked what was behind them. Hal said they were old control rooms for operators who worked the airlocks in the days before the ships had special transmitters and the pilots had the codes to do it all themselves. A passageway joined the rooms so the operator could go from one room to the next as the ship progressed through the three airlocks. He said they were still used on occasion if a ship without a transmitter needed to get through, or if there was a malfunction and a pilot couldn't open a door. Tran asked how the operators got up there, but the pilot said he didn't know.

"We're going through the Hub wall now," said Hal as the thick door of the last airlock opened. Tran's heart speeded up when they passed through the final airlock and its door closed securely behind them. As they flew the remaining mile through the shaft to the Skydoor, what Tran mostly saw was dark gray, which wasn't exciting to see, but he loved every second of it. Finally they hovered above the Skydoor, which was marked with a large red "x." Hal entered another code, and the two giant panels below them dropped down and swung open like bombbay doors. Hal tilted the ship down so Tran could get a good view and lowered the Blocker into Dome 4, then hovered 1200 feet above the ground. "Wow! Look at that!" marveled Tran. Hal grinned. Maintaining the same altitude, he closed the door and then rotated the ship slowly 360 degrees so his passenger could get a good look. Tran leaned forward, staring out the cockpit window, fascinated by the orderly quilt-like patterns of the blocks of buildings connected by networks of cream-colored streets. He could easily see the places he had explored on foot, but this put it all into context and perspective, as if a splendid detailed three-dimensional map had just appeared before him.

Hal dropped to 800 feet and flew to the main warehouse where he landed the ship precisely on its mark in the warehouse yard. As soon as he opened the ship's freight doors, workers swiftly positioned forklifts and anti-g platforms and efficiently unloaded the ship. When the Blocker was back in the air, Hal took the time to fly slowly around the dome one more glorious time before heading back out the Skydoor. He was enjoying Tran's enthusiastic appreciation for something he, himself, was able to see every day. He told Tran it reminded him how much he really liked his job.

Back at the docking bay on Deck 1, Tran thanked Hal and Phillip profusely, saying what a thrill it had been. Then he went to Deck 7 and caught a flight to Vidmar so he could tell Mei all about it.

The Niners ended up winning the championship, three games to one, and Tran received the MVP award for the series, but he didn't feel he or his team played up to their potential, so the whole thing was kind of a letdown for him. In all his years of baseball he had been exposed to two trains of thought. One was "Winning is everything." The other was "It doesn't matter if you win or lose, it's how you play the game." Of the two, Tran agreed more with the latter, but to him it wasn't just a matter of attitude and sportsmanship, it was giving it your all every step of the way. So even though they'd won he was disappointed, because he felt they all got lazy and unfocused and could have played much better. His teammates did not agree.

Not long after the school year was over, Gransom scheduled a trip to the Shaytown mining station and asked Tran and Bobby to accompany him. Shaytown was an independent operation that sold the magtronium ore they mined to the Zenith colony. It was run by Shay Raskin, the first miner to set up an independent operation outside the colony. The station was four days away from Z9, the farthest Tran would have ever been from his place of birth. He was excited to go. For this venture, Gransom had chosen to go light. Only he, Tran, Bobby, a few staff members, and a flight crew would fly in Mirage, accompanied by two Protector ships to insure safe travel. Tran was pleased to learn Shaytown was a closed station like Vidmar, so Protectors were not required there.

Though it seemed strange to be so far from home, Tran was used to being on Mirage in his familiar cabin, and he enjoyed the flight to the mining station, especially because he and Bobby had the luxury of some uninterrupted time with Gransom, something that hadn't happened in quite a while. And, possibly because they were heading to a station whose sole reason for existence was magtronium, Gransom was in the mood to talk about his experiences in the early days on Earth when he was doing what he called his "space rock studies." He told the boys that, back then, he took meteorites and subjected them to both long- and short-term processes, tests, and analysis that no one else had ever thought of doing. He said most of those experiments ended up not going anywhere, but some led to discoveries that had an impact on the entire world.

With a wry smile and laughter in his eyes, Gransom told them some of the worst ones, to amuse the boys, and also to show them his thought processes—how an idea could be a huge failure, but it was still important to keep trying and to think big and outside the box. He told them about flying to the arctic and burying a meteorite and then uncovering it a year later and bringing it home and breaking it down to examine if its magnetic properties had changed in any way. "Not the smartest of ideas," Gransom chuckled. "But you never know until you try, and sometimes it's the crazy ideas that pay off."

During the trip, Bobby attended meetings with Gransom and his staff. Shaytown wanted to expand their operations to include the grinding of the rocks before hauling them to the processing plants. They could haul much more tonnage that way and receive a higher price per ton. Gransom was supportive of the idea, but it was a big step because the grinding had to be done in a very specific way, and the logistics and timeline and terms needed to be worked out. The year before, Bobby had accompanied Gransom to Shaytown and talked to the workers; he was therefore able to contribute additional considerations to the discussions. And, being who he was, he had also made some friends.

Tran wasn't involved in any of these meetings, and that suited him just fine. He wanted to keep training every day, making use of the excellent gym onboard Mirage. He also had a chance to pilot the ship a number of times, and learned emergency procedures from the flight crew that would help him if a navigational system ever failed him in deep space.

As they approached Shaytown station, Tran went to the bridge to have a look. It was a hub-arm configuration, typical of older stations, but larger than he had imagined it would be. The diameter of its main hub was 250 yards wide, and it had three thick arms extending out from it, each 200 yards long. There were also two smaller satellite stations nearby, no more than a mile away.

Shay Raskin was a short, petite woman with the most infectious positive energy Tran had ever experienced. She and about thirty Shaytowners, along with a small band made up of children armed with various musical instruments, were waiting in the docking bay as Gransom and the others disembarked from Mirage. The band played a lively, happy tune with great enthusiasm, though a little off key. The visitors applauded and cheered. The children looked immensely pleased. Gransom said what a pleasure it was to be there, thanked the children for the wonderful song and shook everyone's hand. After that, the formalities were over and the socializing began.

Raskin greeted Gransom as an old friend. Soon they were walking off together, Gransom's tall body bent down so he could hear the woman, who was shorter by perhaps twenty inches. Tran thought they looked comical together, but they were obviously enjoying each other's company, talking, laughing, forgetting about everyone else.

A few of Bobby's friends were there to meet him and Bobby introduced them to Tran. All of them had unusual names—Solara, Misrow, Telmara, Candle. While they were catching up on each other's lives, Tran drifted away and began looking around the docking bay. It was spotless and he wondered if it was like that all the time or if it was because Gransom was visiting. A girl came up and asked him his name. "Tran," he said.

"Oh, I've heard of you. You're that baseball player. My name is Victory. She had a happy, honest face, clear blue eyes, a smudge of grease on her cheek, and a navy blue bandana holding back her blonde hair. Her work clothes were spotted with grease and oil, and somewhat dusty. They had the well-worn look of significant use during hands-on labor. Tran found that surprising since she seemed to be only about the same age as he was.

"I like your name," he said.

"Thanks," said Victory. "The adults out here tend to give their kids unusual names.

"Well," said Tran, "my parents told me they named me after some kind of biochemical process, but then they said I was named after my Dad's favorite professor, so I don't know which to believe. How did you know I was a baseball player?"

"There's a guy who boosts the radio signal of the games just for the outer stations," she said. "They're very popular out here."

"Oh, I didn't know they did that, or that anyone would care. It's not the adult league," said Tran.

"The kids here like the school leagues," said the girl.

Just then someone came in and announced that dinner would be served in the dining hall in an hour.

"I have to go change for dinner," said Victory, smacking her coveralls a few times to dislodge the loose dust. "Do you want to walk with me?"

"Sure!" he said. There was a lot about this girl that intrigued him.

"My flat is on the far end of Arm 2," she said. It's a long walk, but I like it. Gives me a nice spacer after I finish for the day.

As they walked briskly along, Victory greeted all those who went past. Some of them stopped to talk, and she would introduce them to Tran. They all had names Tran had never heard before. He was also surprised by the topics of their conversations. They'd ask her about this ship or that part or what the schedule was for this repair or when they could expect delivery of something and she always knew the answers.

As they resumed their walk, he asked, "What do you do here?"

"I'm a mechanic and the assistant shop manager."

"Really!" He was astonished. "How old are you?"

"I turned fourteen two months ago," she said. "How 'bout you?"

"I'll be fourteen next year. How did you get to be a mechanic at such a young age?"

"Oh, a few reasons," she said. "Out here kids have to have jobs. They can't just sit around and do whatever they want. Of course, they only work part-time, because they have school. But since school always came easy to me, I completed it early, so I asked if

I could go to work full-time, and my dad and Shay said I could, as long as I took some engineering courses, too. The other thing is I've always loved tinkering with engines or any kind of mechanisms. My brain feels at home doing that. I'm hoping to work my way up to head mechanic and then go into engine design. How about you? What do you like to do?"

"I don't know," said Tran. "I feel like a lazy bum compared to you. It's incredible what you've done."

"Don't say that," Victory replied. "We have a lot more time on our hands out here. There's not as many distractions. If I lived on Z9, most likely I'd still be in the third grade." She laughed, a happy open sound that Tran found infectious. "But really," she asked again, "tell me what you like to do."

Tran felt silly and frivolous and shy. He didn't like talking about himself, but he decided to tell her just a little. "Well, I like baseball, obviously. And I like exploring and finding places most people don't know about. And I like words and math and studying how social systems work. And I like reading about animals and nature." The corridor was much more narrow than the ones on Z9, and not as well lit. It made him feel crowded, which added to his discomfort as he talked about himself, so he changed the subject. "Have you ever been to Earth?" he asked.

"No, I've hardly been anywhere. I've only been to Z9 three times. We go to Z35 once in awhile because it's only ten hours away. Have you been to Earth?"

"No," said Tran. "This is the farthest I've ever been from home."

"I'm surprised," she said. "I thought since you were with Dr. Gransom you would have traveled a lot. He's such a great man. How do you know him?"

"He's my adopted grandfather."

"I didn't know Dr. Gransom had any children," said Victory.

"He doesn't. Five years ago Bobby's mom and both of my parents were killed in an accident and he adopted us. I have an adopted mother, too. Her name is Mei. She's the best."

Victory stopped in front of a door and looked at Tran with understanding. "That's so sad about your parents. My mom died when I was young, too. She went to Earth to help when her sister was sick, and when she came back she got sick herself and died, just like that." She punched in a code and opened the door. "Come on in," she said, switching on the lights. "Please sit down wherever. Would you like some water?"

"Yes, please," said Tran. He was curious to see how people lived on this independent station. Victory's flat was pretty much like his own except there were no light panels to provide a feeling of windows showing the colors of the day. It was medium-sized, furnished simply, and looked comfortable. Tran thought it was nice.

"My dad is a long hauler pilot," Victory said, handing Tran a glass of water. "He won't be home for a week. He was disappointed he wasn't going to see Dr. Gransom. He missed him last time, too. He's going to be especially disappointed this time. I know he would have liked to meet you. He listens to as many games as he can. Baseball is his thing. Now, if you'll excuse me, I have to get changed. It won't take me long."

Tran sat drinking his water and thought about how it might have been to grow up here so far away from Z9 and everything he knew. He wondered how Victory kept from getting bored. But she seemed happy and content and comfortable with herself, and Tran realized he couldn't claim the same. He wondered if he could have finished school early. He was smart and got good grades, but he had done only just enough to get by. His world was fastfighting and baseball and exploring, but where were those things going to get him? He decided he would have to give it all some thought at another time. After all, he was only thirteen. Mei had told him repeatedly, "You stay young boy." For now he was going to do just that; he was going to stay present and enjoy his time with this interesting girl.

Victory came out dressed in a simple black top and pants, her straight blonde hair loose over her shoulders, looking trim and fit like Mei. "There, all clean," she said. "A Clean Bean. Do you want more water?"

"No thanks. I'm fine," Tran said. He thought it amusing that she used the term his mother used to say. He always thought it was an archaic colloquialism that only old people used.

With a sigh, Victory sank into the armchair across from him. "We have a little more time," she said. "Do you mind if we relax here till dinnertime? I've been running around all day. Dr. Gransom visiting is a big deal."

"I don't mind at all," he said. "I'm not all that comfortable being around a lot of people anyway."

"Oh, it will be all right," she assured him. "It's just dinner and speeches, and then there's going to be a talent show. I'm in it, actually."

"Really? What are you going to do?"

"It'll be a surprise," she said. She leaned back and closed her eyes. "So tell me what it was like growing up on Z9?"

"Oh, um. It was good," Tran said. "My parents and I lived in a flat about this size in Dome 2. Have you been there?"

"In your flat?" Victory said with a snicker.

"No, silly, in Dome 2." He was liking her very much.

"Yes," she said, "it's beautiful with the flowers and the high dome changing colors with the seasons and times of day. Here it's the same all the time. Of course, for us kids, we've never known anything else so we don't feel deprived or anything. I like living here. It's simple. The first time I saw Z9 I was actually shocked. So much open space! It was like being on a different planet. And so much going on all the time. I think that would be interesting. I'd love to live there with my family someday."

"So you have brothers and sisters?"

"No, it's just me and my dad. I meant, when I get married and have children. That's where I'd like to live."

"Oh," said Tran. "Is that what you want to do with your life, get married and have kids?"

"Yes, of course," she said. "I think having kids is the most important thing you *can* do. I also want to work after they get older, but to be with them when they're little and to see them growing up would be the best thing in life. Don't you think?"

"I don't know," said Tran. "I've never met your kids." It was his turn to snicker.

Victory rolled her eyes. "I'm not saying I want to rush out and get married right away either," she continued, "but when I'm ready, maybe around twenty-two, I'd like to find someone who wants to have a family. Just before the second War of the States, fewer babies were being born than at any other time in human history. Did you know that? I find that sad. I think people were very unhappy because of that, and not satisfied with their lives."

"You're smart to want to go to Z9," said Tran. "There are a lot of kids there."

"I know," she said "but there are a lot of kids on Z35 too. Have you been there recently? That station is getting so big. They keep adding modules to it."

"I've never been there," he replied. "What's it like?"

"It's beautiful, but Z9 has more character and feels more homey to me. 35 is more slick and modern." Victory glanced at the clock on the wall. "I guess we should be going. I'll be right back." She returned with a gym bag and handed it to Tran when he offered to carry it for her.

As they stepped into the corridor, a girl with curly black hair came out a door across the way. "Falteen, I'd like you to meet Tran," said Victory.

"Nice to meet you," said the girl.

"Likewise," he said.

"I'll see you two there," said the girl. "I've got stuff I have to get ready, so I have to run." And she did—literally.

As Falteen sprinted away, Tran asked, "Why *do* kids have such unusual names here?"

"That's an interesting story," said Victory. "Shaytown was founded after Shay rescued orphans during the second War of the

States and brought them out here. When they got old enough and started having kids of their own, they wanted to start anew, to get rid of the history, stigma, and associations with all other names. No more Bill, Joe, Gene, Nancy, Linda, or Maria, but names like Rockline, Loney, Sophira, Willowbend."

"I think it's good they did that," said Tran, who always felt his own name was uncommon. "So you're part of that fresh start. Your parents gave you a wonderful name."

"Yes," said Victory. "It kind of reflects how they felt about getting a chance for a better life. My dad was an orphaned refugee from the wars. His name is Andrew. Shay found him and brought him here when he was eight, like she did so many others."

"Your mom, too?"

"No, her family survived the war pretty well. Then after, she became a lawyer and got a job where she had to travel back and forth from Earth to Midway. That's where they met, on Midway. I only have the slightest memory of her. She died before I was three. Her name was Kathleen. All of us have lost somebody. I guess that's why we're so close. Out here, you realize how precious life is, and how special it is to have a family."

Though they had been walking a long way, Tran had not noticed. Soon the station's hub was just ahead and the flats they'd been passing were ending. The corridor widened on the right into an observation area with a long, tall window. Gransom, Shay Raskin, and their staff members were gathered there. "Victory, my girl, come over here," said Raskin, who immediately put her arm around Victory's shoulders and introduced her to the doctor.

"It's a pleasure to meet you, Victory," said Gransom warmly, bowing and shaking her hand.

"It's an honor meeting you, sir," Victory said with an honest smile. "I'm a great admirer of yours."

Raskin interjected, "Victory's dad was aboard that old cruiser I took from Earth that broke down two weeks from Z9 and you had to come out and rescue us. Do you remember that, Joseph?"

"Yes, I do," he said. "That must have been thirty years ago, but I can still see all those hungry, frightened little faces."

"Victory's a mechanic and the shop's assistant manager," Tran said, adding enthusiastically, "and she's only fourteen!"

"My goodness, that is impressive," said Gransom. "So, Victory, does that mean you're a fellow gearhead like me?"

"Yes, sir. Very much so. I don't like anything better. I was telling Tran I'd like to design my own engines someday."

"Good for you!" Gransom said. "I have no doubt you will make that happen. You're already well on your way."

"Thank you, sir," said Victory gratefully. "That's very encouraging coming from you."

"We'll see you at dinner," said Shay, giving Tran a nod and a smile and Victory a little hug.

In the dining hall, colorful ribbons and paper flowers decorated the long tables positioned around a large raised black platform in the middle of the floor. "That's the stage. Your table is right up front over there," said Victory.

"Will you sit with us?" asked Tran.

"I'm sorry, I can't. You're honored guests, so it wouldn't be proper. And anyway, I have to get ready for the show," she said, taking her gym bag from him. "Can you walk me home after?"

"Yes, I would like that" he said. "Good luck with whatever it is you're going to do for the show."

Finding his chair, Tran sat down and tried to look comfortable. A few people came over and introduced themselves and told him they were happy to have him there. Soon Bobby was sitting next to him and started getting all the attention. Tran was glad for the deflection.

Between visitors to the table, Bobby asked, "Who was that girl you were with?"

"Her name is Victory," said Tran. "Can I ask you something?"

"Sure," said Bobby, smiling and shaking someone's hand.

"Do you ever feel stupid around a girl, like you don't know what to say?"

"Oh, yeah," said Bobby, "all the time. Especially around the ones I really like. I guess it's because we don't want to say the wrong thing and have them not like us. But I wouldn't worry about it. I've never known you to shut up for too long anyway." He elbowed Tran in the ribs. "Welcome to the club, little brother."

The food was good, and the program afterwards was not painful. There were some speeches, but they were not long, and the things people said were interesting—mostly about the long-term supportive relationship between Shaytown Station and the Zenith Colony.

Tran expected the talent show to be a succession of lame amateurish acts, the sort of things that usually happen at such events, but he found himself thoroughly entertained. The children's band played a couple of numbers and a girl with a sweet, warm alto voice sang the *Angnus Dei* from Bach's *Mass in B Minor* accompanied by a boy playing a cello that was almost as big as he was. A number of young men gave an exhibition of martial arts. They were remarkably good, though they did a lot of bouncing around. Bobby and Tran glanced at each other. Mei had taught them to be still, not waste energy bobbing and moving for no reason. Even so, when they talked about it later, they agreed the boys were very good—fast, powerful, disciplined, though it was a completely different style from fastfighting. The next number was surprising and stunning. A young violinist filled the room with a haunting melody while two ballet dancers in full, classic costumes, executed a very credible *pas de deux*. Every act was followed by enthusiastic, affectionate applause.

Then, suddenly, the lights went out. The audience hushed with a stir of anticipation. The black silence continued an uncomfortably long time. Then came a steady beat from a deep-voiced drum. Boom! Boom! Boom! A brilliant white light split the dark. On stage were eight girls dressed in what reminded the boys of Mei's fastfighting clothes, except they were all one piece. Four were in bright red and four were in bright blue. They moved in slow strength to the solemn beat of the drum. Suddenly the beat exploded in a flurry of sharp short strokes and the girls flashed into dazzling combinations of gymnastics and acrobatics—colors a blur with the speed of their graceful and complicated moves. Tran recognized Solara and Falteen, but he thought the best one by far was Victory. She did backwards handsprings across the platform and vaulted herself high into the air, flipping and spinning before landing perfectly balanced on her feet, all synchronized precisely in time with the drums. It was like watching Mei doing her fastfighting.

The number was over too soon. The audience exploded with cheers and a standing ovation. Each of the acts came out and received another round of applause. Then they held hands and bowed together, every face beaming. It was obvious they felt loved and appreciated, a family in a caring place they knew they truly belonged.

During the next three days, Tran was free to explore the station as he wished. Victory was taking care of some tricky engine repairs and didn't have a lot of time off, though she did show Tran around the shop where she worked, and they went for walks in the evenings after dinner. As Bobby predicted, Tran overcame his shyness with her. He found her easy to talk to, and he was captured by her wry sense of humor, ready laugh, and intelligent thoughts. He was excited to give her a tour of Mirage, and enjoyed watching as she marveled at the famous ship. He told her the story Gransom told of how Mirage came to be. Victory listened intently and said after that she had no doubt the story was true.

Too soon their days were up. Tran expected to find Victory among the group that came to see them off, but she wasn't there. He was about to start looking for her when Shay found him. "Victory had to leave early this morning to do an emergency repair on our satellite station," she said. "She wanted me to tell you she's so sorry she didn't get to say good-bye."

Chapter 14: Shaytown Station

It was difficult for Tran to speak past the lump in his throat. "Please tell her I said good-bye and thank her for showing me around the station. I'm sorry I didn't get to see her." He wanted to say more, but couldn't.

Not long after, Gransom and his group were bidding farewell to Shay Raskin and the Shaytowners who were no longer strangers to them. The little children played them a farewell tune as they boarded their ship to leave.

During the trip home, Tran lay on his bed feeling a dull ache in his chest. It was a totally unfamiliar empty place that felt like the size and shape of a girl named Victory. For the first time in his life, he cared about a girl more than training or exploring or even playing baseball. He had always thought if he could go to Earth it would profoundly change his life. Something about being in a different world would make that happen. Now he had been in a different world, not Earth but Shaytown, and it had changed him, but not in the ways he thought. He hadn't expected it to hurt.

Ch 15
Choices

After they arrived back home on Vidmar, life for the boys seemed to widen, deepen, and speed up, both in long-desired and unexpected ways.

For years Bobby had wanted to join the Emergency Response Team. He liked helping people, and he also liked flying fast, so much so that Gransom had to warn him many times about pushing Mirage too hard. The ERT flew Screamers to get to other stations or ships in distress as quickly as possible, and that's the ship Bobby wanted to fly. Aside from the ships with mag-pulse engines his mother had flown, Screamers were the fastest ships in the colony. But the ERT had an age restriction, and that could not be overridden, so he had to wait. Finally he was old enough. On the day he turned eighteen, Bobby submitted his application to be trained as a Screamer pilot. To his disappointment, he heard nothing back from them. By the time he left for Shaytown, it had already been three agonizingly silent months. And when they returned, there was still no word. Wondering if his application had gotten lost, he was about to contact ERT headquarters when an official-looking letter arrived in the mail drop at his flat. He stood with the envelope in his hand, looking at the emblem on the front, excited and apprehensive. Carefully he slit the envelope open, withdrew the contents, took a deep breath, and unfolded the paper. The yell he let out was so loud Gransom could have heard it, had he been at home in is quarters. Bobby danced around his flat, crying, "Yes! Yes! Yes!" Then he called Mei and Tran and shouted over the intercom, "I'm going to be a Screamer pilot in the ERT!"

Inspired by Victory's accomplishments and work ethic, Tran returned from Shaytown with a determination to have a productive school break. Except for Sundays, he spent his days training with Mei in the morning, doing baseball drills in the afternoon, then dinner and a brief rest followed by a fastfighting session with Bobby in the evening.

Bobby's ERT training precluded his coming to the morning sessions, but he felt the need to keep up with his fastfighting. He had to stay in top shape and have stamina for whatever emergencies he might face as a member of the ERT. Besides, he enjoyed fastfighting. It had become part of his life and he loved learning from Mei. When she couldn't be there in the evenings, he trained with Tran. All those extra mornings with Mei had given Tran time to absorb additional techniques, strategies, principles, and skills that he passed on to Bobby, who wasn't the least bit put off by having to be taught by his little brother. He knew how diligently Tran trained, and he was glad to learn from him. All of this kept Tran busy, and letters which had started out fairly frequent between him and Victory became fewer. She was busier too. Eventually they stopped writing each other altogether.

On Sundays Mei and the boys attended church at St. Mark's. Gransom was often visiting other stations around the colony, but the Sundays he was on Z9, he made a point of going to a different church each time. When Tran asked him why he did that, Gransom explained as Chief Director he didn't want to give any one church too much notoriety.

Most of Tran's friends were from school and lived on Z9. One Sunday after church, his friend Chris introduced him to Freetubing. Tran had seen Freetubes before, but never thought of jumping into one and pushing himself up to the higher decks. Chris showed him a few things and taught him the hazards to look out for—gravity turbulence being one, and getting caught in the middle of the tube without any momentum being another. Tran loved it and started doing Freetubing as often as he could. To keep the Protectors happy, he would tell them which deck he was going to end up on, and they would wait for him at that level. It worked out well for everyone, and he enjoyed the solitude inside the tube.

The year was heading into Fall. School would be starting soon. Families on Z9 began preparing for the shift away from summer break to the structured activities that brought a sense of order back into the rhythms of life in the community.

It was also coming to the start of the theater season. Mei liked seeing each musical at least twice. Tran enjoyed watching how excited she was about the shows, and he was happy to accompany her as many times as she wanted to go. Something told him she hadn't had much joy in her life, so he wanted to support her in this way as much as he could. Mei especially loved opening night of the new season. The audience was eager to welcome a whole new troupe from Earth, and the troupe was excited to be performing on the famous space station.

When his school year began, Tran continued in his resolve to apply himself, and attacked his schoolwork aggressively as in the days of high motivation when his parents were alive. Mei approved. She told him, "Now you are round wheel, not flat on one side that goes *blop blop blop.*" When she demonstrated the lopsided wheel, Tran found it so funny that he'd chuckle any time he thought about it. But he also saw the truth in what she said. He was now putting time and energy into everything he did, desiring the same excellence as he had invested in his physical activities. He was a round wheel, able to travel far, his life and priorities in balance that made the journey smooth and productive.

In the evenings, he did his homework at the dining room table while Mei sewed on her machine nearby. He often stopped and watched her, marveling at the graceful speed and dexterity of her fingers. She never used a pattern, and what she made was in the same shape and style as what she always wore, whether for fast-fighting, church, or bed, though the fabrics were different. She used to make her clothes by hand, joining the pieces with neat,

Chapter 15: Choices

tiny stitches, but not long before the trip to Shaytown, Gransom surprised her with a special gift—a sewing machine. One of his staff provided a few lessons, and within months Mei had it mastered.

Now that she had a machine, she could make in hours what used to take her days. She loved giving worn things new life. Old sheets became a wealth of handkerchiefs that she distributed generously to Gransom and the boys. Worn kitchen towels became neat square wash cloths. She even made some clothes for Tran, though finally, at the risk of hurting her feelings, he had to tell her they weren't what kids were wearing. She didn't understand why what other kids were wearing had anything to do with what he wore, but eventually he was able to explain it in a way she accepted. Things like that always caused him to wonder where she was from and how she had grown up. On the other hand, he and Bobby were glad to have more fastfighting clothes, which she made for them in the colors they chose.

When baseball season started Tran was in peak condition. All the players were getting bigger and stronger, and there were usually one or two per team who were already drawing attention from the Adult League scouts. Scouts were not permitted to recruit or even talk to the young players about baseball. But they would watch, evaluate, and talk amongst themselves. As the season went on, Tran was their main topic of conversation. Though he was just an average-sized kid, he played like an adult. When they thought of how good he might be by the time he was nineteen and eligible for their league, they found themselves talking in superlatives that bordered on hyperbole.

On Tran's fourteenth birthday, Gransom announced that he was planning a trip to Earth and said Bobby and Tran could come along. Tran was beside himself with joy. It was his lifelong dream, his heart's desire, his one great ambition. He couldn't have been more thrilled. Gransom had set the departure date for soon after the end of the school year and baseball season to accommodate all of Tran's activities. *Eight weeks until departure,* Tran thought. He could hardly bear it. But he put his mind to the present tasks, and that helped the time go faster.

Bobby was concerned about the trip. He didn't know if he could go, or even if he should. By then he would be done with ERT training and ready to go to work. After much thought, he asked the ERT Office if they would give him a deferment of four months before he would be required to begin active duty, and his request was approved.

Only one thing about the trip dimmed Tran's joy: Mei wasn't coming. When he asked her why, she said she had no desire to go, and then suggested maybe he shouldn't go either, but gave no reason why. Her attitude confused him. He thought maybe it had something to do with the men who attacked them at the horticulture station, but that was over three years ago and nothing like that had happened since, so certainly that couldn't be her reason. But still, no matter what it was, he was going to go to Earth and nothing was going to stop him.

Sooner than Tran thought possible, he was looking at the end of the school year and the last two weeks before his trip to Earth. Just one more thing to do. His team had made it to the championship once again, and was heavily favored to win. Even so, their Manager, seeing that his young team was getting over-confident and too full of themselves, called for an afternoon practice three days before the series began. By running them ragged with multiple laps and drill after drill of the fundamentals, he knocked them down a peg or two. The players dragged themselves to the locker room where their coach laid out more reality. He told them they were to respect the other team and play their best. Nothing was going to be handed to them. They had to work for it. All the games they had already won that year were over. They meant nothing to the outcome of the series coming up. The only thing that mattered was how they played in the games ahead. Then he told his team if they played up to their potential, the other team had no chance against them because they outmatched the other guys at every position. This got The Niners revved up to do their best.

When the manager and the coaches left the locker room, the boys were shouting and clapping and ready for battle. The excitement stirred for sometime before players got showered and changed and started leaving for home.

Tran was putting on his shoes when Brooks, the starting second baseman, called to him, "Hey, Tran! come take a look at this." A few players who hadn't left for home were gathered around the training table looking at a crude object that was something like a catcher's chest protector, but with a hard breastplate and back-plate, a pack on the back, and thick straps. In a low voice Brookes said, "Simmons has an anti-g vest."

"Where'd you get this?" asked Tran.

"My brother paid some guy to make it," said Simmons.

"Does it work?" asked Tran.

"Yeah, watch!" Simmons turned a dial near the bottom of the chest plate. There was a soft humming sound and a small green light came on. He held the vest out and let it go. It floated in mid-air, not going up or down. This didn't impress the boys. Anti-g devices were used every day in the colony. Simmons turned the dial down and the device floated slowly to the floor.

"Have you done any jumps with it?" asked one of the boys.

"No, but my brother has," said Simmons. "He jumped off the radio tower by Ring 4."

"Can I try it on?" Tran asked.

"Sure," said Simmons.

The boys began glancing around. It seemed like the perfect time for a test drive of the contraband. The manager and coaches rarely came back into the locker room after going to their offices. But just to be absolutely sure, a lookout was posted at the door.

Simmons helped Tran strap on the vest. Tran guessed it to weigh about 35 pounds, and at least half of that was the pack on the back which held the battery and magneto. The rest of the weight was the two anti-g plates. Once it was secure, Tran climbed onto the table and stood up. "Turn the dial to adjust it for your weight," said Simmons. "It won't lift you, but you'll feel it. I don't know how to describe it." Tran adjusted the dial until he had a sense of being supported. He stepped off the table and floated there until he turned the dial down and lowered to the floor. After that he tried jumping off the table as high as he could. Resistance to his jump was not less than usual. In fact, because of the added weight of the vest, there was even more. But when he reached the apex of the jump, it felt to him like he were pushing down against a spring that kept him from falling. It was different from being in the Freetube, which was more like complete weightlessness.

"I want to try somewhere higher," said Tran. "Let's go out back to the roof." He took the vest off, Simmons slipped it into his bag, and the pack of boys gathered out back looking as nonchalant as possible while they waited until all the coaches were gone. Tran went out front and told the Protectors who were there waiting that he would be a while longer. Back with the guys, he looked at the roof and declared, "We need something higher."

Brooks said, "How 'bout the steeple?"

"Good idea," said Tran, heading over to St. Mark's which was situated behind the school. It was late afternoon by this time and no one was around the church or the school. Before he began climbing up the church building, Tran activated the vest so if he slipped he wouldn't fall. Soon he was on the roof and began shimmying up the tall, tapered steeple. The boys watched with the peculiar thrill that comes with doing something dangerous and forbidden. Tran had planned to stop when he reached the spire, but once he was there, it didn't seem quite perilous or high enough, so he decided to climb all the way to the top of the pole, stopping just under the cross, two hundred feet from the ground. The climb was quite a workout, so he rested before getting ready for the jump. The view from up there was truly impressive. It reminded him of his flight in the Blocker ship.

Tran figured if he turned the vest on halfway down that should give the device more than enough time to stop his fall. Even so, he was a little nervous as he looked down. A creepy thought crossed his mind, *What if it doesn't come on at all?* But he dismissed that

Chapter 15: Choices

fear as quickly as it appeared. He was used to being in the Free-tube thousands of feet off the ground. *This is no different,* he told himself. With his left hand gripping the pole just under the cross, Tran bent his knees and pushed his feet against the thin spire, then leaned out. Searching with his right hand he switched off the vest. Immediately he felt all his weight on his legs and the pull on his left arm. He paused, wondering if he was really going to do this, but when he looked down, all the guys started clapping, waving, and cheering. This was definitely not the time to back out.

"You go on three," he said aloud to himself. "One, two, three…" With a determined leap Tran pushed off the pole as hard as he could to make sure he cleared the overhang of the roof below. The force threw his body into a half-summersault. Suddenly he was falling head first toward the ground, the wind rushing in his ears as he picked up speed. How intense everything felt! He was fighting not to flip all the way over onto his back when he turned on the vest. It seemed a long time, but finally his momentum began to slow and then stopped. Tran let out a relieved breath, but when he looked down he saw he was still well above the peak of the roof. He turned down the dial and waited impatiently as the device lowered him to the ground. The boys crowded around him, telling him how great it looked, especially coming down head first. Tran wasn't listening. To his mind it hadn't been the least bit spectacular. He asked Simmons if the battery had enough charge for another jump and if he would mind if he tried again. "You could probably do a couple of more jumps from that height on one charge," said Simmons. "Go for it!"

Tran hurried back up the steeple, his mind calculating and re-figuring. Now that he knew what to expect, he was really going to pay attention to where he was in the air and wait longer before turning on the device. Reaching the top, he got set, counted to three and launched himself into the air. This time he was falling just right—his belly down and his arms and legs stretched out. It was exhilarating. *This is fun!* he thought, extremely pleased. Instead of looking down as he fell, Tran looked out so he could better judge how high he was. He was nearing the peak of the roof. *Wait... Wait...* He passed the peak. *Wait...* He reached the bottom edge of the roof. *Now!* He turned the vest on. Soon he could feel his momentum slowing. With immense satisfaction, he thought, *This is going to be perfect.* Then he glanced down. To his horror, the ground was still rushing up to meet him. Out of reflex he tried to flip over onto his back. There was a deep, horrible thud and a loud, thick crack. A flame shot through Tran's right shoulder and chest. His lungs deflated like popped balloons. He seemed to be shattered into a thousand pieces.

Faces crowded around him, ashen with fear. "Tran, are you okay?" Their voices were shaky with worry. Some of the boys ran to get help. Protectors rushed over and emergency sirens howled in the air of Dome 2. Tran was fighting hard to breathe when the ERT arrived. Quickly they assessed his injuries, loaded him into the air ambulance and sped him to the Health Station, vest and all.

Tubes were everywhere—in his nose, in his arms, in his chest. Mei sat by Tran's bed, eyes blurry with tears. He looked small under all the bandages. It made her think of the eight year-old boy she'd asked to care for, so still under the covers that he barely seemed to breathe. She had been praying ever since she got the news and had rushed to the Health Station, terrified of what she might find. Machines hummed and beeped, monitoring Tran's functions, letting everyone know he was still alive. Mei whispered a fervent "Thank You" to God.

Dislocated shoulder, broken collarbone, five fractured ribs, both lungs punctured. They had collapsed, but the Emergency Response Team was able to re-inflate one during transport or Tran would have suffocated to death within minutes. Mei shivered at the thought. Tran had landed hard on his right side, severely bruising his face and body but the doctor told her it could have been much, much worse. "We'll need to keep him a week or so," he

Chapter 15: Choices

said. "I'm not anticipating any problems, I just want to be sure he's here if any surprises crop up."

The day Gransom and Bobby left for Earth, Tran stood by the giant window of Vidmar Delta watching Mirage glide slowly past the asteroids and fade into the blackness. For weeks he had imagined the three of them starting the journey together. Instead, here he was, suffering the consequences of his stupid choices. To make it worse, because of the nature of Tran's injuries, Gransom had postponed the trip for two weeks. The delay dragged across the optimum orbit window, which meant their flight time and absence from Vidmar would now be longer. Reluctantly Bobby requested an extension from the ERT office and fortunately they approved, but it would be more delay before Bobby would actually be able to begin active duty in the service he'd waited so many years to do. This made Tran feel even worse.

In the days before the trip, he had tried desperately to convince Gransom and Mei to let him go. "I can get well on the way," he had pleaded, peppering them with logic he'd been assembling in his head. "I'll just be sitting in Mirage for six weeks anyway. What's the big deal?"

"Out of the question," Gransom had said. "If something happens to your lungs while we're in the middle of the trip, how would we get you any help?"

Mei was more direct. She made it very clear that once he jumped off that steeple he had given up his privilege to go on the trip. "If you had not got hurt, you still would not go," she said. "You stop asking now."

Tran had also missed the Championship series. He felt lousy about that too. The Niners won without him. The day after the big win, his coach and some of the players came to the Health Station with the trophy. "We couldn't have gotten there without you," they said, trying to convince him he had been part of it. He forced a smile and congratulated them, but he didn't feel any part of it and he didn't feel any better. In fact, he felt even more lousy, and totally alone.

Mirage had been long out of sight when Tran turned from the window and began walking slowly up the ramp to his flat. How empty Vidmar Delta already felt without Bobby. *Four and a half months!* He was used to Gransom being gone, but Bobby had always been there. He missed him already, and the ache was deep and grievous in his heart.

When he got home, Mei was stirring a pungent liniment in the kitchen. "This smell is not good," she said, dipping a cloth into the amber liquid. "but it will make you heal faster." She wrung out the excess fluid and deftly folded the cloth into a therapeutic wrap. "Come sit here," she said, pointing to a chair.

Tran wasn't in the mood. "What do I care? I'm not going anywhere anyway. Might as well just heal slowly."

Mei pointed to the chair.

Tran shrieked, "I don't need your stupid, stinky medicine!"

Mei looked him squarely in the eye. Cooly she said, "You do foolish thing and you scream at me? No. You will not act like that." She wasn't loud, but there was a tiger threat in her voice.

Tran barked, "You didn't want me to go to Earth in the first place! I did you a favor. You should thank me for it."

Mei kept her eyes on his and pointed toward the hall. "You go to your room now. You think about what you have done and what you have said."

He glared at her, stomped off to his room, and slammed the door. He was tempted to start ripping down posters and throwing things against the wall but controlled the urge to do so. He knew it would only make things worse. Fuming, he flung himself on his bed, jarring his right side, sudden fresh burning pain reminding him how his foolish, rash, stupidity was hurting him yet again. He was furious—so mad he felt crazy. So mad he wanted to scream and scream and scream. But not at Mei. No, not at Mei. He wasn't mad at Mei. He was mad at himself. He messed up. No trip to Earth. No Championship games. He wanted to go back in time and erase it all. But now, more than anything else, he was ashamed of the way he had just treated Mei.

The light panel glowed orange and red, dimmed to deep blue, and turned black before Tran quietly opened his door and walked hesitantly to the kitchen. Mei was drying dishes and singing softly in her language. He stood a few feet away, but it felt like a hundred miles with a chasm between. She didn't look up or stop singing. He listened, feeling awkward and completely at a loss of what to do. The hurt between them was unbearable. Finally he asked carefully, "What is that song about?"

Mei didn't look at him. In an icy voice, she said, "A bird lost in storm who cannot find home." A painful silence followed. She wasn't singing anymore.

"Mei, I'm sorry! I didn't mean it." His words felt small and hollow, but he struggled on. "I was mad at myself. I'm sorry I yelled at you. I'm sorry I jumped off the steeple. It was stupid and I'm so sorry!" Mei's eyes filled with tears. Tran rushed to her and wrapped his arms around her. "I'm really sorry. I didn't mean to hurt you. I'm so sorry I hurt you."

"I could have lost you," she said in the barest of whispers. "I don't want to lose you. We have both lost so much."

Chapter 16
Restoration

For the first time in his life, Tran was facing a school break without being able to do the things which usually crowded his days. He was allowed to do light walking, but the doctor said he was restricted from any strenuous physical activities. For someone as active as he was, this was its own unique brand of torture.

In his room trying to get his mind off his painful ribs and figure out how to fill his time without going nuts, his eyes fell on the book Gransom had given him when they met—*The Future of Magtronic Space Travel.* It sounded horribly boring, but he remembered his promise to read it someday, and he didn't have anything else to do, so he took it from the shelf, thinking it would at least lull him into a nice nap. To his surprise, he was instantly drawn into another world. The book wasn't only about technology and engineering. It told how Gransom discovered magtronium, the ugly battles over getting it recognized as a new element, and how its secret properties were discovered, making deep-space travel and gravitational manipulation possible.

The political and scientific battles that Gransom fought over magtronium were fierce. World governments, corporations, scientific organizations, and politicians all wanted a piece of the booming technologies and the vast financial rewards magtronium generated. If they could have done away with Gransom, they would have. The thing that kept him safe, alive, and not imprisoned under false charges was his proprietary knowledge. He was the only one who knew how to extract magtronium from meteorites and asteroids, and how to process it to make use of its special properties. If something happened to him, the technology would be lost. In the book, Gransom stated openly that it was

170

an accident brought on by a mistake, not his genius, that led to the breakthroughs. That meant it would be nearly impossible for anyone to duplicate or reverse engineer his discoveries, which he believed were the result of Divine Guidance.

Since the entire world wanted what magtronium had to offer, it became impossible for Gransom to satisfy the ever-increasing demands. At that time he had only two processing plants and a small fleet of ships going back and forth to an eccentric orbit of asteroids hauling space rock back to Earth, some of which ended up not containing any magtronium at all. It became obvious a permanent settlement was needed where mining and processing could take place. That's when he gathered a group of gifted and like-minded individuals and headed out to start the colony.

Tran paused, picturing Gransom writing the book while he and his team were on their way to build a station which would eventually lead to the creation of Z9 City and the Zenith Colony, a complicated endeavor which would have been impossible without another of his inventions: PiMar.

Gransom had already amassed a huge fortune with his PiMar technology. Program Induced Mitosis Active Resin was a bio-synthetic resin which could be programmed to multiply, divide, and grow into any continuous structure or shape imaginable. It happened in much the same way the human body develops its different parts according to its internal codes, except PiMar was much faster. Light, strong, durable, odorless, non-toxic, all but a few Zenith stations and ships were formed from it, along with a number of space cities that orbited Earth.

Tran grew up surrounded by PiMar. From the book, he learned that the research that went into its development had taken place some 60 years before he was born. Until Gransom's discoveries, PiMar simply did not exist. It made Tran appreciate something he had always taken for granted.

The last part of the book detailed magtronic engine design and its contribution to the advancement of high-speed and deep-space travel. Most of it was too technical for him to understand, but he decided not to skip any of it. And though it took him weeks to get through it, he read every word. Much to his surprise, he began to see how things interacted and fit together, giving him a sense of the functions and inner workings of engines he had never known before, and an even closer connection to Mirage and the other ships he was privileged to fly.

When he finished the last page and closed the old brown cover, Tran sat on his bed thinking. When Gransom wrote that book, he was on his way to create something new. None of it existed back then. All he had was some technology, some ideas, and some visions of what could be. He and his team were about to find out if they could materialize their dream, and together they were able to create a place where hundreds of thousands of people could live and work in safety and peace.

For Tran, the Zenith Colony and Z9 had always been and would always be. Now he had looked through a window into a different world and a different time. It gave him a much bigger picture of where he lived, and he was proud and amazed at what it had become.

After two months under Mei's care, consisting of ointments, wraps, many mugs of bitter tea, a lot of rest, and a check up, the doctor was convinced that Tran was ready to resume light physical activities as long as he took it slow and didn't try to do too much too soon. The very next day he went to the ballfield with Mei who led him in some simple stretches and easy exercises. He felt stiff and his ribs still hurt, but Mei's ministrations had worked wonders in healing breaks and bruises and easing his pains. As they stood on the ballfield together, Tran felt again the connection with her that let him know they were back to normal. It put him in great spirits.

That evening they celebrated by going to the theater. It was the opening of the first show of the season with the new acting troupe from Earth. Had it really been a year since he and Mei and Bobby and Gransom were there together on this special occasion?

The lobby was a bustle of anticipation as they made their way up the stairs and down the corridor that led to Gransom's reserved box. As they took their seats, the curtain rose and the audience fell into expectant silence. Once more Tran witnessed the transformation of Mei's face as she was drawn into a fictional world where people sang through their troubles, joys, and sorrows.

The musical was a space-spoof comedy with tongue-twisters, intrigue, multiple mistaken identities, and elaborate sets. The fast-paced lyrics and peppy music kept the show going at top speed, and all of it was delivered by actors who could pull off athletic physical comedy while singing articulately on key at the tops of their lungs.

It was a dazzling and dizzying show. But the most dazzling of all, in Tran's opinion, was the actress playing the main character. She could make the audience laugh with just a look, a flip of her hair, the dip of her hip, or the shrug of her shoulders. The cast was in colorful costumes, weaving in and out in complicated choreography, but in her sparkling long red dress, that actress was easy to spot at any moment. She moved confidently about the stage, owning every inch of it. Tran was thoroughly caught up in the performance until he became aware that Mei had gotten out of her seat. She was leaning forward, hands gripping the balcony rail, her eyes following the actress wherever she went. He was just about to ask what was going on when she spun around and hurried out the door. He followed.

The corridor was deserted except for the Protectors waiting watchfully in the distance. One started their way, but Mei waved him away. Without a word, she slumped against the wall, then slid to the floor. She covered her face with her hands and began weeping softly. Tran was stunned "What is it, Mei?" he asked anxiously. Kneeling by her side, he offered her his handkerchief. "What's wrong?"

She looked up at him, wiped her eyes, and managed a faint, unconvincing smile. She took his hand and squeezed it tightly. In a hoarse whisper she managed, "That girl is my best friend."

"What? Who?" asked Tran.

"In red dress," Mei croaked.

"The actress?" He almost yelled the words.

Mei hushed him, then nodded.

Tran pulled the program from his back pocket and glanced through it. "Her name is Lin Thompson," he said. She's part of the Earth acting troupe." He kept his finger on the name as he handed her the program. "You mean, you know her from Earth?"

Mei nodded again. "Yes. Best friend." Tears brimmed in her eyes.

"Well, Mei, that's wonderful," said Tran. "You can see her at the reception after the show."

"No," said Mei, standing up and wiping the tears away. Tran stared at her, completely confused. In a steadier voice, she said, "I cannot be seen with her. It could be dangerous for her. You will meet her for me." Carefully she tore a page from the program and quickly folded it into a figure like the dolls Fe Lin had made as a child. "You give this to her. But you say nothing. Do not bring attention. She will tell you what to do. You listen to her."

Mei didn't go back in to see the rest of the show. She told Tran she would wait for him at the ship. She instructed all the Protectors to stay with him, slipped out a side exit and headed back to the docking bay.

After the opening performance of a new season, the theater always hosted a lavish reception so the patrons could meet the new troupe. Tran had attended a few of them before. They weren't his favorite thing, but they had good food. He parked himself by the hors d'oeuvres tables, sampling the fancy finger food as he waited for the actors and director to make an entrance.

When Lin Thompson came out, Tran didn't recognize her. Without her stage makeup, she looked much younger than the character she played. She also didn't act like the character. She was friendly, but not flashy, dressed in a simple linen sheath of celadon green. Enthusiastic patrons had already lined up to meet this talented young lady, but eventually the crowd thinned out and Tran wandered over and stood at the end of her line. Finally it was just the two of them.

"Hello there," Lin said with a lovely smile. Tran smiled back, pulled the paper figure from his pocket and handed it to her. Instantly her brown eyes widened, but just as quickly she composed herself. "Oh, thank you," she said, slipping the doll into her pocket. She stepped towards him and kissed him softly on the cheek, and whispered in his ear, "If I meet you tomorrow, can you take me to her?" Tran nodded. Quietly the actress continued, "I will meet you in the park a few blocks from here at eleven hundred hours. Do you know this park?" Tran nodded again. Lin stepped back. "Thank you very much, young man. It was a pleasure to meet you. I'm so happy you enjoyed the show."

The ride to Vidmar that night was quiet except for Tran's report of his encounter with Lin and the arrangements that had been made. Mei glanced at him with a look he couldn't understand, except he knew that meant it would do no good to ask questions.

When at last Mei and Tran sat at the dining room table, she said it was time now to say things it would not have been good to say before. She told him about her life on Daoqin. The killing of babies and young children. Being taken in by the monks, being a grub, living in caves, learning fastfighting. She spoke of the loss of her family, and about Taal, how he had led her to hope when she didn't think any was left. She told him about Great Master Yaang, and Park, Master Suun, and Taal's murder. She told him about becoming the Supreme Master, and the mistakes she made which led to more sorrow and the death of so many, including her friend, and why she had to leave the people she loved and her beloved island. And she told him about Fe Lin, her best friend through it all, the girl who refused to let the hardships and ugliness swallow her up. Mei said how much she admired her and was lifted up and strengthened with courage by her indomitable spirit.

Though Tran knew Mei loved him and was committed to his well-being, there had always been gaps in their relationship that bewildered him and made him sad. Part of her always seemed to be someplace else. Now he knew where. There was that deep sadness, the grief that was heavy upon her that never seemed to be emptied. Now he understood. As far as he was concerned, she had done nothing wrong. She did the things that needed to be done; it just didn't come out for the best. It was not her fault. It was the evilness of others. But he didn't tell her. He didn't think she would believe him.

It was past 0200 by the time Tran climbed into bed. He tried his best to sleep but his mind was full of imaginings. As he pictured the little girl learning to live in the hard society of fighting monks, growing into a woman who would create a refuge for others in the rocky hollows of the island mountain, he suddenly realized he finally knew her. Any shadowing of the real Mei in his mind was gone. A fierce love for her welled up in him—smooth and untroubled like water filling all silences, deflections, worrisome unknowns. In that deep security, he went to sleep, all questions answered, all doubts destroyed.

By 1045, Tran was seated on a bench by a bed of large red flowers in the center of the park away from the avenue. A little before 1100, he saw Fe Lin coming his way. Her stride was almost identical to Mei's—comfortable, confident, in perfect rhythm and balance. She smiled as she came near. "I see you have guardians like Dr. Gransom," she said. "Who is he to you?"

"He's my adopted Grandfather," said Tran.

She sat down next to him on the bench. "And may I ask who you are to Mei?"

"I am her adopted son."

Fe Lin's head snapped around to look at him so quickly that it startled him, her brown eyes intent on his face. Then, seeing his reaction, she reached out and gently touched his shoulder. "I'm sorry," she said, "but that is quite a surprise to me. Is Mei with a husband now?"

"Oh, no, nothing like that," said Tran. "She took care of me after my parents were killed in an accident and I've been with her ever since. It's been six years."

"What is your name?" she asked.

"I'm Tran. And Mei told me you are her best friend Fe Lin."

"Yes, but here you say only Lin. Here I cannot be Daoqin."

"I understand," said Tran. "Shall I take you to see Mei now? Once we get to the ship, it's a short twenty-minute flight." To his surprise, Lin did not immediately jump up. She sat silent on the bench, tears falling from her eyes. Tran stood quietly waiting, every one of her tears confirming the words Mei had spoken to him only hours before. Finally Lin said, "Yes, I go with you now."

When they arrived at Vidmar Delta, he escorted her through the station. Stunned by the massive window wall, she couldn't stop staring, her eyes fixed on the asteroids. "I have never seen anything like this," she said. "It's beautiful! Is there any fear they will hit this place?"

"That's what I worried about, too," said Tran. "As long as they're not disturbed by some other force, they won't change their position. We all move through space together." He wanted to point out more things to her, but decided to stay quiet. He could tell she was thinking about seeing her friend and he didn't want to get in the way.

"Here we are," he said, sliding open the door to the ballfield. He led her up to the landing where Mei had first revealed the field to him. They could see her in centerfield gracefully going through fastfighting forms.

Fe Lin stood silently watching, her hands pressed over her heart, tears spilling down her cheeks. Suddenly she cried, "Mei! Mei!" and ran down the stairs and onto the diamond. But when she reached the infield grass she fell to her knees, burying her face in her hands. Mei hurried to her friend and knelt by her side, murmuring her name. Holding each other tightly they wept, words flooding past sobs in the language of childhood, of secrets, of dreams. Tran watched for a moment, then quietly slipped out the big green door, closing it softly behind him.

Chapter 16: Restoration   177

Chapter 17
Taken

Though Fe Lin had a flat on Z9 in a complex near the theater, she preferred staying with Mei and Tran on Vidmar, leaving the station only to do her acting duties. Vidmar Delta was in a classified location with restricted access that could only be reached by navigating there using special codes. Mei wasn't worried about being seen there with Fe Lin, but the two of them never went to Z9 together.

Now that Fe Lin was staying with them, Mei indulged in cooking Fe Lin's favorite meals. That meant frequent trips to Z9 to pick up supplies at Earth Island, the specialty store on Deck 3 that carried unusual foods from all over the world. While she shopped, Tran wandered among the aisles, smelling the herbs and spices that he recognized from his life with Mei, looking at rows of glass jars with pale plant parts floating in clear liquids—roots, shoots, thick-sliced something or other, and thin sticks of something else. There was an entire aisle of canned fruits. He liked looking at the pictures on their labels, especially the pineapples, wondering what it would feel like to hold one in his hand.

When Mei was done shopping, Tran helped her carry her purchases home, anticipating wonderful things to eat that would delight Fe Lin, whose exclamations of appreciation made Mei smile. He noticed Mei smiled much more often now, and she laughed a lot too. It was as if a river in her heart had been stuck, and being with her best friend unblocked it and let it flow. When the two of them were with him, they always spoke English, but often when he was doing homework at the dining room table, he would hear them in Mei's room, talking in their language together, words that flowed like rippling water.

Fe Lin began doing fastfighting with Mei after seven long years of separation, and Mei quickly and happily outfitted her with fastfighting clothes. Tran sat watching them mirror each other flawlessly while doing the most elaborate fighting moves—jumping, spinning, kicking, and landing in perfect form with exact timing—each series a stunning work of art. They would start slow, then begin another series, then another, each set of moves executed ever faster, difficulty and intricacy increasing with each sequence. It seemed impossible to him that they could remember everything, much less perform it all so perfectly together.

He loved watching them—except when they sparred with each other. That was shocking to him. Because Fe Lin had to be on stage, Mei never struck her in the face. Other than that they didn't seem to hold back at all and injuries ensued. It upset Tran to see how violent it was. Once again he was reminded how different their childhoods had been from his. For him, fastfighting was a fascinating sport and a personal challenge. For them, it had been a matter of survival.

Tran marveled at the skill and stamina of each of the women and couldn't see any difference in their abilities. To him, they looked identical. But it was clear that Fe Lin considered Mei the Supreme Master, and although they were the same age, she gave her the deference and respect due the elder sister.

Because of Mei's careful ministrations and his own mindful, cautious exercises, Tran's health was improving rapidly. He no longer needed the wraps, liniment packs, or the physical adjustments she gave him to relieve and realign his sore, beleaguered body. He wasn't back to where he had been before his injuries, but he was starting to feel he could get there. For several weeks now, he had been able to resume his fastfighting training.

One early afternoon Mei asked Fe Lin to show Tran some defensive moves, so he and Fe Lin went to the ballfield and warmed up. Tran was curious to see whether Fe Lin would teach like Mei, who seemed a vast reservoir of endless new things. What could Fe Lin teach him? He had been at this for three years now, and he had long ago left the ranks of neophytes and undisciplined beginners. Fe Lin asked him to spar with her and told him not to hold back. She wanted him to try to make contact. She also said not to worry about defending himself because she wasn't going to throw any strikes. She would do only evasive moves and blocks.

Tran acknowledged her instructions then set himself and began. He threw flurry after flurry of hand strikes and kicks and landed nothing. He wasn't surprised. He had expected as much. But then she asked him, "What do you notice, Tran? What do you see about my movements? Try to lock and see if you can notice it." At that moment, he realized he hadn't been locked at all. Once she told him she wasn't going to throw any strikes, he had become so focused on trying to make contact that he had forgotten all about locking. He felt foolish. After hundreds of hours of Mei's diligent teaching and his assiduous practice, he had fallen back into the same trap he did when he was first learning. It was an important reminder for him. He got set and locked and they started again. This time he notice something. Fe Lin barely moved at all. She was always close to him yet he couldn't touch her. She was like a ghost.

He and Bobby had experienced this same phenomenon when they sparred with Mei. Bobby called it the gnat defense. He told Tran that on Earth, there were these tiny insects so light that if you tried to swat them while they were flying around your face, the air pressure from your hand would push them out of the way and you would never hit them. He said trying to hit Mei was just as frustrating.

When Tran told Fe Lin what he noticed, she explained that when you slip or slide or duck from an attack, you must move only as far as you need to. "Short precise moves slow down time," she said. "In fastfighting you want time to be as slow as possible. If you make long moves, time will move quickly and overtake you." She taught him to move his head and body only slightly, just enough for the strike to miss. "It only needs to miss a small amount, not long distance," she said. "This way your counterattack will come much quicker. If you move far, your opponent has time to recover from their miss and strike again."

Tran trained with Fe Lin for hours, beginning to learn the precise kinetics of distance and minute movement. As evening deepened, Mei came quietly in and stood watching. After a while Fe Lin asked her to spar with him so she could test his progress. Tran shook out his arms and faced Mei. She threw a hand strike to his head and he slipped it nicely. "Good," said Fe Lin, "but watch your balance." Mei threw another hand strike to the head followed by a spin kick, both barely missing Tran's chin. "Yes. Good," said Fe Lin. They sparred for a few minutes with Tran successfully evading most of the strikes. The ones that got through didn't hit him with much force, due to Mei's masterful control.

Fe Lin asked Mei to speed things up and to throw more combinations. This time he slipped each strike perfectly. Mei started throwing combos faster and faster—so fast that he could not believe he was evading or blocking them. It was as if time had slowed down just as Fe Lin said. He felt relaxed and confident and didn't worry about making a mistake or looking foolish. He was locked, focused, and in the moment. Mei continued mixing the combos in rapid succession. Tran moved with her, feeling the dance, breathing the rhythm, weightless in his soul.

At first he didn't notice the change. It came to his conscious mind slowly, as if any faster could somehow cause him damage. Mei's arms and hands were moving with cadence and patterns that he had never seen. Full geometric shapes appeared, strobing in and out, filling his eyes and mind with their intricacies and beauty. They were mesmerizing. He didn't want to take his eyes off of them. Time skipped, sounds blurred, quiet came, thoughts stopped altogether. When he finally came to himself, he was standing on the ballfield alone with Fe Lin. "What happened? Where's Mei?" he asked. He felt strange and disoriented.

Fe Lin helped steady his balance. "Welcome to a new level of fastfighting," she said. "Let's go have dinner."

Tran wanted so badly to learn how Mei did what she did with the movements of her hands, and she was willing to teach him in small increments, but cautioned him that it was a long and difficult process. It would take many years of training for him to get even the basics down. To make sure he understood what she meant, she showed him a few of the hand shapes and movements he would need to know. They were so precise, intricate, and difficult that he couldn't do them at all. His fingers and muscles refused to act independently. Mei assured him if he worked at it it would come with time.

When he asked how she learned the technique, she told him she and Fe Lin had come up with it when they were little girls making shadow figures on the walls of the cave for entertainment. One day as they were sparring in their fastfighting class, Fe Lin made a couple of the hand shapes just to fool around when the master wasn't looking, but it had so distracted Mei that Fe Lin was able to put her on her backside. After that, they experimented until they perfected all the different shapes, patterns, and movements that they found effective.

Tran practiced the hand shapes as much as he could, but school was in session and his teachers were assigning quite a lot of homework. He also had baseball season coming up, so he couldn't spend as much time doing fastfighting as he wanted.

Meanwhile, Fe Lin was busy rehearsing her part in a new musical while still performing in the space-spoof comedy, so she was gone most of the time, staying at her flat on Z9, visiting Mei only on her off days.

Since Mei had not seen all of that show, she and Tran went to a Thursday night performance so she could see Fe Lin in it before it closed. As Tran followed Mei through the lobby towards the staircase, he noticed a beautiful blonde woman coming their way through the crowd. When she was very near, she tried to slip something into Mei's hand. Instead of taking hold of the object, Mei snatched the woman's wrist, swiftly bending and twisting it to activate pressure points, then locking it in place with her left arm.

Once she did that, the woman had no choice but to go wherever Mei led, the two of them looking like good friends walking arm in arm. The three Protectors shadowing Mei and Tran picked up on the trouble and closed in, but Mei gave them a signal to stand down. When the woman tried to raise her voice, Mei applied more pressure and the blonde went instantly silent. Steering the stranger to the empty reception hall located behind the main staircase, Mei pulled open one of the large doors and ushered the woman inside. Tran followed and the Protectors guarded the doors from the outside. Mei released her grip on the woman who immediately backed away rubbing her wrist. Eyes black with rage, she shrieked, "What do you think you're doing?"

Mei was calm. "What is it you tried to give me?"

"I-I don't know," stammered the woman. "It's a letter, I guess. Someone told me to give it to you."

"Who told you?" Mei demanded.

The woman snapped, "I don't know! I never saw him before. He told me to come to each performance and wait until I saw you. Well, here you are. You finally showed up."

Mei prodded, "What does this man look like?"

"Just some old guy," answered the blonde sullenly.

Watching her face intently, Mei asked, "Why do you do this for him?"

"Because he gave me a thousand tags to deliver it," she said. Abruptly she flipped the envelope at Mei. It spun wildly and landed on the floor. "There! Mission accomplished. It's delivered."

Mei's voice was even. "You leave now."

The woman gave Mei a wide berth as she passed. At the doors she turned and glared at Mei, her pretty face distorted with hatred. She roared, "Next time I'll take you down, you pureblooded freak!" She spun around and flung herself at the double doors, which might have been an impressively dramatic exit, except the Protectors were holding them shut. Mei shouted for them to let her out.

Tran stared at the doors. He had never heard anyone say such ugly, hateful words. Poison still seemed to hang in the air. He glanced at Mei as she picked up the envelope and put it in her pocket.

"Don't you want to know what it says?" he asked.

"I will read it at home," she said. "We need to go watch Fe Lin now."

Mei never told Tran what was in the letter. When he asked her about it the next day, she told him it was none of his concern. He knew better than to ask again. But in the following two weeks he noticed a disturbing change come over her. She was distant and sad, almost depressed. She spent long periods of time in her room, even leaving some of her work undone. The flat was not as orderly and clean, and a few times she told him to eat at the cafeteria because she had not made lunch or dinner. When Fe Lin visited, they spent long hours in Mei's room talking in their language in hushed tones.

Tran felt excluded, shunned, forgotten. Mei looked far away—farther than in the old days when they knew nothing of each other. Finally he asked if she was angry with him. He saw recognition come into her eyes, as if she were seeing him for the first time in a long time. Gently she touched his face with her fingertips, then drew him close, enfolding him in her arms. She assured him she was not angry with him. She said she loved him and everything would be all right.

The next morning as Tran was getting ready for school, Mei seemed herself again. She was making breakfast and singing. She told him Gransom had sent word that he and Bobby would be home in two weeks. Tran could hardly wait. As he was leaving, Mei asked him if he could meet her at Earth Island after school to do some shopping. He told her he would.

"You will not forget?" she asked.

"I won't forget," he said. "I'll see you there." He gave her a quick hug and a kiss on the cheek, slung his backpack over his shoulder, and dashed out the door.

Tran rushed to his first period class and managed to sign the attendance sheet just before the bell rang. As he walked down the aisle towards his desk, a girl glanced up from her seat, smiled and said, "Hi." Tran had been going to St. Mark's with the same kids for years so he knew her name was Jessica, but he had never really noticed her before. This time, however, he felt as if he'd been smacked in the head with one of Bobby's roundhouse kicks.

Sitting in class, he replayed Jessica's "Hi" in his mind. Something in the way she said it made him think there was something more to it. His desk was in the row on the right next to hers but four desks farther back. Hoping to catch another glimpse of her, he leaned to the left, but all he could see was her wavy brown hair.

When the teacher had to briefly step out of the room, everyone started talking, and Jessica chatted with the girl across from her, three desks ahead of Tran's. He kept stealing glances at her, and every once in a while she looked in his direction, and then they would both quickly look away.

By the time the teacher returned and restored order, Tran had devised a plan. He would coordinate his exit from class so he would reach the door at the same time as Jessica and start a conversation with her. He didn't know what he was going to say, but he figured he'd think of something. Finally the bell rang, but she was out the door before he had time to pick up his books.

You're imagining things, he told himself. *All she did was say hi. It's nothing more than that.* He decided to put her out of his mind. Only he couldn't. She kept showing up in his thoughts throughout the rest of his school day.

When the last bell rang, Tran grabbed his backpack and headed out to meet Mei. He took one of the many Smartcarts going to the North Gate where the kids swarmed in front of the lifts. Tran wanted to let the crowd dissipate before he went down to Dome

3. That way he could be alone on his walk to the store. He sat on a short wall by the entrance to the lifts, bouncing his heels off its surface. Just as the last chattering kids disappeared, another Smartcart pulled up. To his astonishment, it was Jessica. She walked directly over to him. "Hi, Tran," she said. "It's so funny you're here. I wanted to ask you something."

"You did?" he said.

She set her book bag on top of the wall. "Yes, I was wondering who that woman is I see you with from time to time."

"Oh, that's Mei. She's my adopted mom."

"She's very beautiful," said Jessica. "My mom thinks so too."

"I guess," said Tran, looking down at his shoes.

Gently Jessica said, "I still remember the day your parents died. The whole school went over to the church and prayed for you."

"I didn't know that," said Tran. Thank you for telling me." A quick thought came to his mind, *Maybe that's why Mei came into my life.*

Jessica asked, "What are you doing here? I've never seen you here after school before."

"I have to go meet Mei at Earth Island," he said as he hopped off the wall. "Actually, I should get going."

"Oh! I love that store!" she said. "It's near my house. Can I walk with you?"

"Sure," he said, surprised but pleased.

The sky of Dome 3 was bright blue and warm eddies of autumn air brushed their faces as they walked through Jessica's neighborhood. "This is one of my favorite houses," she said, pointing at a tidy one-story home whose front yard was cheerful with bushes of white and yellow daisies growing in Zenith soil. "My dad says a lot of the houses in Dome 3 look like the ones on Earth from the old days. Have you ever been to Earth?"

"No," he said. "Have you?"

"No, not really. We moved here when I was two, so I don't remember anything. Dad has been back a bunch of times, but I stay here with Mom."

Chapter 17: Taken

"What does your dad do?" asked Tran.

"He's the Energy Procurement Secretary for the Central States," she said. "His job keeps him there a lot, or he's busy going back and forth. He's there right now. He says someday he'll move us back there so we can all live in one place, but I hope not. It's safer here, and I would miss my friends terribly."

Tran was thoughtful for a moment. Earth had always been an adventure to him, a frontier filled with undiscovered wonders. He had never considered it as an actual place to live, one with dangers he didn't know much about. "I don't really want to go where there's a lot of people," he mused, "but I'd like to walk in the forests and stick my feet in the ocean and stuff like that."

"I would love that too," said Jessica enthusiastically.

A few blocks later, Jessica pointed across the street at a white two-story house with a large yard full of neatly trimmed hedges and bushes of different colored roses. "There's my house right there. If you wait a minute, I'll walk the rest of the way with you."

"Okay, sure," said Tran.

Jessica sprinted across the street, up the steps, and into the big house. A few minutes later she was back. "I told Mom I was going to the store with you. Sorry I didn't ask you in. You said you're in a hurry and my mom would want to talk."

"Thanks," said Tran. "I do need to get there."

"Then let's cut through the park," she said. "It's faster." Tran didn't really want to get there faster. He wanted to spend as much time as possible with this girl.

They walked through the well-kept park, with plentiful shrubs, flowers, and small trees. Little kids were climbing on the equipment in the playground, their parents watching from nearby benches. Tran was overwhelmed with happiness—a strange and foreign sensation for him. It was a perfect halcyon afternoon—the light, the sounds, the very special girl at his side. For some reason when he looked at her, she was more in focus, more real than anything he had ever seen. He wanted to say something about it, but knew he wouldn't.

Suddenly the air was shaken with the roar of a loud ship, and another, and another. Three gray ships flew low overhead and hovered about two blocks to the east. One quickly dipped behind the buildings and out of sight. Startled, Jessica stopped and stared. "What's going on? What kind of ships are those?"

"I don't know," said Tran. But a moment after the words left his mouth, he did know. *Rhinos!* The same kind of ship he had seen in the docking bay after the attack on the horticulture station. A thought quickly flashed in his mind, *How did they get through the Space Gate?* Urgently he said "Jessica, please go straight home. I have to go get Mei." Not waiting for a reply, he ran as fast as he could, his mind crowded with fear about what might happen to Mei. His Protectors, trailing about half a block behind, ran to catch up with him.

When Tran reached the street he headed east towards the store. Three doors down was a fabric shop. Just beyond that the street curved to the left and on that curve was Earth Island, It was a large store, set back from the street, with a wide impressive walkway leading up to its eight doors. Tran ran to the side wall of the fabric shop and peered around its corner. One of the Rhinos had landed right in the middle of the curve causing a traffic jam of Smartcarts. The other two ships remained hovering overhead. Two bodies lay on the ground close to Earth Island's doors. Tran was pretty sure they were Mei's Protectors, the ones who would have been waiting outside. He didn't see any signs of Mei or her third Protector. *They must be in the store,* he thought.

Two men holding neuroblasters stood facing the store on either side of the Rhino's open starboard hatch. People came out of the shops wondering what was going on, but ran for cover when loud blasts sounding like cannons thundered from the Rhinos overhead.

Tran ran across the street and crouched behind a planter along the sidewalk. Right then his three Protectors reached the wall of the fabric store. To Tran's horror, one of the hovering Rhinos shot jagged bolts of intense blue light that struck the Protectors, one after the other. Without a cry they fell to the ground and lay mo-

188   *Chapter 17: Taken*

tionless. Tran didn't know what to do. These were his guys. Were they dead? He had to find out. Expecting at any moment to be hit by the same weapon, he ran back to his Protectors and checked their pulses. They were unconscious, but still alive. *Hopefully the ERT will help them soon.* He ran back to the planter. He was trying to figure out how to get into the store when Jessica came running up and crouched beside him. Breathlessly she whispered, "What's going on, Tran? Who are these people?"

"I don't know," he said. "What are you doing here?"

"I can't go home while all this is going on in my neighborhood." Earnestly she added. "I want to help."

Tran kept his eyes on the Rhino in the street, fully aware that armed attackers on the other side of the ship were keeping watch. Suddenly he knew what he needed to do. Without looking at her, he said, "Jessica, please go inside somewhere safe so you don't get hurt." With that he was gone, dashing to the ship, climbing up its side. In five seconds he was on top of it. *Lock,* he told himself, and jumped off the other side landing directly in front of the unsuspecting invaders. Before they could react, he side-kicked the one on his right in the gut and spin-kicked the one on his left to the side of the head. The first man had doubled over. Tran slammed his right elbow to the base of the man's skull. The other man was dazed but still on his feet. Tran gave him a hand strike to the throat and a wheelhouse kick to the other side of the head. Within seconds, both men were down and out.

The ships above released an ear-splitting cacophony of canon blasts, but Tran ignored them and made a dash for the store. He was almost to the door when a big man stepped out with a neuroblaster aimed at him, but a split second before he pulled the trigger, Tran kicked the barrel and the blue bolt went just over his head. Tran could feel the heat from it. A salvo of kicks to the side of the man's head and neck brought him down. Tran kicked the blaster away and, crouching low, crept quietly into the store. Inside he saw clerks and customers lying on the floor by the checkouts stands. They glanced up at him with frightened faces. He crawled over to one of the clerks and whispered, "How many are there?" She stared at him in shock and terror. Tran took her hand and looked her straight in the eye. "It's going to be okay," he said. "Just tell me how many there are."

"I don't know," she said in a shaky voice. "Seven or eight, I think. They came in shooting in the air and told us to get down."

"You'll be okay," he said reassuringly. "They're not here for you. Stay down." The clerk nodded nervously and tried to smile. Lightly, Tran leapt to his feet and ran up the empty aisle in front of him. When he reached the back aisle, he dropped to his belly and peered around the corner of the shelves. Three rows to his right stood a man with a blaster, his eyes scanning back and forth across the room. Periodically he yelled, "Stay down and you won't be hurt."

Tran didn't know what to think, so he ran quickly and quietly and checked the other aisles, careful not to let the man see him. He saw frightened customers and employees, all lying on the floor, but he didn't find Mei.

In the center of the wall at the back of the store was a pair of swinging doors that led into the storeroom. *Mei has to be back there*, he thought. He grabbed a couple of cans off the shelf, then peered carefully around the corner. The lookout was still standing in the back aisle off to his right. Tran hurled a can to the far right side of the store where he knew there were no people. It hit with a sudden, violent crash, glass jars shattering on the floor. The man turned sharply towards the source of the racket. As he started to walk that direction, Tran immediately threw the other can to the same spot. As soon as it hit with a loud crash, he bolted across the back aisle and slipped through the doors. Heart pounding, he hid behind a pallet of boxes, waiting to jump on the man if he came through the doors. But no one came.

When Tran looked around, he was surprised to find himself in a large warehouse instead of the smaller storeroom he had expected. In front of him were long rows of tall racks from one side of the store to the other. The racks were double-deckers with a catwalk

Chapter 17: Taken

twelve feet off the ground that gave access to the second level. He had no idea where to look for Mei, but he thought the second level might be the safest place to search from. He crossed the front aisle, climbed the stairs and followed the catwalk to his right, looking down the rows as he passed them, not seeing anyone.

He came to a corner where the catwalk turned to the left. Looking down over the edge, he saw it was following a wide aisle extending towards the back of the storeroom. On the other side of the aisle, rows of racks continued to the far wall. *This aisle must go back to the loading docks*, he thought, and he decided to follow it. The light was so dim that he couldn't see very far ahead. Periodically he looked down over the edge, at one point seeing Mei's other Protector lying unmoving, face-down in the aisle. Then he heard voices coming from the rear of the storeroom. He crept along, careful not to bump anything or make noise. The voices were louder now, and his hopes rose. By the time he was near the end of the catwalk he could clearly understand what people were saying.

Carefully he peered over the edge. There was Mei! She was just across the aisle from him, standing in neutral position without fear or alarm on her face. Some fifteen feet in front of her were five men and one woman. All the men had blasters and all the blasters were pointed at Mei.

"I'll make a deal with you," said the woman in a silky, chilling voice. "If you beat me, I'll let you walk out of here. How's that?"

"If you wish to fight, we will fight," said Mei.

"Knock it off, Angel," one of the men complained. "We don't have time for your games. We need to get out of here."

"Shut up or I'll drop you right here and now," the woman snapped. "Me and this pureblood have a score to settle." Immediately Tran recognized the ugly sound. It was the blonde from the theater. She stalked towards Mei and crouched into her fighting stance. Mei watched her calmly, standing upright and relaxed, her arms at her sides.

The attack came swiftly, so fast that Tran barely saw it. The blonde threw two spinning back kicks. Mei ducked both, sprang up and landed a spinning back kick of her own that arched over the top of the woman's block and struck her in the face. The blonde touched her mouth with her fingers and they came back bloody. Shrieking, she released a full-on attack, throwing kick after kick and hand strikes by the dozens. Teeth bared, she was powerful, fast, savage, and determined. Mei blocked or evaded each strike, then counterattacked with a flurry of kicks that knocked the blonde backward to the floor. It was all Tran could do to keep from cheering out loud.

Quickly the blonde jumped back up into her crouching stance. This time Mei attacked first, throwing combinations of hand strikes at a moderate speed. The blonde easily blocked or evaded them all. Tran knew this strategy. It was like a change-up in baseball, only reversed. Mei threw slower hand strikes to get her opponent used to blocking that speed, building their confidence, then she would attack at full speed and break their defense.

"Oh, my!" mocked the blonde. "From all the stories, I would have thought you'd be much better than this!" Immediately Mei released a barrage of hand strikes—quick and sharp as arrows. The woman slammed back against a stack of pallets and sank to her knees, frightened and confused. Suddenly Mei was behind her. Deftly she secured her in a deadly neck lock and stood her up.

"You are beaten, yes?" she said.

"Yes," panted the blonde.

"You will let me go now?" Mei said. It wasn't really a question.

"I said I would," the woman scowled.

"We will walk out together like this," Mei said. "If they try to shoot, you will die."

"Lower your blasters," ordered the blonde, and the men obeyed.

"Just a moment," boomed a male voice. Tran couldn't see who was speaking or determine where the voice was coming from. It wasn't one of the five men. "If you don't come with us now," said the voice, "I will have no choice but to carry out the threats I made

192   *Chapter 17: Taken*

to you in my letter. Are you ready to accept that responsibility, Champion of Daoqin?"

"You wrote the letter?" asked Mei.

"I did," said the voice.

"Maybe I come kill you," said Mei.

"I doubt that," the man said dismissively. "Weapons up." Quickly the men pointed their blasters at Mei. "And in case you're wondering," said the voice, "I don't care if you kill Angel. She's been quite the disappointment to me."

"You tell me what is in letter," Mei demanded.

"It says seven a week. One a day on your head. And also that little orphan boy you seem to care so much about. Does that refresh your memory? If you come with us now, I can promise you none of that will happen."

Tran saw Mei steel herself, then release her hold on the blonde. Without defiance, defeat, or surrender, she stated simply, "I will go with you."

"Very good decision," the voice said. "Take her to the ship."

Tran heard the man's footsteps walking away.

Smirking, the blonde grabbed a blaster from one of the men and aimed it at Mei. "Have a nice trip," she sneered, and pulled the trigger. Mei fell to the floor.

With a shriek, Tran jumped down from the catwalk, startling everyone. He was relentless, throwing everything he had at them, his mind on one thing only: rescue Mei. But he was a fourteen-year-old boy and there were six of them. Two of the large men held him with powerful arms and hard, cruel fingers.

"Pick up the trash and let's get out of this dump," commanded the blonde. "It stinks in here."

A burly man bent over Mei, grabbed her by the wrists, violently yanked her up and slung her over his shoulder. Tran screamed in a fury. "Leave her alone! Leave her here! MEI! MEI!" He was thrashing, twisting, kicking. "MEI! MEI!" The men held onto him as if they were merely restraining an unruly puppy.

With a wicked smile, the blonde sauntered over to Tran and said, "Nightie-night, sweetie pie!" and cracked him hard in the forehead with the butt end of the blaster.

"Tran... Tran... Tran... Wake up! Wake up!" Tran had been here before. This was the Echo World you slipped into to protect yourself from the cruelty of reality.

"Let me go," he murmured. "Let me go."

"Tran, wake up! Please wake up!"

Tran blinked open his eyes. Everything was blurry and unfamiliar and smelled like many things all mixed together. "Mei," he mumbled groggily, "I have to find Mei."

Jessica was kneeling by his side. "Just lie still till help comes. You have a nasty lump on your head."

"It doesn't matter. I have to find Mei." He tried to sit up but his head spun and Jessica gently eased him back down.

"She's gone, Tran. They put her in that ship and took off. I saw them." Tran's head was pounding. He felt sick, and now his worse fears had come to pass. He tried drifting back to Echo World but Jessica wouldn't let him. "You have to stay awake," she said firmly. "I'm sure you have a concussion. You need help, and things are getting crazy. People are saying other decks were attacked, and other stations too."

"If that's true," said Tran, "no help will come for a long time. Help me up and we'll get out of here. I need to go find Lin."

"Who's Lin?" asked Jessica as she helped him to his feet.

"Mei's sister," he answered, reciting what he was coached to say. He stood unsteadily, hoping the room would stop moving. Suddenly he lurched a few steps forward and doubled over, his right hand hitting the floor. Thinking he was falling, Jessica grabbed at him, but he straightened back up, swaying a little. In his hand was Mei's red hair band. He slipped it on his wrist. Then he stood, steadying himself with a hand on Jessica's shoulder. "How long since they took off?" he asked, wobbling a little as they started to walk.

　　　　　　　　　Chapter 17: Taken

"Twenty or thirty minutes." Then in a rush she said, "I couldn't find you. I searched all over the store first. It took me awhile to build up the courage to come back here. It's really scary, and then I found that other man lying in the aisle." She shivered. "I think he was still breathing though—barely…"

Tran stopped and looked at her. She hardly knew him, but as frightened as she was, she'd come searching for him. "I can't believe how brave you are," he said. "Thank you for helping me." Jessica smiled shyly.

The two of them made their way out of the storeroom, through the empty store, and into the remaining afternoon.

Out on the walkway, people were gathered around the unconscious Protectors. A woman ran up and announced that the ERT was on their way.

"They shot another man in the back storeroom," Tran told her. "Can you make sure they get to him?" The woman said she would.

"I need to go tell my mom I'm okay," said Jessica. "She might be worried because of all the noise." The street was still backed up with Smartcarts and people talking, wondering what just happened and why.

"We'll have to walk," said Tran, who was moving more steadily now.

The pure blue sky was dimming in the late afternoon as they cut through the now completely deserted park. When they reached Jessica's house, he asked her not to tell her mom about Mei. She gave him a puzzled look and asked, "Tran, what's going on?"

"I don't know yet," he said, "but please don't say anything."

"Wait here," she said. "I won't be long." A few minutes later, she was back. "Mom said all the neighbors came out when they heard the big booms, but no one knew what was going on. I told her some ships flew in and made a bunch of noise and flew back out. I didn't tell her anything else. She's not worried now, so I can go with you."

"With me? Why?"

"Because you're hurt and upset and you need someone with you. That's why."

"Okay," said Tran, thankful not to be alone.

Jessica started toward the street. "So where are we going?"

When they arrived at the theater, the front door was unlocked so Tran led them inside. Since it was Wednesday, there was no performance that evening, but Tran knew Fe Lin was supposed to be rehearsing that night. They found the director and a few stagehands moving props on the stage. When Tran questioned him about Lin, the director said he hadn't seen her all day. She hadn't shown up for rehearsal that morning and it wasn't like her at all. Then he noticed the bruised lump on Tran's forehead and asked if he was okay. Tran said it looked worse than it was.

A few blocks away was the complex where Fe Lin had her flat. She didn't answer her door, but Tran knew the code because she had sent him over there a few times to get things for her while she stayed at Vidmar. Nothing was out of place or looked suspicious. All her clothes were still neatly hung up in the closet and there wasn't so much as a dish in the drainer or a spoon in the sink. *She's just as fastidious as Mei,* he thought, and it made him miss them even more.

It was dark now, and outside Fe Lin's building, Dome 4 was eerily deserted. "I'll take you home," said Tran, looking at Jessica with concern.

"Tran, you need to see a doctor," she said.

"First I have to see if Lin made it to Vidmar," Tran countered. "After that, I'll have them check me at the Health Station."

"Just please make sure you do," Jessica said with a worried look. "I know you're upset about Mei and everything, but you can't do her any good if your brain doesn't work right. You go ahead and go. I can make it home on my own." She made her face look brave, though the silence was creepy and everything felt ominous and uncertain.

"No, I'm taking you home first," he insisted. "I don't want to worry that you didn't get home safe."

"Okay, I'd like that," she said with a relieved smile.

On the way to her house, Jessica started asking questions about the people in the ships and why they wanted to take Mei. Tran told her he didn't know but said he was determined to find out. Then he asked her again not to say anything about Mei or Lin. He said he would explain more when he could. She looked into his troubled eyes with deep compassion and promised she wouldn't say a word.

After Jessica was safely home, Tran went to the docking bay and found Mei's pilot still waiting for her there. As they flew back to Vidmar, Tran radioed the Protectors' office to let them know about Mei's abduction and the wounded Protectors. They reported back that they were contacting Dr. Gransom on Mirage and sending out Protector ships to search for Mei. Tran wanted to hope, but he knew there was little to no chance of finding her. In his mind he could see Mei waking up on a strange ship surrounded by those horrible people. His heart ached so hard for her that he could barely stand it.

Ignoring his pounding head, he went quickly to the flat. Fe Lin wasn't there. He hurried to the ballfield. She wasn't there either. Standing in the special place where they had spent so many hours together, now horribly silent and empty, the entire day began to crash down on him. He felt weak, sick, and exhausted. All he wanted was to go lie down in the outfield and go to sleep, but he knew he shouldn't. Nearly delirious, he stumbled to the Health Station. He had been running on adrenalin for hours. It was now late evening and he hadn't had anything to eat or drink since noon. The staff at the Health Station took one look at him and put him in bed with an IV and radioed for the doctor. They said he would be staying there awhile so they could monitor his sleep and wake him up periodically. He didn't care. He didn't feel much like going back to the empty flat anyway. He lay there in the strange bed, floating between sleep and agonizing sorrow, and cried.

Chapter 18
Changes

By the time Gransom and Bobby returned from Earth, word about the attack on Dome 3 had spread throughout the entire colony, and some of the Zenith people were demanding answers. How could the security of the capital city be so easy to penetrate that three ships could fly into a dome, terrorize its citizens, injure some brave agents, and fly right back out again never to be found? And where was the Chief Director during this failure? It was a troubling incident and citizens wanted Gransom to answer for it, some even suggesting he should retire, saying he was too old, too rich, too out of touch.

Gransom was not new to dealing with contention within the colony. He acknowledged the concerns, agreed they were valid and that he was to blame for the failure, and said immediate changes would be made. But he also warned that an increasing number of entities from Earth were acquiring ships with long range capabilities to reach the colony, and some freedoms which the Zenith people were accustomed to may be lost in order to increase security. "Space is a difficult place to defend," he said.

After five days in the Vidmar Health Station, Tran was released. His injury turned out to be more severe than he thought. He had double vision, dizziness, and nausea for days, on top of his worry and grief for Mei and Fe Lin. Leaving the Health Station, he went home and packed his clothes. He couldn't bear to stay at the flat without Mei. He thought of going to the compound but decided instead to stay at Bobby's. When Bobby returned a week later, he helped his little brother set up the spare bedroom, and Tran moved in permanently. He was relieved when Bobby and Gransom arrived home, but he didn't get to spend much time with either of them. Bobby had to go to work right away with the ERT, and Gransom was busy organizing the search for Mei and Fe Lin, as well as dealing with the maelstrom of political issues and taking steps to increase security around the colony. In a way, Tran was thankful for this. He wanted to be alone with his sorrow.

Late one Friday afternoon, a month after Mei's abduction, Jessica answered a knock on her front door. It was Tran.

"Hi!" she said, surprised. "How are you? How's your head?"

Tran gave a crooked smile and rubbed the spot. "It's okay. I have a hard one."

"You haven't been to school…obviously," she said lightly, but with a concerned look.

"I have to go back on Monday," he said without enthusiasm.

"Oh, good. I'm glad," she said, stepping outside. "Let's sit down." There was plenty of room for both of them on the wide top step of the porch. "I've been worried about you but couldn't figure out how to see you."

"I'm sorry," he said. "I should have come sooner. I wanted to… I mean, I wanted to thank you for everything."

Jessica squeezed his arm gently. "Don't be sorry. You've had a lot of difficult things to deal with. And anyway you already thanked me."

"I did?" he said, absently rubbing his forehead.

"Uh-huh. Right after. You probably don't remember."

"I guess not. I was pretty much out of it. Anyway, I wanted to tell you, you really were incredible. Thank you for not going home when I told you to."

Jessica smiled and said staunchly, "We Z9ers have to stick together, right?" Then carefully she asked, "Is there any word about Mei or her sister?"

Tran frowned. "No. They've searched all the outposts from here to Earth and they're still looking, but nothing yet. Who knows what route the attackers took? Space is a big place. And once they go dark by turning off their comms and transponders, no one's going to find them."

"I'm so sorry," said Jessica, "but I'm glad they're still looking."

"There's other stuff going on, too," Tran said, "political and financial pressure. I don't know much about that kind of thing, but I can tell Dr. Gransom is working hard to make things happen. Right now, all I can do is wait and see and pray for the best. But really, the reason I came is to find out how you're doing."

Jessica glanced up into the pale blue overhead. "I'm okay. I've had a few nightmares. Mostly about ugly, gray ships flying inside domes and being in that creepy backroom. But I'm not going to let it get me down. I've always been able to go anywhere on Z9 without a worry and I want to keep it that way." She sounded brave and almost defiant. Then she looked at him. "Speaking of that, do you want to go for a walk?"

"Sure," he said. He was glad he had forced himself past his own turmoil to come to see her. She was not afraid of talking about painful things, and she left space for thoughts and sadness. He found it soothing to be with her.

After Jessica told her mom she was going to be out with Tran, they stepped into the late afternoon sun, walking west at an easy pace, the opposite direction from Earth Island. "I went to a few of your games to see if you would be there," she said. "Are you going to play tomorrow?"

"I'm not playing the rest of the season," he said. "I already told my coach. I just don't have it in me this year."

"Was it a hard decision?" she asked.

"Not really. I kind of almost didn't want to play this year anyway. I don't care about baseball right now. It's just not important to me."

Surprised, Jessica asked, "How did the coach take it?"

"I think he understood," said Tran. He's not a 'win at any cost' kind of manager, and I really like that about him. He did warn me that some people were going to be upset, but he wanted me to know I had every right to do what I thought was best for me."

Chapter 18: Changes

"Good for him," Jessica said.

"Yeah, I really respect him," said Tran. "He didn't try to pressure me into playing, though he asked me if I'd consider coaching a junior team—kids 8 to 10."

"Are you going to do it?"

"I'm not sure yet. I told him I'd think about it and let him know."

They walked along in the subtly changing afternoon light. Some little kids were playing kickball in the street, their sounds bringing Tran a sense of normalcy—something he desperately needed.

Jessica filled him in on what he missed at school, and amused him by telling him what he was fortunate to have missed. Before they knew it, they were at the dome wall. Instead of heading back, they walked the perimeter path until they came to the West Gate. "Hey, would you like to go down to Deck 6 where the birds are?" he asked.

"Yes, I would love that," she said. "I haven't been there in ages."

The ride in the lift was a rough one, but neither of them noticed. They chatted undisturbed, both of them adjusting their balance without having to think about it. They left the lift, crossed the Ring, and Tran led Jessica to a bench under the trees, where they sat listening to the birds and the slight whir of the Smartcarts speeding along the Ring in the distance. He told her starlings had various calls, but since he didn't know how many, they started counting, though they couldn't always remember what they'd already heard. Eventually they found themselves simply listening, soothed by the sweet sounds.

After a while, Jessica broke the silence. "I was glad to hear your Protectors survived," she said.

Tran let out a long sigh. "Yeah, those neuroblasters are nasty. The doctor said getting shot by one is similar to having a stroke. The guys outside were hit by a gunship blaster. They're more powerful than the ones like rifles, so it was more damaging to their nervous systems. Those guys are just now getting better. The Protector in the storeroom was shot with one of the rifles. He recovered in half the time. That's what I'm hoping for Mei."

Jessica looked horrified. "They shot Mei with one of those things?"

"That's how they knocked her out," said Tran. "You said you saw her, right?"

"Yes," said Jessica. "After you disappeared over the top of the ship, I ran farther up the street and across to the other side so I could see everything better and not have that ugly ship in the way. I could see the two guys on the ground beside the ship and the one by the store's front door. About twenty minutes later all those creepy people came out and one of the guys had Mei over his shoulder. When I saw her beautiful long hair hanging down, I just started crying. It hurt me to see her like that. The creepy guys got the three men up off the ground and they all loaded into the ship and took off. That's when I went into the store. I didn't know if Mei was alive or not, but I didn't want to tell you that so I just said they took her."

"I watched the woman shoot her," said Tran. "The only good thing is that the blaster wasn't dialed up to be lethal. Gransom said a lethal bolt is red-colored, but I know the bolt that hit Mei was blue."

"Oh, thank goodness!" said Jessica. "But what were all those loud explosions?"

"Gransom thinks they were intimidation blasts," said Tran. "Loud blanks to make people take cover and stay away. He said those were used a lot in the War of the States when squads got pinned down and ran out of real ammo. By the way, there weren't any attacks on other decks or on other stations. Thankfully those were all rumors. Gransom said it's a common thing that happens when there's a lot of shooting and loud explosions and stuff like that. The 'fog of war' is what he called it."

"I kind of figured that out after a while," said Jessica. "I'm so glad. I don't want things to change on Z9."

Though only domes had projected skies, light on the Rings and other areas outside the domes still represented the time of day, and as the light dimmed on Deck 6, the starlings settled into chirps and the flutter of wings till they were quiet and still. Jessica turned to Tran and asked, "Are you going to tell me now?"

Tran sat wordless for a time, looking down. Then he began. "Mei is from an island," he said. And starting with that he told Jessica everything he knew about Mei. What she had been through on Daoqin. How she had come to the colony. What she had done for him. The attack on the horticulture station. About fastfighting. About Fe Lin. He told her things he promised Mei he would never say. But he had to. He needed to tell someone how incredible she was and how important she was to him. How she had saved his life, raised and loved him as her own, and how afraid he was that she was now gone forever. He had to say it or he would explode.

Jessica listened without a word, barely able to comprehend that someone could have such a difficult, tragic, yet valiant life, or that others could be so evil. She knew that living in the colony had shielded her from many things, but she had no idea how out of control things were in other places or how inhumane human beings could actually be. It scared her to know that people like that had been able to invade the colony, and wondered if they would come again. "Why do you think they took her?" she asked.

Before answering, Tran studied the leaves on the branches above them. It was a painful place for his mind to go, but he chose to answer her nonetheless, "Gransom seems to think it's because she's still so important to her people that their enemies are going to use her as some kind of example. But I don't know for sure. I could drive myself crazy thinking about all the reasons and possibilities, especially the bad ones. I can't be consumed with hatred towards these people. Mei told me that hating an evil person does not make you a good one. She said her friend Taal told her that at a very critical time in her life. I wondered why she was telling it to me, but now I think I know. She knew this day was coming."

Tran fell silent, considering his words. He decided it was best not to tell Jessica about the letter he had found under Mei's pillow. For a long time he had sat on her bed holding it in trembling hands. With a knot in his gut, he finally unfolded the dreaded message and read, *Champion of Daoqin: When it comes time, you will return with us to your island for trial and possible execution. Failure to do so will result in the death of one Daoqin child per day, and that of the orphaned Z9er. We will come for you shortly. Do not resist.*

Tran sat in deep sadness that Jessica did not break. Without a word, they stood up and started back to her house, both of them lost in their own thoughts.

As they stepped out of the lift on Dome 3, Jessica pointed to a little cafe with blue curtains in the windows and cheerful music and warm yellow light coming out the open blue door. "Look, Tran," she said, "That's my favorite restaurant. Let's go have dinner." She took his hand and pulled him inside, as if it were a ship that had come to rescue them.

The staff welcomed Jessica as an old friend and seated them right away. Homey smells were coming from the kitchen. They reminded Tran of his mom's cooking—a comforting wholesomeness that instantly put him into a better frame of mind. The atmosphere was lively but not loud, and the lighting was just right so you didn't have to squint to see the person next to you or your food, which was one of his and Bobby's biggest pet peeves.

Jessica was not shy, but she tended to be interested in other people and not inclined to talk about herself. It took a little prodding, but Tran finally got something out of her. She told him she was a runner, but chose not to be on the track team because she didn't really care for competition. She liked reading literary classics, particularly the works of JRR Tolkien and CS Lewis, though she confessed that *The Space Trilogy* was beyond her brain, saying *The Chronicles of Narnia* were more her speed. "*The Horse and His Boy* is my favorite," she said, and added with a sigh, "I would love to have a horse."

Chapter 18: Changes

She said she got her love of classics from her mom, who enjoyed creative works that had stood the test of time. She told Tran her mom was an accomplished pianist who used to tour concert halls throughout the Central States. "That was before I was born," she said. With further prodding, Jessica said she, herself, loved piano and played it pretty well. When Tran asked her for her definition of "pretty well," she admitted she had done a few concerts of her own, though she was quick to add it was for small, private gatherings around Z9. She explained how interesting it was growing up in her house because her dad, who also played the piano, only played jazz and her mom only played classical, and to make them happy and not hurt the feelings of either of them, she learned to play and love both styles.

Tran told her he didn't have a musical bone in his body, but he enjoyed music and would really like to hear her play sometime. Then he asked if she would like to go to Vidmar Delta with him on Sunday after church, and she said she would like that very much.

The food was good, their bellies were full, and their moods and steps were lighter when they left the restaurant and walked the rest of the way to Jessica's house. At her front door, she gave him a light kiss on the cheek and said she would see him on Sunday.

It was late in the evening when Tran began walking up the incline to the compound on Deck 2. The cool air felt refreshing and the stars were bright. By the time he reached his room, he had made a decision. He changed and went to the courtyard. For a month he had not done any fastfighting training. *Time to get back to it*, he thought. In his white fastfighting clothes, he began the familiar warmup moves, aligning with what was true and good.

When he was on Vidmar that morning, he hadn't felt any reason for having hope again. But now he saw that things could get better. In her own way, Jessica had shown him there was still life out there worth his living, but he had to make the choice to enter into it. He knew he would never give up wanting to find

Mei, and he would miss her terribly until he did, but he would go on without her. Mei herself had made sure that he could.

With night blooming jasmine scenting the dark air, he moved gracefully through the forms specifically for balance. Water trickled into the koi pond, lights glowed in the vista below, stars passed overhead, and Tran, focusing on nothing, saw it all, his heart locked on hope.

On Sunday, when Jessica saw the Window Wall on Vidmar, she reacted to it the same way Tran had when he first saw it—shock, wonder, awe, and some apprehension about its safety. He assured her it was safe.

They walked the entire length of the concourse, flanked the whole way by the spectacular window. She was taking it all in, looking up and around, soaking in the sights and sounds.

The koi pond was another big hit. Like Tran, she had never seen live fish before. He told her all their names, including the blue and orange one he had finally given a name.

"Dachee," she repeated "What does it mean?"

"Fish," he said with a little laugh. He had to pull her away from the koi just as Mei had done on the day he met Gransom six years before. Tran told Jessica she could come back another time, but for now there were other things he wanted her to see.

Into the corridors they went, Tran leading the way. When they reached the white doors, he opened them with a code. "What beautiful carpeting," Jessica said, admiring the rich burgundy as they stepped into the room. Then she saw the 9-foot concert grand in the far corner. "Oh, Tran! Look at that piano! It's gorgeous!"

Tran's face was beaming, "I couldn't wait to show it to you," he said. "You can play it if you want."

"Really? No, I couldn't...I just couldn't," she said, all the while walking towards it.

"It's just a piano." he said.

"Tran, this is a Bellashin. They're very rare and completely made by hand. They created some of the most famous pianos ever!" Her eyes were glowing as she spoke.

"Well," said Tran, "I've banged on it a few times and I can't even play, so I think you should give it a shot."

Jessica walked around the instrument, studying it and lightly running her fingers over its shiny ebony surfaces, careful not to leave any marks. "Are you sure it will be okay?" she asked.

"That's what it's here for," said Tran. "I think it will be happy to be played. He pulled out the bench for her. Gingerly Jessica sat down and carefully lifted the key cover while Tran opened the piano's lid. She put her fingers tentatively on the smooth whites and blacks testing a few notes. "Mmm…Like butter!" she murmured. The keys responded to her touch, releasing shades and nuances from whispers to roars. Whatever she wanted, it gave. Blissfully she closed her eyes and began to play—a delicate gavotte by Bach that deepened into Beethoven, then flowed into Chopin, then Mozart, then Liszt. Tran watched as she played, her fingers graceful yet powerfully flying over the keys, notes coming in showers, but never colliding or murky or muddy, then softly coaxing forth a quiet, dreamy passage. And when the medley of classics was complete, she played the same pieces again, but in a jazz style.

When she finished, there was wild applause and cheering. Gransom, Bobby and some of Gransom's staff had come into the room unnoticed. Jessica hid her face in embarrassment, but they talked her into taking a bow. "No one has played that piano so well, said Gransom, still applauding heartily, "and it's been played by some very famous pianists. Brava! to you, young lady."

Jessica became a frequent visitor to Vidmar. Gransom and Bobby were happy to welcome her into their world. She was smart, funny, engaging, and attentive. They could easily see why Tran wanted to be with her so much and so often, and it was a relief to them to see the positive effects she had on him.

Late one Saturday afternoon when Jessica was visiting on Vidmar, Gransom invited her and the boys to take a ride with him in Mirage. "I want to show you something you have never seen before," he said. "It's about a ninety-minute ride from here, and afterwards we can take Jessica back to Z9."

As Mirage sped along, they tried to guess what they were going to see. They begged Gransom for clues, but he was being especially secretive and wouldn't divulge even the slightest hint. Finally they gave up and sat in the galley talking and eating snacks until they felt the reverse thrust of the engines.

Over the intercom, Gransom said, "You three go down to my study. I'll be there right after I make sure we're in position" With heightened curiosity they took the lift to the bottom deck where Gransom's study and private quarters were located.

Jessica was surprised the study was so spacious. On one side was Gransom's enormous desk, its wide top accommodating piles of papers and books. Nearby was a work table cluttered with papers, pencils, pens, and a lot of erasers. On one wall were shelves of books. On the others hung photographs that expressed the surreal beauty of natural places on Earth at the times of day that most revealed their stunning shapes and colors. Overhead, the curved blue ceiling gave the feeling of being outdoors in a wide open place. It was an uncrowded space where new ideas were invited to freely come.

When Gransom arrived, he said, "I think we're about ready," and walked to the far wall. "Come have a seat, everyone," he invited, sliding open a panel door revealing a room with chairs facing a wide floor-to-ceiling window.

Only about a quarter of a mile away, two ships were positioned close together stern to stern, both with bright search lights aimed at the darkness behind them.

"What are they doing?" asked Jessica.

"You'll see in a moment," said Gransom.

Presently the ship on the right began to move slowly away. Illuminated by the lights, a thin, silvery material unfurled between the two ships as the distance between them increased. A quarter mile, half a mile, three-quarters of a mile, the long, shimmering material undulated between the spacecraft.

When the ship on the right stopped, the other ship inflated the material with a smoke-like substance, transforming it into a startling shapeshifting sphere that jittered and shimmered and danced in the light.

"It looks alive," said Jessica.

Suddenly the smoke dissipated and the sphere became transparent but still glistened in the light.

Gransom's voice was excited but hushed, "There! Right there! You see that?" A capsule had been released from the back of the left ship and was now floating inside the sphere. "That's the PiMar starter cells. I wanted you to see that because this is a special moment for you boys. You are witnessing the very beginning of Z51, the Johnson-Moore Flight and Science Station named after your parents."

"Wow!" whispered Jessica.

Bobby and Tran were speechless. When they were finally able, they thanked Grandfather for his kindness and generosity, and for not forgetting their parents. Gransom received their thanks without words. In his eyes, they could see he was remembering three gifted human beings who had also been his friends.

Throughout the following months, Bobby and Tran were like expectant fathers watching in wonder the gestation process that was taking place. They took Jessica often to Z51 to keep track of its progress, the three of them marveling at how quickly the PiMar cells generated and developed the structure. In only one month, the first of three decks had formed with all its walls, windows, electrical and plumbing channels and air shafts in place. At that time, the station was still entirely inside the sphere. A few weeks later it broke through to the vacuum of space. The PiMar cells continued to multiply and take shape and after another six weeks the structure was complete. Crews installed space doors. Environmental pumps were placed and activated, the station sealed and pressurized.

With PiMar, one never knew what the exterior color would be when it hardened. What would Z51 look like? Scattered through the colony were stations of all colors—amethyst, sapphire, amber, jasper, topaz, garnet—and all of them luminescent. They were like jewels flung out in space. When the outer PiMar cells hardened on Z51, they turned a bright emerald green. The three watchers couldn't have been more pleased.

Work began on installing the interior doors and other accessories, all of which were grown and shipped from several PiMar processing stations in the colony.

As time went by, Tran and Jessica spent most of their time together. Tran stayed at the compound so he could be closer to her house and they could be together as much as possible. At night he did his fastfighting training in the compound courtyard. He was determined not to let what happened at Earth Island ever happen to him again. *Mei warned me never to act out of emotion during a fight,* he chided himself, *Maybe I could have saved her if I hadn't lost my head.* He pushed himself to get faster and stronger and to always stay locked during a fight no matter what.

In his mind he played his fight with Mei's abductors over and over, analyzing every move he had made and then correcting them, working the fight out physically and mentally, rewriting the results until he had defeated them all and was able to get Mei to safety. Finally, after months, he was satisfied. Then he was able to move on, concentrating his efforts on the things Mei had been teaching him before she was taken.

Tran decided to coach the junior baseball team, and it turned out to be a perfect fit for him. Jessica became his assistant coach. She knew baseball well and really enjoyed working with the kids. After practice, they would walk or run to her house, have something to eat, then do their homework. The only thing they didn't share was the love of Freetubing. Jessica wasn't a fan, so Tran went less often. He didn't mind. There were so many other things they enjoyed together.

Chapter 18: Changes

One day at school, Tran noticed Jessica was withdrawn and subdued. It puzzled him because he'd never seen her like that before. Between classes he asked if anything was wrong or if he had done something that upset her. She said she would tell him later but assured him he hadn't done anything wrong. This was unusual behavior for her, and it worried Tran all day. Finally, that evening, as they were sitting on the top step of her front porch, he asked her again what was going on and she started to cry. "What is it, Jess?" he asked.

She looked at him with her deep brown eyes full of tears and said, "My dad says we have to move to Earth."

The words hit Tran like a bolt from a blaster. With a shaky voice he managed to get out, "For how long?"

"Forever!" she said, and burst into tears. They held each other for a long time, neither wanting to let go.

"When?" he asked.

Jessica bit her lip and collected herself. When she spoke again her words were flat, as if she'd pressed them down before she could get them out. "We have to pack up the house and be ready to go in six weeks." She started sobbing and pressed her face against his chest. Then in a soft, heart-broken wail, she said, "I can't believe he's doing this to us! I don't want to leave here! I don't want to leave you! I feel like dying!"

Tran wanted to console her but couldn't think how. Desperately, he blurted, "Maybe I can come with you! What's the difference if I complete school here or there? Gransom won't care. He can put me up in a place there."

At the time, Tran actually believed what he was saying. But Gransom did mind. When he heard that Jessica and her family were leaving for Earth he was deeply saddened, but immediately put an end to Tran's thoughts about moving to Earth.

Tran couldn't believe how fast the six weeks went by. Before he knew it, he was sitting on the front steps of Jessica's empty house just hours after a tearful good-bye at the docking bay. He wasn't sure why he was there. He just didn't know where else to go.

Chapter 19
The Trap, cont.

From his hiding place by the pathway, Phillip hurries to Tran, who lies on his side with fresh blood on his face. "Are you all right, Mr. Moore?" he asks anxiously. Stiffly, Tran struggles to sit up.

"I'm okay," he says with a little groan as his Protector helps him to his feet.

"It hurt to watch that," says Phillip.

"It didn't feel so great from where I was either," Tran chuckles, straightening his bloodstained clothes. "They went for it, though."

"They did indeed!" says Phillip, "Just like you thought." Phillip makes a quick visual assessment of Tran's injuries. The head-butt had looked severe and he's unsteady on his feet.

"Go ahead and get the Smartcart and let's get to the compound," says Tran. I want to join the team as soon as they radio in."

Three weeks earlier, as he was running up to the compound after coaching his junior team, Tran noticed two suspicious looking men watching him from the shadows. Immediately they brought to mind the attackers at the horticulture station and Earth Island. He thought about confronting them right then and there, knowing his three Protectors were not far behind, but instead he started assembling a more far-reaching plan.

For the past year, there have been attacks of vandalism against Z9 and other stations, resulting in the costly destruction of property and ships. Tran thought maybe these men had something to do with it. He also hoped they might have information about Mei's whereabouts. It's been two years since she was taken, and so far, there is still no trace of her. Even the leads they thought were viable had turned cold.

Tran decided to deliberately set himself up to see what these men would do, in hopes that he and his Protectors could find out where they were staying and get information about their operation. His plan included establishing predictable patterns—always running the same route home each Monday and Wednesday night after coaching the kids. Emphatically he told his Protectors not to be seen or to come to his aid if he was attacked. "If it gets too bad, I can take care of myself," he told them. "It's more important that you follow them without being detected." The agents were not too keen on this plan. Their job was to protect, not let their charge be attacked, but Tran was insistent. Grimly they hid themselves along the path and waited, but they never saw the suspicious-looking men again—until tonight.

Back at the compound, Tran washes the blood from his face, quickly changes his clothes and runs back to the Smartcart. "Any word, Phillip?"

Philip has been monitoring a hand-held radio. "Nothing yet, sir," he says. "Hopefully we'll hear something soon."

They wait, tense with anticipation. After fifteen minutes a low voice comes over the radio, "Alpha, this is Omega. Dome 1, section seven, block 12, unit 17. We're in position across the street."

Phillip clicks the radio twice, acknowledging the message was received.

As their Smartcart speeds to the South Gate, Tran says, "That section is all storage warehouses. It's mostly deserted with not much activity. If they see or hear a cart anywhere near there, they might think something is up. We'll have to go in by foot."

"Understood," says Phillip. "Are you up to running twelve blocks?"

Tran shoots Phillip a challenging look and says with a grin, "Try to keep up with me, old man."

Very few lights are on in this section of Deck 1, and the light cast from the South Gate fades to nothing as Tran and Phillip run towards the center of the dome and Omega's position. "I can barely see the street," Phillip says in a low voice. "Don't run us into a wall."

Tran laughs softly and says, "I thought *I* was following *you!*"

Suddenly they see flashes of blue in the darkness at their eleven o'clock position.

"Blaster fire," says Phillip.

Then over the radio they hear, "Alpha, we are taking fire. Repeat, we are taking fire and are being pursued."

"Copy that," says Phillip. "We are five blocks out. Can you head for the South Gate towards us?"

A breathless voice comes back, "Negative. We are cut off. Estimate five attackers. We're heading for the East Gate. Trying not to get flanked."

"Copy that," says Phillip as he and Tran increase their speed. "We're on our way."

"It's faster if we take the perimeter path," says Tran.

"Got it!" Phillip confirms. "And I'll radio the Enforcers."

When they reach the wall, they turn left onto the perimeter path heading towards the East Gate. Phillip calls the Omega team on the radio but gets no answer. He and Tran see a flash from a blaster at their 10 o'clock position. "We can beat them there," gasps Tran. "I'm going to the gate. You cut over. Get in behind them."

Phillip protests, "I'm staying with you."

"Do what I say," Tran orders, and sprints ahead. Reluctantly, Phillip veers off to the left.

There are dim lights every ten feet along the perimeter wall. Tran stays to the left of the path, keeping in the shadows as much as possible while maintaining his speed. He is feeling the distance and the sustained effort, especially after being attacked, but he forces his mind to stay locked and present, focusing on his breathing, not the fatigue or the distance still to go.

At last he can see the lights from the East Gate a few blocks away. As he gets closer he sees his two Protectors run up to the gate, but from where he is, he can't tell if they make it into an

Chapter 19: The Trap, cont.

open lift. Twenty yards from the gate he hides by a warehouse on his left. From the shadows he's able to see that the Omega team is no longer there. Moments later three men run up and stop by the wall, leaning against it as they struggle to catch their breaths. All three are carrying blasters with thick leather shoulder straps. *That's why we beat them here,* thinks Tran. He crawls along the ground ever closer to the attackers, careful to stay in the deep shadows.

"All that running for nothing," gripes one of the men.

"Manny's not going to be happy," says another. "What are we gonna do now?"

"We need to dump these blasters and get back to the ship as fast as we can," says the tallest man. "Clem, you get rid of them."

"Why me?" Clem grumbles. "Why not Rep?"

"Do what Krat says," Rep snaps with a glare.

"Shut your ugly face," Clem growls.

"Quit griping, Clem!" orders Krat. "Throw the blasters behind that warehouse over there." He points in Tran's direction. The two men unstrap their weapons and hand them to Clem.

He's thirty feet from Tran. Now twenty. Now ten. As he gets closer, Tran hears him mumbling in a low voice, "Sure thing, Krat. Anything you want, Krat. Why do I always get stuck doing the stupid stuff?" The blasters are bulky and heavy and Clem is still panting. One of the blasters slips and he almost drops it. He curses darkly. He's now five feet from Tran. "Forget it!" Clem mutters under his breath. "I'm throwing them from here." He flings the weapons towards the warehouse, spewing one last parting remark before going back to the lift. Tran lets out his breath.

When the lift door opens, the three men step inside, but just before it closes, Tran runs in. Startled, the men jump back into defensive stances. "Whoa!" Tran says, holding up both hands. "Sorry to scare you guys. I'm just out for a run."

The men glance at one another and then back at Tran. "It's just a kid," says Krat, and drops his defensive stance. When the other two see that, they do the same.

Tran looks at the control panel. "Oh, good," he says. "You're going to 7, too."

Krat eyes Tran suspiciously. "Kind of late for running," he says.

"I do it all the time," says Tran. "I have to do my homework first. After that I get to go for a run."

"In the dark?" asks Rep.

Tran answers with a reassuring smile. "I just run in a straight line to the West Gate and back again. That gives me a good four miles."

"Good for you, kid," says Rep, and he walks over to the seats and sits down.

The lift begins its descent then stops for passengers at Decks 4 and 5. Tran averts his face hoping not to be recognized by anyone who comes in. A lady sits down next to Rep and gives him a friendly hello. He acknowledges her with a grunt and a nod.

Reaching Deck 7, the three men quickly exit the lift, board a Smartcart and head towards the docking bays. Tran follows, staying well behind them. At Section 4, the men jump out of the Smartcart and hurry into the docking bays' main corridor. Tran rushes to get inside so he can see which direction they take. He wishes the corridor were more crowded, but at this time of night there aren't that many people so he has to stay far back, his eyes fixed on the men. When they enter Bay 42, Tran stops at a nearby radio booth and calls Flight Control. In a low, clear voice he asks that no ships be allowed to leave Bay 42, then radios the Enforcers and waits impatiently for them to arrive. It takes only five minutes, though to Tran if feels much longer.

Quickly he explains to the sergeant what's going on. The sergeant tells him they have been on alert ever since Phillip's call from Deck 1 and says a second four-man crew is on its way. Not long after, the crew arrives. Armed with Blaster Shields and Thumpers, the Enforcers open the bay door and go inside.

Uneasy about having to wait outside, Tran reminds himself to stay present, not be preoccupied with what might be going on inside the bay. In the quiet, he hears footsteps hurrying his way. A

216   *Chapter 19: The Trap, cont.*

moment later, he sees a large man walking quickly his direction. When the man is about twenty feet from Bay 42, Tran sees him hesitate for a split second as if he wants to change direction but decides to continue moving forward. As he passes, he glances at Tran. The instant their eyes meet, Tran knows it's the man who head-butted him on the path. The man takes off running. Surprised, Tran hesitates a few seconds before chasing after him.

Ahead of Tran by thirty yards, the man bursts out the doors of the docking bays. By the time Tran is out, the man is speeding away in one of the Enforcers' Hovercarts. Tran jumps into the other cart and quickly scans its controls. It's a manually controlled vehicle, similar to the kind on Vidmar. *Hope it works the same*, he thinks, and gives pursuit.

The Enforcer vehicle is faster than any cart Tran has ever been in. He struggles to manage it, and he worries about the safety of other Z9ers on the lanes. In his caution, he's falling well behind the other cart. Just ahead is the Hub. As he merges onto the Ring, more lanes open up so he can go faster without endangering anyone.

Tran opens up the throttle and speeds around the Ring until he sees the other cart pulled off by the North Gate. He jumps out of the cart and rushes to the lifts, but he has no idea which lift the man took or which deck he went to or what to do next.

"He went that way," says a voice. Tran glances around and sees an elderly woman sitting on a bench. "He went into a door down there," she says, pointing. "It looked like he's up to no good."

"Thank you!" Tran shouts over his shoulder as he sprints to the access door of the freight tunnel. Hurriedly he enters the code, opens the door and steps into the dimly lit passageway. *The guy knew the code to the door so he knows what this place is and how to use it,* Tran thinks. *He's not hiding in here. He's using the tube.* For a brief moment he considers what he's about to do, decides it's worth the risk, runs to the Freetube entrance and launches himself up and away from the deck floor to the other side and begins his ascent. If there's ever a time for a record-setting pace, this is it.

But that's not what's foremost in his thoughts. What comes to Tran is what Mei taught him. *Lock—just be and see. Rely on your training.* He pushes off again and again, and then sees the man doing the same above him. By the time they reach Deck 5, Tran has closed the gap and is close behind.

Halfway to Deck 4 the man grabs a side rung and stops. Tran is only seconds behind, flying in feet first. The attacker throws a side kick which Tran blocks with his feet. They collide in a bone-jarring crash. The attacker is big and agile. Tran does his best to fend him off, but the man lands sharp strikes to his body that take his breath away. Tran kicks the attacker in the gut and they break apart and scramble for position, facing each other, each with a hand grasping a rung and one foot on the side of the tube for traction and leverage. With a fast, hard left hand the man throws a salvo of strikes. Tran blocks them with his right arm, but the barrage is fierce and unremitting. Trying to distance himself and regroup, he pulls himself up a few rungs. The attacker stays with him, throwing strike after strike, sometimes letting go of the rung to attack with both hands. The tube echoes with the thuds of landed hits. Tran lands quite a few strikes to the attacker's face, but he has taken too many direct hits and knows he cannot continue this way. He stops blocking and starts evading the punches with head-moves. This works better, and he can tell the man is starting to tire. Then a kick out of nowhere hits Tran sharply on the side of the head. Stunned, he loses his grip and skids along the side of the tube. The attacker is relentless. He's on Tran now, punching him in the head and face. Tran evades some punches and delivers a series of his own, but his vision is starting to close down. The attacker is just too powerful for him. Finally Tran maneuvers himself free and pushes off the wall for the other side. The man does not pursue, but instead climbs the rungs up to Deck 4.

Panting, Tran waits until he sees the man climb out of the tube, then pushes his way up to Deck 4 with barely enough strength left to pull himself out of the tube. He lies on the cool floor trying to collect enough energy to go on. Taking deep breaths, he struggles to his feet and races down the tunnel and out the door. Ahead of him, only 50 feet away, is the attacker walking to a Smartcart. Tran follows quickly after him. When he's close, he says in a strong, steady voice, "Hey!"

The attacker whirls around and stares hard at him. Disdainfully he sneers, "Haven't you had enough, kid?" Tran stands his ground, unmoved by the man's bravado. Sizing him up, the man says dismissively, "Look, I know the pureblood trained you and all that, but you're in way over your head with me. Go on home to your Grampa and enjoy what little time you have left with him."

Tran walks slowly forward with menace in his eyes. "How do you know who trained me?" In the light of Dome 4, he sees clearly that the attacker has not escaped uninjured.

The man fixes his eyes on Tran's and pauses. Then, in a different voice, he says, "Listen, kid, you can't beat me but you might be good enough to slow me down until help arrives. I'm not about to spend ten years in a Zenith prison, so I'll make a deal with you. I'll give you some information about Mei if you let me walk. I don't really care what happens here. I was paid to do a job and I've done it. I give you what you want. You give me what I want. Then I'll be on my way. You'll never see me here again."

Tran's heart almost leaps from his chest. He controls the tremble of excitement that can cloud his thinking. Carefully he ventures, "How do I know you'll tell me the truth?"

"You don't. You'll have to trust me. Give me your word that you'll let me go, and I'll tell you what I know. But I need your decision right now."

"First answer me this," says Tran sternly, "Is Mei alive?"

The man hesitates a brief but agonizing moment, then lets out a long breath. "She was the last time I saw her. Do we have a deal?"

"We have a deal," says Tran. "Where is she?"

The man persists. "You give your word?"

"I give my word. Where is she?"

"Let's get going first," orders the man, climbing into the front seat of the Smartcart. Tran pauses, uncertain, then climbs into the back. When the cart starts moving, the man turns to Tran, resting his arm on the back of the seat as if they're going on a leisurely ride. "The last time I saw Mei, she was in prison on Daoqin."

"How long ago?"

"Three months. Just before I left to come here."

"Is she all right?"

"Better than can be expected, considering that MedTrust isn't the best of hosts."

The way he says it makes Tran want to go back on his word. With irritation he asks, "I mean is she sick or hurt?"

"Not that I know of, but I'm no doctor," says the man.

"How did you happen to see her?"

"I interviewed her before coming here. I got nothing out of her."

Tran scowls. "Interviewed?"

"Well, I *am* paid to be persuasive, but I know it's a waste of time with her." Tran can barely control his urge to beat the man senseless, but at the same time the bluntness of his answers gives him a reason to believe he's telling the truth. The cart pulls up to the South Gate. "That's all I have for you. I'll be going now," says the man.

"Wait! What about Fe Lin?" asks Tran.

"What about her?"

"Is she all right? Is she there, too?"

"She's not part of our deal, Tranny boy," says the man, and quickly walks away.

When Tran arrives back at the docking bays, the Enforcers have the three attackers in custody. Tran's Protectors—Phillip, Peter, and Karl—are there, having apprehended the two other attackers. Tran is relieved to see his Protectors are all alive and well. The sergeant has some choice words for Tran about taking his cart. Tran listens politely and apologizes. The officer's face softens. "You don't look so good," he says.

"I'll be okay," says Tran.

Chapter 19: The Trap, cont.

"And the other guy?" asks the sergeant.

Tran says simply, "He got away."

Back at the compound, Tran lets the shower run a long time to wash off the grime and smell of the battle. He feels fatigue in every cell of his body. Wiping fog from the mirror, he scans the wounds on his face and applies ointment Mei made for him. In the kitchen, he makes a pot of bitter tea for his sore muscles and sits at the table, looking at Mei's empty chair, remembering how she told him the more you need the tea, the less bitter it tastes. Wryly, Tran notices that it tastes pretty good tonight.

Exhausted, Tran climbs into bed, but he's still too wound up to get to sleep. He keeps replaying what the man told him, believing what he heard about Mei to be true. It gives him more hope than he's had since she was taken. He now knows for certain where he must go. Silently he promises Mei he will get there. At last he falls asleep…but not for long.

Chapter 20
Emergency Response, cont.

"There he is at 2 o'clock," says the Growler copilot, pointing to a tiny silver object flashing in the distance.

"Got it!" confirms the pilot. "Let's go get him!" As they near Bobby's erratically flying pod, the copilot radios Flight with their coordinates. Racing in front of the pod, the Growler matches its speed. With thrusters and jets, the pilot expertly angles the Growler 90 degrees, positioning its side hatch directly in front of the pod. A crew member in a space suit opens the hatch and gives directions to the pilot over the radio. "Left. Hold. Down. Hold." The pod dances around so violently that the crew finds it difficult to keep it aligned, and if they try to grab it, it will most likely snap off their capture arm, or come tumbling into the ship and tear it apart. The pilot aborts the attempt and maneuvers her ship out of danger. She reports the situation to the Flight Leader and awaits instructions.

After a few minutes, a radio call comes back. "Growler 3, this is Flight. All we can do is wait until the pod runs out of propellant for the thrusters. Estimated time is ten minutes."

"Copy that, Flight. We will track and capture when safe." The Growler crew knows what this means. As the propellent for the thrusters runs out, so will the oxygen for life support. They wait, solemn and concerned.

After only five minutes the pilot bravely decides to get her ship into position early. Once again she matches the pod's speed and aligns it with the side hatch. The crewman in the compartment gives directions. "Left. Hold. Up. Hold. Right. Hold." They perform this dangerous dance for seven minutes, maintaining optimum alignment to facilitate the capture as soon as it's safe.

Eagerly the crew watches as the pod's thrusters start to sputter. At last they stop working all together. Carefully the crewman taps the spinning pod lightly with the soft grabber on the capture arm. It slows the tumbling until he's able to lock onto it. Carefully the pod is brought into the ship.

As soon as the compartment is pressurized, med techs John and Zach rush in and open the hatch. Bobby's face is gray. "No pulse," says Zach. There's no time to be gentle. They whip the straps off and yank Bobby out of his seat, laying him on the floor. Zach shoves a Cardioplate under Bobby's back and positions another on this chest. The plates glow red and pulse in the rhythm of a normal heartbeat. At the same time, John secures a mask over Bobby's nose and mouth and turns on the high-flow oxygen. Quickly Bobby's color returns. He opens his eyes. Zach is monitoring Bobby's vitals. "He's good," he says. John nods and removes the mask. Hoarsely, Bobby whispers, "My crew!"

"They're okay," Zach tells him. "Don't you worry. Beth and Jason are fine."

"Thank you. Thank God," murmurs Bobby with relief.

Tran is sleeping so deeply that he doesn't hear the voice calling him over the intercom. "Mr. Moore," the voice repeats more insistently. The urgent tone triggers something in Tran's tired brain. He forces open his eyes. The voice calls again, "Mr. Moore, are you there?"

Painfully Tran climbs out of bed and presses the Talk button on the intercom. "Yes," he rasps groggily. "What is it?" A glance at the clock says it's only been three hours since he made it to bed.

"I'm sorry, sir," says the voice, "but we know you would want to be informed. Mr. Johnson was involved in an ERT event and he's been transported to an outer Health Station near Z17."

"An event? What kind of event?"

"An explosion, sir. The reports we've received say his ship was destroyed, but all crew members were recovered."

Tran asks anxiously, "Is he okay?"

"That's all the information I have, sir."

"Have Mirage prepared for flight and find a copilot for me," says Tran. "I'll be there right away."

"Yes, sir."

Tran is fully awake now, hoping and praying Bobby is all right. *An explosion.* He can't believe it. *Not again!* His imagination conjures up endless horrible possibilities. He tries to contain his thoughts, but even his prayers are scattered.

Tran pushes Mirage hard and as always she responds to the challenge. As soon as the bay pressurizes, he's off the ship and into the Health Station. He hurries into Bobby's room, astonished to see him sitting up with a tray of food in front of him. Bobby looks at Tran and gives a long whistle. "Whoa! What happened to you? You jump off another steeple?"

"Very funny," Tran says dryly, but inside he's relieved to find Bobby his jaunty, joking self. "How are you feeling?"

Bobby frowns. "I feel fine. I'm ready to go home, but the doctor says I have to wait till tomorrow." He eyes his little brother. "But you look worse than me. Are you all right?"

Tran sits down in a chair by the bed. "Yeah. I'm okay."

Bobby persists, "Tell me what happened."

Many words crowd into Tran's mind, thoughts and facts he wants his brother to know, but the first thing he tells him is, "Mei is alive!"

They talk deeply into the night with multiple questions, interruptions, comments, conjectures, and details. What does it all mean? They can only guess, hoping they can find the thread that ties it together, so they continue to tell each other what they can remember of what's happened to them, filling in the days of hours since they had dinner together at Rodgers on Saturday night.

Chapter 21
The Meeting

On their way to Vidmar Delta, Bobby and Tran stop at Z9 to drop off the copilot and pick up Dengie, who is practically vibrating with excitement. He's freshly scrubbed and wearing his best red plaid shirt hoping to be dressed appropriately for his meeting with Dr. Gransom. Excitedly, he sits nearby as Tran maneuvers the ship out of Bay 1, punches the navigation code into the system and speeds towards the hidden station.

Dengie admits his nervousness about having to meet Dr. Gransom, but says being able to fly on Mirage is well worth the anxiety. With a covert smile, Tran increases thrust to give Dengie a feel for what the ship can do. Dengie's face lights up like an engine plume. "Wow! All these years in space and I've never done anything like this! Fantastic!" Tran pushes the speed a bit more. They have plenty of time before the meeting starts so if they overshoot a little it won't be a big deal. Dengie's eyes widen, and the sounds of his unabashed appreciation make Tran and Bobby chuckle.

Tran is feeling pretty good, all things considered. Once he and Bobby finished updating each other, he spent the night on Mirage docked at the Health Station enjoying hours of deep, uninterrupted sleep. The second application of Mei's ointment and liniment and a couple of doses of bitter tea have also worked their wonders. The swelling on his face has gone down considerably, the purple bruises have faded to a vague yellowish hue, and the soreness in his muscles and joints has almost disappeared.

Bobby's feeling much better, too. The doctor released him without any restrictions, declaring him to be in perfect health. In the comfort of his quarters on Mirage, he's had a long shower and is thankful to now be in clean, comfortable clothes.

Leaving the east docking bay and entering Gransom's private station, Dengie looks almost as thrilled as when he first stepped onboard Mirage. As they walk towards the conference room to the right of the koi pond, Dengie stares wide-eyed at the unique features of this very special station.

Outside the conference room, Mr. Shapiro is waiting for them to arrive and asks to talk to Bobby privately. Tran and Dengie wander over to wait by the pond. The koi, recognizing Tran's footsteps, immediately begin crowding together, looking at him with hope in their huge, unblinking eyes.

It's not long before Bobby comes over. "There's been a little change in schedule," he says. "Dengie, I'm going to take you to another room where you can wait, and then I'll come get you when we need you. Is that okay?"

"That's okay with me," says Dengie. "but I'd rather stay out here in the courtyard if that's okay with you. It's so beautiful."

"Sure," says Bobby. "Make yourself at home. If you're hungry or thirsty, go through that passageway. To the right is a small cafeteria. Get whatever you like. They don't charge visitors. If you're not out here I'll find you there."

Bobby and Tran go into the conference room and are about to pour themselves some tea when Gransom comes in through the back door. It's been three months since they saw him last and they're shocked. He's thin, his body bent, his gait shaky, his face drawn and tired, but his eyes light up when he sees them, and in a weak, raspy voice he says, "It's so wonderful to see you boys. It's been too long." They rush to him, greeting him with hugs, and help him to his chair at the head of the table, then take their seats, Bobby on the side to his right and Tran on the side to his left.

As usual he gets right to the point. "Bobby, I'm sorry I didn't come to see you at the Health Station. I was laid up in bed. I'm having complications that the doctors can't quite figure out. Of course, being ninety-five has something to do with it. But I still wanted to know what was happening with you. I stayed in contact

Chapter 21: The Meeting

with your doctor by radio and he told me you were going to be fine. Did he tell you I spoke with him?"

"He did, sir. Thank you for checking on me." Bobby serves the tea and looks at Gransom with concern. "Are you feeling better today, Grandfather? Are you up to this?"

Gransom takes a mug and sits back in his chair, his reedy voice belying his reassuring words. "Oh, yes, of course. Much better today. I've been dealing with things and putting out fires all morning." Gransom shoots a look at Tran. "Which brings me to you, young man. Since when are the Protectors your own personal strike team?"

Tran is surprised. He had a feeling this was going to come up, he just didn't think it would be this soon. "Well, sir. I saw an opportunity to find out some information and I took it. It didn't turn out exactly as I hoped, but it did work."

"At what risk?" says Gransom. "You could have gotten one of your men killed or seriously injured, or the same could have happened to you, or to an innocent bystander."

Staunchly Tran replies, "With all due respect, sir, you assigned those men to me to protect me and maybe even die for me. I only used them in a proactive way instead of a protective one." Tran takes a sip of tea and sits back, confident in his irrefutable logic.

Gransom's face is stern, his voice now surprisingly deep and strong. Straightening in his chair, he fixes his eyes on Tran. "This is a problem that continually comes up with you, Tran. You're headstrong and do things only because you want to. You do not think things through or consider the negative ramifications your actions may bring about. You only see your ultimate goal. This is not a good way to be. Mei and I have warned you about it before. You hurt yourself and the others around you when you act in this way. It pains me to have to tell you this—all three of the Protectors who worked with you the other night have been fired. They should not have gone along with your plan in any way. They should have reported it to Mr. Shapiro who would have put a stop to it. Their job was to protect you, not put you at risk. That is the job they accepted and that is the job they should have done."

Tran is horrified. Earnestly he pleads, "Grandfather, please. It was all my fault. Don't punish them for what I made them do."

"I am not punishing them or you. You have brought this about yourself, and now you have to deal with the consequences of your actions. Can you honestly say you believe if you had told me about this plan that I would have gone along with it?"

Tran is seething with anger and regret. He never wanted the Protectors in the first place. And now this? Phillip, Steve, and Peter losing their jobs because of him. It's a nightmare. "I ask you again, Grandfather. Please don't do this to these men. They were not responsible! I was! It was all my idea. I made them go along with it. They didn't want to but I made them. They are good men."

Gransom's voice softens, and so do his eyes. "I'm sorry, Tran. It's already been done. They may be good men, but I can no longer trust them. If a sixteen-year-old can talk them into something they know they shouldn't do, what else could they be convinced of doing?"

Tran glares at Gransom. He can see the sadness in Gransom's face and knows the man is not taking satisfaction or pleasure in saying these things, but this only makes him more angry. Eyes blazing, he slams his mug down on the table and storms out of the room.

For a few long moments, Gransom and Bobby sit in silence. Bobby sighs. He sees the weariness in Gransom's face. "I'm not saying Tran was right in doing what he did, but he did find out some important information about Mei."

Quietly Gransom replies, "When he cools down, I look forward to hearing it." He drinks a little tea and sinks back in his chair. "The men in custody have given us some information about their operations. Unfortunately, they don't know much. They're low-level mercenaries, all ex guards from Daoqin. But I do have news about Mei from someone who's seen her. I wanted Tran to hear

Chapter 21: The Meeting

that, but felt it was important to deal first with his waywardness. Should we go on without him?"

"No," Bobby says, getting up, "let me go talk to him. I think he'll come around."

"Very good. We'll meet back here in one hour."

Bitterly Tran is hurling fastballs at the net behind home plate. His mind is on the Protectors who no longer have jobs because of him. *What will they do? Are they married? Do they have children?* he wonders, but he doesn't know. Their job is to protect, not to be his friends. Getting to know them, sharing anything personal, or even talking to them is discouraged. They are ghosts that follow him around. Except for Phillip, Tran has never liked the arrangement. But now he might have damaged people's lives and that's not what he wanted. His heart is a turmoil of fury and anguish.

"Is it safe to talk to you?" Bobby ventures as he walks towards his brother.

Tran frowns and continues firing fastballs at the net. "Depends what you want to talk about," he says through clenched teeth.

"It's about Mei. Grandfather has some information about her that he wants to share with us."

"Why didn't he tell me that in the first place," Tran cries with fire in his eyes.

"I think he was concerned you might go off on your own without thinking things through or hearing other people's ideas or advice, including his.

Tran scowls. "Is that what you think, Bobby?"

"Does it matter what I think?"

"Yes, of course." Tran throws one more furious pitch at the net and then goes to the dugout and sits down.

Bobby sits next to him as they look out over the baseball field full of years of memories. Gently Bobby says, "I think you want to find Mei so badly that you will do almost anything. I don't blame you for feeling that way. I admire your loyalty. I want to find her too. But we can't be blinded by looking at only what we want. That, I think, is what Grandfather is hoping you will learn.

You know that throwing a spin kick isn't always the best move. Sometimes it can get you into more trouble or worse. You have to be locked and open to everything but thinking about nothing. Grandfather knows things that we don't. He has insights, experience, and intuitions that we can't even fathom. Not to mention the influence he has. He is locked in ways that we can't be. You need to take advantage of that. Doing anything less is not doing the best thing for Mei."

Tran keeps his eyes on the outfield. "Okay, I can accept all that, but he didn't have to fire the Protectors!"

"I would have," says Bobby. He can feel the shock of his words hit his brother like a hand strike to the heart, but he continues in a quiet voice. "He was their boss. Not you. They went against his implicit orders, the very thing he hired them to do—to make sure no harm came to you. Look, Tran, I know it's a hard pill to swallow. I'm sorry you have to go through it, but you can't blame Grandfather for it." Bobby glances at his watch. "Anyway, that's all I wanted to say. We're going to meet back at the conference room in a half hour. I hope you're there." Bobby starts to leave but then turns back. "Oh, by the way, Tran. Let's try to go easy on the old guy. You saw him. Something is seriously wrong. I'm worried he won't be around much longer." Bobby turns quietly away. He does not see Tran hang his head or the tear slide down his cheek.

On his way back to the conference room, Bobby spots Dengie sitting at a table by the spiral ramp eating his dinner. "Sorry this is taking so long. There have been some unforeseen delays. Is there anything I can do for you while you wait?"

"Don't even think about it," says Dengie, his mouth full and his eyes bright. "I'm enjoying every minute here, and this food is fantastic! Do you think I have time to walk the concourse before you need me?"

Bobby smiles and pats Dengie on the shoulder. "Sure, go right ahead. I'll get a cart and come looking for you if you're not here. It's going to be a while yet."

Chapter 21: The Meeting

Coming into the conference room, Bobby sees Gransom sitting in his place at the head of the table talking with a woman seated on the side to his left. Her voice sounds familiar, but since she's facing away from him, all he can see is her dark auburn hair tied back with a narrow band of forest green. He's still trying to place her when Gransom notices him there and calls, "Oh, good, Bobby, I'm glad you're back, I'd like you to meet a good friend of mine, Dr. Hale." The doctor turns in her chair and looks up at him. Her eyes are a deep green, the color of tiranium. For a few surprised seconds they look at one another. Then, with a slight, amused smile, the woman says, "Hello, Bobby."

He replies in a formal tone, "Hello, Dr. Hale." then adds with an amused smile of his own, "How's your space lag?"

The smile she returns is open and her eyes are alight with laughter. "Much better, thank you, It didn't last long, just as you said. And please, it's Eliesia."

"Have you two already met?" Gransom asks.

"Only briefly," says Eliesia. "Bobby was kind enough to help me pick up my errant groceries after I spilled the bag the other day."

"Isn't that something!" says Gransom. "It certainly is a small solar system."

Bobby sits down on Gransom's right, across from Eliesia, and pours her some tea, "So how do you two know each other?" he asks.

"I've known Eliesia's parents for many years," says Gransom. "They were instrumental in helping me start the hospital on Daoqin, and now she is following in their footsteps."

"You've been to the island?" asks Bobby.

"Oh, yes, many times, Even before I became a doctor I worked there. And now, thanks to Dr. Gransom, I'm able to go back quite frequently."

Tran slips into the room and sits next to Bobby. Quietly he says, "I'm sorry, I'm a little late."

Gransom greets him warmly, "I'm glad you joined us, my boy. I'd like to introduce you to Dr. Hale. Dr. Hale this is my grandson Tran."

"Hello, Dr. Hale," says Tran politely.

"Hi, Tran. It's a pleasure to meet you. And please call me Eliesia."

Gransom continues, "I asked Dr. Hale here because she has worked at the hospital on Daoqin and has some important information to share about Mei. Eliesia, please go right ahead."

"Thank you, sir. I'll get right to it. Ten weeks ago I was brought to the number 3 prison outside of Gonqin village to examine a female prisoner there. Because of the added security around her and the prison itself, I suspected that prisoner to be Mei, and that has since been confirmed. She was in fair condition, though there were some issues with her health. She had a low-level kidney infection, she was suffering from dehydration, and her legs were greatly atrophied. I believe she had just been brought down from orbit where she must have been held in zero-g conditions for an extended period of time. She was quiet and calm and all neurological testing showed her nervous system was functioning properly.

"During the examination, we were closely monitored and not allowed to talk except when she needed to answer my questions about her condition. But there are other ways of knowing a person's state of being besides blood pressure and heart rate. When I recommended an antibiotic for her kidney infection, she asked that instead she be able to drink some tea that is made from a combination of plants on the island. The administrator in charge of her care refused that request. But the fact that Mei made it at all told me her spirit is still strong and unbroken, as are her mind and will. They are in tact. She has not forgotten who she is or what she knows. And she was not afraid to ask.

"After I gave her the shot and started an IV for fluids, eight guards took her out of the room and I presume back to her cell. A week later, just before I left the island to come here, I asked to do a follow-up exam but that request was denied."

Tran asks anxiously, "Do you think she's still okay?"

Chapter 21: The Meeting

"I think her health must have improved, and that's why they didn't allow me to see her again," says Eliesia. "They obviously wanted her to get well or they wouldn't have asked me to check her in the first place."

"But maybe she died after you saw her and they didn't want you to know it," says Tran.

Eliesia looks into Tran's troubled eyes. "I understand your worries, and I pondered that frightening possibility myself. But Mei's condition was not life threatening, even if the antibiotics didn't work effectively, and there was still heightened security around the prison when I asked to see her again, so I'm convinced she was alive and her condition had improved."

Gransom adds, "My sources verify what Dr. Hale has just said. Nothing has changed around the prison. However, the security around the island has now been increased threefold. They're not even trying to hide the fact that they have Mei there now."

Tran shifts uncomfortably in his chair, his face more anxious than ever. "What does all this mean?" he asks.

As gently as he can, Gransom says, "Remember the letter you found?"

That fear had always been in Tran's mind, but he had suppressed it, convincing himself it was only a threat to get Mei to do what they wanted. For the two years since she was taken, he has battled imaginations of the full meanings of the words. Now, suddenly, he is about to be told the reality contained in that letter. He's afraid to hear and afraid not to.

Solemnly Gransom says, "They plan on executing her." His words hang heavy in the air. Bobby and Tran look down, hardly able to bear it. Gransom continues, "But they can't do that right away. Other things would have to happen first. Mei is a huge problem for MedTrust. They can't just kill her outright or her legend would live on and grow even larger, much as it has since she left the island. She is considered by villagers and monks alike to be their true leader. The 'Champion of Daoqin' movement and revolt has caused MedTrust severe problems and cost them a lot of money, and it's been getting worse. What they intend to do is crush the hopes and spirit of the Daoqin people once and for all, and the only way to do that is through the complete humiliation of their leader. That's why they couldn't just let her go on being free, a living legend out there somewhere in the universe—a symbol of heroism and hope and physical proof that things can change. If she can do it, so can they.

"In a mock trial they will find Mei guilty of treason or some such thing, and then parade her in front of her people for months, starving her until their champion is reduced to a suffering wisp so weak and ruined that the Daoqin people will welcome her death.

"Of course, our job is to get there before this happens. But we can't go in with weapons blazing or countless people will die, including innocent Daoqins. We need a plan. And to make it worse, they know we're coming."

Eliesia sits forward and looks intently at the boys, "Because of our combined knowledge of the island and its people, Dr. Gransom and I agree the best course of action and the best bet for success is through the order of the monks. We need to get on the island. Go up into the caves and explain to them what's about to happen to Mei, then work on a plan together."

Tran cries, "I'm ready to go right now!"

"Me too!" says Bobby.

Gransom holds up a staying hand, "Unfortunately, it's not that easy. The heightened security around the island is going to make it very tricky. We're not even sure that we can get Eliesia back to the hospital. They may not allow it. And if we do succeed in finding Mei, we still have to get her off the island. And the most difficult thing is there can be no repercussions against her people. We have to figure out a way to end this once and for all, but only if it's what the people of Daoqin want. They may risk their entire culture to end it. We certainly can't make that decision for them."

Catching Eliesia's eye, Tran asks, "What about Fe Lin? Did you see her there?"

"I'm sorry, Tran. I didn't see any other prisoners while I was there. Besides, I couldn't identify Fe Lin by sight. I would only know it was her if she had extra security around here like Mei."

"They may still be holding her on a ship in orbit," says Gransom. "If so, my guess is they would bring her down just before the mock trial."

Urgently Tran interjects, "I have things to tell you, Grandfather. The man who attacked me told me he saw Mei three months ago, just before he came here."

Gransom asks, "And how did this conversation come about?"

"Well, sir, he offered to give me information about Mei if I let him go on his way. He was afraid I was going to slow him down until the Enforcers got there. I thought it was a good deal, so I took it."

"What exactly did he tell you?"

"He said he saw Mei three months ago on Daoqin. When I asked if she was okay, he said she seemed fine to him but he was no doctor. I believe he was there to torture her for information, but he said he knew it would be a lost cause, so I'm hoping he didn't try…"

"He must have seen her on the ship in orbit," says Eliesia. "She couldn't have been on Earth for two weeks before I saw her. Her muscles wouldn't have been as atrophied."

"Yes, exactly," Gransom says. "He probably didn't want to let on she was on a ship."

Gravely Tran looks into Gransom's eyes and says quietly, "He also had a message for you, Grandfather. He said to tell Gransom that we're coming for him. Tell him his days of calling all the shots are over. That's what he told me after he and another man ambushed me and knocked me to the ground. He's big—tall, but stocky. I think I know his name. When I was hiding by the lifts after the Protectors got away, I heard one of the other men say, 'Manny's not going to be happy about this.'"

"Oh," moans Gransom. "Now that is trouble. Frankly, Tran, I'm surprised you're still alive. Manny is one of the most ruthless people I know of. He is one of Eclos' top mercenaries. One of Porter's boys."

"Porter?" Tran asks. "Who is Porter, Grandfather?"

Gransom suppresses a look of disgust. "Porter is the man who forced Mei and Fe Lin to leave the island—a man I hope you never have to meet."

Respectfully Bobby interrupts, "Grandfather, it's getting late and we still need to meet with Dengie. Maybe we should take a break now and let Tran and Eliesia go. Then you and I can meet with Dengie so I can get him on a flight back to Z9."

"Good thinking, my boy" Gransom nods. "The four of us will meet back here tomorrow morning at 0800 and start working on a plan."

Bobby asks, "Eliesia, are you also going back to Z9?"

"No," she says. "Dr. Gransom was kind enough to put me up here so we can start first thing tomorrow morning."

Dengie is not in the courtyard, so Bobby heads through the passageway to the concourse, finds an available cart, and climbs into the driver's seat. He likes the manually driven carts on Vidmar more than the Smartcarts on Z9. They're slower here because Vidmar is much smaller than the capital city, but he likes being in complete control of them. He's almost all the way to the west wing before he finally spots a bright red shirt and finds Dengie staring out the window wall.

As Dengie hops into the cart, he asks, "Are you guys ready for me now?"

"Yes, I'm sorry it's taken so long, but Dr. Gransom is there waiting for you."

Dengie's eyes are wide with wonder. "Dr. Gransom is waiting for me? My mom and dad would never believe this!"

"It's a great honor to meet you, Mr. Chief Director," says Dengie, shyly offering his hand, which is visibly shaking.

Gransom warmly grasps the boy's hand. "Wonderful to meet you as well, Dengie. Bobby tells me you did some repair work on Mirage's transponder."

"Yes, sir. She's a magnificent ship. One of a kind."

"Thank you, son," Gransom says gesturing to his left. "Have a seat and tell me what you found."

It's obvious Dengie is nervous, but the more he talks about his work the less self-conscious he becomes. "Well, sir, while I was working on the transponder I came across some suspicious code trapped in the receiver's buffer. Originally I thought it was just typical code clumping, but when I examined it further, its syntax looked very strange to me. When I checked farther downstream, I didn't find anything else until I thought to look at the navigational system's firewall chain. I found even more suspicious code in its pre-buffer, and that's when I was convinced there had been a hack, or at least, an attempted hack.

"I didn't have the clearance or security codes to go any farther, so Bobby called in an Overseer. Overseer Turry is the one who came. Once he arrived and got me past the firewall chain, I did a thorough scan of the nav system, especially looking at the history logs. I didn't see any signs of malicious code or unauthorized access, so all that was left to do was eradicate the trapped code from the buffers. That took care of the problem."

Gransom sits back, his hand rubbing his chin. "Hmm. That sounds like an old-style hack I haven't seen in ages. It was used with great success before the implementation of alternating firewall chains. In those days it included a subcode compiler, and that was the secret of it. Once the compiler was activated by a normal code stream, it would reconfigure the so-called harmless looking clumped code, and then you had a big mess of malicious code on your hands. Did you find any signs of that subcode?"

"Yes, sir, I did, and I got rid of it. But I didn't say anything about it at the time because I wasn't exactly sure what it was. I looked it up later in the library." Dengie pauses, looking thoughtful. "And that's what confuses me."

"What's that?"

"Well, Overseer Turry had to have seen that subcode was there, and yet he didn't say anything about it."

"He did say it was an old hack from Earth," Bobby adds.

"I'll have to have a talk with him," Gransom says, almost to himself. "But just to be clear, are we confident that the navigational history wasn't compromised?"

"Yes, sir," says Dengie. "It was a primitive hack. It couldn't breach the firewall chain. But still, there's something else I don't understand. If someone is skilled enough to hack a carrier wave and has the advanced equipment to do so, you'd think they'd be smart enough to know a hack like that wouldn't work."

"Yes, that does seem quite curious," says Gransom. "I'll see what Mr. Turry has to say about all this. It's unlike him, but he may have simply missed something."

Gransom starts to get up but falls back into his chair. Alarmed, Bobby jumps up and puts a steadying hand on his shoulder.

"Are you all right, Grandfather?" he asks anxiously.

"Yes, yes. I just got a little dizzy."

"Should I get the doctor?"

"No. I'm fine. It's been a long day. Mr. Shapiro will get me to my quarters and Gracie will have a good dinner for me. That should take care of it."

It's 2100 hours by the time Bobby gets to the cafeteria. First he had to get Dengie settled in his quarters on Vidmar so he would be available the next day in case more questions came up after Gransom talked to Goldwyn Turry.

This late in the evening, there are only a few others in line, maintenance people who work the swing shift. Bobby knows them all. As he fills his plate from the buffet, he talks briefly with them about the stuck launch door in Bay 3, then sits down at his usual table looking out on the concourse. Gratefully he takes a big forkful of mashed potatoes, careful to dip it first in the well of rich, creamy gravy. *Heavenly*! he thinks, breathing the savory steam rising from one of his favorite foods. He's about to really dig in when he notices Eliesia at another table. She has just picked up her tray and is heading his way.

"May I join you?" she asks.

Bobby gets to his feet. "Yes, of course," he says, pulling out a chair for her. "You're eating rather late."

Eliesia chuckles, "This is my second dinner. I confess I was here earlier, but I just had to come back. The food here is fantastic!"

"There are lots of good places to eat throughout the colony," Bobby says. "It's something Zenith people insist on. But this is one of my favorites. Dr. Gransom's chef, Gracie, comes up with many of the recipes."

"Oh, that explains it. I met her this morning. Breakfast was exceptional. I told her so, too. Raved, actually. She just smiled and nodded at me."

"Miss Gracie doesn't speak," says Bobby. "Dr. Gransom says she can, but in all the years here I've never heard her."

"Well, there's something special about being able to make things taste so good." Eliesia says. "Were you fortunate enough to grow up here?"

"Sort of," Bobby says. "I went back and forth between Earth and Z9 a couple of times while my parents were trying to work things out. When they failed to do that, I came here for good. I was twelve, so I've been here close to half my life. And you?" he asks. "Where did you grow up?"

"Oh, all over the world. Both of my parents are missionary doctors, so we traveled country to country, clinic to clinic. That's how I first went to Daoqin." Eliesia gestures with her spoon to help her with the math. "Let's see, I was nine then, so that was fifteen years ago. This was before Dr. Gransom started the hospital there. My parents worked out of the small clinic that MedTrust had set up. We went there a number of times."

"Did you ever see Mei there?" Bobby asks.

"Not that I know of, but I heard stories about her. My parents went back when Dr. Gransom started the hospital at Gonqin village, and they stayed there for a year after Mei left the island."

"So they were there for the uprising?"

"Yes, for the whole thing. They treated everyone they could—villagers, monks, soldiers, guards, and Secrets. I don't call them grubs. It was very bloody. They told me they were there to save lives, not assess blame or decide who would live and who would die. It was very hard on them. It's one thing to set a broken arm or clean out an abscess, but the wounds of war are ugly and much harder to heal." Eliesia sighs and stirs some croutons into her soup.

Bobby asks gently, "Were you there with them?"

"No. I was only fourteen when they went back. Things were very volatile on the island and they wanted to keep me safe. I was taking care of my brother full time, and trying to keep up with my studies."

"Really! You were only a kid! Your parents just left him with you?"

"Kind of. They set us up with another missionary family who were on furlough, but Walter was my responsibility. I hate to say it, but that seems to be a common thing with parents who believe they are called to a mission. Many of them sacrifice their own children on the altar of their cause. My parents did exactly that."

"I never thought of it like that," says Bobby, "but I know exactly what you mean. My mother's calling was deep-space flight. She sacrificed everything for that."

"Including you?"

"Including me."

"And your brother?"

"You mean Tran?" Eliesia nods. "Tran is my adopted brother. Dr. Gransom adopted us after my mother and both of Tran's parents were killed in the same accident. We didn't know each other before that."

"Oh, how awful!" Eliesia looks at him with compassion. "That must have been hard. What about your father? Is he still alive?"

"He's on Earth somewhere. He didn't want me to be part of his life, so instead I got to be with Dr. Gransom, Mei and Tran. I couldn't have asked for a better family. How about you? Do you know where your parents are now?"

"I don't know what country. They move around a lot," says Eliesia. "I get letters from them occasionally, and sometimes if I'm close to where they are we try to see each other. They're good people," she says, adding wistfully, "I miss them."

For a few moments, they're silent. Then Bobby asks, "Did you ever get your brother out of Dome 6?"

"No, I've been down there a couple of times since Saturday. I was able to talk to him, but he's all worked up. He thinks I'm an imposter posing as his sister. He gets like that when he's under stress, and the trip to Z9 without me really stressed him out, even though he had his own private quarters and a caretaker on the ship. He's actually very high functioning and brilliant when he's not suffering like that. I was hoping he'd..."

Eliesia stops suddenly as a strange vibration rumbles through the station, and then another, and another. "What is that?" she asks.

"I don't know," says Bobby.

The floor trembles beneath them. Alarmed, they steady themselves as a huge rumble rolls through the cafeteria, sending dishes crashing to the floor. "Come on!" shouts Bobby, grabbing her hand. "We may have been hit by some rogue asteroids. I'll get you to a safety pod."

With haste they run from the cafeteria and onto the concourse, but Bobby stops suddenly and points. "Wait! Look!" Between the window wall and the asteroids, large, gray ships are flying about the station. He recognizes them immediately. "Rhinos!" he cries. "MedTrust ships!" One fires a red pulse of energy at the window wall. A shockwave from the hit nearly knocks Eliesia off her feet. Bobby puts a steadying hand on her back and stands defiantly against the heavy concussion as if it were no more unsettling than being in a shaking lift on Z9.

Tearing his eyes from the ships, he guides Eliesia towards the passageway to the courtyard. "There's a bank of safety pods right around the corner," he yells over the rumbles and roars. "They have beacons. Z9 will send ships out to pick you up."

As the station shakes, Bobby takes Eliesia's hand to help her into a pod, but she steps away from the open hatch.

"Wait, what about you?" she asks.

"I can't go. I have to get up to Missile Defense."

"Then I'm going with you," she says. "I don't want to be stuck floating around waiting to get rescued."

He doesn't have time to argue. "Okay, if that's what you want. Follow me."

Back on the concourse, people are running in different directions trying to get to their assigned emergency posts or to a safety pod while blast after blast shakes the station, the shockwaves knocking some of them to the floor. Bobby and Eliesia stop to help them to their feet. The lights in the station flicker, the eerie strobing making everything even more chaotic and surreal.

Eliesia runs fiercely, looking straight ahead, intent on following Bobby and staying on her feet. They run up a ramp and through a series of corridors, through a heavy black door and up a narrow flight of stairs. At the end of another corridor they reach a secure door. Bobby punches a code into the keypad and pulls Eliesia into a small lift. There's another keypad on the wall. Bobby enters the code. The door closes and the lift begins to move backwards, slowly at first, then picking up speed, traveling up what feels to Eliesia like a steep incline. "What's happening?" she asks.

"It's a lift that travels at an angle," he tells her.

The lift shudders but they continue to move swiftly upward.

As the first blasts shake the station, Tran rushes to the place he believes will give him the clearest view of what is going on. From the mezzanine of Vidmar's trembling second level he studies the ships attacking the station. It's eight Rhinos in a continuous loop, one after another firing on the station. Each ship delivers its burst, then circles around the asteroid cluster, giving it time to recharge its weapon before rushing in and firing again, never giving Vidmar much time to recover.

From reading Gransom's book, Tran knows the resiliency and strength of PiMar. It should hold up to energy weapons and smaller breaching missiles, but he doesn't know what other weapons they may have onboard those strange ships.

Something else from the book flashes into Tran's mind and he takes off running for the east docking bay, adjusting his balance through the swaying, shuddering station until he reaches Mirage. He fires up her engines and calls on the radio, "Mirage requesting departure Bay 1."

"Mr. Moore, is that you?" says a voice over the speaker.

"Roger that. Ready for departure."

"Sir, you do know that…"

"I'm well aware of what's going on," Tran interrupts. "Now open this door!" The door begins to open.

"Good luck, sir."

"Roger that. You too."

Tran flips Mirage on its side and squeezes out the door before it's fully open. He rockets away from the station as fast as the ship will take him.

Exiting the lift, Bobby and Eliesia climb a narrow ladder up through an access tube. When they reach the top, he opens a heavy, round hatch and then another a few feet directly above it. They climb out into Missile Defense.

Bobby secures both hatches then rushes to sit in the high-back gunner's chair and starts punching buttons and turning dials on the control panel. "Sit down here and strap in," he says, turning the chair next to him towards Eliesia. She glances around while adjusting the straps. They're in a transparent turret on the roof of the station. "I'm glad you're here," he says. "I'm going to need your help. This works better as a two-person job."

"What are we doing?" she asks.

"Shooting bad guys," he says, tugging at her straps to make sure she's secure, then strapping himself in. He grabs the control sticks, quickly calibrating them to his touch, then says, "Hold on! We're going for a ride." The turret suddenly moves backwards while simultaneously rotating 180 degrees. It races along the roof from the middle of the station to its rear. Eliesia can see it follows some sort of rail. "Good. No action here," he says, quickly surveying the area behind Vidmar. "They're only attacking from the front." The turret rotates again and speeds all the way to the front of the station where there's a clear view of the asteroids and enemy ships.

"I've never shot anything before," says Eliesia with a worried look.

"Neither have I, except in training," says Bobby. "Pull that launch board with the red buttons up to your chair."

The board is on a floating arm. Eliesia grabs it and pulls it to her. On the board are eight rows of eight round, red buttons lettered and numbered A1 through H8.

"Push down H5," says Bobby.

She presses down on the button, surprised at how much force it takes to move it. Finally there's and audible click and the button stays depressed when she takes her finger away. "Done!" she says triumphantly. "Now what?"

Bobby points out the window with his chin. "You see that ship coming in?"

"Yes."

"Watch." He works the control sticks and fires. A stream of white pulses hit the ship, forcing it to abort its attack.

"The asteroid!" Eliesia shouts, pointing. "Those pulses came from that asteroid! You did that?"

"*We* did that," says Bobby, and manipulates the controls, getting ready for the next shot. "Quick!" he says, "C1!"

"Done!"

He fires. A missile launches from one of the back asteroids. The Rhinos scatter trying to evade it, but the missile homes in on one of them. The explosion is lethal and thorough, and quickly

Chapter 21: The Meeting

sucked up by the vacuum of space. Where the ship had been is now nothing but litter and glitter. Bobby and Eliesia sit stunned. But the other seven Rhinos are circling back. There's no time to work things out in their minds.

Tran banks Mirage hard to port. Now thousands of miles from Vidmar, he goes through the five-step process of deactivating Mirage's throttle safeties, then speeds back towards the station at over maximum throttle.

Tran had read all about the dangers of magtronic engines in Gransom's book. When they're pushed beyond their recommended output, magtronic degradation occurs causing the engine to emit high levels of magtronic distortion and debris in its wake. *Three minutes out,* he thinks. *Lock.*

"Here they come," says Bobby, sitting up alert in his chair, "all seven of them."

"What should I do?" Eliesia asks.

"D1 through D7."

"Done!"

Bobby works the controls swiftly and fires. Seven missiles spread out from an asteroid, but instead of homing in on the Rhinos, they turn and head straight for the station. "They're compromised!" he shouts as he unstraps from his chair. Grabbing the launch board, he quickly pulls the seven buttons back up, rotates them clockwise a half turn, and punches them back down. The missiles self destruct, exploding soundlessly in brilliant white light.

Eliesia cries, "What happened?"

"The missiles are malfunctioning. They may have been hacked. I'll try one more. Bobby presses down D8. Then grabs his controls and fires. The missile flies directly towards the station. Immediately he activates its self destruct and it explodes. "We can't use them," he says, strapping back into his chair. "Let's try the pulse guns again. Give me F5."

"Done."

He fires. "Guns are working. We'll go with those." He doesn't say anything to Eliesia, but he wonders how long they can defend themselves without missiles.

Traveling at mind-numbing speed with screaming unstable engines, Tran struggles to keep Mirage on course. He slows his breathing and heart rate, remembering: *Smaller moves slow time down. Larger moves speed time up.* For what he's about to attempt, he needs time as slow as possible. *One minute out.* He increases throttle even more.

Bobby watches the Rhinos circling behind the asteroids to re-charge their weapons. In the brief pause, he tells Eliesia, "I'll take you back to the access tube so you can get to a safety pod."

"I'm not going anywhere!" she declares, her eyes snapping with fierce green fire. "Those cowards aren't going to defeat us!"

The Rhinos suddenly come charging back in.

"F1 and F2!"

Eliesia punches the red buttons down hard. "You got it!"

Bobby fires and pulses shoot towards the two closest Rhinos, but the ships suddenly serpentine, then break away high above the station. Bobby's commands come quickly now as he tries to stave off the other five—"A1! E6! H7! H8!"

The Rhinos charge in a fury of fire. From the turret, Bobby and Eliesia see multiple ruinous missile blasts flash to their left and right, hitting the station with a salvo of strikes. There's a deep, throbbing boom followed by a tumult of confusion. Buffeted by the raging, rending forces, Vidmar Delta reels and heaves, swaying and rocking like a ship foundering in a furious ocean storm, moaning and shuddering while sharp cracking sounds travel through the giant structure like jagged bolts of lightening. Power goes out. The turret is suddenly dark. The controls dead. Bobby braces for the death blow, the final assault from the charging Rhinos. Instead, except for some creaking and swaying, Vidmar is quiet.

Chapter 21: The Meeting

Expecting another violent attack at any moment Bobby unstraps and fumbles around in the dark.

Nervously Eliesia asks, "What are you doing?"

"There's a hand crank here somewhere," he says. "If we can get back to the access tube we can get out of here. Here it is!" Crouching on the floor, he calls, "Come help me turn this." Eliesia unstraps and crawls on her hands and knees until she reaches him. Kneeling together, they struggle to crank the handle counterclockwise. As they do, the turret moves slowly towards the middle of the station. Moments later, the auxiliary power comes on, giving a dim, but welcome light. Bobby tries the controls. They're still dead. He takes his place beside Eliesia and they continue turning the handle.

"How will we know when we're over the tube?" she asks.

"There's a notch in the rail. We'll feel it when we drop into it."

Tran stares unblinking out the bridge window. The controls on Mirage are now so sensitive they're almost unusable. He'll have only a fraction of a second to make a final adjustment to his trajectory. If he makes the wrong move he could slam into a Rhino, an asteroid, or the station. *Ten seconds out.* He nudges the ship with the tiniest of adjustments ever so smoothly to port. There in front of him is Vidmar Delta. One more hurried and prayerful adjustment and it's over.

A blinding white light fills the turret. Bobby and Eliesia cringe, dreading the violent fatal impact, but nothing comes. A strange glow now lights the blackness outside. When they look out, Eliesia gasps, "What's that?"

"I have no idea," says Bobby.

Between Vidmar and the asteroids, a cloud of charged silvery gray particles is forming, swirling about in a chaos of amassing dust.

Bobby stares hard. On the other side of the cloud, he sees the Rhinos. They are tumbling helplessly towards the sparkling mass. "Look!" he says, pointing at the ships. "Their engines are out!"

Contracting in size, the cloud is coalescing, becoming more dense, its activity accelerating and intensifying. The Rhinos are pulled powerlessly into the concentrating silvery dust. A purple mist begins to form around their still super-heated engine nozzles, glowing brighter with sparks of brilliant purple.

Multiplying exponentially, the sparks flash faster and faster until every particle burns in blinding purple light. Rampant energy rages through the cloud, extreme heat expanding in every direction more brilliant than the sun. Bobby shouts, "That's charged magtronium dust!" They cover their eyes, the searing heat radiating through the turret so intensely that they cry out and fall to the floor. Fiery dust batters against the turret in a deafening, piercing, overwhelming shriek that steals their breath. And then, sudden quiet.

Dazed and astonished to still be alive, Bobby and Eliesia cautiously sit up. "Are you all right?" he asks.

"I think so," she says. "How 'bout you?"

"Aside from being cooked alive, I think I'm all here, But my ears are ringing like crazy. Are yours?"

"What'd you say?" Eliesia yells, and starts to laugh.

"Very funny," says Bobby, but he can't help laughing too.

Stiffly they get to their feet and look out. All they see are distant stars. "Bobby! They're gone! The ships! The asteroids! Everything! They're gone!" She hugs him with relief and joy, saying softly. "It's a miracle!"

Tran begins Mirage's wide turn back to Vidmar. It will take eleven hours to get home. He prays he still has one, and that Mirage will make it there.

Chapter 21: The Meeting

Chapter 22
Following

With a distinct thunk the turret drops into place over the hatch to the access tube. "We're there," says Bobby.

"Thank God," says Eliesia, rubbing her tired arms. "I don't think I could have done that much longer. They had been turning the crank for the past ninety minutes, barely stopping to rest.

He opens the two hatches and they climb down the ladder to the lift. He punches its code, but nothing happens.

"We'll have to go down the emergency escape," he says. Eliesia follows him to another ladder that goes down through a tube. "We can get to the bottom deck from here," he tells her, feeling with his foot for the first rung. The emergency lights are small and dim and it's a long, dark descent, but at last they reach the bottom.

When they step into one of the main corridors, they start to see the damage that previously they had only felt. Vidmar Delta looks like it's been hit by a catastrophic earthquake. Many things that weren't bolted or mag-locked down have toppled. Walls are cracked, electrical cables are sparking, a foul smoke is in the air. Emergency crews are earnestly addressing everything they can, while civilians are doing their best to help.

"I have to find Grandfather," Bobby says. "Let's go to his quarters." As they hurry around a corner, what they see stops them cold. There's a crowd of people there, most of them sitting or lying on the floor as they wait to be treated at the Health Station. Some are bleeding, some are unconscious, others are moaning in pain from broken bones. Two medical techs and several Protectors along with concerned civilians are trying to help as many as they can, but they're obviously overrun and under-qualified.

"Where's the doctor?" Eliesia asks, assessing the needs with practiced eyes.

"On Z9, but we can't reach anyone on the radio," says one of the Protectors.

Eliesia immediately begins doing triage, giving orders on who should be seen first and what should be done. Kneeling next to a man who lies shuddering on the floor, she carefully pulls back his blood-soaked shirt and shakes her head. Looking up at Bobby she tells him, "We need to get some of these patients to a larger Health Station with more doctors. Can you take care of that?"

Bobby sprints to a maintenance bay where he commandeers a flatbed cart and hurries back. They're able to fit six of the most seriously injured patients onto the flatbed. Some uninjured people volunteer to stay with them. Carefully Bobby drives all of them to the east docking bay and into a small cargo ship. "Make sure you give them a smooth trip," he tells the pilot. The pilot assures him he will.

Leaving the ship, Bobby passes his hand over his forehead and lets out a long sigh. *At least they're safely on their way*, he thinks. Noticing that some of the ships have been damaged, he runs to Bay 1 to check on Mirage. She's not there. Alarmed, he rushes to the Control Center. Anxiously he asks, "Where's Mirage?"

"Mr. Moore took her, sir," says the controller.

"When?"

"During the attack, sir."

"Has he called in?"

"No, sir, but I've only been able to communicate with ships inside the station. Nothing on the outside, not even other stations."

"Try him now, please," Bobby says, doing his best to calm his alarm.

"Yes, sir. Mirage, this is Vidmar Delta control. Come in please."

A voice comes over the radio, but it's not Tran's. "Vidmar Delta, this is Overseer Turry. Are you all right? We've heard reports of some sort of attack." His voice is thick with concern.

Chapter 22: Following

Bobby takes over the mic, relieved to be getting through to someone like Turry. "Mr. Turry, this is Bobby Johnson. You heard right. We've been attacked and need medical evacuation and assistance right away. Send all you can. I will transmit the navigational codes."

"That won't be necessary, Mr. Johnson," Turry replies. "I already have them."

Frowning, Bobby asks, "What do you mean?"

"I mean exactly what I said. I already have the codes."

"Did Dr. Gransom send them to you?"

"That old fool?" Turry scoffs. "Of course not. I took them. In fact, I have the codes for everything. Gransom wanted the security improved, remember? I did that. It's my job. I'm the Senior Overseer. I thought you would have figured me out by now."

"We have!" booms Gransom, striding into the Control Center with surprising strength.

"Ah, is that the great Dr. Joseph Gransom I hear?" says Turry in an oily voice. "How are you, Joey Boy?"

"Enlightened," says Gransom with a smolder in his steady gray eyes.

"Are you now?" Turry mocks.

"I can't understand your thinking, Goldwyn. Why are you doing this? It's insanity."

"I don't need to explain myself to you. Right now all you need to know is all your communications are jammed and I will destroy any ship that tries to leave Vidmar Delta or attempts to come to its aid, and that includes this cargo ship that just left your east dock minutes ago."

Alarmed, Bobby cries, "That cargo ship is transporting injured civilians to the Health Station on Z9. You must let it pass!"

"Must?" Turry says imperiously. "Only I decide what I must or must not do, Mr. Johnson, and that ship is now no more."

Anxiously Bobby asks, "What do you mean, 'no more?'"

"Eliminated," says Turry in a chillingly placid tone. "Don't ever think I don't mean what I say."

Chapter 22: Following   251

The radio goes dead.

"Turry! Turry!" Bobby shouts. "Come in! Come in!" Dismayed he rushes to the Ship Tracking System. "Why are there no readings on STS?" he demands.

"It malfunctioned minutes before the attack, sir," says the controller. "We haven't been able to fix it."

At that moment, Gransom steps forward and takes the mic. Bobby looks at him in astonishment. The elderly man is no longer bent and frail. He's tall and commanding, a veteran of many wars, a leader stirred by the critical needs of his people, strengthened by the call to one more desperate battle. Mic in hand, he makes a station-wide announcement. Over the loudspeakers his deep voice is steady. Zenith people hear the authority of decades of faithful leadership. It stirs the hearts of even the most frightened persons there—like a trumpet calling the troops to battle. "Attention, everyone. This is Chief Director Gransom. Insurrection and treason have come to us on Vidmar Delta. Overseer Turry has compromised most of our systems, and at this time we are essentially cut off from the colony. I want all ships prepped for flight and all able pilots and crew members readied and in the east docking bay within one hour. More information will follow. That is all." Gransom's face is set like granite. "Let's go, Bobby," he says. "We have a lot of work to do."

In the docking bay, Bobby finds a Protector and sends him to the Health Station to inform Eliesia he's been called to other duties. He instructs him to try to get her anything she needs, and let her know that no flights are available off the station. He's relieved he doesn't have to face her to tell her what happened to her patients. That will come later.

Many questions are crowding his mind as he climbs into the back seat of a cart and sits down next to Gransom. Carefully Gransom's Protector begins to drive the cart around the rubble and hurrying people.

"Tran and Mirage are missing," says Bobby. "I think he caused the magtronic storm."

"Oh, that boy," moans Gransom. "He never stops surprising me. I pray he is safe and that Mirage held together."

"I was trying to contact him when Turry came over the radio," says Bobby.

"We'll keep trying to reach him," says Gransom, "but right now Turry is jamming all radio signals. Even the emergency signals from the safety pods are not getting through. We have to figure out a way past the blockade before those people run out of air, and before Turry launches another attack. I don't think he wants to destroy Vidmar outright. I think he wants me to surrender it to him so he can claim it as a trophy, but I don't want to wait around to find out. If Tran did cause that storm, he bought us some precious time."

"Where are we going?" asks Bobby.

"To my lab," Gransom says. "I have ships parked outside right next to the station so Turry can't detect them. They're close enough to send STS data to my lab over a scrambled frequency. It shows Turry has 24 more ships surrounding us on all sides. They're positioned completely around us in a net-type grid. With only that many ships, they have to stay quite a distance away from the station to keep us from just speeding through the gaps, but their missiles greatly increase their coverage."

Bobby asks, "How did you figure out it was that snake Turry?"

"It's what Dengie said about him not mentioning the subcode, and why anyone would go to all that trouble to hack something if they knew it wouldn't work. I couldn't get that out of my head, so instead of going to my quarters, I went to the lab and looked at the system backups for Mirage that were run after you arrived. I discovered that Turry never sent Dengie's extraction code to remove the hack from Mirage's system. Instead he sent a different code, which I suppose he had stored in his interface. That hack made the transponder act normally again, but it broke through the firewalls and then transmitted Mirage's navigation history to Turry over the carrier wave. He set everything up from the beginning. I could think of a number of easier ways he could have done it all, but knowing the conceit of the man, I suppose he wanted to show just how much smarter he is than everyone else. He's always been overly proud of his intellectual prowess, but I certainly didn't see any signs of a treacherous heart in him, until now."

"I didn't either," says Bobby. "When he finished the session on Mirage the other morning, I thanked him and said we were in his debt. He brushed me off and said it was his job. Then he said he couldn't do enough to repay you for what you've done. Of course, that means something totally different now."

Bobby notices a flicker of something in Gransom's eyes—a recognition, a connection, a memory?

"At any rate," Gransom says, "once we get out of this predicament, we have to find out how many other systems Turry has corrupted throughout the colony, and who else might be working with him. It's going to take a huge amount of time and effort from a lot of people." Gransom's voice becomes solemn and weary. "Sixty years of colonial peace, security, and prosperity away from the grasp of Earth is over, Bobby. I knew it was going to happen some day, but it's a shock now that it has. And it's an even bigger shock that it started deep from within."

Bobby puts an encouraging hand on Gransom's shoulder. "We'll make it through, Grandfather. Like Eliesia told me in the turret, 'We're not going to let these cowards beat us.'"

Arriving at the lab, Bobby is surprised to see Dengie there, but before he can say anything, Gransom asks, "What did you find, Dengie?"

"Well, sir, like you suspected, Turry's hack propagated into Vidmar's systems. I just don't know how many areas are affected. I'm at a huge disadvantage not being familiar with the architecture of the systems you put together here. It's going to be difficult to track it all down."

"I understand," says Gransom. "We will work on it together. I don't want to get anyone else involved. Quite frankly, I don't know who I can trust right now. Turry may have gotten to some members of my data team. He has a lot of influence. Until I can

Chapter 22: Following

interview them at length, I can't risk it. But right now we have to come up with a plan to get through the blockade and get some help."

Dengie is visibly upset, tears standing in his troubled eyes. "I'm sorry I brought this to you, sir. It's all my fault. I should have run my own clear check on Mirage instead of relying on that man's word."

"No, dear boy," says Gransom in a kindly voice. "That man was the Senior Overseer of the colony. You were supposed to take his word. None of this is your fault. It is Turry's and mine. But let us not be discouraged or overwhelmed. We have a battle to win. Let's get to work."

Still five hours from Vidmar, Tran slowly paces the bridge. It's been an agonizing trip back. Mirage is struggling. He can feel it. Her usually smooth, fluid and responsive controls now vibrate with resistance, and her engines are strained. But worse than all of that, he hasn't received any replies to his hundreds of radio calls to Vidmar or any other station or ship, and there are no readings on STS. The equipment seems to be working correctly, but nothing is coming through.

He plays the flight past Vidmar over and over again in his mind, wondering if it worked. But he flew past the station so fast that his senses didn't have time to gather any information. He truly was flying blind. *Or maybe*, he thinks, *by faith.*

The east wing docking bay is crowded with personnel. Bobby finishes his briefing to the pilots and crews on what needs to be done and orders everyone to their ships. "We launch in fifteen," he says, giving time for the crews that are flying out of the west wing to get to their ships and ready.

Walking to his ship, he's surprised to see Eliesia riding up in a cart driven by the Protector. She looks disheveled and worn out, and beautiful. She runs over to him.

"Hi," he says. He can't think of anything else to say.

Chapter 22: Following   255

Eliesia looks steadily into his hazel eyes. "You make sure you come back to us, Bobby," she says softly. She gives him a light kiss on the cheek, runs back to the cart, and leaves.

For a moment, Bobby is too stunned to react. Then, hearing the sounds of urgent preparations hastily going on around him, he shakes himself back into the moment and boards his ship. It's a Cutter, one of the fastest and most maneuverable mining ships there is. There are only three in the entire fleet, used primarily for detonating especially hard asteroids and chasing down and gathering up the fractured pieces. He goes through his checklist and fires up the engines. The pilots of the seventeen other flight-worthy ships do the same.

Gransom's voice comes over the radio. It's strong and sure, and the very sound of it raises the spirits of the pilots who are well-aware of their peril and the reason they are choosing to face it.

Into each cockpit rings the clear voice of their leader, "All ships, this is Control. Prepare to launch on my mark. Remember, because of jamming, all radio contact after launch will be lost. God speed."

Bobby winds up the engines.

"5, 4, 3, 2, 1, mark." The ships shoot out of the bays, all eighteen flying in the same direction, quickly gathering close together. Bobby keeps his ship behind a Breaker in the middle of the pack. He watches as a Scout flies in from above, coming ever closer to the top of the Breaker. Deftly the pilot positions the Scout, aligning with the big ship, then with precision, drops down and docks with it. It's a bold move at these speeds without radio contact. Bobby is relieved to see that both pilots pull it off brilliantly.

As soon as the Scout is docked, the ships increase their speed. Bobby can feel the turbulence from all the engine wash, but every ship is flying fast and precisely on the prescribed course. He checks the STS. For now, the Rhinos are holding their positions.

The landing lights flash on the Breaker and the other ships around him. Bobby flashes his. Three minutes to go. They increase their speed. He checks the STS again. The Rhinos at his 2 and 10 o'clock positions move to close the gap the group is heading for.

At two minutes out, his landing lights flash and all the ships alter course, heading for the 10 o'clock position. Thirty seconds later the Scout undocks from the Breaker and flashes its lights. Bobby dives below the Breaker, his ship almost touching the big ship's belly. The eight ships in front of the Breaker break away to the upper left. Simultaneously, the eight ships behind break away to the lower right. Now it's just the Cutter and the Breaker heading for the gap that the enemy ship has left open. Bobby checks the STS. The Rhinos are scrambling to readjust their positions to compensate for the two groups of Vidmar ships.

The Breaker has reached its top speed. Bobby is resisting the urge to go faster, but he holds the Cutter back staying tucked in under the Breaker's belly. *Lock,* he reminds himself. *This is it.*

On STS, he sees one of the enemy ships leave its position and speed his way. Seconds later, the two groups of Vidmar ships break for home, remaining well out of the range of the Rhino's weapons. The two ships chasing them now turn and rush towards the Breaker. Bobby is tempted to make a run for it, but decides to wait.

When the first enemy missile hits on the Breaker's starboard side, he's amazed at what little impact it has on the big ship. The next three are almost as ineffective, but then a missile hits one of its engine nozzles. The Breaker swerves violently as its stern, fueled by a magtronium breach, starts to torch. Barely able to keep his ship from being struck by the swerving bulk, Bobby gives the Cutter full throttle. It rockets away from the floundering Breaker just before it explodes in a massive ball of purple flame. All three Rhinos break away, trying to avoid the debris, giving Bobby the distance and cover he needs to make his run for Z9.

Glancing at STS he sees that another Rhino is at his 2 o'clock with an angle to intercept him. Applying reverse thrust, he drops his speed and then power banks hard to starboard to dodge the ship. It shoots past him. Cutting back to port, Bobby hits full throttle. The enemy ship has to swing back around to try to catch him. It can't make up the distance. Bobby has broken through. He tries his radio. "Mayday! Mayday! Z9 Control, do you read?"

A young man's voice comes back immediately. "This is Z9 Control. We read you. State your emergency."

"This is Bobby Johnson aboard a colonial Cutter. Vidmar Delta has been attacked by foreign enemy ships. We need immediate help. I'm ready to transmit navigational codes."

Another voice breaks in. "This is Senior Overseer Goldwyn Turry. Authentication code 102455. That man is an imposter, an intruder. He is flying a stolen colonial ship armed with explosives and is attempting to ram Z9. You must take defensive action and destroy that ship immediately!"

"No! He's lying!" yells Bobby. "Overseer Turry is a traitor. He attacked Vidmar Delta with foreign ships."

"Uh…I'm connecting my supervisor," says the controller in a shaken voice.

Bobby is racing towards Z9 even as the staticky silence seems to go on and on. At last he hears someone activate a mic.

"This is Flight Control Supervisor Sonja Guardado. Please state your emergency."

"Sonja! Thank God it's you! This is Bobby Johnson…"

On the way back to Vidmar Delta, Bobby flies the Cutter slightly above and behind one of the three giant Transports as it leads a squadron of other formidable ships from Z9 towards the last line of enemy vessels barricading Vidmar Delta. As soon as they're within range, the Rhinos fire upon the Transport. They land direct hits but the weapons have no impact on the massive ship with its thick, high-compact PiMar hull. The Transport unleashes on the Rhinos a volley of shots from its anti-pirate plasma cannons—balls of shifting light and color that fry their electronics. Now uncontrollable, the gray ships float helplessly, unable to avoid the approaching behemoth. The Transport pilot tries to avoid the disabled ships but can't change course fast enough.

The ship bashes into them full force, smashing them into rubble. Quickly the rest of the Rhinos flee, vanishing into the vast black.

Bobby flies ahead to Vidmar followed by an armada of relief ships. Immediately Growlers begin retrieving safety pods, expertly bringing them inside with their skillful capture arms.

As Bobby slowly approaches Vidmar, he can't see through the window wall, so he doesn't know that, on the other side, people are cheering and crying—relieved, thankful, and once more filled with hope.

In very familiar territory now, only ninety minutes from home, Tran is startled when the radio suddenly comes to life. "Is this the little orphan boy?" says an ominous voice.

Instantly a jumble of emotions flood through Tran's entire being. Even over the radio he recognizes the voice. It's the man from the storeroom in Earth Island. The one he couldn't see. The one who wrote the letter. The one who threatened and took Mei. He picks up the mic, and forcing himself to be calm, he says, "This is Tran Moore. And who are you?"

"This is Overseer Goldwyn Turry. I see your ship is damaged. Normally I wouldn't even try chasing down Mirage, but I think I have you at a disadvantage because of your foolish little stunt. If you're wondering how I found you, well, you're leaving a trail of magtronium dust that any moron could follow."

"It's fitting you put it that way," Tran replies dryly. There is silence on the other end. Tran climbs into the pilot's seat and straps in. "Mirage is unarmed," he says. "Are you going to attack an unarmed ship?"

"Of course," chuckles Turry. "If Gransom isn't smart enough to arm his ships, that's not my problem. Only the strong and wise survive. You do understand this is war, don't you?"

"I understand that you're a coward and a traitor," says Tran.

"A traitor? To what?" demands Turry. "The protection of pure-bloods? The fight against the longevity drug? Traitor to a bunch of idiots sitting inertly in space barely advancing? Enough talk!"

Tran doesn't wait around, he fires Mirage's engines and banks hard right and down into a wide corkscrew so he can get a glimpse of what he's up against. He sees he is being pursued by a Rhino and a larger gray ship that is shaped somewhat like Mirage. He straightens his path and flies at three-quarter throttle to find out what Mirage can still do. She struggles, the damaged engines causing her to surge erratically forward and back. An e-pulse missile strikes her port side shaking her violently. The ships are following close behind. Tran banks hard right and downward, putting Mirage into a half roll, then quickly pulls back up to continue on the same trajectory. The other ships fall for the deke and he gains critical distance. A thought comes to him, a plan that might just work. "Only a little more, girl," he says, his eyes seeing without looking, sensing the truth of the movement and his placement as he hurls through space.

Without STS, Tran is at a huge disadvantage, though he senses the enemy ships are not far behind. He commits full power to the engines, but it's too late. Two e-pulse missiles slam into his ship's starboard side. Mirage begins to roll rapidly, floundering hopelessly out of control. The predators rush closer in savage pursuit, their weapons trained on their target. Like ravening wolves in full bloodlust they close in for the kill.

Mirage flies erratically, swerving suddenly wide left, then veering wide right. The pursuing ships stay close, their prey's distressed throes signaling their victory is near. Mirage dives then sweeps steeply upwards, increasing in speed. The other ships follow. Mirage's front thruster jets fire at full velocity. Streaking swiftly upwards, she abruptly arches sharply backwards. Unable to match her angle, the predators rush past, slamming into the tough membrane sphere of newly developing Z52. The larger ship punches through the diaphanous layers and tumbles out of control, pieces of the membrane wrapping around it like a spider securing her dinner. Shreds of membrane undulate around the Rhino's stout body. Suddenly strands of the silvery material are sucked into its cooling ports. Immediately its engines super heat and the ship

Chapter 22: Following

explodes. Tran is alone in the black and starry expanse. There is no one left to pursue him. "Way to go, girl!" he shouts, patting Mirage on the console. With relief, he points the ship towards home.

A voice intrudes on the moment. "Are you there, orphan boy?"

"I'm here," says Tran cooly.

"Before we meet again, you and Bobby may want to ask Gransom why your parents really died. I think you will find that interesting." Before Tran has time to respond, the radio goes silent.

Chapter 23
Preparation

Hastily Bobby enters the recently completed cafeteria on Z51 and wearily flops into the bench seat across from his brother. His face is tired and worried. "Grandfather's getting worse," he says. "As much as I want to be part of getting Mei back, I can't leave him like this. I have to stay here. I'm sorry."

Tran has been concerned that this might happen. It will be a huge disadvantage to go on this perilous mission without Bobby, and frightening in many ways, but he would never expect him to leave Gransom in a time of need. "Don't be sorry," Tran says, "you're doing the right thing. I'm going to miss you, though."

"Yeah, me too," says Bobby. "I know this trip is about Mei, but I have to tell you, I was really looking forward to watching you experience Earth for the first time. I wanted to be there for that. But listen, we need to find you another pilot. I know a guy who might be the perfect fit. He used to be a long-haul Transport pilot who's made probably over fifty hauls to Earth so he knows all the tricks, but he switched to flying experimental craft, and he has experience with mag-pulse engines, too. Do you want me to set up a meeting?"

"Yes!" says Tran earnestly. "Having someone like that on the trip would be a huge relief. Thank you!"

"I wish I could do more," Bobby says regretfully, "but I'm glad I can at least do this much. I'll try to get him here tomorrow." Bobby lets out a long sigh. "Well, I better get back to Grandfather now."

"I'll go," says Tran. "I need to spend as much time with him as I can before I leave. You stay here and relax. I got this for you," he says, pushing a tray of Bobby's favorite foods towards him.

"Have some tea and eat. You've been running ragged since we left Vidmar. I'll see you later."

Bobby leans his head against the window and shuts his eyes. Tran's right, he hasn't rested at all. After the attack, Gransom decided Vidmar was unsafe and needed to be vacated until it was repaired. Most of the people who lived there went to Z9, but he and a team of others moved to Z51 to plan Mei's rescue.

For two weeks Tran and Bobby have been learning to fly the new ship—a sleek pearl-white vessel that Gransom named Redemption. It's not as long or as tall as Mirage, but a luxury-class space yacht nonetheless. And it has weapons. Flying the ship is fairly straight forward, but learning how to manage the mag-pulse engines is difficult. Their power comes from always running on the edge of instability, so they demand special attention and extra care. Cynda Johnson was the master of pushing these engines to their maximum. Experiencing them firsthand has given Bobby a much greater appreciation for what his mother accomplished.

His mind drifts to Eliesia, something it does a lot these days, though they haven't had much time to get to know each other. She's been hurrying to get everything in order before leaving with Tran. Bobby has been tied up assisting Gransom in a myriad of logistics, but even so he has been doing everything in his power to help her.

After the move to Z51, Eliesia's main priority was getting her brother settled. She was not going to leave him to live on Dome 6 while she was gone, and he refused to stay in the group home she had arranged for him on Z9. Knowing her predicament, Gransom hired a team of caretakers that could live with Walter full-time on Z51. They had a beautiful suite readied that had many of the things Eliesia knew her brother liked—things that made him feel secure and comfortable. Now the hard part was to get him there. When Bobby found out that Walter had a fascination with spacecraft, he and Eliesia flew to Z9, entering Dome 6 through the Skydoor, then landing near where Walter was staying. It didn't take long before he came out. "What kind of ship is this?" he asked, running his hand over its smooth nose.

"It's a Scout," said Bobby. "It's a special ship used for finding asteroids containing magtronium."

"And you're its pilot?" he asked cautiously.

"I am today," Bobby said.

Carefully Eliesia asked, "Do you want a ride in it, Walter? We're going to a place that has a lot of ships."

Walter smiled widely and his eyes lit up. "I will get my things," he said, and loped off into one of the twisted structures, returning swiftly with his bags.

As soon as they arrived at Z51, Gransom's chef Gracie took Walter by the hand and led him into the kitchen where she fed him a wonderful meal. After that, he ate most of his meals with her, and the two became fast friends—Gracie who never spoke, and Walter who could talk non-stop about almost anything. A week later, Eliesia told Bobby that Walter was the healthiest and most emotionally stable he had been in years.

Bobby opens his eyes and glances at the array of good things Tran has amassed for him to eat. His stomach growls and he realizes he's actually rather hungry. He takes a bite of mashed potatoes and gravy, grateful for the familiar flavors even though they're only slightly still warm. Soon his mind returns to his current worries. Turry and his band of ships are still causing serious problems in many of the more distant stations. The colony has lost some of the smaller stations to the enemy, and innocent citizens have been killed or injured. There's a rush to arm as many ships as possible, but it's a slow process.

Squadrons of armed colonial ships looking for enemy vessels now patrol the colony, but even that is complicated and hazardous. Because of his deep access into the systems, Turry had transponders in the enemy ships registered as legitimate colonial ships, and that's how they show up on STS. When Flight Control coders removed them, they would pop back up a day later. So now, until a solution is found, all ships have to radio in and go through a long validation process before they're allowed to approach any station. It's a huge mess that has slowed everything way down. And now some colonial ships have been stolen so it's even more difficult to figure out who is who.

With Gransom in a weakened state, much of the responsibility to deal with these problems has fallen on Bobby, and he is definitely feeling the burden. The Zenith people are frightened and worried. Their peaceful lives have been greatly disrupted and threatened. But Bobby has seen the resiliency and spirit in them. They have pulled together, united in purpose. They are fighting back. They want the Zenith Colony to be safe once more, and Bobby is determined to do his best to help make that happen. He prays for God to give him the wisdom, strength, and fortitude to make it so.

The evening before leaving for Earth, Tran flies to Z9. He has dinner at Rodgers and goes to watch a couple of innings of a baseball game on Deck 2, but keeps well away from the crowd.

On his way to the compound, he passes his old flat once again. The memories are still so strong he feels if he walked into the flat right now his parents would be there. He wishes it were true.

At the compound, he walks the garden path to the pond and visits all his koi friends. The fish from Vidmar Delta have all survived the transfer here. They crowd towards him as soon as they feel his footfalls and he kneels down and puts his fingers in the water.

Dachee is pushing past Dragon and Cali, mouthing Tran's fingers with his big, round mouth. Tran smiles fondly and is getting ready to toss in some pellets when he hears footsteps approaching. He rises hastily, wiping his wet fingers on his pants.

"Phillip!" he says. Many things come to mind, but he's too astonished to say any of them.

"I'm not going to stay long," Phillip says in a quiet voice. "I know you're leaving soon and I wanted to tell you that Gransom was right. I've talked to Peter and Karl, and all of us agree on this. We're not mad at him or you."

"But I made you do it," Tran objects.

"No, sir. We chose. I chose. I went against explicit orders and my training, and worse, I went against my conscience. Every choice has consequences."

Tran is silent. He hears the trickle of the water and the fish swishing in the pond. Everything he had thought to say to his Protector is gone, except one. "Still," he says softly, "I'm sorry."

"I know," says Phillip. "And Peter and Karl. We all know you didn't want it to turn out this way." He falls silent for a moment, then adds "I just wanted you to know that."

"Thank you, Philip," says Tran with relief. "That's a weight off my soul. I've been feeling so horrible about it. I didn't think you could ever forgive me. Maybe when I get back we can do some exploring."

"No need to wait that long," says Phillip. "I think we'll get some exploring done on Earth."

Puzzled, Tran says, "I don't understand."

"Well," says Phillip, "I went to Dr Gransom to apologize and thank him for teaching me the truth of the matter. He told me he'd been thinking that you needed someone you could trust to go with you on this trip, especially since Bobby can't go. He offered me the job, based on your approval. What do you say?"

"Yes!" Tran exclaims. "Of course! That would be fantastic!"

"Just one thing," says Phillip. "I'm not going as your Protector. I'm going as your friend. I'm going to do what I think is right to keep you safe. Are you okay with that?"

Tran looks Phillip in the eyes and says, "Under one condition. You call me Tran from now on."

"You got it, Tran," says Phillip with a wide smile. "So I'll see you tomorrow."

"Tomorrow," says Tran.

In the quiet evening, Tran stands shaking his head in disbelief. He tosses pellets into the pond, making sure each fish gets its share. "See you guys in a couple of months," he says. "I'll miss you."

Taking a lift to Deck 3, Tran walks down Jessica's street and stops by her house. He remembers sitting on the porch not so long ago, hearing she was leaving, feeling he'd been stabbed in the heart, feeling like his life was over. It doesn't cut as deeply now. Things have changed.

When he arrives at Vidmar, Tran is glad to see crews working diligently to restore the station structural integrity. For eight years this station has been his home. He knows almost every inch of it. Slowly he walks along the concourse. It's so strange to look out the window wall and not see the beautifully lit asteroids. Even stranger to think he's responsible. A melancholy cloud passes over his heart—silvery gray and sad.

It's hardest to go to Mei's flat. His room is almost empty, but hardly anything else has changed. He sits down at the dining table and looks at the kitchen, hearing a spoon stirring, the splash of water rinsing every utensil, plate, and pot before finishing the day, then finds himself staring at the empty chair across from his. He imagines Mei sewing, her fingers flying, her soft songs like rippling water sweetly floating in the air between them. Has it really been two years since he was last here with her? He finds it difficult to believe.

It's a long walk down the corridors to the ballfield. He's done it thousands of times, but today it seems to take much longer. Quietly he looks down from the spot where Mei first showed him the field, the place from which he watched her be reunited with her best friend. Curious, he scans the dugouts, the bleachers, the dark green outfield walls. The ballfield is not damaged in any way. Thoughtfully he walks around the field. The Zenith grass, the Zenith dirt—they feel as real as the first time he touched them with his hands and felt them under his feet. He stretches, takes a neutral stance, then flows through a sequence of favorite moves, remembering all the effort, struggles, and new ways of thinking.

So many years of fastfighting lessons and training. So many good memories!

Looking to left field Tran sees Mei jump up and catch a fly ball with her barehand, landing gracefully, and shrugging like it's nothing. Tears come to his eyes. "I'm coming for you, Mei," he whispers "I'm coming for you."

Chapter 23: Preperation

Chapter 24
Departure

Tran can hardly believe the day is finally here. "Are you going to go out and say good-bye, Vern?" he asks.

"Uh, no. You go ahead," says the pilot. "I've made this trip so many times, it's no big deal. Phillip and I need to finish the check on the weapons."

"Okay," says Tran. "I'll see you in a bit."

Bobby has picked well. Tran liked the new pilot right away. Vern is a big, friendly man with a wealth of flying experience and a vast store of knowledge about how things work on Earth.

There's a small group waiting on the flight deck to bid the travelers good-bye. Gransom is first in line. Tran is glad to see he has improved somewhat in the past days. Moments after the attack on Vidmar, Gransom had mustered all his strength, leading his pilots in a bold move that not only made a way for Bobby to escape past the barricade, but brought every pilot home safely, including the one from the Breaker who had put the vessel on autopilot and climbed into the Scout that undocked only minutes before the enemy ships blew the Breaker to pieces.

While Redemption was being stocked and prepared for the flight, Tran chose to make time with Gransom his priority. For hours he sat by his bed talking with his beloved grandfather, taking notes for him for his new book on mag-pulse engines. Remembering that time together, Tran smiles inwardly. When he's ninety-five himself, will he have enough energy and brain power left to even read a book, much less write one? Now, there on the flight deck is the elderly gentleman, standing free without even a cane, not as tall as in the old days, but strong as an ancient tree whose roots have gone deep through many harsh winters. As Tran approaches

269

he sees in Gransom's eagle eyes his fierce determination to be there and bless his grandson as he prepares to depart.

"Are you all set, my boy?" says Gransom in a thin, but steady voice.

"Yes, sir. Everything's ready. Thank you so much for allowing me to do this and making it all possible. I'm sorry I have to leave at such a difficult time. I would stay and help if I could."

"You're helping us all by doing this," says Gransom. "Our hopes and prayers are with you. You make sure to tell Mei we love her and can't wait to see her."

"Yes, sir. I will."

Gransom pulls Tran into a strong hug. "I'm extremely proud of you, my boy, and I love you very much. Go with God. You will be in my prayers."

"I love you, Grandfather," Tran says softly.

Gransom pats Tran fondly on the back and lets him go.

"Good ride, Tran," says Dengie with a grin, slapping him on the shoulder. He's wearing his best red plaid shirt. "We'll see you when you get back." Dengie has become one of Gransom's top coders for tracking down Turry's malicious code.

"Thanks, Dengie. You take care."

Bobby walks Tran back towards Redemption. Mirage is in the next bay, her engines scheduled to be overhauled. Tran stops and looks at her docked there, serenely blue. "I'm sure going to miss that ship," he says.

"I know. She's part of the family," says Bobby. "But I'll tell you what—she's going to be flying a banner when all of you return."

Tran smiles at the thought. "Thanks, Bobby. Make sure you stay in shape. We're going to spar when I get back."

"You got it, little brother." As they go to hug, Bobby notices the thin red band around Tran's wrist. He swallows hard. For a moment he can't speak. "Tell Mei I love her," he manages at last, concealing tears with difficulty. "Remember to stay locked," he says, pointing to Heaven.

Chapter 24: Departure

They share a knowing nod, a brotherly hug followed by slaps on the back. Tran waves one more time to Gransom and boards the ship.

Eliesia is on the dock waiting for Bobby. "Hi," she says.

"Hi," says Bobby.

"So you think Walter will be okay while I'm gone?"

"I don't think Miss Gracie is going to let anything happen to him," says Bobby. "Those two are quite the combo."

Eliesia laughs lightly. "Thanks for what you've done for us, Bobby. I'll see you in a few months, okay?"

"You make sure you come back to us," he says, giving her a wry smile. There is more to say. He can see it in her eyes. He hopes she can see it in his, because he hasn't words and there is no time. He walks her to the ship and wraps her in a short, honest embrace. Lightly she touches his arm, looking at him with eyes shining. Then she's gone.

Lifting off, Tran powers Redemption slowly to the departure bay. "Z51 Control, this is Redemption requesting departure from Bay 1."

"Roger that, Redemption. Doors are open, you're clear to launch."

"Roger, Control. Thank you."

Tran's heart beats wildly as he applies power to the engines. The ship growls as it presses them back in their seats. The gleaming emerald green of Z51 quickly disappears behind them. Within a half hour a most familiar sight comes into view—the luminous cobalt blue surface of Z9 City, shifting and changing like ripples on a wind-swept ocean. Tran applies more power. The engines respond effortlessly to the demand, launching him to the future, leaving behind everything he has ever known.

Chapter 24: Departure

Made in the USA
Monee, IL
27 December 2022

23686857R00154